Praise for *The Moscow Offensive*

"**S**pectacular . . . The action builds to an exciting, climactic battle. . . . Brown shows once again why he stands out in the crowded military thriller genre."
—*Publishers Weekly*

"**A**n off-the-books mercenary unit is the world's best bet against unchecked Russian aggression . . . A fun read that really shines with the author's convincing knowledge of military aircraft."
—*Kirkus Reviews*

"**B**rown has long been a master at high-tech thrillers, and . . . there is no denying that he knows his stuff. . . . Even with a long-running series, he continues to find ways to keep the action lively and relevant. For the Tom Clancy crowd, Brown remains the go-to guy."
—*Booklist*

"**A** very smart, timely, and terrifying political thriller . . . Current, spot-on, and full of bone-crushing action, Dale Brown's *The Moscow Offensive* is one of his best novels to date and a sure bet to please action junkies who also like heaping sides of politics and next-gen tech."
—TheREALBookSpy.com

Praise for *Price of Duty*

"**A** tense, atmospheric thriller with a ripped from the headlines plot, *Price of Duty* moves at a breakneck pace. Highly readable, enormously entertaining, its twists and turns will keep you glued to the pages."
—Karen Robards, *New York Times* Bestselling Author

"**A** riveting powerhouse of a novel; action on top of action, fascinating and intricate details about the latest military technology and tactics and a forward-thinking geopolitical plot that yanks the reader along by the collar and takes them on a wild ride. Exciting and intelligent entertainment."
—Mark Greaney, #1 Bestselling Author of *Gunmetal Gray*

"**S**trap in, for there are shootouts on every page plus a well-choreographed climactic raid. . . . A compelling, fast-paced, and imaginative techno-thriller . . . There's so much action here it's a wonder there aren't bullet holes and bomb craters on every page."
—*Kirkus Reviews*

"**M**asterly . . . Explosive."
—*Publishers Weekly*

"**F**ans will find Brown in fine form here, and newcomers who enjoy top-notch military fiction will have no trouble diving into the deep end."
—*Booklist*

"**A**ll too real and eerily authentic. One of the godfathers of techno-thrillers, Brown has saved some of his best and most creative story ideas for *Price of Duty*."
—TheREALBookSpy.com

Praise for Dale Brown

THE MOSCOW OFFENSIVE

By Dale Brown

Coming Soon in Hardcover

THE KREMLIN STRIKE

DALE BROWN

THE MOSCOW OFFENSIVE

A NOVEL

wm

WILLIAM MORROW
An Imprint of HarperCollins*Publishers*

THE MOSCOW OFFENSIVE. Copyright © 2018 by Creative Arts and Sciences LLC. All rights reserved. Printed in the United States of America. No part of this book may be used or reproduced in any manner whatsoever without written permission except in the case of brief quotations embodied in critical articles and reviews. For information, address HarperCollins Publishers, 195 Broadway, New York, NY 10007.

First William Morrow premium printing: April 2019
First William Morrow hardcover printing: June 2018

Print Edition ISBN: 978-0-06-244203-1
Digital Edition ISBN: 978-0-06-244202-4

Cover design by Richard Aquan
Cover images © STILLFX/iStock/Getty Images (flag); © Palo_ok/Shutterstock (F-16 jet); © Maxiphoto/iStock/Getty Images (radar screen)

William Morrow and HarperCollins are registered trademarks of HarperCollins Publishers in the United States of America and other countries.

18 19 20 21 22   QGM   10 9 8 7 6 5 4 3 2 1

This novel is dedicated to U.S. law enforcement
and military and civilian security forces located
right here in the United States.
With all the turmoil and conflicts all over the world,
it's easy to forget those who stand watch
over our homes, businesses, and military
and government installations in America.

Thank you for your service, your watchfulness,
and your dedication to protecting our country.
We pray you never have to be used,
but we are thankful you're on the job
if the need arises.

Being defeated is often a temporary condition. Giving up is what makes it permanent.

—Marilyn vos Savant, American columnist

ACKNOWLEDGMENTS

Thanks as always to Patrick Larkin for his skill and hard work.

<u>CAST OF CHARACTERS</u>

AMERICANS

STACY ANNE BARBEAU, president of the United States of America

EDWARD RAUCH, president's national security adviser

LUKE COHEN, White House chief of staff

SCOTT FIRESTONE, admiral, U.S. Navy, chairman of the Joint Chiefs of Staff

KEVIN CALDWELL, admiral, U.S. Navy, director of the National Security Agency

JOHN DALTON FARRELL, governor of Texas and presidential candidate

ANDREW DAVIS, head of Governor Farrell's security detail, former sergeant in the Iron Wolf Squadron and U.S. Army Special Forces

FRANK JAMESON, owner, Jameson Construction

MARTIN CROWN, chief executive officer, Regan Air Freight

HALSEY STUTZ, chief financial officer, Regan Air Freight

TED LOCKE, director of flight operations, Regan Air Freight

RAFAEL DÍAZ, special agent in charge, U.S. Secret Service

CAPTAIN PAUL FRASER, U.S. Air Force, pilot of HH-60G Pave Hawk search-and-rescue helicopter, Barksdale Air Force Base

COLONEL DANIEL KIM, U.S. Air Force, chief of security for Strategic Command Bunker, Wright-Patterson Air Force Base

TEAM SERGEANT CASIMIR "KAZ" OSTROWSKI, U.S. Army 10th Special Forces Group

LIEUTENANT (JUNIOR GRADE) CARLY DE MELLO, U.S. Navy, radar officer, E-2C Hawkeye 2000

LIEUTENANT TIM LAYTON, U.S. Navy, Combat Information Center officer, E-2C Hawkeye 2000

COMMANDER DENNIS NINOMIYA, U.S. Navy, executive officer, CG-53 *MOBILE BAY*

LIEUTENANT BRIAN THORSON, U.S. Navy, tactical action officer, CG-53 *MOBILE BAY*

CAPTAIN BLAIR POLLOCK, U.S. Navy, commander, Naval Base San Diego

KARL ERICSON, National Cable News, broadcast engineer

Amy Maguire, National Cable News, audio assistant

ISLE OF MAN

Francis Xavier Regan, Canadian tax exile and billionaire, owner of Regan Air Freight and FXR Trucking, Inc.

IRON WOLF SQUADRON AND SCION

Kevin Martindale, president of Scion, former president of the United States of America

Brad McLanahan, Cybernetic Infantry Device (CID) pilot and XCV-62 Ranger pilot, Iron Wolf Squadron

Patrick McLanahan, Iron Wolf Squadron training and intelligence expert, former lieutenant general, U.S. Air Force (ret.)

Major Nadia Rozek, Polish Special Forces officer, attached to Iron Wolf Squadron as a CID pilot, and as copilot and systems operator for XCV-62 Ranger

Wayne "Whack" Macomber, commander, Iron Wolf Squadron CID operations, former major, U.S. Air Force Special Operations Command (ret.)

IAN SCHOFIELD, commander, Iron Wolf deep-penetration unit, former captain in Canada's Special Operations Regiment

SAMANTHA KERR, operative, Scion Intelligence

MARCUS CARTWRIGHT, operative, Scion Intelligence

DAVID JONES, operative, Scion Intelligence

SKY MASTERS AEROSPACE, INC.

HUNTER "BOOMER" NOBLE, Ph.D., chief of aerospace engineering, Sky Masters Aerospace, Inc.

JASON RICHTER, colonel, U.S. Army (ret.), Ph.D., chief executive officer

HELEN KADDIRI, Ph.D., president and chair of the board

RICHARD WITT, Ph.D., cyberneticist

RUSSIANS

GENNADIY ANATOLIYVICH GRYZLOV, president of the Russian Federation

VIKTOR KAZYANOV, minister of state security

IVAN ULANOV, president's private secretary

MIKHAIL ARONOV, Ph.D., chief cyberneticist for the State Cybernetics Factory

CAPTAIN YURI BEZRODNY, commander, disguised special operations ship *Brodyaga*

LIEUTENANT SERGEI ROZONOV, commander, Spetsnaz detachment assigned to *Brodyaga*

MAJOR VASILY DRAGOMIROV, field operative for Russian military intelligence (GRU)

CAPTAIN EDUARD NAUMOV, technical officer, GRU Ninth Directorate

CAPTAIN DMITRY LEONOV, 22nd Guards Spetsnaz Brigade

SENIOR SERGEANT ANDREI ISAYEV, 22nd Guards Spetsnaz Brigade

COLONEL GENERAL VLADISLAV NIKITIN, commander, Southern Military District

MAJOR GENERAL MAXIM BOROVKOV, chief of staff, Southern Military District

COLONEL IVAN ZAITEV, commander, S-400 *Triumf* surface-to-air missile battalion

RAZRESHENIYE KONFLIKTOV USLUGI (CONFLICT RESOLUTION SERVICES)—a private military corporation owned by Gennadiy Gryzlov

VLADIMIR KURAKIN, president and chief executive officer, former major general in Russia's special operations forces

KIRILL ARISTOV, commander RKU reconnaissance and security detachment, former Spetsnaz captain

NIKOLAI DOBRYNIN, second-in-command, RKU recon detachment, former Spetsnaz lieutenant

PAVEL LARIONOV, RKU recon detachment, former Spetsnaz sergeant

YURI ANNENKOV, commander RKU covert flight operations base in Moab, Utah, pilot for converted Boeing 737-200F cruise-missile carrier, former colonel, Russian Air Force

KONSTANTIN USPENSKY, copilot for 737-200F cruise-missile carrier, former major, Russian Air Force

ANDREJ FILIPPOV, ordnance specialist, former major, Russian Air Force

COLONEL RUSLAN BARYSHEV, commander, *Kiberneticheskaya Voyennaya Mashina* (Cybernetic War Machine) force, former Su-50 fighter pilot, Russian Air Force

CAPTAIN OLEG IMREKOV, KVM pilot, former Su-50 fighter pilot, Russian Air Force

MAJOR VIKTOR ZELIN, KVM pilot, former Su-34 fighter-bomber pilot

MAJOR ALEXEI BRAGIN, KVM pilot, former Su-27 fighter pilot, Russian Air Force

MAJOR DMITRY VESELOVSKY, KVM pilot, former Su-35 fighter pilot, Russian Air Force

CAPTAIN SERGEI NOVIKOV, KVM pilot, former Su-34 fighter-bomber pilot, Russian Air Force

SWISS

WILLEM DAENIKER, investment banker chosen by Gennadiy Gryzlov to negotiate the secret purchase of Regan Air Freight and FXR Trucking, Inc.

POLES

PIOTR WILK, president of Poland, former general in the Polish Air Force and commander of the 1st Air Defense Wing

COLONEL PAWEŁ KASPEREK, F-16 fighter pilot and commander of the Polish Air Force's 3rd Tactical Squadron

KAROL SIKORA, sergeant, Polish Special Forces, attached to Iron Wolf Squadron deep-penetration unit

HUNGARIANS

TIBOR LUKÁCS, prime minister of Hungary

PROLOGUE

GHEAY NIAR ÇHIARNYS (EAST WIND MANOR),
ISLE OF MAN, IN THE IRISH SEA
Late fall 2019

Willem Daeniker glanced at the security guard seated across from him. A faint bulge beneath the other man's dark jacket showed he was armed. The Swiss investment banker hid a wry smile as he looked away, out through the tinted windows of the big black Mercedes limousine. They were headed north along a winding, rain-slick road.

Overhead, bands of storm clouds drifted slowly across the sky, soaking hills and valleys that had been continuously inhabited for more than eight thousand years. Over the long millennia, wave after wave of peoples—Stone Age tribesmen, invading Gaels from Ireland, warlike Vikings, and then the rival Scots and English—had descended on this small island to hunt and fish and farm. But the old ways were passing fast, supplanted by wealthy newcomers and corporations lured by low taxes and limited regulation. Offshore banking and high-tech manufacturing were the forces driving the Isle of Man's economy now. And so, one by one, centuries-old estates and homes fell into the hands of rich businessmen from around the world.

Men like Daeniker's host, Francis Xavier Regan.

Like many of the world's super rich, the reclusive Canadian billionaire ruthlessly shielded his privacy. Very few people were ever invited onto his property and they were always subject to close scrutiny. Tabloid journalists and other trespassers were met by armed watchmen and snarling dogs.

Tires crunched on wet gravel as the Mercedes swung onto a long drive. East Wind Manor's age-darkened stone façade, turrets, and chimneys loomed ahead through the dreary gray light of the fading day. Beside its massive front door, a somber manservant stood huddled under an umbrella, waiting to greet him.

Once indoors out of the damp, Daeniker eyed his surroundings with interest. Stone floors overlaid by beautiful Persian rugs, dark oak paneling, gleaming suits of armor, ornate coats of arms, and walls lined with expensive paintings conveyed an overwhelming aura of both vast wealth and a distinguished and ancient lineage. The wealth was Regan's by right, the Swiss thought cynically. But since his immigrant Irish father had been nothing more than a day laborer, the noble lineage belonged entirely to this purchased house.

Meeting the billionaire in the flesh did nothing to dispel that cynical view.

Regan, a tall, burly man in his midsixties, nodded curtly to a chair. "Well, Mr. Daeniker?" he demanded. "What have you got for me?"

Unfazed by this rudeness, the Swiss banker opened his briefcase and took out a thick sheaf of documents. The international consortium he represented wanted to buy two of the other man's privately held North American enterprises—FXR Trucking and Regan Air Freight. And the Canadian wanted to sell. Though these midsized transportation companies were the original foundation of his enormous fortune, Regan was not a sentimental man. In President Stacy Anne Barbeau's overtaxed and overregulated America, neither business was worth his continued investment of time and money.

Donning a polite smile, he handed the documents across the desk. "I think you will find everything is in order, Mr. Regan."

"Maybe so," the other man said brusquely. "And maybe not."

Daeniker frowned, feeling uncertain for the first time. Both sides had already agreed on a price. Even more important, neither wanted to trigger any "inconvenient" scrutiny by government tax officials and regulatory agencies. What kind of game was Regan playing now?

The billionaire looked back at him with a cold expression. "Your clients like to live dangerously, Mr. Daeniker. If they'd dicked around with me for just twelve more hours, they would have been shit out of luck."

The Swiss banker nodded. Regan was due to

depart on his annual sailing vacation at dawn the
next morning. Every year, before the worst winter
weather hit the Isle of Man, he took his prized
Dutch-built yacht, *Bear Venture*, on a weeks-long
cruise south to Spain and then across the Atlantic
to his second home in the Cayman Islands. And
he made it a rule never to conduct any serious
business while at sea.

"I regret the various delays," Daeniker said. He
spread his hands. "But when one is dealing with
the different interests of so many prospective in-
vestors, they are sometimes unavoidable."

Regan snorted.

For a moment, Daeniker had the uncomfortable impression the other man knew he was lying.
In truth, his real client had carefully controlled
the timing of their negotiations. From the beginning, his orders had been clear: The deal must be
concluded *only* in the hours just before Regan set
sail from the Isle of Man.

"Unavoidable or not, those delays are going
to cost you," Regan said, showing his teeth. He
stabbed at the contracts with one powerful fore-
finger. "I'll sign these. But my asking price just
went up fifty million euros."

Daeniker raised an eyebrow. "Fifty million euros more? For what reason?"

"For two reasons," the other man told him
coolly. "First, your buyers have inconvenienced
me. They've wasted my time with bullshit. Nobody does that for free."

Regan leaned back in his chair, looking smug.
"And second, as a means of guaranteeing your

clients' continued anonymity. It's obvious that this 'consortium' of yours is nothing but window dressing. And ordinarily, I don't do business with folks I don't know. But I'm willing to make an exception in this case . . . at a price."

Daeniker kept his mouth shut.

"So here's the situation as I see it," Regan went on. "Your real buyers have tried hard to hide themselves." He shrugged. "Maybe because they want to dodge some confiscatory taxes or nitpicking regulations. Or maybe because they're the sort of people who need new ways to make dirty money a little cleaner. So what I figure is that your mysterious principals really don't want my security people poking and prying around to identify them, Mr. Daeniker." He smiled thinly. "My bet is that you're empowered to sweeten this deal to make sure it goes through on time . . . and without any inconvenient truths coming out. Correct?"

Daeniker sat motionless for several moments, thinking fast. At last, he sighed. "Such a circumstance was not entirely unforeseen. I am authorized to go a bit higher, but no more than—"

Regan shook his head. "We are *not* bargaining here." His eyes were stony. "The price goes up fifty million. Or you leave empty-handed. It's your call."

"You are a hard man, Mr. Regan."

The other man nodded. "That I am. Which is why I'm sitting on this side of the desk and you're on the other, Mr. Daeniker."

* * *

An hour later, Willem Daeniker watched the dark stone walls and dim lights of East Wind Manor disappear behind him, swallowed up by night and rain. The Mercedes swung onto the main road, heading back to the airport where a private jet sat fueled and waiting. Frowning, he pulled out his smartphone and typed a short text message to Russian president Gennadiy Gryzlov waiting impatiently in Moscow, sixteen hundred miles due east of the Isle of Man: *Arrangements complete. Cost 50m higher than hoped. Unfortunately, seller still shows regrettable curiosity.*

SPECIAL OPERATIONS SHIP *BRODYAGA* (PROWLER), FAR OUT IN THE ATLANTIC OCEAN
Several nights later

Stars speckled the moonless night sky—tiny points of light glittering in the midst of infinite blackness. Far below, in inky darkness, an elegant craft more than a hundred meters long and with a displacement of over four thousand tons slid gracefully through long, rolling waves. Without any running lights illuminating her superstructure, the destroyer-sized ship was almost invisible.

Seen in daylight and from a distance, *Brodyaga* looked like a luxury mega-yacht, not a warship. Her sleek lines and floor-to-ceiling windows mirrored those of other gleaming, ultramodern private vessels owned by the world's wealthiest men and women, including a number of Russia's leading industrialists and business oligarchs.

In reality, *Brodyaga* was a disguised intelligence and special operations vessel for the Russian Navy. If necessary, she could discreetly slip in and out of foreign ports that were otherwise off-limits to Russia's surface combatants and spy ships. Nor was she routinely trailed by Western warships and aircraft while at sea—which gave her the necessary freedom of movement to conduct any number of covert missions.

Like this one.

Brodyaga's red-lit Combat Information Center was buried deep in her hull, far below the spacious staterooms and luxurious fittings used to fool foreign observers. Crammed full of sophisticated electronics and displays, it was a hive of quiet, purposeful activity.

Captain Yuri Bezrodny leaned over the shoulder of one of his junior lieutenants. Carefully, he studied the low-light images transmitted by a drone flying forty kilometers ahead. They showed a large, two-masted ketch sailing downwind at around four knots. His eyes narrowed. There were no other ships or aircraft within effective radar range. Their sonar reported no subsurface contacts. And the sea state and weather conditions were near optimal.

He straightened up and turned to his executive officer. "Launch the strike team."

* * *

Forty minutes later, a rigid inflatable boat, comparable to the F470 Zodiac rubber raiding craft used by U.S. Navy SEALs, sped across the sea at nearly fifteen knots. A coxswain manned the tiller at the rear and seven more Spetsnaz combat frogmen straddled the gunwale, lying low to reduce their profile. They wore black wet suits and night-vision gear. Compact Groza-4 assault carbines were slung across their shoulders. Fitted with suppressors on shortened barrels, the weapons were designed for close-quarters clandestine action.

Perched on the bow, Lieutenant Sergei Rozonov stared into the darkness as the inflatable boat rose and fell, cresting long Atlantic rollers. If his navigation calculations were even reasonably accurate, he should be able to see their target soon.

There! Something, a fleck of brighter green against the green-tinged sky produced by his night-vision goggles, flickered on the horizon almost dead ahead. The tiny shape vanished again as their boat slid back down into a trough between waves. But when it came back into view, the image was clearer, more distinct. He was seeing the sails of a large yacht running down toward them on a gentle breeze.

Rozonov looked back at the coxswain manning the tiller. Slowly, he flapped his hand twice.

The petty officer nodded and reduced his throttle sharply. Their speed dropped. So did the noise from their fifty-five-horsepower outboard motor and its pump-jet propulsor. Approaching from upwind like this should make it impossible for anyone aboard the yacht to hear them coming, but there was no point in taking unnecessary risks.

Rozonov swung around again. The ketch's towering masts and slender hull were plainly visible now. They grew larger with astonishing speed as the two craft converged. Minutes passed with no sound other than the periodic slap of waves on their boat's rubber hull and the low, throaty growl of its throttled-back engine.

The Spetsnaz lieutenant tensed. Any moment now. There was still no sign that they'd been spotted by anyone aboard the yacht. The two men on watch were either engrossed in keeping an eye on their rigging or, just as likely, dozing comfortably in the cockpit.

One hundred meters to go. Fifty meters. *Now!* Rozonov pumped his fist rapidly three times.

Behind him, the coxswain swung his tiller across. Their assault boat turned smoothly through a tight half circle, sliding in right alongside the big yacht. Quickly, one of the Russian commandos hooked on to its guardrail.

Moving fast, Rozonov slithered up onto the deck and crouched low. They were tied up close beside the main deckhouse. No lights were showing. He unslung his carbine. One by one, the rest of his men swarmed silently aboard.

Rapid hand signals sent two of them forward toward the bow. The other four followed him aft. The yacht's carbon-fiber masts and enormous Dacron sails soared above them.

Gliding soundlessly around the corner of the deckhouse, Rozonov tucked the stock of the

Groza-4 carbine securely against his shoulder. The main cockpit was just ahead. Through his night-vision goggles, he could see one crewman peering down at the navigation console and electronic sail controls next to the helm. Another sailor lounged on one of the L-shaped sofas fitted around the edges of the cockpit. He sipped appreciatively at a steaming cup of coffee.

Without hesitating, Rozonov opened fire. His silenced carbine stuttered.

Hit by multiple 9mm subsonic rounds at close range, the helmsman spun away in a gruesome cloud of blood and shattered bone. His coffee-drinking companion slumped back against the bullet-torn sofa, shot through the chest and stomach.

The Spetsnaz lieutenant dropped lightly into the cockpit and spun toward the nearest companionway. It was open.

Catlike, he drifted down a short set of stairs into the main deckhouse. His commandos followed close behind him. They fanned out across the large darkened room. A long teak dining table ran down the middle, with plush sofas and armchairs in the corners.

Rozonov took just a moment to compare what he saw with the deck plans he'd memorized earlier. Two more doors opened into the immaculately furnished room. One led forward into the yacht's crew quarters. The other passage ran aft, toward the owner's cabin and guest quarters.

He nodded to his men and then jerked a thumb at the forward passage. "*Net zaklyuchennykh.* No prisoners," he mouthed.

They slipped silently through the door one by one and disappeared into darkness. Almost immediately, he heard wood splinter as they started kicking in doors. Silenced carbines cracked briefly, echoed by muffled groans and cries from dying sailors and servants.

Without waiting any longer, Rozonov charged aft.

He ran down a short hallway, broke through an oak-paneled door, and burst into a dimly lit and comfortably appointed stateroom. Bookcases lined the curving wall around a king-sized bed. There, an older man, big and gray-haired, sat bolt upright among the tangled blankets, blinking in surprise.

"Just who the fuck are you?" the old man growled.

"No one you will ever know, Mr. Regan," Rozonov replied. Then he squeezed the trigger, holding the assault carbine firmly on target as it bucked back against his shoulder.

Hit repeatedly, the billionaire sagged back against his torn, bloodstained pillows. White-faced, he struggled to breathe for a few seconds, shuddered once, and then died.

Rozonov turned away.

His senior sergeant met him in the corridor. "The yacht is secure, sir. Everyone aboard has been eliminated."

"Excellent work, Yenin," Rozonov said. "Make sure all the bodies are weighted down before you dump them into the sea. Moscow doesn't want anyone finding bullet-riddled corpses drifting on the wind and waves."

The sergeant shot him a twisted grin. "Well,

that would sort of spoil the mystery of the thing, wouldn't it, Lieutenant?"

An hour later, the Spetsnaz team clambered back onto their rigid inflatable boat and cast off. They motored off to a safe distance and turned to parallel the now-deserted yacht as it glided downwind.

Rozonov glanced down at his waterproof watch. "Ten seconds," he murmured. "Five seconds. Four. Three. Two . . ."

WHUMMP. WHUMMP. WHUMMP.

The scuttling charges they'd placed in the bilge detonated one after another—ripping enormous holes in the yacht's hull from stem to stern. Slowly at first and then faster, the vessel, with its sails still set, slid lower in the water. Within minutes, it vanished beneath the waves, plunging down and down into the lightless depths of the abyss.

Rozonov nodded in satisfaction. President Gryzlov would be pleased. Except for a few small bits and pieces of unidentifiable wreckage bobbing on the waves, nothing remained to explain the disappearance of Francis Xavier Regan.

CHAPTER 1

The world is in greater peril from those who tolerate or encourage evil than from those who actually commit it.

—Albert Einstein, theoretical physicist

IRON WOLF SQUADRON ASSAULT FORCE, MOSCOW, RUSSIAN FEDERATION
Spring 2020

Moscow was burning.

Fires glowed orange-red around the horizon in all directions. Each blaze showed where long-range standoff weapons launched by Polish and Iron Wolf fighter-bombers and drones had slammed home—obliterating Russian surface-to-air missile batteries, military airfields, air defense radars, and command posts.

Sun-bright flashes rippled across the night sky, lighting up a spaghetti-like tangle of wildly corkscrewing smoke trails left by missiles. Blinded by the loss of most of their radars and by waves of electronic jamming and decoys, the city's surviving air defense units were shooting almost at random, hoping to score lucky hits. It was all they had left to fend off any airborne attackers slashing in to strike Moscow's center of political and military power, the Kremlin.

But the Russians were too late. Their enemies were already on the ground, well inside their outer defenses.

Vozdvizhenka Street ran almost due west toward the tall redbrick walls and towers surrounding the Kremlin. On one side of the street, three- and four-story buildings housed a mix of cafés, restaurants, shops, and government offices. A wing of the huge Russian State Library ran along the other.

Now wreckage and rubble blocked most of the street. Oily pillars of black smoke curled lazily away from mangled police cars and BTR-82 armored personnel carriers. Bodies were strewn across the cratered pavement. Flames danced eerily inside darkened buildings blown open by high-explosive rounds.

Nothing seemed to be moving.

And then a twelve-foot-tall humanlike machine emerged from the billowing smoke—moving with terrible, almost predatory swiftness. Two arms carried weapons, a 25mm autocannon and a 40mm automatic grenade launcher. More equipment and weapons packs were attached to its long, broad-shouldered torso. A six-sided head studded with sensor panels swiveled intently from side to side, carefully scanning the surrounding streets and buildings.

It was a Cybernetic Infantry Device—a human-piloted combat robot. First developed by a U.S. Army research lab years before, every CID carried more firepower than a conventionally equipped infantry platoon. Protected by highly resistant composite armor, its powered exoskeleton was faster and stronger than any ten men combined. A special haptic interface translated its pilot's smallest gestures into motion by the exoskeleton, allowing the robot to move with eerie precision and agility.

Very few Russians ever saw a CID up close and most who did died within seconds.

Inside the robot's cockpit, Brad McLanahan concentrated intently, allowing data gathered by a wide array of passive and active sensors to pour into his mind through a neural link with the CID's sophisticated computer systems. Red targeting indicators blinked into existence across his displays. Each identified an enemy infantry squad or heavy-weapons team frantically deploying along his axis of advance. They were taking up concealed positions inside buildings, planning to ambush him with machine-gun fire and RPGs as he charged past.

Sorry guys, he thought, *you can't run and you can't hide. Not from me.* The direct link with his sensors, coupled with advanced computer analysis, gave him astonishing situational awareness. It was like being gifted with a god's-eye view of the world.

With difficulty, Brad fought down a sudden

sense of wild, inhuman glee. Piloting one of these Iron Wolf Squadron combat robots was an incredible thrill ride. You couldn't help feeling an almost godlike rush of power, perception, and speed. But that way lay madness . . . and death.

CIDs were tough . . . but they weren't invincible. Some of his friends had found that out the hard way.

C'mon, McLanahan, get your head back in the game, Brad growled to himself. The Russian soldiers scurrying across his path to the Kremlin were off balance, shocked by this sudden attack and their horrendous losses. They were ready to break. But going in half-cocked was just a way to get killed.

"Wolf One to Wolf Six and Wolf Two," he said aloud, opening a secure channel to the other Iron Wolf Squadron war machines committed to this operation. "I'm roughly four hundred meters from the ramp to the Troitskaya Tower gate. Standing by."

"Six copies," the laconic voice of Colonel Wayne "Whack" Macomber answered through his headphones. "I've got the right flank."

"Two copies, Wolf One. I am in position to guard your left flank," a clear, crisp female voice said a heartbeat later. "Submit we stop pissing around and finish this before the Russians fully wake up. Even *they* will not run around like idiots forever."

Brad couldn't help smiling. In combat, Major Nadia Rozek was tough, fearless, and intensely focused. Off duty and out of uniform, she was astonishingly passionate. But no matter where she was, the beautiful, dark-haired Polish special forces officer was a force of nature. When she made up her mind to do something, you either sided with her or you got the hell out of her way. There were no other choices.

"You heard the major, McLanahan," Macomber murmured.

"Loud and clear, Whack," Brad agreed. Mentally, he commanded his CID's battle computer to assign priorities to every Russian defensive position its sensors had identified—ranking them by the danger they represented. In seconds, its software finished work that would have taken a human staff officer minutes. His targeting indicators changed color and shape to match those priorities.

He took a deep breath, getting centered. "Attacking now!"

Without waiting for a response, Brad sprinted up the street—speeding up with every long-legged stride. Dodging around a wrecked personnel carrier, he opened fire on the move. Rounds from his autocannon hammered an upper-floor window ahead, killing a lurking Russian RPG team. Shards of shattered stone and broken glass spilled onto the pavement.

Another icon blinked insistently at the edge of his vision, highlighting a darkened doorway. *12.7mm heavy-machine-gun team*, the CID reported. *Threat level high*.

No shit, Brad thought. Rounds from that Russian MG might not penetrate his armor, but they

could definitely damage or destroy his sensors
and other equipment. Instantly, he swiveled the
robot's torso and fired a 40mm high-explosive
grenade into the opening. It went off with a dazzling flash.

The threat icon disappeared.

Still shooting on the run, he dashed across
Mokhovaya Street, hurtled over a row of stubby
metal pillars designed to block traffic, and landed
in a wide stone-paved plaza. The Kutafya Tower
rose ahead. This barbican was the Kremlin's main
public entrance. Past its wrought-iron gates, a
gently inclined ramp sloped up to the tall, spired
Troitskaya Tower. To the right, treetops rose
above a guardrail at the plaza's edge. That was
the Alexandrovsky Garden, a narrow tree-lined
stretch of walkways, flower gardens, and lawns
occupying what had once been a moat around the
old fortress.

"Armored vehicles approaching," he heard Nadia Rozek report coolly. "T-90 and T-72 main
battle tanks. I am engaging."

CCRRACK! CCRRACK! CCRRACK!

The sky on Brad's left lit up as she opened fire
with her electromagnetic rail gun, flaring bright
white with every shot. Propelled at Mach 5, small
superdense metal projectiles punched into the
enemy tanks and tore right through their armor.
One by one, wrecked T-90s and T-72s slewed
across the road and shuddered to a stop, spewing
smoke and flame.

"Targets destroyed," Nadia said. "My camouflage worked perfectly. The Russians never saw me."

Brad nodded in satisfaction. In a brutal, close-quarters urban fight like this, every edge counted. When stationary or moving slowly, the advanced camouflage systems carried by their Sky Masters Aerospace–built Mod IV CIDs rendered them almost invisible to enemy IR sensors and even to the naked eye.

Hundreds of small, hexagonal thermal adaptive tiles overlaid each robot's armored "skin"—tiles that could change temperature with extraordinary rapidity. Computers could adjust them to mimic the heat signatures of trees, buildings, and other vehicles. In turn, paper-thin electrochromatic plates covered these thermal tiles. Tiny voltage changes could alter the mix of colors displayed by each plate, giving the CID a chameleon-like ability to blend in with its environment. But both camouflage systems lost effectiveness and drained too much power if they were used when moving at high speed.

Like he was now.

Brad charged ahead, shooting up a glass-walled building used for security screening. The Russian soldiers who'd been firing back at him from inside were hurled backward, either blown apart by 25mm autocannon rounds or cut to ribbons by flying glass.

Flashes winked at him from open arches below the Troitskaya Tower's spire. Rifle bullets thwacked into his CID's torso, shattering a couple of its thermal tiles. He spun away and ducked into cover behind the ruins of the security building.

"Drone imagery and scans downlinked," Ma-

comber radioed. "Looks like the bastards are reacting as expected."

Brad saw new data relayed through his neural interface appear on his displays. Their Iron
Wolf assault team had half a dozen small and very
stealthy drones orbiting high over the Kremlin—
acting as their eyes and ears beyond the reach of
their CIDs' sensors.

At a glance, he could see that the colonel was
right. Most of the Kremlin's elite guard infantry
platoons and armored vehicles were deploying to
protect the walled compound's gates. Anyone trying to breach those entrances would be met by
a hail of antitank missiles, rocket-propelled grenades, and 125mm tank cannon fire. Not even the
composite armor on their CIDs would hold up
against that kind of firepower.

Which was exactly why Brad had never planned
to conduct a real attack on the gates.

With a wolfish grin, he darted away from the
Kutafya Tower, swung over the iron railing, and
dropped lightly into the tree-lined expanse of the
Alexandrovsky Garden. The Russians had bought
his feint. Now it was time to show them why they
should have been thinking vertically instead.

Brad sprinted south, paralleling the Kremlin
wall rising beyond the trees. An antitank missile
streaked after him, impacted against the trunk
of a lime tree, and blew up. He dodged away and
kept running.

Preset targeting icons appeared on the massive
redbrick wall. "Engaging Spider-Man protocol,"
he said wryly. He raised his autocannon, quickly

checking to make sure he had armor-piercing rounds loaded. Then he skidded to a stop and opened fire.

WHANG. WHANG. WHANG. WHANG.

Broken bits of pulverized brick exploded away from the wall. Ragged craters appeared at precisely calculated intervals, rising from near the bottom all the way to the top. Since the Kremlin's ancient defense barrier ranged between eleven and twenty-one feet thick, none of the rounds penetrated all the way through.

But that's not the point, now, is it? Brad thought with a silent laugh. Swiftly, he slid the autocannon and grenade launcher back into his weapons pack, flexed the fingers of the CID's hands, and then started climbing the wall—pulling himself up fast using the craters he'd just blown in the brickwork as handholds.

He reached the battlements and scrambled onto a wide walkway used by guards to patrol the wall. There, he met a disheveled-looking soldier hurrying toward the distant Troitskaya Tower. The Russian was frantically trying to squirm into a bulky set of body armor.

The man stopped dead. He stared up at the huge combat robot in horror. *"Mater' Bozh'ya!* Mother of God!"

Apologetically, Brad shook his head. "Sorry, pal. That's not me." Then he grabbed the Russian with one big metal hand and tossed him off the wall. Shrieking, the soldier vanished into the darkness. His despairing wail ended in a dull, wet-sounding thud.

Brad winced. That had to hurt.

He blurred back into motion and dropped over the other side, coming down on his CID's hands and knees inside the Kremlin compound itself. He was in a small courtyard close to the armory.

Without further thought, Brad stood back up and pulled out his rail gun. It powered up with a shrill, high-pitched whine. The autocannon dropped into his other hand.

He looked around for a way out of the courtyard and spotted a big, solid-looking wooden door into the nearest building. One quick kick smashed it open, revealing a short, well-lit corridor.

Bending low, Brad trotted down the corridor. He ignored a gaggle of panicked clerks and officials scrambling out of his path. They were no threat. None of them were armed.

He smashed through another door and came out onto Dvortsovaya Boulevard. The State Kremlin Palace, a massive and horrifically ugly Soviet-era glass-and-concrete edifice, loomed straight ahead. *Blowing the snot out of that monstrosity would probably be doing the Russians a favor,* Brad decided.

Instead, he swung away and sprinted north toward the Troitskaya Tower gate. His CID burst out into the open, right on the flank of the Russian infantry and armored units deployed to block the gate. Targets crowded his vision.

Brad opened fire with both the rail gun and autocannon, often shooting almost simultaneously at different targets. Tracked BMP infantry fighting vehicles and T-72 tanks shuddered and exploded— ripped open by rail-gun rounds. Infantrymen and antitank missile crews scattered in panic. A few, braver or more foolish, turned to fight. Autocannon bursts knocked them dead or dying to the cobblestone pavement.

He stalked on through a nightmarish tangle of burning vehicles and bleeding soldiers, slowing only now and again to destroy new targets identified by his CID computer. Through the thickening smoke, he could make out the wooded confines of the Kremlin's Senate Square . . . and beyond that, a large, triangular-shaped building, the Kremlin Senate itself. Its yellow walls were studded with tall white columns.

Brad's mouth tightened. Signals intercepts and other intelligence confirmed that building was where Russia's vicious president, Gennadiy Gryzlov, was holed up, along with his closest advisers. He raised his rail gun, aiming at the upper floors. Three or four slugs ripping through those walls at supersonic speeds ought to kick things off with a nice bang.

Suddenly Nadia Rozek broke in over the radio. "Unidentified movement from the west detected. Moving to engage!" She sounded startled. "I cannot get a lock. Repeat, I cannot get a—"

Her voice vanished, replaced only by crackling static. In that same moment, the icon representing her robot abruptly flared orange and then red. It winked out.

Brad swallowed hard against the taste of bile. Somehow, some Russian son of a bitch had just knocked out Nadia's CID. He spun around, looking for the fastest way to her last known position.

"Drop it, McLanahan!" Whack Macomber growled. He sounded like death itself. "Continue the mission. I'm on this." The icon showing the colonel's own CID was already in motion, rushing north.

"Understood, Wolf Six," Brad said through gritted teeth. He turned back toward Gryzlov's lair. It was time to finish this.

More hostiles approaching, his computer reported calmly, reclaiming his attention. *Threat axis at three o'clock.*

Swearing under his breath, Brad glanced to his right. Three more T-72s had just appeared around the far corner of the mammoth State Kremlin Palace. Whirring, their turrets spun in his direction, bringing their main guns to bear.

"Ah, crap," Brad muttered. He slid to the side and snapped off a quick rail-gun shot at the lead tank. Hit squarely beneath its long 125mm cannon, it blew apart. Twisted fragments of the turret flew skyward on a pillar of fire.

One of the other T-72s fired back at him. The armor-piercing shell screamed low over his head, missing by less than a meter. Rocked by the shock wave, his CID staggered slightly and then recovered its balance. A coaxial machine gun chattered. 7.62mm rounds spattered off his composite armor.

Camouflage systems seriously degraded. Minor hydraulic damage to left arm, the computer told him.

Brad stayed on the move, veering unpredictably to make it harder for the Russian gunners to draw a bead on him. His targeting reticle centered on another T-72. He squeezed the trigger. Hit broadside, it burst into flame.

Two down. One to go.

"I see Major Rozek's CID," Macomber said starkly over their secure channel. "It's a total write-off. No life signs. And there's no sign of whatever killed her."

Brad nodded bleakly. Successfully bailing out of a damaged robot under fire was virtually impossible. "Understood, Six." He fired again, smashing the last Russian tank. His threat displays were clear, empty of any new enemies. "I'm going after Gryzlov now. Watch my back."

"Affirmative, Wolf One," Macomber replied. Then his voice tightened. "Holy shit! What the fuck is *that* thing? Am engag—" Abruptly, his CID beacon flared bright red and disappeared.

For what seemed an eternity but couldn't have been more than a second or two, Brad stared at his tactical display in complete consternation. What the hell was happening here? This was a nightmare, a total damned disaster.

Angrily, he shook himself back to full alertness. Disaster or not, he could still kill Gryzlov and accomplish the mission. He owed Nadia and Whack Macomber that much. He turned back toward the Russian president's headquarters.

And then a stream of 30mm cannon rounds hammered the side of his CID with horrific force. Brad crashed into the edge of the cockpit as his robot tumbled off its feet and smacked headlong into the pavement.

Warning. Warning. Sensors severely damaged.

Hydraulic system function down to thirty percent. Ammunition and weapons packs off-line, the computer told him. *Camouflage systems inoperative. Armor breaches in multiple locations.*

Groggily, Brad shook his head, an action emulated by the robot. He forced himself upright. Damaged servos and actuators whined. More failure and damage warnings flowed through his dazed mind.

Moving slower now, he spun around, toward the soaring glass-and-concrete façade of the State Kremlin Palace. That was where the Russian bastards who'd just ambushed him had to be lurking. Fragments and bits of glass were still falling from one of the enormous second-floor windows.

A tall, humanlike machine leaped out through the opening and landed only meters away. Its spindly arms held an array of weaponry.

Brad's eyes opened wide in shock. *Oh, my God . . .*

Before he could react, the other combat robot opened fire again, this time at point-blank range. Multiple armor-piercing rounds tore into his CID, hurling it backward across the cobblestones in a shower of sparks and torn bits of wiring and metal. Sensors were ripped away. Whole segments of his vision grayed out and shut down. Red failure warnings cascaded through his bleary consciousness, each telling a dizzying tale of catastrophe.

Stunned, Brad fought to regain some measure of control over his dying CID. Nothing worked. His computer systems were damaged beyond repair. Through his one working visual sensor, he saw the other robot leaning over him. Slowly, almost gleefully, it took aim with its autocannon . . . and then it started shooting.

Everything went black.

"Battle simulation complete," a smooth, computer-generated voice said in satisfaction. *"Total mission failure. Assault force casualties: One hundred percent."*

CHAPTER 2

The lights came back on.

"*Senior exercise personnel should report to the main conference room,*" the computer said. "*Simulation debriefing is scheduled in ten minutes.*"

Blinking in the sudden brightness, Brad McLanahan squirmed out of the simulator's haptic interface module. Now that he wasn't connected through it to the computers and virtual reality setup, the touch of the gray, gelatinous membrane made his skin crawl. Strapping in or disconnecting always felt a lot like wriggling through a narrow tube full of body-temperature, oozy mud. At the bottom of the cockpit, he tapped a glowing green button.

A metal hatch slid open. Carefully, he squeezed through the small opening, slid down a short ladder, and then, keeping his head low, crab-walked out from under the egg-shaped Cybernetic Infantry Device simulator. Set in the middle of a large opaque dome, the cockpit nested inside a bewildering array of hydraulic jacks.

Once clear of the complicated, Rube Goldberg–looking assembly, Brad straightened up to his full height. For several seconds, he twisted and stretched his neck and shoulders and hips, working out the kinks in muscles that felt cramped and sore. Most of the time he didn't mind being tall and broad-shouldered, but there were a few places where his build was a definite disadvantage.

Yeah, like cramped, instrument-filled aircraft and CID cockpits, he thought with a wry grin. Which just happened to be where he spent a huge portion of his working hours. *Smooth career move, McLanahan*, he told himself, heading for the door out of the dome. He could have been anything from an aerospace engineer to a bartender, but no, he'd wanted to be a combat pilot, just like his old man.

He emerged into a cavernous hangar. Two more of the big domes crowded the vast space. Each looked very much like one of those inflatable planetariums used for traveling astronomy shows. Color-coded fiber-optic and power cables snaked across the bare concrete floor, linking the domes to banks of big-screen monitors and powerful computers.

Ordinarily, the simulators gave rookie CID pilots a taste of what it was really like to command one of the big fighting machines. Once you were strapped inside, the combination of haptic interfaces, full-motion capability, and three-dimensional virtual reality projectors provided an experience that sounded, looked, and even *felt* real. It was a relatively fast, cheap, and easy way to weed out newbies who couldn't hack the job.

Today, though, the simulator domes had been repurposed to run veteran Iron Wolf pilots through a series of immersive combat scenarios. Fighting virtual battles avoided wear and tear on their expensive robots . . . and on the Polish countryside. Live-fire exercises with CIDs might be exciting, but they were hell on equipment, buildings, and the landscape.

Even worse, open field maneuvers risked exposing key intelligence about the lethal machines and their advanced capabilities to Moscow's spies. Warsaw's Military Counterintelligence Service was top-notch, but Poland was a free and democratic country. There was no way to build an iron curtain of secrecy around its armed forces—or those of its high-tech allies, the Iron Wolf Squadron and its corporate parent Scion, a private military company.

And Brad knew only too well that Russia and its ruthless, belligerent leader, Gennadiy Gryzlov, had every reason to pry deeply into their secrets. He felt his mood darken.

For three difficult and dangerous years, the foreign-born pilots, commandos, and intelligence specialists who formed the nucleus of Iron Wolf had helped the Poles and other Eastern Europeans defend their freedoms against Russian aggression. Together they'd stopped Gryzlov's forces cold—in the air, on the ground, and even in the strange digital battlegrounds of cyberspace. But the cost had been high. Too many of his fellow pilots and soldiers were dead.

Right now Poland and its allies were not openly at war with Russia. But neither were they really at peace. Sure, maybe nobody was actively shooting, slipping malware into power grids and banking systems, or lobbing bombs and missiles into cities, but that didn't mean the two sides were ready to beat their swords into plowshares.

This current lull had lasted for more than a year. No one with any common sense believed it would last much longer. Like the leopard who could not change his spots, Gennadiy Gryzlov wasn't going to abandon his ambition of making Russia the most powerful nation on the planet. The only open question was when he would make his next aggressive move . . . and what form it would take.

Warily, Brad poked his head in through the conference room's open door.

Waiting for the hammer to fall was starting to wear on a lot of nerves around the squadron. This morning's fiasco wasn't going to make anyone feel really warm and fuzzy.

Whack Macomber and Nadia Rozek were already seated at the big, oval table. *No surprise there*, he thought. They both got "killed" in the sim before he did. Neither looked especially happy about what had just happened. Like most dedicated soldiers, both were intensely competitive and fiercely determined. Losing gracefully was for the other guys.

Nadia glanced over her shoulder when he came in. A fleeting smile briefly brightened her blue-gray eyes. She patted the empty chair beside her. "Come and join the ranks of the dishonored dead, fellow ghost."

Ruefully, Brad did as she suggested. "Yeah, I guess that's us," he said. "So do they give virtual wraiths government-issued chains to clank around in? Or do we have to buy our own?"

Macomber snorted and looked away. The big man's arms were folded across his chest. From the set of his jaw, he was just about mad enough to go off and bust a few heads in a bar somewhere, preferably one full of the meanest, nastiest sons of bitches around.

Oh, boy, Brad thought worriedly. He knew that look. So would a lot of MPs and civilian cops around the world who'd ever made the mistake of trying to stop Whack from blowing off some steam. There were a lot of stories about the colonel from his younger days in the U.S. Air Force's Special Operations Command. Some of the wilder ones were even true.

Nadia's warm hand slipped into his. Almost against his will, he felt himself relax a little. They'd first met almost three years ago, when she was assigned as Polish president Piotr Wilk's military liaison to Scion and the newly formed Iron Wolf Squadron. If he'd been asked way back then, he would have bet good money this was going to be one of those short-lived "stunning local girl takes pity on lonely foreigner" kind of flings. Instead, whenever duty allowed, they were still spending almost every waking and sleeping moment together. So much, in fact, that Brad was taking a lot of flak from friends who wondered when they were getting married.

He thought about that. If he ever got up the guts to propose to her, would she say yes? Or would she just laugh, tell him not to be an idiot, and then drag him away to their bed to take his mind off the impossible?

Suddenly Nadia shot him an amused, sidelong glance from under her eyelashes. Brad felt himself reddening. Christ, was she reading his mind now?

Fortunately, before he could dig himself in any deeper, another man entered the conference room. Shorter than either Brad or Macomber, the newcomer was in his midsixties, with longish gray hair and a neatly trimmed gray beard. Moving fast, he crossed to the opposite side of the table and dropped heavily into a chair. From there, he surveyed the three Iron Wolf officers with a coldly displeased expression.

Kevin Martindale, once president of the United States, now ran Scion. He was also a close adviser to Piotr Wilk and the other leaders of the fledgling Alliance of Free Nations. They all knew that the high-tech weaponry, innovative tactics, and intelligence expertise Martindale and his people provided were the margin between their continued survival as free nations and renewed Russian domination.

"Well, that was a mess," Martindale said at last,

breaking an uncomfortable silence. "Three CIDs wrecked beyond repair. Three top-notch pilots who would certainly have been killed if they were lucky, and captured if they were not. And all for nothing."

"Yeah, no kidding," Macomber said through gritted teeth. He stabbed a finger back at Martindale. "What the hell was that little bolt-out-of-the-blue bushwhack supposed to prove? That we can get killed in these tin cans? Tell me something I don't already fucking *know*!"

Brad felt Nadia stiffen beside him. Fifteen months ago, during the last round of fighting with Russia, Whack Macomber had led a raid on Perun's Aerie, a secret Russian cyberwar complex buried deep in the icy, snow-cloaked Ural Mountains. They'd walked into a cleverly planned ambush. Charlie Turlock, one of their best friends, had been killed—unable to bail out of her damaged CID before it self-destructed. Whack himself had been captured by the Russians when his own robot was knocked out. He'd been rescued, but climbing into one of the Iron Wolf war machines still put him on edge.

"Adding those simulated Russian war robots was my idea," someone said calmly from the doorway behind them, coming to Martindale's defense. "Consider it a warning shot."

Brad hid a grin. His father, retired U.S. Air Force Lieutenant General Patrick McLanahan, always did know how to make a dramatic entrance.

Heads turned as the older McLanahan came into the conference room and moved to join

Martindale. A motor-driven, carbon-fiber-and-metal exoskeleton supported his torso, arms, and legs, whirring softly as he moved. The exoskeleton, a bulky life-support backpack, and the clear helmet enclosing his head gave the impression he was wearing an eccentrically designed space suit.

In a very real sense, Brad knew, that was exactly what the LEAF, or Life Enhancing Assistive Facility, was . . . a piece of advanced hardware designed to keep his father alive in a hostile environment. Only the hostile environment wasn't just the cold vacuum of space, it was the whole wide world itself.

Years before, Patrick McLanahan had been critically wounded during an unauthorized retaliatory strike against the People's Republic of China. Most people thought he'd been killed. They hadn't been far off. His injuries were beyond the power of modern medicine to heal. Only a CID's automated life-support systems had kept him alive. And so for year after long year, he'd been forced to exist inside a machine designed solely for war, robbed of all normal human contact—able to interact only through the CID's sensors and computers.

Brad swallowed hard, remembering the sorrow he had felt as the man who'd raised him slowly disappeared into a shadowy, inhuman world of binary 1s and 0s. This Sky Masters–designed LEAF, risky and highly experimental though it was, had come along just in time to save his father's sanity. While the suit might look a little weird, at least it let Patrick McLanahan see other people with his own eyes and touch them with his own hands. It also let him speak to them in his own voice.

And that was a precious gift . . . even when what he said with it pissed them off.

"A warning shot?" Whack repeated angrily. "Nobody else has CIDs. Using them against us in the sim was a bullshit move, General."

Patrick shook his head. "I'm afraid not, Colonel." He looked around the small group. "Gennadiy Gryzlov may be a psychopath, but he's also quite intelligent. He knows the kind of force multiplier our combat robots represent. Obtaining CID technology for his own armed forces has to be very high up on his priority list. In fact, I'm pretty sure that's what he was after in that ambush that killed Charlie."

"Maybe so," Whack agreed reluctantly, obviously wrestling with painful memories. Surrounded by overwhelming numbers of the enemy, he and Charlie Turlock had gone down hard— destroying dozens of Russian tanks and armored vehicles in a desperate last-stand fight. "But there sure as shit wasn't a lot left of our gear when those bastards finished shooting us to pieces."

Patrick sighed. "I've spent months analyzing the last few minutes of telemetry relayed from your CIDs, Whack. And I'm afraid more components might have survived intact than we first thought." His mouth turned down. "For example, Charlie's robot lost an arm to a Russian tank shell before it blew up."

"Yeah, so?"

"There are some indications that the impact

point was high up, on the CID's shoulder, and not on the arm itself. In which case, the arm's actuators and control links might not have been severely damaged," Patrick said quietly. "The same goes for your machine, Whack. It took a hell of a beating before the end, but the Russians could still have salvaged any number of functional or near-functional systems from the wreckage."

Brad stared at his father. "You really think Gryzlov could reverse-engineer the CIDs from a bunch of half-fried odds and ends?"

"Let's just say it's a possibility I can't rule out," the older man said. "But we can be sure his scientists and engineers are hard at work studying whatever they retrieved from the battlefield. And now that they know what our CIDs can do—" He shrugged.

"'What one man can invent, another can discover,'" Nadia quoted slowly, looking worried.

Patrick nodded. "Sooner or later . . . hopefully much later . . . the Russians are likely to figure out how to build their own war robots. And when that day comes, Gryzlov isn't going to be shy about using them in combat."

"Facing off against Russian CIDs?" Brad grimaced. "Well, crap, Dad. Based on what we just experienced in the simulator, that would really suck."

His father nodded. "Which is why we better start figuring out how to fight and *win* that kind of battle." He offered Macomber a wry, half-apologetic smile. "Hence the sucker punch today, Whack."

"One thing still bugs me, though," Brad said, thinking back over the way the enemy CIDs had seemingly materialized out of nowhere. "You programmed in those Russian robots with the equivalent of our thermal and chameleon camouflage systems, didn't you?"

"Yep."

Nadia frowned. "But we stripped the thermal tiles and chameleon plates off the CIDs we sent to Perun's Aerie *before* the raid itself. In those arctic winter conditions, neither camouflage system was worth the weight or power expenditure."

"True," Patrick agreed.

"So there's no possible way the Russians could reverse-engineer our camouflage gear. Not from anything they might have pulled out of the wrecks," Brad pointed out.

"Nope," his father agreed again.

"Then why throw that kind of high-tech invisibility-cloak shit at us in the sim?" Whack demanded. "What's next? Force fields and plasma guns?"

"'Train hard, fight easy,'" Patrick said with a grin, quoting the famous eighteenth-century Russian soldier Field Marshal Suvorov. Then his expression turned more serious. He tapped the exoskeleton sheathing his crippled body. "Look, Colonel, most of this complicated hardware is necessary just to keep me breathing. There's no way I'll ever fly a plane or pilot a CID again. So, the way I see it, I have *one* job. Just *one*. And that's to do *whatever* I can to make sure the rest of you are ready for the fight that may be coming."

His lopsided smile returned. "Even if I have to cheat like crazy to do it." He looked around the table. "Anyone here have a problem with that?"

There was a moment's silence. Finally, Nadia cocked her head to one side, looking thoughtful. "No, what you say makes sense." She matched the older McLanahan's grin with one of her own. "Better that we die a thousand times in the computer than get our asses kicked just once on a real battlefield."

CHAPTER 3

D r. Richard Witt stood uncertainly outside the door to an office suite in downtown Reno. A silver-colored nameplate showed that the space was leased to Peregrine Datalytics, ostensibly a small software research firm.

He wasn't used to feeling this nervous. Witt's colleagues at Sky Masters Aerospace often joked that he showed less emotion than the automatons he helped create. He suspected many of them were just jealous of his ability to swiftly analyze complex robotics challenges and software problems, using impeccably rigorous logic. His fellow engineers were slower and less efficient than he was because they allowed trifles—personal relationships, rivalries, and ambitions—to clutter up their working lives.

Sweat beaded his high bald forehead. Logic suggested nobody else at Sky Masters could possibly know or care why he had driven to Reno today. But this was one of those situations where pure reason provided less comfort than he would have wished.

Before he could knock, the door opened inward.

"Come on in, Dr. Witt," FBI special agent Carl Sundstrom said genially. "You're exactly on time."

Witt awkwardly shook hands, aware of how rumpled he must look compared to the FBI agent. The other man was shorter by a head, but trim and fit in a perfectly tailored navy-blue suit and crisply knotted red silk tie. "I don't think anyone followed me," he blurted.

"Relax, Doctor," Sundstrom said, offering him a quick, reassuring smile. He closed the door. "You're not here to do anything illegal after all. Or even immoral."

"Certainly not," Witt agreed stiffly. "I am a patriot and a concerned citizen."

Still smiling, the FBI agent nodded. "And believe me, Doctor, the powers that be in Washington greatly appreciate what you're offering us." He shrugged his narrow shoulders. "I only wish others at Sky Masters shared your sense of patriotism and loyalty."

Witt knew what he meant. It wasn't exactly a secret that Sky Masters covertly supplied high-tech military hardware, including Cybernetic Infantry Devices, to Scion's mercenary forces. Those sales violated a whole slew of executive orders issued by President Stacy Anne Barbeau—orders designed to prevent the United States from being dragged into Poland's bloody no-win conflict with the

Russians. True, a number of federal courts had recently stayed her regulations as unconstitutional, but that was mere legalistic nitpicking. Presidents should make foreign policy, not corporations. *Especially not a corporation so morally corrupt that it would arm and equip Scion's brutal hired killers*, he thought bitterly. Only greed could explain a willingness to support a warmongering madman like former president Martindale.

He followed Sundstrom into a large conference room. Huge windows looked north across the brightly lit Reno skyline. Another man, gray-haired and heavyset, turned away from the spectacular view when they came in. Dark brown eyes looked back at them through a pair of thick, horn-rimmed glasses.

"Dr. Witt, this is . . . Mr. Smith," the FBI agent said. "Let's just say that he works for another department, shall we? One with a much better scientific and technological grounding than my bureau." He smiled again. "We're pretty good at catching crooks and spies. Not so much at understanding gizmos like cybernetic control circuitry and neural interfaces."

Witt nodded, pleased at this confirmation that Sundstrom had taken him seriously during their earlier conversations. This "Mr. Smith" undoubtedly worked for the Defense Advanced Research Projects Agency, or maybe for one of its lesser-known government counterparts. DARPA, part of the Defense Department, was responsible for developing emerging technologies for military use. In fact, Jason Richter, Sky Masters' current chief executive officer, had been working for a DARPA-affiliated Army research lab when he built the first Cybernetic Infantry Device.

He came to a final decision. For weeks after the FBI first contacted him, he'd agonized over the seeming conflict between the demands of his conscience and his sense of professional ethics and company loyalty. Slowly, Witt reached into his coat pocket and took out a small USB flash drive. He handed it to Sundstrom. "In that case, I believe the information I've downloaded onto that device properly belongs to Mr. Smith and his agency."

The FBI agent looked down at the tiny drive he held with undisguised wonder. "*This* little thing contains all the schematics and other data necessary to replicate CID haptic interfaces?"

"As I promised," Witt told him. He looked at Smith. "The password protecting those files is *Prometheus*." Seeing their blank stares, he shrugged in embarrassment. "As in the Titan who stole fire from the gods for humanity? It seemed . . . well . . . appropriate."

Carefully, Sundstrom passed the flash drive to his colleague. "Would you evaluate this material for me, Mr. Smith? But quickly, please." He nodded toward the Sky Masters cyberneticist. "While *I'm* sure we can trust the good doctor here, our political masters will want confirmation."

Silently, Smith nodded and left the room with the drive.

Politely, the FBI agent waved Witt into one of the chairs around the big table and took another.

He leaned forward. "Forgive me for asking again, but you're still convinced that no one at Sky Masters will ever realize you've copied this data for us?"

"*I* wrote the security software for our cybernetics lab," Witt said flatly. "So I know for a fact there are no traces of what I've done in the system."

Sundstrom visibly relaxed. He shook his head. "I really don't understand why you haven't been promoted higher up the Sky Masters corporate ladder, Dr. Witt. Your abilities are quite extraordinary."

Witt frowned. That was a sore subject. By rights, he should long since have been named head of the Sky Masters Cybernetics Division. No one else in the lab had anything approaching his technical knowledge or analytical skill. But every time he applied for the job, Richter fobbed him off with some lame excuse or another about the difference between scientific and technical expertise and people skills.

"I think I've also been remiss in not extending my condolences for the death of Ms. Turlock," Sundstrom said suddenly. "I understand she was a valued colleague of yours?"

Charlie Turlock? Just hearing her name spoken aloud and thinking about what might have been . . . no, damn it, what *should* have been, made Witt feel as though he'd been stabbed in the stomach. He felt the blood drain from his face.

"Dr. Witt?" the FBI agent said, sounding concerned. "Are you all right?"

Fighting to regain control, Witt forced himself to nod. "I'm fine," he rasped. He took a shaky breath. "Yes, Ms. Turlock and I worked very closely together. She was a superb engineer. Her death was a real blow. To our team, I mean."

Liar, he thought bitterly. He'd wasted so many months and years. Always admiring Charlie Turlock, hell, *loving* her, and always being too afraid to say anything about it. Then one day, before he could work up the nerve to tell her how he really felt, off she'd flown to take part in one of Martindale's insane mercenary operations. Somewhere deep inside Russia, he'd heard. And it killed her. She was gone. Gone forever.

With one part of his mind, Witt heard Sundstrom still talking, trying to engage him in the kind of nonsensical chitchat that other people seemed to need to fill uncomfortable silences. He did his best to respond. But most of his being was lost in grief for what *might* have been—if only he'd been bolder sooner.

He only fully reentered the present when the mysterious "Mr. Smith" rejoined them.

"It is as Dr. Witt has said," Smith told Sundstrom, flourishing the USB drive. "Everything we need is there."

Later, after the Sky Masters cybernetics engineer was gone, ushered out with profuse thanks on behalf of the U.S. government and President Barbeau, the heavyset man who'd called himself Smith turned to his younger and better-dressed colleague. "*Kakoy debil!* What a moron!"

"Come now, Eduard," Major Vasily Dragomirov said in mock reproof. "Be kind. Why should the good Dr. Witt look further than the carefully forged FBI identity card I showed him?" He shrugged. "Like so many others in life, he sees what he wants to see. Now he has what he wanted, revenge against Sky Masters and Scion. If he thinks he has achieved that by helping his own government, instead of ours, well, so much the better for us, eh?"

"But how the hell did you get onto him?" Captain Eduard Naumov asked. Unlike Dragomirov, he wasn't a field operative for Russia's military intelligence service, the GRU. He was a technical officer in its Ninth Directorate, a group charged with acquiring and analyzing foreign military technology. He'd only flown in to Reno a few days before, standing by solely to verify the data they hoped to obtain in this covert operation.

"From our friends in Beijing," the major said. Seeing the confusion on the older man's face, he explained. "A few years ago, the Chinese hacked into the computer archives of the American OPM, their Office of Personnel Management. They stole millions of individual security clearance files." He smiled cruelly. "And those files include enormous amounts of information on candidates for sensitive positions—embarrassing information on everything from shaky personal finances to substance-abuse problems to potential psychological weaknesses."

"Like those of Dr. Witt," Naumov realized.

Dragomirov nodded. "Our masters in the Kremlin paid Beijing huge sums for access to certain files, chief among them those of any scientists and engineers connected in any way to Sky Masters or Scion."

"Well, it was money well spent," the older man assured him. He shook his head in wonder. "With the data I have already transmitted to Moscow, our robotics experts should not have any trouble reproducing these advanced haptic interfaces."

"Which means Mother Russia will soon have combat robots of its own," Dragomirov said in quiet satisfaction. While preparing for this mission, he had studied every GRU file on the Iron Wolf Squadron's fighting machines. He had been awed by their lethality and power. His eyes were cold. "And then the world will change forever."

CHAPTER 4

THE WHITE HOUSE, WASHINGTON, D.C.
Several days later

President Stacy Anne Barbeau kept her oh-so-charming, professional politician's smile fixed firmly in place while her aides ushered the members of her cabinet out of the Oval Office. She dropped it the moment the doors closed, leaving her alone with Luke Cohen, her White House chief of staff and longtime political adviser, and Edward Rauch, her national security adviser.

Good God, she thought caustically, pretending to respect the mediocrities she'd appointed to head various Executive Branch departments was sometimes tiresome. But she'd deliberately surrounded herself with sycophantic second raters at the cabinet level. As president, she could bully lower-echelon appointees into doing her bidding. If anyone balked, she could dump them without igniting a political firestorm. She couldn't ax a

recalcitrant secretary of state or defense or trea-
sury with the same impunity. So she'd picked men
and women who were politically reliable and pli-
able, rather than competent.

After all, Stacy Anne Barbeau knew better than
to trust anyone who might prove to be as shrewd,
devious, and power-hungry as she was herself.
For decades, she'd clawed her way up through the
rough-and-tumble world of American politics.
Washington, D.C., was full of onetime allies and
rivals she'd first charmed, then outfoxed, and finally discarded.

Well, by God, now she was at the top of the
heap. She was the queen bee of the American political scene. And like it was in a hive, there wasn't
room for another queen. Nor, for that matter, a
king.

"And most especially not that swaggering son
of a bitch John Dalton Farrell," she muttered.

Luke Cohen nodded solemnly. He'd been
sounding the alarm about the state of her reelection campaign for weeks, ever since it became
clear that John D. Farrell had effectively locked
up the other party's nomination to run against
her in November.

Farrell was the current governor of Texas,
but that wasn't what made him a dangerous general election opponent. As the incumbent president, Barbeau had a lot of advantages—including
virtually unlimited campaign funds and all the
TV-camera-friendly pomp and circumstance surrounding her as America's commander-in-chief.

Even with the nation's economy sputtering along in low gear, no ordinary, run-of-the-mill politician should be able to shake her hold on the White House.

But as both Cohen and his boss knew, John Dalton Farrell was about as far away from a conventional politician as it was possible to get and still be a viable presidential candidate. Born into a hardscrabble farming family, the Texan had made his substantial fortune as a wildcatter in the energy industry. Time after time, he'd played hunches and beaten the big players—Exxon Mobil, Chevron, BP, and the others—to new oil and gas fields. And then he'd made them pay through the nose for the rights to develop his discoveries. Along the way, he'd also cemented a reputation as a no-nonsense, plainspoken, tough-as-nails defender of free markets and enemy of crony capitalism. Straight from the long-ago days when his sole asset was one battered, secondhand drilling rig, he'd blasted the kind of backroom special deals career politicians loved to cut with favored big businesses and unions.

And now Farrell was out there every day on TV and at big campaign rallies pounding on the president's handouts to major corporate donors, especially in the defense and finance industries. He was also savaging her for allowing NATO to fall apart while the Russians pushed hard on Eastern and central Europe. All of those attacks were starting to bite, eating into her narrow polling edge.

Coldly, Barbeau looked across her big desk at

Cohen and Rauch. "Okay, no more bullshit. I need straight talk and straight answers."

Rauch, gray-haired, pale, and painfully thin, looked confused. "About what, Madam President?"

"About finding ways to spike Farrell's guns before he kicks the living shit out of me in November," Barbeau snapped.

Rauch stared back at her, suddenly looking even more uncomfortable. Before joining the administration, he'd devoted his working life at different Beltway think tanks to producing research papers on U.S. defense policy. Unfortunately, crafting careful academic analyses on subjects like strategic force modernization and base reorganization had turned out to be poor preparation for serving a president far more interested in politics than in policy. He cleared his throat. "Campaign tactics and strategy aren't exactly my forte."

"No kidding, Ed," Barbeau retorted. She pointed at Cohen. "That's Luke's patch." Her eyes glittered. "But you *are* minding my national security shop, aren't you?"

Cautiously, he nodded. Since both the secretary of defense and the head of the CIA were amiable, unambitious nonentities, more and more of the White House's day-to-day business with the defense and intelligence agencies flowed through his hands. Despite Rauch's occasional misgivings about some of her decisions, Barbeau knew it was tough for him to resist access to that kind of power.

"Then figure out how I can push back against the crap Farrell's peddling about our national security strategy," she demanded. "Every time I turn on the damned TV, he's out bitching somewhere about how we're letting Gennadiy Gryzlov run wild. Or how we're blowing billions of taxpayer dollars on bloated defense contracts for weapons systems that won't work as advertised."

Rauch looked down at his hands for a moment, thinking. "For one thing, the Russians *aren't* running wild," he said. He perked up a bit. "Oh, they've made some very limited territorial gains—in eastern Ukraine, for example. But otherwise Moscow has achieved nothing of any real strategic consequence. President Gryzlov's offensive operations against the Poles and their allies have yielded only a continuing stalemate."

"No thanks to us," Cohen pointed out carefully.

Early in her term, unwilling to risk a clash with the Russians, Stacy Anne Barbeau had abandoned the Poles—refusing to send help when Gryzlov unleashed his armies and airpower against them. Then, to her surprise and chagrin, former president Kevin Martindale's band of high-tech mercenaries managed to fight the Russian onslaught to a standstill. Feeling betrayed by the United States, the Poles and their Eastern European neighbors had broken away from NATO and formed their own defense pact, the so-called Alliance of Free Nations.

She had taken political heat for that outcome, especially from the kind of armchair generals who were always eager to send other people's kids off to fight and die. *Well, screw them*, she thought.

Nothing in Eastern Europe was worth a single American soldier or airman's life.

"Yes, no thanks to us," Rauch agreed, echoing Cohen. "But that's precisely my point. Despite the odds, the Poles and their allies have contained the Russians so far—without any financial or military cost to us. So, in a strategic sense, the president's policies have produced the best of all worlds for the United States." He had the grace to look embarrassed. "And that isn't the result I would have predicted using any kind of conventional political or military analysis."

Barbeau eyed him coolly. She'd known her national security adviser thought she was crazy for standing aside every time Gennadiy Gryzlov got a burr up his ass about the Poles. If she hadn't needed Rauch to ride herd for her on the labyrinthine defense and intelligence communities, she'd have shit-canned him a long time ago. That made watching the onetime academic eat crow even more enjoyable.

"Not bad, Ed," Cohen said admiringly. His eyes were full of mischief. "We can definitely sell that. Every time Farrell mouths off about unchecked Russian aggression, we'll point out how little all their 'mighty tank divisions, bombers, and cyberwar geniuses' have really achieved. He'll come across like a whiny dick for trying to make Gryzlov look ten feet tall. And the president will end up looking pretty damned smart for showing so much restraint in the face of both Russian *and* Polish provocation."

"You run with that, Luke," Barbeau agreed. "But see if you can filter that angle out through our allies in the media. Let them make the case for us first. That way it'll look more like unbiased analysis and less like special pleading."

The New Yorker nodded. There was always a revolving door between the media and an administration like Barbeau's. Political people leaving the White House found jobs as pundits, reporters, and even news anchors on the networks. And, in turn, friendly journalists rotated in to act as press secretaries or speechwriters. Incestuous the process might be, but it guaranteed the president and her staff a first crack at spinning any story in the direction they wanted.

Barbeau turned back to Rauch. She offered him a wry smile. "You may be better suited to political infighting than you imagined, Ed."

He didn't look quite as pleased by that as she expected.

"We're still going to bleed every time Farrell slams our big-ticket weapons procurement programs," Cohen warned. "The flyover country rubes he's whipping into a frenzy are buying his crap about crooked deals with defense contractors."

"We *need* those new fighters, strategic bombers, and missiles," Barbeau said flatly. "My unlamented predecessors, like that scumbag Martindale, ran around the world picking senseless fights. And every stupid war they started ate deeper and deeper into our force structure. Those glory-grabbing morons left this country with a hollowed-out Air Force. For Christ's sake, we've been limping along with a handful of aging bombers and fighter squadrons full of F-15s and F-16s that were old twenty years ago! So now it's my job to put the pieces back together."

Left unspoken were the obvious political benefits of pumping tens of billions of federal dollars into states whose electoral votes she was going to need in November. Not to mention the hefty contributions the big defense companies and labor unions were funneling into her reelection campaign and those of her political allies. All of which just made her strategic rearmament program a win-win-win situation as far as she was concerned.

Rauch looked pained, which meant he had something to say that she wasn't going to like hearing. "Governor Farrell is not opposed to rebuilding our defenses, Madam President," he pointed out. "Instead, he's arguing that there are better, faster, and cheaper ways to do the job."

"Oh, let me guess. Big Tex is a fan of all those pie-in-the-sky wonder weapons Sky Masters peddles," Barbeau said with icy disdain. "All the super-duper combat drones, hypersonic missiles, and other Buck Rogers baloney they've been pushing at the Pentagon for years. Right?"

Rauch nodded reluctantly.

Cohen snorted. "Well, that's a dead giveaway as to who's pulling Farrell's strings."

"Martindale." Barbeau's lip curled in disgust. As president, Martindale had been a big believer in the cutting-edge military hardware developed by Jon Masters, the founder and chief scientist of Sky Masters. Masters himself was dead, killed years ago by domestic terrorists. But with his ex-wife, Helen Kaddiri, at the helm, the Nevada-based company kept rolling out new concepts for manned and unmanned aircraft, sensors, weapons systems, and other equipment. And despite her best efforts to stop them, Sky Masters was still selling Martindale the high-tech weapons and combat robots he needed to fight his own private, highly profitable wars.

She frowned. No wonder Martindale and his corporate allies wanted her out . . . and Farrell in. They were counting on the Texas oil man to shovel billions in new Pentagon contracts their way come next January. She looked at Cohen. "Well, now we know what good old John D. was really doing in Warsaw last fall."

He nodded.

Shortly after announcing his candidacy, Farrell had jetted off on what he called a "fact-finding trip" across Europe and Asia. Pundits and blog-gers on Barbeau's side had mocked him for the obvious effort to paper over his total lack of for-eign policy experience. When he added Warsaw to his itinerary, Barbeau had privately dismissed the visit as a publicity stunt designed to embar-rass her. She should have known better. Besides hobnobbing with Poland's president, Piotr Wilk, and other leaders in the Alliance of Free Nations, he must also have been making a deal with Mar-tindale for his support.

From the dubious expression on Rauch's pale face, she knew he didn't buy the idea that Farrell was acting as a stalking horse for Martindale and Sky Masters. She ignored him.

Like many former academics, her national security adviser still longed for the life of the ivory tower where truth was determined by agreed-upon facts and clear evidence. Politics was a very different game—one where intuition reigned supreme and where taking an opponent's actions and words solely at face value was never the smart play.

"If Farrell *is* tied in with Sky Masters through Martindale, they'll pull out all the stops to make him look good," Cohen said thoughtfully. "They could put on one hell of an air show with some of those experimental aircraft and drones they're sitting on."

Barbeau nodded slowly. After she learned that Kaddiri and her new chief engineer and CEO, Jason Richter, were shipping arms and equipment to Scion's mercenaries, she'd ordered a full FBI-led investigation into the company. Reading those reports had been an eye-opener. Sky Masters had at least one hangar full of flyable prototypes.

Common sense told her that most of those X-planes must be duds, either unsuited for real-world military use or too expensive to mass-produce, operate, and maintain. Unfortunately, none of those considerations would matter much to the voters Farrell was wooing. They'd only see a slew of futuristic-looking aircraft and drones already winging through the air . . . while most of the new fifth-generation air-superiority fighters and long-range bombers her administration backed were only on drawing boards, or, at best, crawling through the Pentagon's interminable review processes. The contrast would be damning.

Irritably, Barbeau swiveled away from her desk and glared out across the White House lawn. What could her administration do to counter a Sky Masters dog and pony show? Static models, mockups, and computer animations weren't going to wow anyone. While F-35 Lightning IIs were finally coming off the production line in reasonable numbers, individual examples had already been seen at air shows in the States and around the world for years. The only thing different now was that the Air Force could finally field a complete active-duty squadron of the stealth multirole fighters.

Suddenly it occurred to her that she'd been coming at this from the wrong direction. She didn't need to *counter* whatever Farrell, Sky Masters, and Martindale had planned. She needed to *preempt* it. The old axiom about the best defense being a good offense was as true in a political campaign as it was in war.

Barbeau swiveled back. "Dr. Rauch," she said formally. "Am I right that the defense contractor for the new B-21 Raider long-range stealth bomber has promised us a flyable prototype by midyear?"

"Yes, ma'am," Rauch said guardedly. He shrugged his narrow shoulders. "But schedules tend to slip, especially in a program as complex and expensive as the Raider."

Her eyes went stone-cold. "Then you are going to get on the horn to those *gentlemen* and inform them that there will be no such slipups in this case. That bird *will* fly as promised. Or heads will roll . . . and contract penalty clauses will be invoked."

The national security adviser winced. "With respect, Madam President, there's no way I can make that a serious threat. Merging all the electronics, weapons and flight controls, navigation and communications systems, and passive and active defenses in a totally new airframe is a massive, incredibly intricate undertaking. There's no way any court will uphold a judgment against a defense contractor for unforeseen delays in so difficult a project."

"You misunderstand me, Doctor," Barbeau snapped. "I don't give a damn if that B-21 prototype is combat-ready . . . or even close to it. All I want for the moment is a really deadly-looking, brand-new bomber that can take off, fly around for a few minutes, and then land safely."

Interested now, Cohen leaned forward. "What's your plan?"

"The hell with Sky Masters and its piddling X-planes," she said, with a wide, wicked grin. "We'll put on our own goddamned show. A show that'll totally undercut Farrell's attacks on my defense programs. And best of all, it won't cost the campaign one thin dime."

Cohen raised an eyebrow. "How so?"

"Because *I'm* the commander in chief, Luke," Barbeau said, still grinning. "So when I order a major Air Force readiness exercise featuring a whole damn bunch of our nation's most advanced combat aircraft, that's official business . . . not politics." She chuckled. "Picture *Air Force One* arriving at an air base jam-packed with shiny-new F-35s. Thousands of officers and enlisted personnel are lined up at attention in full-dress uniform to salute me. And then, just as I come sashaying down the aircraft stairs with 'Hail to the Chief' playing, our beautiful new B-21 Raider bomber comes roaring in, orbits low over the field, and lands."

Cohen whistled softly. "Oh, hell, yeah. Those would be some seriously good visuals." He leaned back in his chair. "So when would we stage this 'readiness exercise'?"

"The when's easy," Barbeau said confidently. "This summer. After all the primaries are over and before the political conventions kick off. The press will be dying for something exciting to cover, so that'll be the best time to knock the wind out of Farrell's sails."

Cohen nodded, thinking that through. "And the where?"

"Barksdale Air Force Base in Louisiana," she told him smugly. "Bomber country. Right where I was born."

CHAPTER 5

**STATE CYBERNETICS FACTORY,
ON THE OUTSKIRTS OF AKADEMGORODOK,
IN THE CENTER OF SIBERIA, RUSSIA**
Several days later

Vladimir Kurakin climbed out of the armored limousine that had brought him from Novosibirsk's Tolmachevo Airport. A gentle breeze from the south rustled through the tall pine and birch trees surrounding the huge, windowless robotics factory. He buttoned his suit jacket. Even in the spring, Siberia was cold.

He looked around. In the distance, dozens of older buildings rose above the forest. Founded in the heyday of the old Soviet Union, Akademgorodok's research institutes and labs had been a haven for the sciences like genetics and cybernetics considered heretical by the Communist Party hierarchy. Tens of thousands of scientists and their families had lived a relatively sheltered existence here—better fed and somewhat freer than ordinary Russian citizens.

Then, when the Soviet Union collapsed, Akademgorodok fell on hard times. At first, the new Russian Federation had little money to invest in pure research. But private venture capital sparked a renaissance in the mid-1990s. The town again became a thriving center of scientific research and development. American journalists had even called it Russia's "Silicon Forest."

Akademgorodok was still thriving, Kurakin knew. But not quite in the same way.

Spurred on by Russia's young and charismatic leader, Gennadiy Gryzlov, Moscow had moved in—pouring billions of rubles into research and development work on weapons-grade lasers, cybernetics, industrial automation, and applied genetics. With government money and top-secret government contracts came new restrictions and controls. Whole sections of the once-open town were now off-limits to foreigners or anyone without top-level security clearances.

The State Cybernetics Factory was one of those places.

Soldiers in camouflage battle dress and body armor guarded every entrance to the huge robotics installation. With their AK-400 assault rifles at the ready, several headed in his direction.

"*Pokazhi mne svoye udostovereniye lichnosti!* Show me your identification card!" their leader, a young, tough-looking captain, demanded. "This is a restricted area."

Silently, Kurakin handed over his ID card.

The captain glanced down at it. His eyes widened slightly. He stiffened to attention. "Major General Kurakin! My apologies."

"None are necessary, Captain," Kurakin said, with a thin, humorless smile. "Nor is any formal military ceremony. Officially, I have retired. I am now only a civilian."

A civilian. The thought was still strange. Kurakin, now in his early fifties, had served in the military since he entered Moscow's High Command Training School as a teenager. Commissioned as a lieutenant in the ground forces, he'd risen steadily in rank, seeing combat in Chechnya, South Ossetia, the Ukraine, and other hot spots. For the past two years, he had led Russia's shadowy special operations forces, its equivalent of the U.S. Special Operations Command. Hard work and rigorous, realistic training had honed the professional officers and soldiers under his command into an elite, highly capable force. From there, a post on the general staff and further promotion beckoned.

And then, several months ago, with a single urgent summons, the Kremlin had upended the smooth progression of his planned career and sent it careening off in a direction he could never have imagined. He shook his head, still feeling slightly dazed. The state, under Gennadiy Gryzlov's rule, moved fast. You either kept pace, or you were swept away.

Still smiling dryly, Kurakin took back his identity card from the worried-looking captain. He nodded toward the factory door. "Am I cleared to go inside?"

"Oh, yes, sir," the other man assured him quickly. He swallowed hard. "Sir, I apologize for the confusion. I expected—"

"You expected to see someone in uniform," Kurakin said quietly. He leaned closer to the captain, keeping his reproof between them. "And so your assumptions clouded your vision. Do not make this mistake again."

Leaving the shaken captain and his soldiers behind, Kurakin entered the huge cybernetics factory alone. He stood still for a moment, taking it all in. Industrial robots crowded around a single assembly line that ran straight down the middle of the vast open space. Each robot sprouted multiple, flexible limbs, which ended in a variety of tools and other devices. Eerily, they seemed more like giant metal spiders lying in wait for prey than manufactured machines. Windowed bays high above the tiled floor showed where human technicians monitored computers that must control the entire facility.

His breath steamed in the air. It was almost as cold inside as outside. He shook his head in sudden understanding. Of course! Why waste precious heat on soulless machines? Especially since their electronic components were undoubtedly more efficient at lower temperatures.

"Impressive, isn't it?"

Kurakin turned to face the ruggedly good-looking man who'd been waiting off to the side. "Extremely impressive, Mr. President," he said. He waved at the array of silent, waiting industrial machines. "It looks like something out of a science-fiction film, in a scene set in the distant future."

Openly amused, Gennadiy Gryzlov came forward to join him. He nodded at Kurakin's dark gray civilian suit. "So how does it feel, Vladimir? Running your own private company?"

"Strange, Mr. President," Kurakin admitted. He shrugged. "I've been a soldier all my life. It feels odd not to operate within a clearly defined command structure."

"Ah, there you are mistaken," Gryzlov said, turning on him with a fast, slashing grin. "Like any good businessman you must, ultimately, obey your shareholders. Or, in this case, your *only* shareholder. *Me.*" His gaze hardened. "What I direct, you will do. I set the strategic objectives. And then you will employ whatever means are necessary to achieve my objectives. Is that clear?"

"Very clear, Mr. President," Kurakin agreed quickly. In public, Gryzlov was always charming, self-assured, and calm. But those who served Russia's president closely learned very early on to be wary of his hair-trigger temper. Few walked away unscathed from one of their leader's towering, manic rages.

Recovering his good humor, Gryzlov clapped him on the shoulder. "Cheer up, Vladimir. Forget the fancy civilian suits and your impressive-sounding title. They're just window dressing. Where it counts, you're still a soldier under my orders."

Kurakin nodded again. Nominally, he was the chief executive officer of a brand-new private military corporation, *Razresheniye Konfliktov Uslugi* (Conflict Resolution Services). Long thwarted by the actions of the American-owned Scion, Gryzlov had decided to create his own deniable mercenary force. On paper, if not in practice, RKU was an independent commercial enterprise. Like Martindale's Scion, it should be able to conduct clandestine military operations without the political constraints and risks that inevitably accompanied any open Russian military action.

That was the president's theory anyway, Kurakin knew. Whether other governments, especially that of the United States, would react as he predicted was an open question.

"And why should they not?" Gryzlov had assured him at their first meeting to discuss his plans. He'd shown his teeth. "After all, I took that fat cow Stacy Anne Barbeau at her word when she swore that her country wasn't responsible for the actions of Martindale and his mercenaries."

"You think she lied?" Kurakin had asked.

Gryzlov had only shrugged. "What does it really matter? Her countrymen, whether paid solely by the Poles or not, have served America's interests. Besides, even if she spoke the truth, Barbeau will not govern the United States forever. Some future American president will undoubtedly make use of Scion and its hired Iron Wolf killers." His eyes had gleamed with a predator's hunger. "Are we not entitled to use the same methods in our own national interest?"

Kurakin shivered, remembering the president's expression. For years, Gryzlov's longtime chief of staff, Sergei Tarzarov, had acted as a brake on his wilder impulses. The wily Kremlin insider had been the only one ever able to dissuade the younger man from reckless action. But now Tarzarov was dead, killed by those same American mercenaries during their escape from the ambush at Perun's Aerie. Which meant that Russia's undisputed leader was free to follow his aggressive instincts . . . without restraint.

"What is the status of your forces?" Gryzlov asked abruptly, dragging him back to the present. "Are you getting the quality of recruits you need?"

With an effort, Kurakin pushed away both his memories and his lingering worries about the future. Whatever his "official" position, he still had a duty to his country.

"Yes, Mr. President," he assured Gryzlov. "Between the promises of high base pay and bonuses and pressure from their superior officers, we've been able to hire some of our toughest and most experienced Spetsnaz troops and GRU covert operatives. They are all proven veterans, many with superb language skills. A number of them can pass as natives of the United States, Poland, the Baltic States, Germany, or other NATO countries."

"And your weapons?"

"A mix of Russian and Western small arms, heavy weapons, explosives, sensors, aircraft, and missiles," Kurakin said.

"Your men will use some American-made equipment?" Gryzlov mused.

Kurakin nodded. "Also weapons manufactured

by the Poles and other nations—chiefly the UK, Germany, and France."

"That should certainly add to the confusion after any operation," Gryzlov said dryly.

"Yes, sir." Kurakin forced a smile. "We have obtained most of the equipment we need from existing Spetsnaz stockpiles, but we'll have to buy the rest on the international arms black market. That will be expensive, especially since we need to cover our tracks very carefully."

"I don't give a damn about the money, Vladimir," Gryzlov said emphatically. "What matters to me is whether or not your RKU action groups can handle the missions I assign them."

"My men are already among the most lethal special forces troops in the world. By the time I'm finished with them, they will have no equal," Kurakin promised. He hesitated. "But I can't guarantee success against every potential opponent. Especially not—"

"The Iron Wolf Squadron and its combat robots?" Gryzlov finished for him.

"*Da*, Mr. President," Kurakin admitted. He'd studied the available records of every known clash between Russian forces and the enemy's Cybernetic Infantry Devices. At best, they were sketchy, since very few friendly troops survived long enough to report many details. Despite that, it was blindingly obvious that no conventionally equipped special forces unit could hope to go up against those human-piloted war machines and win.

"Then come with me," Gryzlov said simply. "And I will show you the future." He led Kurakin down the long factory floor toward a distant pair of massive doors.

Once there, he keyed in a code on a security panel. Smoothly, the doors slid open. Powerful overhead lights blinked on one by one—revealing a row of immobile, human-shaped machines.

"My God," Kurakin murmured, staring up at the robots. Each stood more than three meters tall, with thin, agile arms and legs and long torsos. Eyeless spheres bristling with antennas and other sensor arrays took the place of heads.

He swung toward Gryzlov in amazement. "We have our *own* combat robots?"

"Yes, we do," Gryzlov said with a smug, satisfied smile. He waved a hand at the row of silent man-shaped automatons. "Our *Kiberneticheskiye Voyennyye Mashiny*, our Cybernetic War Machines, will be ready for operational use in weeks. We lacked only the special devices needed to meld human pilots with their controls and computer systems. Now we have the technology required to build haptic interfaces of our own. The first production models are already emerging from our labs."

"And the men to control these . . . KVMs?" Kurakin asked. He stared back at the menacing shapes. "Where will we find them?"

"I've already found them," Gryzlov said flatly. "At my orders, several of the best fighter pilots from our Aerospace Defense Force will shortly be resigning their commissions to accept employment with your company. Once the new haptic interfaces are installed, they can begin their combat training."

It made sense to use fighter pilots, Kurakin realized. Men trained on advanced combat aircraft like the Su-35 and Su-50 already knew how to fly and fight without being overwhelmed by the flood of information from multiple sensors and computers. Strapping into a war robot would be far less alien to them than it would be for any of his old-school, rifle-toting Spetsnaz soldiers.

"Then, while your new KVM units are working up, your conventional strike groups will take on their first assignments—safely infiltrating deep into the nation I've selected as your first target," Gryzlov said bluntly.

Startled, Kurakin blinked. "What? You're sending my men into action? So soon?"

"Calm yourself, Vladimir," Gryzlov snapped. He shook his head. "I'm not asking your mercenaries to fix bayonets and assault an enemy fortress. Not yet at least. Only to carry out certain necessary preliminaries to a much larger and more intricate campaign."

"What sort of preliminary missions?" Kurakin asked carefully, still stunned by how swiftly the other man was moving.

"Mostly close reconnaissance of selected sites," Gryzlov told him. "Although they will also need to set up a number of clandestine bases to house larger strike forces."

Slowly, Kurakin recovered his balance. What the president was asking of him was not impossible. The Spetsnaz and GRU veterans he'd recruited for RKU were old hands at covert reconnaissance inside enemy territory.

"Well?" Gryzlov demanded. "Will your men be ready to move on my orders?"

"Yes, Mr. President," he said confidently. His mind was already busy working out different schemes for smuggling the necessary men, weapons, and gear into Poland. Or the Baltic states. Or Romania. It should not be too difficult. Drawing up such plans was a routine part of any experienced Spetsnaz commander's preparation for wartime operations. "I can have teams in place around the Iron Wolf base at Powidz or near important political and military targets in Warsaw, Bucharest, and other cities in a matter of days."

"Poland? Romania? No, you misunderstand me, Kurakin," Gryzlov said with a dismissive laugh. "I haven't created your force to fight another meaningless border skirmish with the Poles and their allies. Those preliminary actions are over. They've served their purpose in finding and fixing the primary enemy threat to us, Martindale's Iron Wolf mercenaries. Now, with them tied down in the wrong place, we move on to the main event."

"The main event?" Kurakin asked cautiously.

"*Operatisya Shakh i Mat*, Operation Checkmate," Gryzlov told him. His eyes were ice-cold, full of cruel anticipation. "Those who've plagued Russia for so long—destroying our air and missile bases, suborning our allies, killing our brave airmen and soldiers—*they* are about to learn what suffering truly means."

CHAPTER 6

REGAN AIR FREIGHT AIRFIELD EXPANSION PROJECT, NEAR MOAB, UTAH
Several days later

Pale red dust swirled high in the air, drifting away from where bulldozers, front loaders, graders, dump trucks, and road rollers rumbled back and forth along a strip of high desert south of Moab. Cranes swayed elsewhere, carefully hoisting sections of prefabricated steel buildings into place. Tall sandstone cliffs rose scarcely more than a mile away to the east and west.

Frank Jameson pushed back his hard hat and rubbed distractedly at his sweaty forehead. His construction company had bid for this rush job and stood to profit handsomely when it was finished. But he still couldn't figure out what on earth Regan Air Freight, a privately owned air cargo company, really had to gain here.

Moab's old Grand County Airport had been abandoned since 1965, the victim of a failed bid to entice the U.S. Air Force into building a base at a newer location, Canyonlands Field. In all the long years since, its sole paved runway had sat idle, slowly deteriorating in southeastern Utah's arid climate. Mule deer, coyotes, and jackrabbits roamed unchecked, joined only occasionally by drag racers who used the mile-long strip for their meets.

Now all that had changed. Regan Air had swooped in out of the blue and bought the land for a pittance. They were paying Jameson and his workers a princely sum to repair and extend the old runway and erect new buildings on the site.

Although Frank Jameson wasn't one to kick about a contract that would put his company in the black for the next year, he still couldn't help being curious about what Regan Air had in mind. With the uranium mines closed, the Moab-area economy relied heavily on tourism. And mountain bikers, base jumpers, and hikers didn't exactly need much in the way of air freight services.

He said as much to the shorter, well-dressed man standing at his shoulder.

"Access to the next energy boom, Mr. Jameson," Willem Daeniker replied with a slight smile. As a representative of Regan Air's new owners, the Swiss banker had flown in earlier that day to inspect their progress. "Our company believes there will be substantial profits to be made flying in equipment and supplies for new power projects in this region."

Jameson raised an eyebrow. "Energy boom?" He shook his head. "Well, I sure hope your folks know what they're doing, because the geology's all wrong. At least right around here. The nearest oil and gas deposits are a hundred miles north . . . and Salt Lake City's got better road connections to 'em."

"Oh, I am not speaking primarily of oil and natural gas," Daeniker said, still smiling. "The boom I refer to is mostly in renewable energy, in wind and solar power. With the tax incentives and other subsidies offered by your federal government, we believe many companies will be interested in building such plants in the surrounding area—especially with a new air freight hub able to handle their cargos."

"That sort of depends on who wins the election, doesn't it?" Jameson carefully pointed out. "Last time I checked, J. D. Farrell wasn't a big fan of all this 'green energy' stuff."

Daeniker shrugged. "There are always risks in any significant investment, Mr. Jameson. Evidently my employers believe your President Barbeau will be reelected." He glanced up at the taller man with narrowed eyes. "But that is of no real importance to you as far as this construction project is concerned, is it?"

"No, sir," Jameson said quickly. Arguing politics with clients was never good business. Regan Air's new owners might be wasting its money here, but that was their lookout. Besides, if they were right about new wind and solar plants going up around Moab and the rest of southeastern Utah, his company had a good shot at landing a lot of that work. "My guys will have that runway extension finished and those buildings up within ten days."

"Excellent," Daeniker said. "My employers will be pleased."

DRAWSKO POMORSKIE MILITARY TRAINING AREA, NORTHWEST POLAND
A few weeks later

The muffled *crump* of artillery and heavy mortar fire echoed across a wide, shallow valley flanked by beech woods on all sides. Its grassy slopes were torn by crisscrossing tank tracks and smoldering shell craters. Gray and black smoke stained the near horizon.

Secure in a bunker built into the hillside, Polish president Piotr Wilk focused his binoculars through an observation port. Senior military officers and government officials from half a dozen different Eastern and central European countries did the same at other firing slits and ports.

Suddenly two light gray shapes screamed down the valley at low altitude. Small bombs tumbled from under their delta wings, slamming into the ground and exploding in brief, blinding flashes. Dozens of decoy flares streamed behind the Hungarian JAS 39 Gripens as they rolled away and climbed, turning with incredible agility.

Enviously, Wilk followed them though his binoculars. *Good planes. Good pilots*, he thought. Like the American-built F-16s he'd loved flying during his days as a veteran pilot and charismatic air-force commander, those Swedish-designed single-engine fighters were superb air superiority and ground-attack aircraft. Wiry, middling tall, and not quite fifty, Poland's president still occasionally found himself longing for the days when he could strap into a cockpit and go head-to-head against his nation's enemies. Unfortunately, he reminded himself, service to Poland and the cause of freedom now demanded that he engage in the subtler and sometimes darker arts of politics, strategy, and diplomacy.

Like now, Piotr, he reminded himself with a wry grin.

Wilk lowered his binoculars and turned to his Hungarian counterpart, Prime Minister Tibor Lukács. The other man, notoriously touchy and xenophobic, had been one of the leaders most reluctant to join the fledgling Alliance of Free Nations. Only the overwhelming evidence of Gennadiy Gryzlov's aggressive plans had persuaded him to sign on. All of which made buttering him up whenever possible a priority. "Please pass my compliments to your pilots and their commanders, Tibor. That was an excellent attack run."

A thin smile creased Lukács's broad face. "Coming from an old aviator like you, my friend, that is high praise indeed." The Hungarian prime minister waved a hand toward the nearest firing slit. "My generals assure me our troops and pilots are gaining much-needed experience in this war maneuver wonderland of yours."

Wilk nodded. That was true. Drawsko Pomorskie was Europe's largest military training area, with more than a hundred and thirty square miles set aside for live fire exercises and battlefield maneuvers. No other country on the continent except Russia could boast of anything comparable. The Polish Army had used the area since 1945. Now the combined forces of the new AFN held their spring and summer maneuvers among its forests, fields, low rolling hills, abandoned villages, and swamps. Decades of combat training had left the exercise area littered with burned-out hulks used for target practice—among them, old Soviet tanks and self-propelled guns, surplus U.S. Army M-60 tanks, Huey helicopters, and stripped-down F-4 Phantom fighter jets.

"Local enemy air defenses are judged as suppressed," one of the exercise control-team officers reported over the intercom. *"Iron Wolf Squadron strike team inbound. Follow-on conventional armored and infantry forces in movement from Phase Line Alpha."*

Wilk raised his binoculars in time to see a large, twin-engine aircraft in mottled dark green, light green, and gray camouflage roar in just above the treetops. It banked left over the valley in a steep, tight turn, slowing fast. Its huge propellers were already swiveling upward, turning into rotors. The Sky Masters XV-40 Sparrowhawk tilt rotor had the same basic lines as the V-22 Ospreys flown by the U.S. Air Force and U.S. Marine Corps, but it was smaller and more agile.

Rotors spinning, the Sparrowhawk touched down in the middle of the valley. Immediately, its rear ramp whirred open. Two tall, menacing shapes unfolded out of the troop compartment and glided down the ramp. Without any pause, the two Iron Wolf combat robots darted away at high speed, heading down the valley toward a distant ruined village defended by a simulated Russian motorized rifle battalion. As soon as they were off the ramp, the XV-40 leaped into the air and veered away, accelerating fast as its rotors transitioned to level flight.

Explosions erupted among the buildings as the CIDs opened fire, using their autocannons, rail guns, and grenade launchers. One after another, old BMP-1 infantry fighting vehicles went up in flames. Puffs of smoke and debris flew away from foxholes dug amid the rubble. Within minutes, the two Iron Wolf machines had fought their way through the village and disappeared into the surrounding woods, leaving only smoldering wreckage in their wake.

"*Bámulatos!* Amazing!" Lukács murmured from beside Wilk. "So much power. So much speed." He leaned closer. "Now I understand better how your country has dared to defy Moscow for so long."

The Polish president concealed a smile. That was exactly the kind of reaction he'd hoped for. Although Kevin Martindale had been understandably worried about the security risks entailed in showing off the CIDs in these open-field maneuvers, he'd insisted they were necessary—both on political *and* military grounds.

Battle drills blending the capabilities of the AFN's conventional air, armor, and mechanized units with the Iron Wolf Squadron's robots, drones, and deep-strike recon and commando forces built much-needed teamwork. Equally important, they helped strengthen the alliance by reassuring its political leaders that their combined armed forces could hold their own against Russia if another open war broke out.

"But can your squadron field enough of those robots to defend us all?" Lukács asked pointedly, after a moment's reflection. "I understand the Americans have made it difficult to obtain replacements and new machines."

"President Barbeau's sanctions and legal threats have made the buildup of our CID force slower and more expensive than I would have liked," Wilk agreed. "Despite that, we now have six operational fighting machines and twelve trained pilots."

"Only *six*?"

"Three years ago, fighting in coordination with my country's ground and air forces, just *two* CIDs were able to first delay and then defeat two full-strength Russian armies," Wilk reminded the Hungarian prime minister dryly.

"But then you had the element of surprise," Lukács commented. "Gryzlov and his commanders will not make the same mistakes again."

"No, they won't," Wilk said. He nodded toward the valley below their bunker. An assortment of Polish, Romanian, and Hungarian armored vehicles were coming into view, deploying from march columns into battle formation as they advanced. "Which is why exercises such as this are so important. As are all the modernization programs our armed forces are undertaking."

Every member of the Alliance of Free Nations, even the tiny Baltic states, had agreed to strengthen and modernize its air and ground forces—replacing antiquated and worn-out Soviet-era tanks, APCs, artillery, and aircraft with newer, more capable weapons. At the same time, they'd toughened their training and increased combat readiness. Timeservers and careerists had been weeded out in favor of younger, more energetic officers.

It was a difficult and expensive process, but Wilk was convinced that it was working. Together with their CIDs, the alliance's conventional ground forces were now strong enough to stop an offensive by Russia's tank and motorized rifle divisions. In the air, the combination of upgraded Polish and Romanian F-16s and Hungary's JAS 39 Gripens, working in tandem with Iron Wolf's stealthy MQ-55 Coyote drone missile launchers and Scion's other high-tech weapons, stood an excellent chance of blunting raids by Russia's fighters and bombers. The same held true for any new cyberwar campaign orchestrated by Moscow. Since the last onslaught, the alliance had steadily strengthened its defenses against computer hacking and destructive malware.

The Hungarian sighed. "I only wish the costs were not so high, Piotr," he said. He looked pained. "Every new defense bill draws more and more opposition in my country's National Assembly."

Wilk nodded somberly. He faced the same

political difficulties. Even after two Russian attacks on Poland, there were still some members of the opposition parties who fought him tooth and nail over every zloty for national defense. "Well, I think it's better to spend money now than to spend lives and risk our freedoms later," he said quietly.

Grudgingly, Lukács acknowledged the power of his argument.

At least I've convinced you that we can hold our own against Moscow, Wilk thought, looking at the Hungarian. *Then why am I still so worried?*

Much later that evening, after a dinner and reception in honor of the ranking political and military leaders attending the exercises, Wilk finally got the chance to pose that same question to some of his closest advisers. They were gathered in his hotel suite in Szczecin, eighty kilometers west of Drawsko Pomorskie.

He looked carefully around the sitting room, taking each of the attendees in.

First, Kevin Martindale, looking smooth and well polished as always in an elegant black dinner jacket and bow tie. Next, Major Nadia Rozek, his former military aide, in her dress uniform as an officer in Poland's special forces. And finally, Captain Brad McLanahan, tall, broad-shouldered, and blond-haired. The young American wore the dark, rifle-green uniform jacket, collared shirt, and black tie of the Iron Wolf Squadron. A patch on his shoulder showed a metal-gray robotic wolf's head with glowing red eyes on a bright green background.

"You're right, Piotr," Martindale said, after listening to Wilk's concerns. "We are missing something. My Scion intelligence analysts have been picking up signs of unusual activity involving Russia's most elite Spetsnaz and combat aviation units. But I'll be damned if I can make the pieces fit together into anything that makes sense."

Suddenly intent and focused, Brad leaned forward. "What kind of activity? Like they're moving to higher readiness? Getting ready to take another crack at us?"

"That's what's strange," Martindale said, shaking his head. "As far as my people can tell from very limited data, these units are *not* training for a renewed war. If anything, it looks as if their preparedness is actually slipping."

Nadia frowned. "Slipping? In what way?"

"For one thing, a significant number of previously scheduled maneuvers have been abruptly canceled," Martindale told her. "Regular tank and motorized rifle brigades don't seem to be affected, but it doesn't appear as though any Spetsnaz unit has conducted serious combat training for several months. And now, over the past few weeks, we've seen the same pattern with those fighter units equipped with top-of-the-line interceptors like the Su-35 and Su-50. Suddenly they're not engaging in any air-to-air combat exercises or even flying routine patrols."

Perplexed, Wilk shook his head. The former American president was right. This was very odd.

Maintaining air-to-air combat skills required constant effort. Fighter pilots left sitting on the ground, even with access to advanced flight simulators, soon lost their edge. The same thing went for the specialized skills needed by Spetsnaz teams. But why would Gennadiy Gryzlov suddenly pull the plug on training for his best troops and pilots?

"We've also lost track of some key personnel in those units," Martindale went on. "Either because they've been reassigned somewhere we don't know about . . . or because they're being demobilized."

Brad snorted. "Demobilized? I wouldn't bet on that. Gryzlov's not the kind of guy who'd let his best people just walk away. No, that Russian son of a bitch is up to something all right." He grimaced. "But like Mr. Martindale over there, I'm damned if I can put my finger on what it might be."

Nadia's blue-gray eyes darkened. "I really do *not* care for the idea of just sitting around waiting to find out the hard way what Moscow has up its sleeve."

"Nor do I, Major," Wilk assured her. He turned to Martindale. "I assume you have a plan to remedy our ignorance? And probably one that is both highly dangerous and of questionable legality?"

A wry grin flashed across the former American president's face. "I see that my reputation precedes me." He leaned back in his chair. "But yes, I do, Piotr. In fact, I've already set a covert op in motion."

"Without my authorization," Wilk said flatly. There were moments when it became clear that even though his private military company was employed by Poland, Martindale viewed himself as an independent actor on the world stage.

"Correct." The other man shrugged. "This is a strictly Scion-initiated intelligence-gathering operation, not an AFN- or Polish-ordered action. If it goes badly, that might give your government a modest amount of diplomatic cover."

"And why, precisely, would we need such protection?" Wilk asked coolly.

"Because I'm sending a team of my best operatives deep inside Russia to get some answers," Martindale replied. "And try as they might, I suspect they're not likely to end up being very subtle about it."

"Which means the odds are this team of yours is going to need a fast ride out," Brad guessed.

"So that is why you are telling us about this mission now, rather than simply reporting its results later," Nadia said. Her tone was cold.

Martindale nodded. "Quite true, Major Rozek. I may need help from the Iron Wolf Squadron to extract my agents."

Brad sighed. "I suppose you want us to warm up the XCV-62 Ranger?"

He didn't sound especially eager and Wilk could not blame him. The younger McLanahan and Nadia had flown the Ranger, a stealthy, short-takeoff-and-landing tactical airlifter, on the raid against Russia's Perun's Aerie cyberwar complex. Two members of their nine-person assault team had been killed and another seriously wounded. While the survivors had escaped through a tightly drawn net of Russian interceptors and SAMs, it was only by the narrowest of margins.

"Not this time," Martindale said, shaking his head. "The Ranger's a highly capable machine, but the area my people are going to be operating in probably won't offer any decent landing zones big enough to accommodate an aircraft of its size." He turned to Nadia, eyeing the silver eagle pilot's badge on her uniform. "No, for this mission, I have something a bit more mundane in mind."

CHAPTER 7

**REGAN AIR FREIGHT FACILITY,
INDIANAPOLIS INTERNATIONAL AIRPORT,
INDIANAPOLIS, INDIANA**
That same time

Sited just seven miles from the state capital and near the junction of several major interstate highways, Indianapolis International Airport was the eighth busiest air freight hub in the United States. More than a million metric tons of cargo flowed through its distribution centers and adjoining warehouses every year. So when Francis Xavier Regan expanded his namesake Regan Air Freight's operations into the American market, it had made perfect sense to choose Indianapolis as its new corporate headquarters.

In the months since the reclusive billionaire sold his interest and then vanished at sea, Regan Air's top executives had carried on managing the company's day-to-day operations without much interference or even guidance from the new owners. At first, they'd all agreed that it felt peculiar to be out from under the old man's cold and ever-calculating eye. Gradually, though, CEO Martin Crown and his closest subordinates had begun enjoying their unanticipated freedom of action. For the first time in their tenure with the company, they felt fully in charge.

Now, Crown thought dourly, it looked very much like those short-lived glory days of power and total control were coming to an end. Together with his chief financial officer, Halsey Stutz, and their director of flight operations, Ted Locke, he'd been "invited" out to the airport to watch Regan Air's newest acquisition, a Boeing 737-200F freighter, arrive.

Sweating profusely in the heat rolling off the tarmac, the big, paunchy American unbuttoned his suit jacket. He glanced at the shorter, slimmer man who'd summoned them here out of their comfortable air-conditioned offices. This guy Daeniker was their liaison with the new owners, all of whom were based overseas. He also had the lean and hungry look Crown associated with men who didn't mind being the bearers of bad tidings—like mass layoffs or poorly conceived corporate restructurings that usually ended in bankruptcy.

"There it comes," Daeniker said suddenly, pointing to the twin-engine narrow-body jet flaring in to land on Runway 5L about a mile and a half from their position in front of Regan Air's shipment center. The air freighter was already painted in Regan's trademarked kelly-green and gold stripes, with a large, stylized *R* on its tailfin. The Swiss checked his watch. "Precisely on schedule," he said with satisfaction.

Crown exchanged a pained look with Stutz and Locke. Given the current state of the economy, none of them would have approved buying another aircraft—let alone a model so old and outdated. After all, the last 737-200 had rolled off Boeing's production line more than thirty years ago. And out of more than a thousand built, fewer than a hundred were still flying.

Daeniker smiled politely, seeing their expressions. "Do not worry, gentlemen. We negotiated a very good price when purchasing this aircraft from its former owners. And though it may be old, it is still in good flying condition."

Crown merely nodded, this time working harder to hide his dismay. Like most people without aviation industry experience, Daeniker obviously believed the up-front purchase price for an aircraft was what mattered most. But that was peanuts in the bigger scheme of things. What really counted was how much the plane cost to maintain and operate over time. And on that score, he was pretty sure this 737-200F was going to prove a massive headache. Compared to newer jets, it was a fuel hog. Besides that, keeping the damned antiquated thing flying was going to soak up precious maintenance hours that would have been far better spent on more efficient aircraft. Hell, he was willing to bet that the guys at the regional Chinese airline that used to fly this hunk of junk couldn't believe their luck when they were offered more than the scrap-metal price.

Engines whining shrilly, the cargo jet taxied off the runway and over toward them.

As the jet rolled to a stop, Ted Locke leaned in closer to Crown. "Jesus Christ, Martin," he muttered. "They've put a fricking gravel kit on this bird."

Crown nodded, seeing the telltale gravel deflector, shaped like a wide ski, attached to the 737's nosewheel, and the long, thin vortex dissipators mounted in front of both engines. By protecting the engines from debris kicked up on takeoffs and landings, gravel kits allowed aircraft to use shorter, unpaved runways. In its early days, Regan Air Freight had equipped some of its planes with the same kind of kits so they could fly into rough rural airfields in Alaska and the wilds of northern Canada. But over time, those routes proved totally uneconomical and were dropped. He scowled. Just what were the new owners planning?

Invited by Daeniker to inspect the aircraft more closely, Crown and his team soon realized the gravel kit was the least of its modifications. The 737's forward main cargo door was now much larger than that of any standard model. Not only that, but the door had been completely reconfigured so that it would slide smoothly back along the fuselage, rather than pop open. In addition, the freighter's main deck now featured a high-speed overhead cargo handling mechanism and guide rails slotted into the floor.

"What's the game here, Mr. Daeniker?" Crown demanded when they finished walking through the heavily modified cargo jet. "None of these fancy new gizmos is of any real use in our current lines of business."

"That is quite true," the other man said blandly. "But since the company's owners plan to use this aircraft to explore a new business opportunity, it is also immaterial."

"What new opportunity?" Halsey Stutz asked, with a sharp edge in his voice. As Regan Air Freight's chief financial officer, he spent a lot of time hunting for ways to improve the company's efficiency and market share. Clearly, he found the idea that he'd missed something obvious insulting.

Daeniker offered him a conciliatory smile. "One quite far afield from your current operations, Mr. Stutz. And somewhat untested."

"Untested, how?"

"Your company's new owners are interested in ferrying equipment, parts, and supplies to oil and gas fracking operations and wind-turbine and solar-power installations in remote parts of the United States, Canada, and Mexico," Daeniker said. "They believe there is money to be made out of these new green-energy industries. Significant amounts of money. In fact, I believe they have already recruited a small group of experts who will soon arrive to staff a new division within your company."

Stutz looked even more worried. "With respect,

Mr. Daeniker, where on earth do you think the money's going to come from to pay for this new venture of theirs? We're in a very competitive industry here and practically every dollar we make is already fully committed. There is absolutely no way we can expand into a risky new field right now. Not if we want to stay profitable."

"Relax, gentlemen," Daeniker said, still smiling calmly. "You need not worry about the costs. The owners fully understand Regan Air's current financial constraints. They assure me they will fund this experimental endeavor out of their own resources, rather than using profits from your current operations."

For the first time since the Swiss banker appeared in his office, Martin Crown allowed himself to relax a bit. He could tell the others had the same reaction. If the people who'd bought out old Francis Xavier Regan wanted to risk even more of their own money, more power to them. If nothing else, playing around with this wacky idea of supplying the air freight needs of green-energy projects might keep them busy and out of his hair. And if they actually managed to turn a profit at it, well, so much the better. Facing competition from bigger rivals like FedEx, UPS, and DHL, Regan Air could use every extra dollar it could rustle up.

Standing in the open forward cargo door of the 737-200F, Willem Daeniker watched the American

business executives drive away. Gennadiy Gryzlov
had chosen wisely in buying this company, he realized. Its executives and employees were used to
accommodating Regan's sudden whims and top-
down style of leadership. That rendered them
easier to manipulate and less curious about matters they saw as outside their immediate respon-
sibilities.

"Do you have new instructions for us, Herr
Daeniker?" a lightly accented voice said behind him.

He turned around. The 737's pilot, a stocky,
fit-looking man in his forties, stood in the door
leading to the cockpit. "No, Colonel Annenkov,
I do not. Moscow's original orders stand. Once
you're refueled, you will proceed to the Grand
County Airport outside Moab in the American
state of Utah and await further orders."

Colonel Yuri Annenkov nodded. "*Ya ponimayu.*
I understand."

The former Russian Air Force officer now
worked for Major General Kurakin's "private"
military company, RKU. His passport and other
documents, like those of the other flight crew
aboard, identified him as a German national employed by Regan Air Freight. Under close scrutiny by American law enforcement or intelligence
agencies, it was unlikely their cover stories would
hold up. Fortunately, Daeniker knew, no such
scrutiny was likely as long as they stayed safely
aboard their aircraft or inside the newly fenced-in
perimeter at the Moab base.

JOHN D. FARRELL PRESIDENTIAL
CAMPAIGN RALLY, ERIE INSURANCE ARENA,
ERIE, PENNSYLVANIA
A short time later

Tall, with the broad shoulders and powerful arms he'd first developed working on oil rigs and now kept through rigorous exercise, John Dalton Farrell strode right out in front of the podium as he came to the finish of his stump speech. "And so, friends, I say: May God bless the United States of America! Now . . . let's get to work! Let's get this great nation of ours moving again!"

With a deafening roar of enthusiasm, the eight thousand people crowding the arena were on their feet—chanting in unison and waving campaign signs and flags. Smiling broadly, Farrell took the brown Stetson cowboy hat handed him by an aide and swung it in lazy circles in the air above his head. The clamor rose even higher.

His big, openhearted smile turned into a wide, toothy grin. Early on in his presidential bid, some high-priced political consultant had tried to dissuade him from wearing that hat in public, arguing that it was too stereotypically Texan. "Hell, son," Farrell had retorted. "I *am* from Texas. You hear that drawl? There's no hiding where I'm from. So I might as well make it work for me."

Like most of the gambles he'd taken throughout his life, this one had paid off. After nearly four years of increasingly bureaucratic rule by buttoned-down Washington insiders, people were hungry for a candidate who seemed fresh, alive, and genuine—a candidate who wasn't afraid to break stale, old political rules.

With a final wave to the shouting, cheering, foot-stomping crowd, Farrell clapped his cowboy hat firmly back onto his head. Making sure to shake every hand he could reach, he left the stage and passed through doors into a hallway that led out back, where his motorcade was waiting. His security detail closed in on all sides.

As soon as they stepped outside into the warm, humid evening, a throng of reporters mobbed them, yelling questions in his direction. Bright klieg lights lit the scene. Cameras clicked and whirred.

Farrell held up a hand. "I'm real sorry, ladies and gentlemen." He grinned at them. "Ordinarily I love talking with y'all, but right now my security folks tell me we've got to get a move on."

A young blond-haired woman wearing a CNN press badge elbowed her way out of the crowd. "That's my question, Governor. Who are these all-powerful security people of yours exactly? They're not members of the Secret Service. Why not? Surely, as the nominee of your party, you're entitled to Secret Service protection."

Farrell shook his head. "I hate to correct you, ma'am, but I am not yet the nominee. That won't come until we hold our convention in a few weeks."

"Isn't that just a formality?" another journalist asked. "You've got the delegates you need to win sewed up."

"Maybe so. But I learned a hard lesson after drilling my first dry hole," Farrell said. "There's no such thing as sewed up in life." He grinned again. "Except if you wave a bunch of taxpayer dollars in front of corporate big fish, they're guaranteed to cut you a nice, fat campaign check." That drew laughter. "And President Barbeau's sure got *that* routine down cold," he added.

This time, his quip drew a mix of pained laughter and sour looks. *No surprise there*, Farrell thought in amusement. Most of the press corps were not so subtly rooting for Stacy Anne Barbeau. Their slant was something he had to factor into every political calculation he made. At least in this day and age, between the Internet and other new media, he had more ways to get his message to the voters without running headlong into their ideological buzz saw.

"Anyway," he said, "I don't plan on using the Secret Service for protection even if I win the nomination."

"And why is that?" the CNN reporter pounced. "Don't you trust them?"

"I've no doubts at all about the professionalism of the Secret Service," Farrell said patiently. "But I'm not in this race to cost the taxpayers even more of their hard-earned dollars. So I'm sticking with the folks I've brought to this dance—a collection of fine men and women from the Texas Capitol Police and the Texas Rangers, together with several decorated veterans of our nation's armed forces." He nodded at the grizzled, tough-looking man standing next to him. "Men like Sergeant Davis here."

Former U.S. Special Forces sergeant Andrew

Davis looked pained. Years of covert fieldwork for the Army and later for Scion and the Iron Wolf Squadron had taught him to avoid the limelight, not to relish it.

"But those Rangers and Capitol police officers are paid by your state's taxpayers, aren't they?" the woman CNN reporter said with an audible sneer. "So isn't this just a PR stunt?"

"No, ma'am," Farrell said politely, with just the barest hint of an edge to his voice. "As it happens, I'm reimbursing the good people of Texas out of my own pocket. When I'm not conducting official business in my own state, nothing I do costs any Texan one red cent. Unlike some candidates, I pay my own freight." He donned another wide grin and doffed his hat to her. "You know, the country might be better off if more politicians did the same."

With that parting shot, he climbed into the big black SUV idling at the curb and waited while Andrew Davis took the jump seat across from him. The doors slammed shut and they pulled away—followed by several more SUVs carrying his staff and the rest of his security detail.

Farrell sighed and closed his eyes briefly. "Good God," he muttered. "What a snarling, snapping pack of hyenas."

"Comes with the turf, Governor," Davis said unsympathetically. "Nobody forced you into politics, did they?"

"Nope," Farrell admitted with a self-deprecating smile. "That was all my own big damned ego at work." He looked at the other man. "Sorry about

THE MOSCOW OFFENSIVE 97

turning the spotlight on you back there, Sergeant. I know that's not real comfortable for you."

Davis shrugged. "Like I said, it comes with this turf." With a grimace, he shifted in his seat. "I figure not many people would think having their picture taken was rougher than getting shot at by the Russians or some other goons."

Farrell nodded. Davis had been invalided out of the Iron Wolf Squadron after being badly wounded in a raid on Russia's cyberwar complex. After months of intensive physical therapy, the veteran special forces noncom had recovered enough to find himself bored as hell in civilian life. He and Farrell were from the same part of rural Texas, and when mutual acquaintances suggested Davis would be a good fit for his campaign security team, Farrell had jumped at the chance to bring him on board.

"Do you miss it?" he asked seriously. "Fighting for the Poles and Scion?"

"Do you miss wildcatting?" Davis asked him in return.

Farrell thought about that, remembering the sheer thrill involved in staking every penny he had on the chance of striking oil in desolate places conventional geologists had already ruled out. "Sometimes," he admitted. "But then I figure that shooting for the presidency's a pretty big gamble all on its own. And God knows, this country needs someone better than Stacy Anne Barbeau and her crowd running things."

Davis raised an eyebrow. "And you figure you're that someone better?"

Farrell shrugged with a wry half smile. "I do."

"There haven't been many really good presidents," the other man said meditatively. "Washington, Lincoln, Reagan . . . maybe a few more."

"You seriously think I'm on that level?" Farrell asked, still smiling ironically.

Davis shook his head. "With all due respect, Governor . . . hell no."

"Then why exactly are you working for me?" Farrell wondered. "Since I'm a miserly son of a bitch, I sure as hell know it's not the pay."

"Not hardly," Davis agreed with a snort. He grinned. "Mostly, I guess, it's because you're smart enough to hire guys like me who'll tell you straight out when you start sounding like you're full of shit."

Laughing now, Farrell tipped his hat in salute and then sat back to enjoy the rest of the ride to the airport.

CHAPTER 8

RKU SPECIAL WEAPONS EXERCISE AREA, IN THE KUZNETSKIY ALATAU MOUNTAIN RANGE, SIBERIA, RUSSIA
The next day

More than two hundred kilometers east of Novosibirsk, rugged, stream-cut foothills rose higher and higher—climbing steadily toward the iron-, manganese-, and gold-rich slopes of the Kuznetskiy Alatau Mountains. Dense fir and pine forests covered most of the region. Digital and paper maps showed only a handful of dirt roads, mostly used by logging companies cutting local timber.

Those maps were out-of-date.

For several months, troops from the Russian Army's 60th Engineer Regiment had labored under enormously long stretches of carefully erected camouflage netting to cut and pave a new road through the woods. Wide enough for heavy trucks, this concealed thoroughfare tied into the P-255

Novosibirsk-Irkutsk highway. It ended at a new
top-secret military training area set aside for use
by RKU's *Kiberneticheskiye Voyennyye Mashiny*, its
Cybernetic War Machines.

Flanked by his bodyguards, Gennadiy Gryzlov
left the half-buried concrete bunker that had kept
him safe during a recently completed live-fire
exercise. His eyes gleamed with excitement and
pleasure. Years of carefully laid plans were coming to fruition. Russia's first operational KVMs
had all the mobility and firepower their designer,
Dr. Mikhail Aronov, had promised and more.

Quickly, Gryzlov strode off along a winding footpath, savoring the sight of burned-out
armored vehicles and explosion-shattered mock
buildings scattered through the nearby woods
and clearings. Soldiers scurried in all directions
putting out fires. Others scrambled to drag new
camouflage panels over wrecked vehicles and ruined structures, hopefully hiding them from satellite view.

Abruptly, a voice blared out from concealed
loudspeakers. "*Preduprezhdeniye! Preduprezhdeniye!*
Warning! Warning! The next hostile satellite pass
will occur in thirty minutes. Repeat, the next satellite pass will occur in thirty minutes. Expedite all
preplanned concealment operations."

His pleasure momentarily derailed, Gryzlov
scowled. This continuing need to hide their activities from America's spy satellites was an unwelcome
reminder that he did not yet fully control all of
Russia's frontiers. The day must come, he thought
coldly, when his country dominated both the world

and the cold dark vacuum of space around it. Nothing less would do.

The sight of one of the KVMs stationed beside the path restored his good humor. Lean and lethal-looking, the war robot towered over Vladimir Kurakin and Dr. Aronov. Bulky weapons packs were attached at various points around its long torso. From his emphatic gestures, the portly professor of cybernetics was explaining something to Kurakin.

Both men stiffened to attention when Gryzlov joined them. "My congratulations on a successful training exercise, gentlemen," he said easily. "But carry on. Don't let me interrupt you."

"Yes, Mr. President," Aronov stammered. "I was just discussing proposed weapons load-outs with General . . . I mean, with Mr. Kurakin."

"And what have you decided?" Gryzlov asked.

"That the guns and missiles carried by our KVMs must be tailored precisely to each planned mission," Kurakin said. He tapped the dull gray metal and ceramic leg of the robot beside him. "As powerful as these machines are, they have limitations."

"It's mostly a question of battery power and volume, sir," Aronov explained apologetically. "The more weapons and ammunition a KVM carries, the more power it consumes when moving. Excessive weight will greatly reduce their effective combat range. And autocannons, antitank missiles, and the like are all quite bulky. We only have room to carry so many of them at one time."

Gryzlov nodded his understanding. He'd been

fully briefed on the weapons systems Kurakin
had selected to equip RKU's combat robot force.
While Russia's scientists and engineers had not
yet been able to re-create the remarkable electromagnetic rail guns used by Martindale's CIDs,
their own fighting machines would still be able to
bring a deadly assortment of armament to bear in
any battle.

For heavy firepower, each fighting machine
would employ a massive Russian-made GSH-30-1
30mm autocannon. Used by fighter and ground-
attack aircraft, it was an extremely powerful and
accurate weapon. As a plus, the GSH-30-1 was in
service with more than twenty countries around
the world, many of them third-world nations with
notoriously lax control over their armaments
stockpiles. Directly tying the use of these autocannons to Russia itself would be a difficult task
for any investigator.

The same thing applied to the other weapons
Kurakin had chosen. For example, on missions that
might involve contact with enemy armored forces,
each KVM could carry up to three Israeli-made
Spike fire-and-forget antitank missiles. More than
two dozen nations had those missiles in their inventory. Best of all, they were also used by Poland's
mercenary Iron Wolf Squadron. Gryzlov allowed
himself a quick, predatory smile at that thought,
imagining Martindale and that Polish piece of
shit Wilk desperately claiming *their* robots weren't
responsible for the havoc Kurakin's KVMs were
about to wreak.

"Very well, Dr. Aronov," he said. "Make sure

all the pilots, unit commanders, and technicians understand *exactly* what these machines can and cannot do."

"Yes, Mr. President."

Gryzlov turned to Kurakin. "Are your plans to infiltrate the combat robot force complete?"

Kurakin nodded confidently. "They are, sir." Again, he patted the robot looming above him. "Thanks to Dr. Aronov's cleverness, each KVM is completely modular. They can be broken down into their separate components, all of which are easily concealed inside shipments of heavy machinery— especially the kind of machinery used in power plants and other energy industry facilities. Once at their final destination, the robots can be reassembled in a matter of hours."

Gryzlov smiled. "It's fortunate that a Russian-owned firm routinely exports such equipment to Mexico, is it not?"

Kurakin shot him an answering smile. "Fortunate indeed, Mr. President."

"*Otlichnaya rabota!* Excellent work!" Gryzlov said. "You are authorized to begin shipping your KVMs immediately. I want them ready for action as soon as possible."

While Kurakin hurried away to issue the necessary orders to his pilots and technicians, Gryzlov turned back toward a camouflaged landing pad built behind the observation bunker. Once the American spy satellite completed its pass over this area, his light Ansat-U helicopter could safely depart. A nondescript private jet stood by at Novosibirsk for the longer flight back to Moscow.

With luck, no one outside his inner circle would ever realize he'd been gone.

To his surprise and irritation, Aronov tagged along with him. "You have something else to report, Doctor?" he asked. "I've already read all of your technical assessments of these robots. Is there some new development I should know about?"

"It's not so much an assessment of the KVMs themselves," the professor said, hesitating a bit. "More a concern about possible psychological effects their pilots could experience."

"Go on," Gryzlov said with deceptive mildness.

Aronov swallowed hard. "I'm worried that prolonged operation of these powerful machines— especially the mental and physical isolation involved when connected to their neural interfaces—might give pilots a dangerous sense of almost superhuman invulnerability. If so, the consequences—"

Gryzlov cut him off with a dismissive, offhand gesture. "War is not a place for weaklings, Aronov," he said. "These men have already proven themselves in high-performance fighter aircraft, under maximum stress while pulling high-Gs. Compared to that, running around in those metal suits of yours will be like a stroll in the park."

CHAPTER 9

**HEADQUARTERS, 22ND GUARDS
SPETSNAZ BRIGADE, BATAYSK,
NEAR ROSTOV-ON-DON, RUSSIA**
A few days later

Russia's 22nd Guards Spetsnaz Brigade was based on the eastern outskirts of the little city of Bataysk, roughly ten kilometers south of the much larger city of Rostov-on-Don. The Taganrog Gulf, the northeastern tip of the Sea of Azov, lay about forty kilometers due west. The Spetsnaz compound contained troop barracks, vehicle parks, a parade ground, indoor close-combat training ranges, and a large, two-story headquarters building. Outside its wooded perimeter, the surrounding streets were lined with old, Soviet-era concrete apartment blocks, a few grocery stores and pharmacies, and a couple of light-manufacturing and aircraft-repair plants.

Late in the afternoon, a green UAZ-3163 Patriot SUV pulled up in front of the headquarters building and parked. Almost immediately, a trim, efficient-looking colonel with jet-black hair and ice-cold blue eyes got out from behind the wheel. For a brief moment, she stood with her hands on her hips, surveying the area with a disdainful expression. The black-and-gold patch on her right sleeve showed the medieval helmet and crossed sword and marshal's baton of Russia's general staff. A big, beefy man wearing a dark black civilian suit climbed out behind her. His broad, clean-shaven face was harder to read.

Every building in sight had dirty windows and peeling paint. Trash cans stacked beside them were full to overflowing. Gravel walkways were rutted and unraked. At first glance, the Spetsnaz compound looked almost completely deserted. Apparently, most of the brigade's officers and men were away for the weekend or off duty for other reasons.

"It seems our information was correct," Colonel Irina Zakharova said to her companion. She shook her head in disbelief. "If this is what passes for an *elite* unit, I would hate to see what a ragtag conscript force looks like. My aged grandmother and two of her arthritic friends could take this place over without breaking a sweat."

Thoughtfully, the big man nodded. "Perhaps, Colonel. But I suggest we find out just how deep the rot goes before coming to any firm conclusions. After all, appearances *can* be deceiving."

"True enough," she agreed with a faint smile.

Together, they trotted up the steps, entered the headquarters building, and strode briskly toward the security desk blocking the front hall.

The senior sergeant on duty rose to his feet as soon as they came through the door. Andrei Isayev, a hard-bitten veteran of combat in Chechnya, Ukraine, and Poland, frowned slightly. He knew trouble when he saw it. And these two looked like trouble. Wiping the frown off his face, he threw a quick, precise salute to the woman colonel. "How may I help you, sir?" he asked politely.

"*We* want to see the officer of the day," she snapped. "Immediately."

Without delay, Isayev picked up a phone and relayed her demand to his immediate superior, Captain Dmitry Leonov. Moments later, the captain, who looked absurdly young for his rank, appeared—hurriedly buttoning his uniform jacket and then straightening his tie. From his rumpled look, he'd probably been caught napping after a heavy lunch in the mess.

Swallowing hard, he straightened to attention. "Welcome to the Twenty-Second Guards Spetsnaz Brigade, Colonel . . . ?"

Wordlessly, the two strangers exchanged disgusted looks and then showed the young officer their identification cards. He stared at them in surprise.

"My name is Zakharova," the colonel told him coldly. "I am assigned to the Main Army Command." She indicated the big man at her side. "This is Oleg Solomin. He works for the Ministry of Defense, in the Financial Inspectorate. Our orders are to conduct a snap inspection of your brigade's personnel records, equipment inventory, and other relevant files."

If anything, her expression grew even icier. "Your unit's most recent readiness reports have been found to be highly unsatisfactory, Captain." Her voice hardened. "And I must inform you that the ministry and the general staff are not at all pleased by this sorry state of affairs."

Oh shit, Leonov thought. With his commanding officer on leave in St. Petersburg, he was the one in the hot seat here. And if there were a worse time for Moscow to start poking its nose into the brigade's internal activities and readiness, he could not imagine when that might be.

Recently promoted from lieutenant, Leonov had been transferred to this Spetsnaz unit from a regular motorized rifle battalion only weeks before. But already he could tell that things were in a bad state. Too many key officer billets were either vacant or filled by greenhorns like him. Except for a couple of diehards like Sergeant Isayev, the same thing could be said about the brigade's enlisted ranks. Everyone at Bataysk seemed to be just going through the motions, with little evidence of the rigorous standards of physical fitness, marksmanship, and discipline he'd been assured were the hallmarks of Russia's vaunted Spetsnaz troops. He gulped.

"Don't just stand there gawping at me like some useless peasant, Captain!" Zakharova said. Her voice cracked like a whip. "Are you prepared to cooperate with this inspection? Or not?"

Desperately, Leonov fell back on the military courtesies pounded into him as a fledgling officer cadet. He threw his shoulders back, stiffened to rigid attention, and clicked his heels together. "Of course, Colonel! I will do whatever is necessary to assist you."

"Fortunately for us and, I suspect, for you, that will not be much," Zakharova said, with thinly veiled amusement. "For now, all we require is access to your database. And an office to work in."

Thoroughly cowed now, Leonov escorted them down the hall to the small room set aside for the officer of the day. With a muttered apology, he swept the old newspapers and tabloid magazines stacked next to his computer screen and keyboard into a trash can. From the disgusted sneer on her attractive face, Zakharova probably thought he should have been boning up on weapons and tactics manuals instead.

Sweating, he brought the computer screen to life and typed in his user ID and password.

"Good," the colonel said flatly. She jerked her head toward the door. "Now you can go, Captain Leonov." Her eyes flashed. "But don't go far. Depending on what we find in your unit's records, we may have more questions for you."

Nervously, Leonov checked his watch. The two bigwigs from Moscow had been locked away inside his office for almost an hour. He wished he had some clearer idea of how much longer they would be there. He supposed it depended on how far back in time they were digging into the brigade's files.

Like all organized armies around the world,

Russia's ground forces made a fetish of record keeping. You wanted a new rifle or pair of boots? *Fill out the required form, Corporal.* Going on leave to visit your family? *File your request through the appropriate channels, Sergeant.* Organizing a training exercise for your platoon? *Complete the necessary requisitions for ammunition, firing-range time, and transportation, Lieutenant.* The only difference now was that almost everything was stored in digital form rather than being kept on paper.

"You don't look too happy about this situation, Captain," Sergeant Isayev commented quietly from his post at the security desk.

Leonov forced down a bitter laugh. "What's there to be happy about?" He stopped pacing and waved a hand toward his office. "We both know nothing good can come out of this surprise inspection."

"If there's a problem, Colonel Andreyev may have more to worry about than you," the sergeant pointed out, referring to the absent commander of the 22nd Guards Spetsnaz Brigade.

Leonov snorted. In a just world that would be true. Whatever deficiencies this Colonel Zakharova and the accountant Solomin turned up ought to be laid squarely at the feet of Andreyev and his battalion commanders—not pinned on someone like him, a freshly minted and very junior captain. Unfortunately, justice was not usually a concept associated with Russia's armed forces. If Moscow was really pissed off, the brigade commander was going to be hunting around for scapegoats . . . and blame, like raw sewage, always flowed downhill.

And even if Andreyev went down instead, nobody on his staff could hope to escape being tarnished by the same aura of sloth, incompetence, and possible corruption.

"No matter how this plays out in the end, one thing's sure: I'm royally fucked, Sergeant," he said gloomily.

"Well, that depends," Isayev said slowly.

Surprised, the captain looked up. "Depends on what?"

"On whether those two really are who they say they are," the sergeant replied.

Leonov stared at him. While he'd been moaning about his fate, Isayev had obviously been thinking very different thoughts. "Zakharova and Solomin? Who else would they be?"

"I don't know, sir." The sergeant lowered his voice even more. "But their arrival sure seems conveniently timed to avoid awkward questions. I mean, here we are on the weekend with all the senior officers away. And then, bang, two total strangers storm in flashing identity cards and demanding access to all our files?" He shrugged. "Doesn't that seem sort of odd to you?"

"Well, that's the whole point of a surprise inspection!" Leonov argued. "To catch people off their guard."

"Maybe in books, sir," Isayev said patiently. "But that's not the way the game is usually played. See, higher-ups like Colonel Andreyev almost always have pals or connections on the staff who give them a little friendly warning—quietlike—about things like this before they happen. The system's set up so that nobody gets embarrassed and everybody looks good." He swung around in his chair to glance carefully down the hall. "All of which makes me wonder who these people really work for."

Leonov felt cold. "You think they're foreign spies?"

"Maybe." The sergeant hesitated. "Or they could be some of our own spooks." His mouth tightened. "Those rat bastards in the GRU or the FSB might be running a no-warning security exercise on us. If so, letting them poke around in our databases isn't going to look too good." He looked back at the captain. "Either way, sir, you'd better check up on these people."

For what felt like an eternity, Leonov stood frozen. *My God*, he thought, fighting down a rising sense of dread. Isayev was right. His situation was bad enough if this were just a genuine probe into the brigade's records. If, instead, it turned out that he'd given spies—whether foreign or domestic—unchallenged access to their computer systems, he was a dead man walking. Unless, that was, he could find out for sure in time to stop whatever they were doing.

"The colonel has a direct link to the Ministry of Defense in his office," the sergeant reminded him.

"Yes! That's right," Leonov realized abruptly. He shook himself like a sleeper throwing off a nightmare. "Make sure those two don't leave until I confirm their identities, Sergeant."

Isayev nodded. The veteran Spetsnaz noncom's eyes were expressionless. "No problem, Captain."

With that, Leonov spun on his heel and hurried away down the hall.

Inside the captain's office, the big man who called himself Oleg Solomin sat in front of the computer, rapidly scanning through files and then copying them onto a special, ultra-high-speed USB flash drive.

"How's it going?" his companion asked. Zakharova leaned casually on one corner of the desk, keeping her eye on the door.

"Almost finished," he grunted.

Her smartphone buzzed once. She fished it out of her uniform jacket. "Yes."

"You've got trouble, Sam," the lilting Welsh voice of David Jones, their backup man, told her. "Someone on that base just placed a secure call to Moscow, to the Ministry of Defense. I doubt that's a coincidence."

Samantha Kerr frowned. "Understood," she said. "We're pulling out now." She looked across at Marcus Cartwright, her fellow Scion field operative. "We're blown. Or in the process of being blown."

"That's unfortunate," the big man replied calmly. "But not wholly unexpected." With quick, economical movements, he detached the USB drive and slipped it into his own coat. Then he got up and moved toward the door, taking the lead.

The hard-faced Spetsnaz sergeant who'd first greeted them stood waiting in the hallway right outside. "Going somewhere, Mr. *Solomin*?" he asked Cartwright with a mocking smile. "So soon?"

The big man offered him a polite smile and nodded. "The colonel and I have finished our work, Sergeant Isayev. You should be glad to get us out of your hair."

Smoothly, the Russian unholstered his sidearm, a 9mm Udav pistol. "If you are who you claim to be, you have my apologies." His smile turned uglier. "But if you are what I *suspect*, your next of kin will have my condolences."

Ashen-faced with fear, Cartwright sagged to his knees. He raised his hands. They were visibly trembling. "Please, this isn't what you think." Words spilled out of his slack mouth in an almost incoherent jumble. "Really, I swear. We are not—"

Phut. Phut.

Shot twice by Samantha Kerr at point-blank range with a tiny, Russian-made PSS pistol, the sergeant stumbled backward. He slid down the wall, smearing bright red blood across dingy white paint. His mouth opened for one last desperate cry. And then Marcus Cartwright lunged upward, crushing his trachea with one powerful hammerblow.

Working swiftly, the two Scion agents dragged the corpse back into Leonov's office and dumped it behind his desk.

"Well, that's annoying," Sam said quietly, reloading her little pistol—originally developed by the Soviets for use in covert assassinations by KGB agents and Spetsnaz operatives. Though its slow-moving 7.62mm subsonic rounds were almost useless beyond twenty-five meters, the weapon was almost perfectly silent. "I hate it when the opposition wakes up just a bit too soon."

In the brigade commander's much larger and better-furnished office not far down the hall, Captain Leonov was on the phone. Grimly, he listened to the dry, disinterested voice of the personnel clerk he'd finally been able to reach. Finding someone at the Ministry of Defense who was willing and able to answer his questions had taken much longer than he'd hoped.

"Colonel Zakharova? Irina Zakharova?" the clerk said. "Yes, there is such an officer attached to the general staff. But she is on medical leave, or so my records indicate. Apparently, she had suffered a mild heart attack last month. Why do you ask?"

Leonov clutched the phone tighter. He *had* been tricked. "Because she—"

Behind him, the door into the office swung silently open. Sam Kerr leaned around the doorframe with her pistol in hand and a look of intense concentration on her face. Coolly, she squeezed the trigger twice.

Hit by both shots, Dmitry Leonov crumpled across the desk. The phone dropped out of his hand.

Cartwright scooped it up. "This is Senior Sergeant Isayev."

"Isayev? What's going on there? Where is your captain?" the clerk in Moscow asked, obviously puzzled. "And what is this business about Colonel Zakharova?"

"Apparently, we have an impostor on the base," Cartwright explained. "Captain Leonov is taking a squad to deal with the situation immediately. But he wishes me to thank you for your extremely valuable assistance." Then, without waiting for a reply, he hung up.

The big man looked at Sam. "That's torn it. I'd estimate we have about thirty minutes before all hell breaks loose here. Probably less."

She nodded. "I'm on it." Taking out her smart-phone, she tapped in a one-word text message— *DAMOCLES*, the request for an emergency extraction. *Message sent*, her phone reported.

CHAPTER 10

**HEADQUARTERS, SOUTHERN MILITARY
DISTRICT, ROSTOV-ON-DON, RUSSIA**
A couple of hours later

The Southern Military District had its headquarters in a five-story neoclassical building
in downtown Rostov. If it weren't for the iron rail
fence and small white guard post blocking access
to a door bearing the double-headed eagle em-
blem of Russia's armed forces, passersby would
ordinarily have thought it was just another luxury
apartment building, art gallery, store, or bank.

No one could have made that mistake now.

Armed soldiers in camouflaged battle dress and
body armor patrolled the neighboring streets.
Police cars barricaded every major intersection.
Staff officers streamed into the building in twos
and threes, summoned back to duty by emergency phone calls to suburban homes and country
dachas. One by one, lights flicked on behind tall,
curtained windows on every floor.

Short and stocky, still built like the tank commander he had once been, Colonel General Vladislav Nikitin stormed into the crowded operations center in a foul temper. It was irritating enough that this sudden emergency had ruined a delightful romp with his newest mistress, a beautiful blond soap-opera actress. Arriving to find his staff scurrying around in what appeared at first glance to be total confusion was worse. Everywhere he turned, phones were ringing off the hook. Cigarettes smoldered in overflowing ashtrays. And throughout the room, groups of officers clustered around maps, gesturing wildly while they argued about which units should be deployed where.

Scowling, Nikitin shoved past them, ignoring their startled looks and frantic salutes. He found his chief of staff, Major General Maxim Borovkov, hunched over a map of his own. This one showed the entire region around Rostov, stretching from Ukraine and the Sea of Azov in the west, to Georgia and Azerbaijan in the south, and the Caspian Sea and Kazakhstan to the east. Even Borovkov, tall, wiry, and ordinarily as cool as ice, looked ruffled.

"How bad is this?" Nikitin demanded.

"Pretty bad," his chief of staff admitted. He pointed to Bataysk. "Earlier this afternoon, a captain and sergeant of the Twenty-Second Guards Spetsnaz Brigade were murdered—gunned down inside the headquarters building there. Their bodies were discovered after a Ministry of Defense official reported receiving a strange, interrupted telephone call from this Captain Leonov. The captain was trying to check up on the identity of two strangers on base, one of whom claimed to be a colonel on the general staff."

"*Sukin syn!* Son of a bitch," Nikitin muttered. Donning his reading glasses, he glared down at the map. "So was this a terrorist attack? Or some sort of espionage operation that went wrong?"

Borovkov didn't hesitate. "Probably the latter. The sentries at the gate confirm there were only two visitors during the time in question, a man and a woman. Both had what seemed valid identification papers. From what we can tell, these people drove straight to the Twenty-Second's headquarters, spent roughly an hour inside, and then left. Searches haven't turned up any evidence they planted explosives or other destructive devices, as one would expect terrorists to do."

Nikitin nodded, thinking that over. The other man's assessment made sense. But what in the hell could spies have been looking for at Bataysk? The Spetsnaz units based there hadn't seen active service since the short, abortive war with Poland three years ago. Why target them now?

"The local police found the vehicle the attackers used, a UAZ Patriot SUV, abandoned several kilometers away," Borovkov continued.

"So they've switched cars."

"Quite probably," Borovkov agreed. He shrugged. "Unfortunately, we don't have any description of this other vehicle. The police haven't yet been able to find any witnesses who saw the switch."

"Better and better, Maxim," Nikitin said acidly.

He took off his reading glasses, closed his eyes for a moment, and pinched the bridge of his nose. He could feel a headache threatening to develop. "So, what is being done to find these enemy agents?"

"All airports, railway stations, bus terminals, and border control points are on high alert," Borovkov reported. "We've also established roadblocks on all the major highways and secondary roads leading out of Bataysk and Rostov."

"Who's manning these roadblocks?"

"Mostly the local police," Borovkov said. "I've ordered more troops flown in from the Seventh Guards Mountain Air Assault Division and the Fifty-Sixth Guards Airborne Brigade, but they won't arrive for several more hours."

Sourly, Nikitin nodded. Unfortunately, most of his active-duty army units were scattered widely across the vast Southern Military District—either on occupation duty in eastern Ukraine and the Crimea or guarding the border with Georgia and Azerbaijan. Aside from the 22nd Guards Spetsnaz Brigade itself, his immediately available forces were limited to a relative handful of military police troops and a few motor-rifle platoons detached from their parent units to act as guards for key installations in and around Rostov.

"Get those paratroops here as fast as possible," he ordered. "I want a solid cordon around Rostov and Bataysk before dawn tomorrow. Let's try to pin these spies close to the city. Then, if necessary, we can send in our soldiers to go house to house hunting them."

"Yes, sir."

"And tell the air defense forces I want every SAM regiment in this area at maximum readiness. Then contact the air base at Krymsk. I want some of our Su-27 fighters aloft as soon as they can be armed, fueled, and made ready."

Borovkov raised an eyebrow. "Do you think someone will try to fly the enemy agents out?"

Nikitin shrugged. "Hell if I know. But now that we know we have burglars prowling around, let's not make the mistake of leaving the windows open."

SCION SIX, OVER SOUTHERN RUSSIA
Later that night

Beneath scattered clouds, isolated points of light marked the small towns and villages dotting a darkened landscape. This part of southern Russia was mostly farmland. Even with spring planting well under way, many fields still lay fallow. In the distance, off to the northeast, the city lights of Rostov-on-Don glowed pale yellow on the horizon.

With Major Nadia Rozek piloting from the right-hand seat, a specially modified PZL SW-4 light helicopter skimmed low over the ground, heading east at nearly one hundred knots. Called the *Puszczyk*, or Tawny Owl, by its Polish designers, this particular single-engine machine had been configured for covert missions deep in enemy territory by Scion technicians.

The helicopter's fuselage and tail boom were

covered with a special Israeli-invented radar-absorbent paint. This coating soaked up the electromagnetic energy from incoming radar waves and shunted most of it off as heat. Some energy would still get back to the emitting enemy radar, but only in greatly reduced and scattered form. And like most stealthy aircraft, a film of vapor-deposited gold covered the helicopter's cockpit. Radar waves that would ordinarily penetrate the cockpit and reflect back off pilots, passengers, seats, and controls were deflected away by this ultrathin metal coating. To further reduce its radar signature, this PZL SW-4's landing skids retracted tightly into what had once been a baggage compartment. Overall, the Sky Masters–modified helicopter had a radar cross section about that of a Hellfire missile, just a bit bigger than that of the U.S. Army's canceled stealth RAH-66 Comanche helicopter.

The Scion-owned helicopter's small size and ability to fly nap-of-the-earth, together with these modifications, made it difficult to detect—even by Russia's most powerful air defense radars. A suite of advanced threat-warning sensors and defensive countermeasures systems further enhanced its abilities to undertake clandestine missions in hostile airspace.

Even so, Nadia Rozek was only too aware that penetrating this deep into Russian territory without being spotted was a lot like threading a needle. Wearing thick gloves. In the dark. At high speed. And with the ever-present risk of crashing into some of the electric power transmission lines and pylons strung across her flight path if her concentration wavered for even a fraction of a second.

A high-pitched tone pulsed sharply in her earphones, signaling the detection of yet another active enemy air-search radar. From the sound, it was close. Maybe dangerously close. She fought back against the instinctive reaction to jink away. She was flying just a little more than one hundred feet off the deck. At this low altitude, sudden, violent maneuvers were far more likely to slam her helicopter into the ground than to avoid trouble.

"That's an S-band search radar at two o'clock," Brad McLanahan reported from the left-hand seat. For this mission, the powerfully built young American was acting as Nadia's copilot and systems operator, a reversal of their usual roles. Thanks to her Polish special forces training, she had a lot more stick time in helicopters than he did. Out of the corner of her eye, she could see him leaning over to study one of the large, softly glowing MFDs, multifunction displays, set between them. "The computer figures it's about thirty-five nautical miles away. We should be okay."

"*Zrozumiany*. Understood," Nadia said, relaxing slightly. That was the 96L6E "Cheese Board" air-search radar system operating with the S-300 SAM regiment based around Rostov's international airport. At this altitude, even if the Russians had the radar set's forty-meter-tall mast fully extended, the helicopter was still several nautical miles below its horizon.

She heard another soft *ping*, this one indicating

they had just received a compressed and encrypted radio signal.

"We're in contact with the team," Brad said, reading the message sent by the Scion intelligence operatives they were here to retrieve. "They're at Rendezvous Point Alpha and in the clear. At least so far."

"*Dobry*," Nadia said, with a tiny nod.

From the moment they crossed into hostile airspace, Brad had been monitoring radio and cellphone transmissions that showed Russian army and police units were conducting a large-scale manhunt for the "foreign terrorists" who'd shot up the headquarters of the 22nd Guards Spetsnaz Brigade. Fortunately, the Russians were focusing their roadblocks and patrols along the roads heading out of Rostov and Bataysk. They seemed to be acting on the logical assumption that their quarry would want to put as much distance as possible between them and the scene of the crime.

For now, this rural backwater closer to the coast of the Sea of Azov was a lower priority. Nadia couldn't fault the Russians' reasoning. After all, in daylight, strangers would stand out like sore thumbs among the area's farms and small villages. But now that the sun had set, those same farmers and peasants tended to stick close to their own homes—which gave the Scion team room to maneuver without being spotted. Of course, every passing hour allowed the Russians to bring in more troops from their outlying garrisons. Given enough time, they were bound to cordon off the coast and start sweeping inland.

So the trick was to deny them that time.

Brad rapidly tapped virtual "keys" on the MFD he'd set to navigation guidance. "RP Alpha coordinates laid in."

"*Bardzo dobrze*. Very good." Nadia tweaked the cyclic gently, altering course to follow the new steering cue transferred to her heads-up display.

Fields, orchards, and distant houses glowed an eerie green in her night-vision goggles. Several kilometers ahead, a blinking LZ icon highlighted an empty, unplanted field. Rows of trees planted as windbreaks lined its west and east sides.

Nadia started working the cyclic, pedals, and collective to reduce their airspeed while still in horizontal flight. The field they were heading for grew larger in the windscreen as they slid lower.

She thumbed a control on the cyclic. Hydraulics whined as their landing skids swung down out of the fuselage. A new icon flashed on her HUD.

"Green light. The skids are locked," Brad confirmed. "We're go for landing."

Totally focused, Nadia brought the helicopter in low across the field, just a few feet off the ground. A cloud of dust and dirt kicked up by the rotors whirled behind them. Slowing fast, they flared in and touched down with a gentle thump.

With the rotors still turning, Brad grabbed the Polish-made Radon assault carbine stowed next to him. Then he popped the cockpit door open and dropped out onto the ground.

"Be careful," Nadia said quietly.

He grinned back at her. "Yes, ma'am, I will." His smile tightened. "But if there's company we're not expecting out there, yank this crate into the air and get out fast."

Without waiting for a reply, Brad swung away and moved off toward the eastern tree line. His pulse accelerated. In the darkness, every sound—the muffled *whump-whump-whump* of their helicopter's slowly spinning rotors, the soft crunch of his boots on freshly turned dirt, and even the gentle breeze sighing through the nearest trees—seemed magnified.

Fifty meters from the windbreak, he dropped to one knee. He pulled a tiny, high-powered infrared flashlight out of one of the pouches on his assault vest and a monocular night-vision scope from another. If those hidden somewhere in the shadows ahead were friendlies, it was time to confirm his own identity. *Or to make yourself an even bigger damn target if they're Russians instead*, he thought grimly.

Quickly, he pointed the flashlight toward the trees and clicked it on and off six times, signaling that he was Scion Six. Almost immediately, a tiny, answering dot of light blinked three times in reply.

Brad breathed out in relief. That was the correct countersign.

Three people emerged from the shadows and came out to meet him. Two of them were men—one of them tall and heavyset, the other short and whip-thin. The third was a slender young woman. Even in the darkness, he could tell that she was very good-looking. And that she seemed awfully familiar.

Abruptly, he recognized her. It was Sam Kerr. She'd helped him evade both Russian and FBI surveillance in Mexico three years ago, back when he'd first been secretly summoned to join Scion and what would later become the Iron Wolf Squadron.

"Nice to see you, McLanahan," she said cheerfully, with an impish grin. "But the timing's still bad for a quick roll in the hay." Then she glanced around the rural Russian countryside. "Although I've gotta say there *is* a lot more hay here than there was in Cancún."

Brad felt himself turning red with embarrassment. Before he found out Samantha Kerr was a Scion agent, he'd tried to pick her up for a little light, no-strings-attached, beach-resort sex. Suddenly he was very glad that it was so dark and that Nadia was well out of earshot. Even though his encounter with Sam had occurred before he met Nadia, he was pretty sure that was a part of his past he'd rather not have to explain to the woman he loved.

The big man, Marcus Cartwright, saved him. "Go easy on this guy, Sam," he said with a soft chuckle. "Somehow I don't think we're going to find another ride out of here anytime soon."

Still blushing, Brad led Sam and Cartwright and their backup man, David Jones, across the field to the waiting helicopter. One after another, he helped them into the tiny passenger cabin behind the cockpit. It was a tight squeeze. This PZL SW-4 was only rated for a pilot and four passengers and that was before Scion technicians had packed in all their added sensors and other electronics.

Once the Scion team was strapped in, he climbed back into the copilot's seat and reconnected his headset. Immediately he heard a repeated series of high-pitched tones from their threat-warning system. He tapped one of the MFDs, bringing up a visual defensives systems display. The computer's evaluation scrolled across his screen. *Multiple airborne X-band search radars detected.* A map opened up, depicting the estimated positions and courses of those hostile radar emitters. They were off to the west, over the Sea of Azov, and flying what looked like a north–south racetrack oval.

"Well, that sucks," Brad muttered, drawing Nadia's attention to the display. "Someone out there just decided to bar the barn door *before* the horse gets out."

"Is there a problem?" Cartwright asked from behind them.

"Yes, a bit of a problem," Nadia told him. Her voice was cool, almost completely unruffled. "The Russians now have at least four Su-27 fighters patrolling across our planned flight path."

"Can we sneak past them?"

"Not a chance," Brad said, glancing back into the crowded cabin. "Those Su-27s are equipped with upgraded radars that can detect us pretty far out, even with all the stealth features our guys added to this helicopter."

"So how about flying around them, then?" Sam asked.

This time, Nadia answered. "I am afraid that is not possible either. We do not have enough fuel for any detour that would evade both those fighters and the SAM units stationed at Rostov and in the Crimea."

Brad nodded. Off-the-shelf SW-4s had a maximum range of nearly five hundred nautical miles. And while the Scion techs who'd worked on this one had squeezed in some extra fuel capacity, it was just enough to offset the added weight of its stealth coating and new electronics. Toss in the fact that penetrating Russian air defenses required flying long distances at extremely low altitude, which significantly increased fuel consumption, and the reality was that they were already dancing right on the ragged edge of their available fuel. As it was, safely reaching their planned refueling point, a covert Scion airstrip in unoccupied western Ukraine, was going to test Nadia's piloting skills to the limit.

Sam looked more irritated than scared. "So we're basically screwed?"

"Not if the contingency plan Captain McLanahan developed for this mission works," Nadia assured her.

"What kind of contingency plan?"

"Sometimes the mountain comes to Mohammed," Brad said as he brought up a com window on his display and typed in a short message. The system beeped once as it compressed, encrypted, and then sent his message as a single, millisecond-long burst via satellite uplink. "But other times we have to persuade Mohammed to fly off to the mountain."

TALON FLIGHT, OVER THE BLACK SEA
That same time

Two Polish F-16C Vipers circled low over the
sea, only a couple of hundred meters above wave
height. Their mottled light and dark gray camouflage made them difficult to spot visually and
their current altitude rendered them effectively
invisible to the Russian radars painting the night
sky along the Crimean and Caucasus coasts.

"Talon Lead, this is Air Operations Center South,"
a Romanian-accented voice said through Colonel
Paweł Kasperek's headset. *"Execute WRIGGLE
ONE. Repeat, execute WRIGGLE ONE."*

He clicked his mike. "Acknowledged, Center. Executing WRIGGLE ONE." Briefly, he
glanced down at the cockpit map display set to
show the current position of the MQ-55 Coyote
drone data-linked with his F-16. He smiled under
his oxygen mask. The stealthy unmanned aircraft
was right where it should be—orbiting very low
above the sea about two hundred kilometers south
of the Crimean Peninsula.

Just about the size of a small business jet, the
Sky Masters–built Coyote had a flying-wing configuration, twin wing-buried turbofan engines,
stealth coating, and just enough avionics to allow a ground- or air-based pilot to fly it remotely
or to follow simple, preprogrammed flight plans.
Originally designed as a missile truck, a low-cost
platform capable of carrying up to ten AIM-120

advanced medium-range air-to-air missiles in its internal weapons bay, this MQ-55 was intended to play a very different role tonight.

"Time to strut your stuff, little bird," Kasperek murmured. He activated the data link and punched in the command needed to trigger a new flight plan buried in the Coyote's tiny onboard computer.

Four hundred kilometers east of where the Polish F-16s were stationed, the MQ-55 drone broke out of the slow, lazy circle it had been tracing over the Black Sea and headed due west. Its turbofan engines whined louder, powering up as the Coyote climbed steadily into the cloud-speckled night sky.

COMMAND POST, S-400 TRIUMF SURFACE-TO-AIR MISSILE BATTALION, FEODOSIA, CRIMEA
That same time

"I have intermittent contact with an unidentified aircraft approximately two hundred kilometers south of our position," one of the battalion's radar operators reported suddenly. His voice cracked with mingled excitement and frustration. "But I can't lock it up for very long. The target keeps fading in and out on my screen."

Colonel Ivan Zaitev spun toward the boyish-looking lieutenant. His eyes narrowed. "Intermittent contact? Are we being jammed?"

"No, sir."

"What is the estimated course and speed of this contact?" Zaitev asked.

"Direction of flight is roughly two-six-five degrees. Speed is more than six hundred kilometers an hour."

"Altitude?"

"Perhaps one thousand meters," the lieutenant said hesitantly.

"That certainly sounds like a stealth aircraft of some kind," Zaitev's executive officer commented from his station.

The colonel nodded. His lips thinned. "So it does." His fingers drummed on a console in time with his speeding thoughts. "And if it is, now we know right where those spies the whole Southern Military District is hunting have got to."

"Should we fire now?" his XO asked. He sounded uncertain. "At that speed, they'll be out of our effective engagement range in less than ten minutes. I know we haven't got a tight lock on this bastard, but maybe if we put enough missiles in the air—"

"Fire? Without confirming we have a valid target? Christ, no!" Zaitev snapped. The sky over the Black Sea was full of commercial airliners crisscrossing to and from Europe, Turkey, and the rest of the Middle East. Lobbing effectively unguided missiles into that tangle would be insane. The diplomatic repercussions if his battalion accidentally blew a passenger jet out of the air would be horrific. Just imagining the Kremlin's likely reaction to such a disastrous mistake was enough to make his skin crawl.

"Then what can we do?"

"We make the flyboys earn their pay for once," Zaitev said, coming to a decision. He stabbed at the button that opened his direct secure link to the headquarters of the Southern Military District. "This is Colonel Zaitev. I need to speak to Colonel General Nikitin immediately!"

While he waited for Nikitin to come on the line, his executive officer frowned. "But what can those Su-27 pilots do that we can't? Our radar is better than theirs . . . and if we can't lock up this contact, how will they?"

"The old-fashioned way, Yevgeni," Zaitev said with a lopsided smile. "With their own eyes. After all, we're getting enough data off this unidentified contact to vector them into the right sector. And then, if this really is one of those damned Iron Wolf stealth planes, our fighters should be able to shoot it down without too much trouble."

SCION SIX, ON THE GROUND IN SOUTHERN RUSSIA
A short time later

Peering down at his display, Brad saw the icons representing the Russian Su-27s suddenly break out of the racetrack patrol pattern they'd been flying and head southeast at high speed. He whistled. "I'll be damned. My cockeyed idea actually worked."

"So Mohammed really is going to the mountain?" Sam asked from the darkened cabin behind him.

"Just as fast as their afterburners can take them, Ms. Kerr," Nadia said matter-of-factly. She throttled up. Overhead, the PZL SW-4's rotors spun ever faster. She pulled up on the collective, changing the pitch of the rotors, and pressed down on her left pedal—counteracting the torque produced by the three big blades.

The helicopter lifted off.

"So now we get you back to Poland," Nadia continued. "And then we see if what you discovered at Bataysk was really worth all this trouble."

CHAPTER 11

**REGAN AIR FREIGHT SPECIAL CARGO HUB,
GRAND COUNTY AIRPORT, NEAR MOAB, UTAH**
The next day

Squinting against the sudden brightness, Yuri
Annenkov stepped out of the portable trailer
he and his crews were using as a flight operations
control center. Heat waves shimmered across the
concrete apron. Several ground support vehicles
with the Regan Air logo surrounded their Boeing
737-200F aircraft. One was a tanker truck, busy
refueling the twin-engine cargo jet after its most
recent round-trip flight to Mexico. The rest were
"K" loaders assigned to unload the freight contain-
ers Annenkov and his copilot had just ferried in.

For a moment, the former Russian Air Force
colonel stood watching his small ground crew at
their work. By military standards, this clandestine
RKU operation was shorthanded, with each man
at the Moab base being expected to handle several different tasks as needed. While that made

turning their aircraft around between flights a slower process, it was also less likely to arouse unwelcome suspicion. Even the Americans, he supposed, might notice the sudden arrival of a large number of foreign aircraft mechanics, cargo handlers, and refueling specialists. As it was, he knew the locals were puzzled that so few of Regan Air's new employees ever ventured outside the fenced-in airport perimeter.

So far, his security detail, the only really fluent English speakers working for him, had handled this potential problem by explaining that Moab was a high-stakes, start-up operation for the company. "Until we start cranking out profits, the bigwigs back at corporate expect our guys here to put in ridiculously long hours. We're on call practically twenty-four hours a day, seven days a week," he'd heard one of his guards tell a caterer delivering prepackaged meals. "By the time we're off shift, basically all we want to do is watch a little TV and then crash."

"Sounds like working on one of those offshore oil rigs," the caterer had replied with a knowing grin. "Good way to save up a lot of money. Of course, then a lot of guys blow their savings on a spree when they finally get off the rig."

Smiling back, the guard, a veteran GRU agent, had agreed this was pretty much the same kind of arrangement.

For now, at least, Annenkov was satisfied that their cover story would hold up. The bigger question was whether or not this base would be ready to conduct active operations when Moscow finally gave the word. He turned on his heel and strode toward the big prefabricated steel building they were using as a warehouse and "special materials" assembly plant.

The air-conditioned warehouse was brightly lit. Crates and cargo pallets stacked halfway to the high ceiling filled the front half. A couple of workers in grease-stained coveralls were comparing the contents of one crate with a manifest. They stiffened to attention when they saw him. With a tight-lipped frown, Annenkov waved them back to work. Some of his people still had trouble remembering they were no longer "officially" members of Russia's armed forces.

He threaded his way through the stacks, heading toward the rear of the big steel building. Sound-canceling partitions screened off the area. The armed sentry posted at the only entrance stepped aside at his terse nod, allowing him to pass.

Workbenches littered with tools and other pieces of equipment lined the back wall. More crates, most of them opened, were scattered across the concrete floor. Several technicians were busy at various tasks.

"Come to inspect our progress, Colonel?" their leader, a short man with thinning hair, asked.

Before joining RKU, Major Andrej Filippov had been an air-force ordnance specialist. His narrow face was always serious. He rarely made jokes. Unlike those lured by Major General Kurakin's promises of higher pay and spectacular bonuses, Filippov had personal reasons for joining this covert operation. Three years ago, his older brother, a fighter pilot flying Su-35s, had been shot down and killed by the Poles and their mercenary American allies. This was his chance to exact a measure of revenge.

"If you can spare the time, Andrej," Annenkov said dryly, "I'd just like to make sure that all the flights I've made to Mexico, Canada, and other godforsaken spots across the U.S. have served some real purpose."

"Of that you can be certain," Filippov replied. He led the way to the nearest bench. Several desktop computers and printers in various states of disassembly covered the work surface. They were all manufactured by different companies. "For example, these came in today."

Annenkov raised an eyebrow. "Are you planning on opening an office supply store, Major?"

Filippov forced himself to smile. "Not exactly, sir." He pulled off the case on one of the computers, revealing a mare's nest of electronic components and wiring. "You see?"

"Just for a minute, Andrej, pretend that I am nothing more than a simpleminded old aircraft pilot," Annenkov said with deliberate patience. "And not a rocket scientist."

"Oh," the other man said blankly, obviously recalibrating his thoughts. Then, with a quick shrug, he reached inside the open computer case and carefully detached a gray metal box. "You see this?"

Annenkov frowned. "So? What is it? Some sort of hard drive or power supply unit?"

"That is precisely what a customs agent would assume, if he x-rayed the computer or opened the case," Filippov said with quiet satisfaction. "In reality, it is the inertial control system for one of our Kh-35UE cruise missiles."

"Ah, I begin to understand."

First designed as anti-ship weapons comparable to America's Harpoon missiles, Russia's Kh-35 subsonic, short-range cruise missiles could be launched by ships, helicopters, coastal defense batteries, and aircraft. In attack mode, they were sea-skimmers, able to fly at extremely low altitude to evade enemy detection and countermeasures.

Filippov opened another computer. With pride, he plucked out several more components to show the colonel. Pieces that masqueraded as everything from DVD drives to video cards and memory card readers turned out to be things like radar altimeters, servo units, and missile fuel system controllers.

Annenkov offered praise where praise was due. "*Ochen' umno*, Andrej. Very clever." He looked at the other benches. "But what about the rest of the components we need? You can't smuggle everything inside computers and other electronic gear."

"Quite true," the other man agreed. With the colonel in tow, he moved over to a large container in one corner of the warehouse. The words WIND ENERGY SYSTEMS, INC. were stenciled across its exterior. Smaller boxes and crates that had been packed inside were being opened and inspected by one of Filippov's technicians.

Annenkov peered into one. There, surrounded

by foam packing material, he saw a sky-gray aluminum-alloy cone nearly a meter long and around forty centimeters in diameter. "A Kh-35 missile nose cone?"

"To us, yes," Filippov agreed. He shrugged. "But according to the official paperwork filed with U.S. Customs, this is the nose cone for a wind turbine rotor hub."

Annenkov raised an eyebrow. "Who would believe that? It's too small, isn't it? I've seen wind turbines. They're enormous. Some of them have blades that must be forty meters long."

"Those are industrial-sized machines," Filippov explained. "Turbines come in all sizes." For a brief instant, it looked as though he might actually smile again, but the moment passed. "The paperwork for our shipments describes them as 'experimental, high-efficiency small wind turbines intended for modular installation in disadvantaged and isolated rural communities.'"

"And customs officials actually buy that line of bullshit?" Annenkov asked in disbelief.

"They do." One corner of the other man's mouth twitched slightly. "In fact, thanks to the American government's renewable-energy incentives, we receive a significant discount on the import duty and taxes for this equipment."

Annenkov grinned. What could be better than seeing the Americans actually help make President Gryzlov's planned operations that much cheaper? Still enjoying the irony, he paid close attention while Filippov showed him other disguised missile components. Kh-35 active radar homing seekers were concealed inside cylinders mocked up to look like the generators used to convert the mechanical energy of turbine blades into electric power. Missile flight control surfaces were camouflaged as tail vanes that kept turbines themselves facing into the wind in all conditions. Fuselage pieces were hidden in plain sight as sections of pipe or nacelle.

"Smuggling in the missile warheads and their turbofan engines is the trickiest part of the business," Filippov admitted. "The Americans take more care to check for weapons and explosives crossing their borders. And engines are difficult to disguise as anything but themselves."

"But it can be done?"

"Oh, yes, Colonel," Filippov said with total confidence. "We have several shipments of oil and gas exploration equipment slated for your next flight." Seeing Annenkov's look of incomprehension, he explained. "Small explosive charges are commonly used in oil exploration and production—in seismic surveys to find potential fields and in the newly completed wells themselves."

"So the explosives required for our Kh-35 warheads can be safely included with these apparently legitimate energy industry shipments," Annenkov realized. Filippov nodded. "And our missile engines? What about them?"

"The turbofans are camouflaged as parts of large diesel motors used to provide power for oil-drilling rigs," the ordnance specialist answered simply. "They should be effectively undetectable by any routine visual or X-ray inspection."

Annenkov shook his head in admiration. Filippov and the men in Moscow's RKU logistics branch were geniuses. Once the rotary launchers being sent by sea and then truck arrived here and were installed aboard his 737-200F, he would possess a powerful strike force. He knew both Gryzlov and Kurakin put more emphasis on their prized, ultra-advanced war robots, but the colonel was something of an old-fashioned warrior. In his experience, if you put enough air-launched weapons on target, you could destroy virtually anything.

CHAPTER 12

IRON WOLF SQUADRON HEADQUARTERS, POWIDZ, POLAND

The next day

Kevin Martindale finished reading the intelligence report prepared by his top Scion analysts. With a frown, he flipped the manila folder closed, revealing the red security designations stamped on its cover, *Nazbardziej Tajne, Nie Kopiować* in Polish and *Most Secret, Do Not Copy* in English. Then he looked up, suddenly aware of the awkward silence.

Four others sat around the conference table: Brad and Patrick McLanahan, Whack Macomber, and Nadia Rozek. They were the key members of the joint Polish–Iron Wolf command team. And all of them were watching him with equally serious expressions.

He opened his mouth to begin. "I suppose—"

"If you really say, 'I suppose you are all wondering why I have called you here,' I will personally shoot you in the kneecap," Nadia interrupted bluntly.

"And then I'll break the other one with my bare hands, sir," Macomber promised. He nodded toward the folder. "We know you're dying to fill us in on what your guys uncovered at Bataysk, so let's just cut to the chase, okay?"

Outwardly, both Brad and his father winced. But neither could completely hide his amusement.

Martindale forced himself to smile. There were moments when he wished these people didn't take so much pleasure in baiting him. Then again, he guessed they'd earned the right by repeatedly risking their lives at his request. And, he supposed, he did have the occasional tendency to pontificate. Maybe you couldn't spend years in politics and the White House—even in the unconventional way he'd played his part as president—without catching the disease.

"Very well, Colonel," he said calmly. "You're quite right. This"—he tapped the Scion intelligence report—"confirms our earlier speculation. Certainly as far as the Twenty-Second Spetsnaz Brigade is concerned."

"You telling me their combat readiness really *is* collapsing?" Brad asked. The younger man could not hide his skepticism. No one who'd gone up against Russia's elite special forces troops in battle could ever take them lightly.

Martindale nodded. "My best intelligence analysts have gone over every file Kerr and Cartwright retrieved from the Bataysk database and there's no other possible conclusion. The Twenty-Second has been hollowed out."

"Hollowed out how?"

"Over the past several months, some of its most experienced platoon and company leaders, scouts, snipers, demolition, and language specialists have requested permission to resign from active duty in the armed forces."

"You say *some*," Nadia said carefully. She looked at Martindale. "How many . . . exactly?"

"Fifty-two," he said. "All of them with top-notch fitness reports."

Whack Macomber whistled. "You're right. Having that many of your best people dump out on you like that would leave a hell of a mark on any military unit. But in a commando outfit?" He shook his head. "That brigade's fucked."

Martindale nodded.

On the surface, the resignation of fifty-two officers and senior enlisted men didn't seem like much—not out of a force with a total strength of thirteen hundred soldiers. But this was a case where quality counted for a lot more than raw numbers. In any military organization, a relative handful of natural leaders created the unit cohesion that was essential to combat effectiveness. That was especially true in the special forces, where so much depended on skill, initiative, and courage at the individual and small-unit level. In wartime, as casualties mounted, new leaders might emerge amid the stress of battle. In a peacetime army, with all its inherent bureaucratic sluggishness, it was much harder to rebuild a leadership cadre once it was lost.

"And the Russian high command is just sitting back and letting those guys leave?" Brad asked in astonishment.

"'Just sitting back' would imply a level of passivity which does not exist," Martindale said quietly.

"Meaning what?"

"Far from fighting these resignation requests, Moscow actually expedited them. In fact, when the brigade commander, a Colonel Andreyev, filed a protest with his superior officers, he was threatened with disciplinary action for daring to stand in the way of any officer or soldier who wanted to return to civilian life."

Patrick McLanahan's frown was plain through the clear visor of his LEAF life-support helmet. "Tactics, marksmanship, and demolitions?" He shook his head in disbelief. "Those aren't skill sets in high demand in the civilian world."

"Not in ordinary civilian life, no," Martindale said, with a thin, humorless smile. "But that's *not* where these men are actually heading."

There was a momentary silence around the table.

Finally, Brad sighed. "Okay, I'll bite. Where are these Spetsnaz soldiers really going?"

"Fortunately, the Russian armed forces, like all government bureaucracies, amasses paperwork—even if in digital form—like a ship accumulates barnacles," Martindale explained. "The records my agents captured include copies of every request for separation made by every departing officer and enlisted man. All of them report that they've been offered employment by a company called *Razresheniye Konfliktov Uslugi.*"

Nadia raised an eyebrow. "Conflict Resolution Services?" she translated automatically.

"Which is what? In real life?" Macomber wondered.

"That's still an open question, Colonel," Martindale said flatly. "My people haven't been able to learn anything of substance about this company. Russian commercial databases show only its name, without any details about its financing, officers, facilities, or operations."

"Then this Conflict Resolution Services is a dummy corporation, nothing more than a shell," Nadia said coldly.

"Yes. And one almost certainly established by the Russian government for its own purposes, or perhaps more accurately, for Gennadiy Gryzlov's purposes," Martindale agreed. He smiled wryly. "Since I have some small experience of my own in setting up clandestine enterprises along those same lines, the pattern is unfortunately familiar to me."

His smile disappeared. "But that's not the only information we've gleaned from the Twenty-Second Brigade's files." He looked around the table again. "Like all Spetsnaz units, its armories included significant quantities of Western small arms, ammunition, and other hardware—probably for use in covert operations against NATO or other American allies."

"That's not exactly news." Macomber shrugged

his massive shoulders. "Hell, our people do the same thing, only in reverse." He showed his teeth in a quick, fierce grin. "Over the past couple of years, our Iron Wolf recon units have amassed a pretty good-sized collection of Russian assault rifles, grenades, RPGs, and other military gear. It's SOP for any well-trained special forces outfit."

"Yes, it is standard Spetsnaz operating procedure," Martindale said, speaking with care and precision. "Which makes it all the more remarkable that those inventories of Western-style arms and equipment have now been completely zeroed out. Everything's marked as 'transferred for sale to state-approved buyers in the private sector.'"

"Which would be that so-called Conflict Resolution Services," Brad guessed, with a sinking feeling.

"Undoubtedly."

"What about Russia's other elite units?" Patrick pressed. "Is the same thing happening to them?"

"It seems probable," Martindale said. "Obviously, we can't run the same kind of intelligence-gathering operations against more Spetsnaz and air-force units now, but it's a safe bet that their troops, equipment, and pilots are also being acquired by this front company."

"Well, that's just fucking swell," Macomber growled. "Gryzlov's decided to recruit his own private mercenary army. He's out there creating a Russian version of Scion and the Iron Wolf Squadron."

Martindale looked pained. "Quite so, Colonel.

And while imitation may be the sincerest form of flattery, in this case, I could easily live without it."

RKU RECONNAISSANCE TEAM CHECKMATE-ONE, NEAR BATTLE MOUNTAIN, NEVADA
A few days later

The hitchhiker trudging stolidly along the shoulder of eastbound Interstate 80 never even looked up at the cars and trucks slashing past him at speeds that were uniformly ten or fifteen or twenty miles an hour over the posted limit. The whirling, dust-laden gusts kicked up by their passage tore at his jeans, Army-surplus jacket, and faded black nylon backpack. Behind dark sunglasses, his eyes were narrowed to slits against the glare of the early-morning sun. His mouth felt gritty, as dry as the Kazakh Steppe in high summer.

The sudden deep *blaaat* of an air horn made him turn around.

A big truck, painted kelly green with gold stripes, thundered past and then pulled off the highway onto the shoulder. It braked to a full stop about a hundred yards ahead of him.

For a moment, the hitchhiker stood motionless, as if considering his options. Then he shrugged and plodded on over to the waiting big-rig. He came up on the cab's right side and yanked the door open. Then, wearily, he climbed up inside and plopped back against the seat with a deep sigh.

"Long night?" the driver asked sympathetically.

"Oh, you could say that, Dobrynin," former Spetsnaz captain Kirill Aristov said with a glare. He turned his head, hawked, and spat out onto the ground. "I think I've swallowed half of this damned Nevada desert in the past twelve hours."

Nikolai Dobrynin chuckled, checked his mirrors, and then pulled back out onto the highway. "Where to next, sir?"

"Just keep heading east for now," Aristov told him. "We'll report in to Kurakin from Salt Lake City tonight. After that, who knows?" He shrugged. Orders from RKU's chief had kept them on the hop for days, sending them rushing from place to place across the length and breadth of the U.S. to scout potential targets for *Shakh i Mat*, Operation Checkmate.

He closed his mouth on a powerful, jaw-cracking yawn. There were more and more moments when the details of this seemingly unending trek began to blur together in his travel-worn mind. *The general had better give us time for a little R&R before the balloon goes up*, he thought darkly. *Or we'll be too tired to take on even a couple of those American Girl Scouts peddling their overpriced cookies.*

With an effort, Aristov forced himself to sit up straighter. At least Moscow had been right about their disguise. There were so many millions of commercial trucks coming and going on this country's highways and byways that no one paid any real attention to them. It was the next best thing to being invisible.

He glanced at Dobrynin. "So what did you and

the others learn while I was out there all night crawling around like a snake?"

While Aristov conducted an up-close and personal reconnaissance along the outer perimeter of Sky Master's Battle Mountain facility, the rest of his team had spent the night parked at an isolated side road. Using the surveillance equipment built into their concealed hideout inside the big-rig's trailer, they'd monitored radio signals, cell-phone and landline calls, and other electronic emissions from the American compound.

"Not much," Dobrynin admitted. "Sky Masters has done an excellent job of screening its activities from nosy visitors like us. All radio and phone transmissions, whether from the air operations center or roving security patrols, are encrypted beyond our ability to decipher. We couldn't pick up any signals from wireless computer networks, which means either they're heavily shielded, or more likely, their networks are hardwired."

"What about their airport radar?"

Dobrynin grimaced. "Extremely powerful. It's certainly far more capable than any other system in regular civilian use." He shrugged, keeping his eyes firmly fixed on the road. "There's obviously a lot going on inside those hangars and office buildings, sir. But short of getting one of our people on the inside, there's no way to find out for sure."

Aristov nodded. The other man's assessment matched his own observations. He'd gotten close enough to the fence enclosing McLanahan Industrial Airport and the rest of the Sky Masters facility to identify a remarkable array of passive and active sensors guarding every centimeter. Sneaking through that perimeter would be an impossible task. In fact, nothing short of a full-on assault employing heavy weapons was likely to breach Sky Masters' security.

A slow smile spread across his tired face. Which made it fortunate that was probably precisely what Major General Kurakin and President Gryzlov had in mind.

CHAPTER 13

THE WHITE HOUSE SITUATION ROOM, WASHINGTON, D.C.
That same time

President Stacy Anne Barbeau had spent decades mastering the art of charming powerful men she otherwise loathed. For all their supposed intelligence and sophistication, a great many members of Washington, D.C.'s self-proclaimed elite were surprisingly easy to manipulate—at least by an attractive woman willing to use every weapon at her disposal, including her sexual favors, if that became necessary. Flattering useful idiots who weren't fit to kiss her dirty high heels had required an enormous amount of self-control. Screwing them while smiling took even more.

Unfortunately, former U.S. president Kevin Martindale was one of the very few men who'd seen through her right from the start. He'd immediately perceived her ruthless willingness to do whatever was necessary to achieve her desires.

Well, of course, he pegged me early on, she thought viciously. For all his bullshit about protecting the free world, Martindale was just as much a Machiavellian manipulator as she was. That was one of the reasons she'd always hated, and secretly feared, the devious son of a bitch. So it was a relief now to be able to drop the mask and confront him openly.

Even if it was only via a secure video link to Warsaw.

She'd condescended to listen to Martindale's pitch only after several urgent requests by the Polish government made through diplomatic back channels. She'd hoped it would give her a chance to learn more about his latest schemes—with a special emphasis on figuring out just how far he was prepared to go to help John D. Farrell beat her in November. But within the first couple of minutes, she'd realized this call was a waste of time.

"The intelligence my people have gathered is clear and undeniable, Madam President," Martindale said quietly. "It's highly probable that Gennadiy Gryzlov is organizing his own mercenary force on the sly. Coupled with his reckless personal nature and worldwide geopolitical ambitions, that's an extremely unsettling and dangerous development. I've no doubt that Gryzlov will use these mercenaries against his enemies—against us—while claiming his own hands are clean."

Oh, Christ, I should have known better, Barbeau thought with unconcealed disdain. For all his celebrated cleverness, ultimately, Kevin Martindale was just a one-trick pony. The Russians, the Russians, the Russians. It was always the goddamned Russians.

"Spare me the histrionics, *Mr.* Martindale," she retorted. "What's your proposition?"

"It's high time we set our personal and political differences aside," Martindale replied without any evident hesitation, somehow managing to sound surprisingly sincere. "Wherever he intends to strike first, Gryzlov poses a serious and growing threat to all of us—to NATO, to the Alliance of Free Nations, and to the United States itself. But if we openly pool our military and diplomatic resources and fully share our respective intelligence assets and information, we might be able to deter the Russians from acting rashly. At a minimum, our combined forces would be strong enough to—"

That was enough, she decided.

"Cut the Cold War crap, Martindale," Barbeau snapped, interrupting him in midsentence. "Do *not* expect me to fall for your old and very tired line of bullshit. And *don't* come crying to me because you and your hired killers—and the morons in Warsaw who pay you—are suddenly running scared. Did you really think you could end-run international law with your own goddamned private army and air force without anybody else deciding to follow your lead?"

Angrily, she shook her head. "My number one priority is to protect the citizens and national security interests of the United States. It sure as hell isn't to save your sorry old playboy ass when the bear you've been batting around suddenly bites back."

Visibly annoyed, Martindale leaned forward. "Madam President, I can assure you that saving my sorry old ass, as you so eloquently put it, is *not* what this is about—"

"Bull! You and that lunatic Patrick McLanahan set an incredibly dangerous precedent when you decided you could play toy soldiers with real people and real countries," Barbeau continued, overriding him. "Well, that was a fucking stupid game to play and it ended up killing McLanahan. Now it may be your turn. Tough shit. I guess you and the Poles are just going to have to learn to live with the consequences of your own illegal actions. In any case, you can sure as hell forget about hiding under my skirts! If Gryzlov really does send his own mercenaries after you and Piotr Wilk and the rest of your gang, you're on your own."

Contemptuously, she tapped a control on the keyboard at her elbow, cutting the secure link to Warsaw.

The wall-sized screen went black.

Barbeau swiveled her chair to look at Luke Cohen and Ed Rauch. Her chief of staff and national security adviser were the only two people she'd trusted to hear what passed between her and Martindale. Bringing more staffers into the loop only multiplied the odds of a leak to the press and that was something she simply could not risk. Rumors from Warsaw wouldn't gain any traction. Nobody important would believe them.

But at this stage of the campaign, having anonymous, high-level White House sources confirm that she'd been in secret contact with Martindale and the Polish government could be disastrous. Public and congressional support for her foreign policy in Europe hinged on a belief that cutting ties with Poland and its half-baked Alliance of Free Nations was a rational move—one in America's best interests. Anything that suggested she might be rethinking that could seriously damage her credibility . . . and lay her wide open to Farrell's political attacks.

Barbeau snorted in disgust. Did Martindale really think she was that dumb? Reversing course now to forge new defense and intelligence links with Poland and its allies would be political malpractice of the highest order. It would split her own party right down the middle—dividing it between those who would loyally toe whatever line she took and those who genuinely wanted a new détente with the Russians. That kind of division could easily cost her a closely contested election. If she'd ever doubted the former president was in bed with her opponent, there was her answer.

She could rely on Cohen keeping his mouth shut about this aborted conversation because the lanky New Yorker's political future was entirely tied to hers. Without her, he would be nothing . . . just another washed-up White House toady who'd be lucky to land a paying gig at some rinky-dink cable news network.

And Rauch was trustworthy because he was smart enough to know that he could never spill anything like this to reporters and get away with it. Leaking confidential and classified information was a federal crime. The general rule in D.C. was that leakers never paid a price. But Barbeau was willing to bet that her skinny, gray-haired national security adviser knew damned well she was vengeful enough to make him the exception.

"Comments?" she snapped.

"Assuming the intelligence information he shared is accurate, former president Martindale could be right," Rauch said reluctantly. "At least about the potential danger a deniable Russian mercenary force represents."

Barbeau's lip curled. "You're not really going to tell me that a couple of hundred ex-Spetsnaz troops could threaten this country's survival, Ed?"

"Our survival? No, Madam President," Rauch said quickly. He looked worried, though. "But a clandestine force of that size could inflict some serious damage on a U.S. military installation, either here, or more likely, in Europe."

"Get real, Dr. Rauch," she retorted. "There's no *way* the Russians could hope to sneak that many men into this country or one of our NATO allies . . . not without getting caught. They'd be lucky to infiltrate ten men successfully. Trying the same thing with even twenty would be one hell of a risk." She shrugged. "What could Gryzlov really hope to accomplish with a handful of former Spetsnaz thugs with small arms and maybe some RPGs and explosives? That's not a strategic game changer. Not even close." Reluctantly, Rauch dipped his head, acknowledging her point.

Barbeau turned her cold-eyed gaze on Luke Cohen. "Anything to add, Luke?"

Her chief of staff nodded. "Sure, Gryzlov's ballsy. But he's not stupid enough to come after us. Not without good cause," he said confidently. "He's got to know that we'll retaliate for any attack on us or our real allies . . . no matter how hard he tries to spin it as some phony-baloney mercenary operation."

"Okay, that's a solid point," she agreed. She looked back at Rauch. "Well, Ed?"

"I can't argue with Mr. Cohen's analysis, Madam President," he said. The pale little former academic looked thoughtful. "But fear of us won't stop Gryzlov from attacking the Poles again, using his 'private' covert-action units to sow terror and confusion ahead of a more conventional offensive."

"Is the CIA or anyone else in the intelligence community picking up any hints that Moscow's planning a new war against Warsaw and the AFN?" Barbeau asked sharply.

"Not really," Rauch admitted. He spread his hands. "But our intelligence assets—our satellites, intercept stations, and HUMINT sources—are all almost exclusively oriented against Russia's official military and political establishment. If Gryzlov really has created an off-the-books mercenary force, our people might not even be looking in the right direction."

"Great," Barbeau muttered, chewing that over in her mind. What if that nutcase Gennadiy Gryzlov actually had his own private army and somehow managed to kick the crap out of the Poles and their piddling allies? Russian success in Eastern and central Europe now could make her look weak in the unsophisticated eyes of too many swing-state voters. The enduring political problem she faced had once been defined by General George S. Patton. Americans loved a winner. And they would not tolerate a loser.

But Luke Cohen only shrugged when she expressed her fears.

"So the Russians hit the Poles again? So what?" the New Yorker said with a callous grin. "It doesn't matter how many badass Spetsnaz commandos Gryzlov's got on his personal payroll. If the shit hits the fan, they're still completely outmatched by Martindale's Iron Wolf robots." He shrugged. "We've all seen the intel on those machines. They're basically death on steroids."

With a quick grimace, Barbeau nodded. Just thinking about those unearthly war robots made her skin crawl. In the past, she'd had her own terrifying encounters with Cybernetic Infantry Devices. Those experiences were *not* something she ever wanted to repeat.

"Even if they got lucky, the best the Russians could hope for would be just another blood-soaked stalemate," Cohen continued. "And no one who matters is going to blame you for refusing to shove American fighting men and women into that kind of a no-win meat grinder."

He offered her a cynical grin. "Besides, looked at the right way, every dead Spetsnaz goon and every shot-up Iron Wolf combat robot is just one less threat to our national security. In the bigger scheme of things, another round of fighting between Russia and Poland would be a win for us."

Slowly, Stacy Anne Barbeau nodded. Years ago, Martindale and that warmongering slimeball Patrick McLanahan had effectively stolen the technology for those Cybernetic Infantry Devices from its rightful owner, the U.S. government. So why not let the Russians pay the blood price necessary to pare down Scion's inventory of the deadly machines?

OFFICE OF THE PRESIDENT, BELWEDER PALACE, WARSAW, POLAND
That same time

With a bleak look on his face, Polish president Piotr Wilk leaned over the desk and snapped off the power to his computer monitor. The field of gray static left when Barbeau cut the secure teleconference link to Warsaw vanished. Then he sat down across from Martindale. "You made a valiant effort," he told the American. "At first, I really hoped she might listen."

"Unfortunately, listening to others has never been Stacy Anne's strong suit," Martindale said. "Especially when they're asking her to admit she might have made a mistake. Like too many politicians, she confuses rigid thinking with strength of purpose."

"She is certainly astonishingly petty and willfully blind." Wilk shook his head in disappointment. "Your country deserves better."

"Maybe so, Piotr. We'll see what the voters say in November." Wry amusement flickered in Martindale's eyes. "Otto von Bismarck once said that God looked after fools, drunkards, and the United States. There are many times when I wish my fellow Americans weren't so willing to test that proposition to its limit."

"In the meantime, it appears we must look to our own defenses."

"That's about the size of it," Martindale agreed. He sighed. "I just wish I could shake the nagging worry that we're missing something. Something important."

"Such as?"

"Such as the fact that, try as I might, I can't figure out what Gryzlov hopes to gain by forming his own mercenary force," Martindale said, with a frustrated look. "He's got to know that conventionally equipped Spetsnaz commandos are no match for the Iron Wolf Squadron and our CIDs. So what's his real plan?"

Wilk nodded. Even at Perun's Aerie, where everything went wrong, it had taken an ambush by a battalion of Russian tanks and other armored fighting vehicles, together with massed artillery fire, to destroy the two Iron Wolf combat robots piloted by Charlie Turlock and Whack Macomber. And so far, they had no reports that would indicate Moscow was supplying Gryzlov's

RKU mercenaries with tanks, self-propelled guns, or other heavy weapons.

"The Russians could still hurt us badly in a sudden surprise attack," he pointed out. "After all, there are only six CIDs in our order of battle. We cannot defend every vulnerable point in the Alliance of Free Nations."

"Sure, Gryzlov's mercs could inflict some pain," Martindale said evenly. "But not nearly enough to swing the outcome in a new war." He looked at Wilk. "We'd just roll with the first punch and then tear them to shreds."

"Perhaps friend Gennadiy is more optimistic about his chances against us than you are," the Polish president countered in a dry voice.

"Oh, I'm sure he is," Martindale agreed. "But he's still not crazy enough to see using hired Spetsnaz veterans as a winning play. Gaining a measure of plausible deniability for violent covert action may be useful from a diplomatic and political point of view, but it doesn't change the fundamental military equation."

"He may not define winning in quite the same way we do," Wilk warned. "Russia's armed forces still outnumber ours. Moscow can trade pawn for pawn and still come out ahead. Maybe Gryzlov has decided to erode our strength with a series of pinprick raids using his 'mercenaries'—confident that we will be unwilling to escalate in retaliation."

Martindale frowned. That was a nasty thought. A prolonged covert war of attrition would not

succeed in destroying Poland and its allies outright, but the military and economic strain involved in fending off a seemingly unending
series of commando attacks and sabotage would
be enormous. It was no secret that a number of
governments in the Alliance of Free Nations were
fragile, dependent on small parliamentary ma-
jorities and narrow margins of public support. If
those governments fell, either by losing elections
or because of massive public discontent, their
successors might be more willing to cozy up to
Moscow in return for peace. Having failed in his
earlier all-out military and cyberwar campaigns,
was Gryzlov now willing to play a longer game?

He shook his head. The willingness to fight a
slow war of attrition seemed out of character for
Russia's aggressive leader. On the other hand, it
was a classic mistake to assume that an opponent
could not learn from his earlier mistakes.

Which led directly to another piece of the puzzle that he could not make fit. Crazy or not, there
was no way that Gryzlov could hope to skate away
from responsibility for any attacks launched by
Russian-made aircraft and missiles operating out
of Russian-controlled air bases. So why was this
RKU outfit recruiting veteran fighter and bomber
pilots?

CHAPTER 14

Yuri Annenkov stood up to greet the two men who entered his sparsely furnished office at one end of the trailer. Despite their business suits, neither of them could really be mistaken for a midlevel corporate executive, no matter what it said on their false passports. While only of average height, both were remarkably fit and moved with the easy assurance of men used to handling advanced aircraft under high-Gs in combat conditions.

"How was your flight?" he asked.

"Uneventful from a security standpoint, but damned noisy," Colonel Ruslan Baryshev, the older of the two, answered. His thin-lipped smile stopped well short of his pale blue eyes. "Some fat American woman's brat screamed all the way from Toronto to Salt Lake City."

Annenkov winced in sympathy. No real pilot, especially not a former Su-50 stealth-fighter squadron commander like Baryshev, could enjoy being forced to travel as a mere passenger at the mercy of some other flier. Doing so in the sort of dingy, jam-packed horror shows that passed for commercial airliners these days must have seemed like a foretaste of hell itself.

Baryshev nodded toward his companion. "This is my wingman, Captain Oleg Imrekov."

"Technically, I'm your former wingman, sir. And no longer exactly a captain," the younger man said with a more genuine smile. He sketched a salute to Annenkov. "KVM Senior Pilot Imrekov reporting for duty."

Baryshev shook his head in mock despair. "And thus you see how discipline dies in the glorious private sector, Yuri. Once I could have had this young whelp shot for disrespect. Now the best I can do is contemplate giving him a bad performance review."

Annenkov laughed. He waved them into the two chairs in front of his desk and sat down himself. "The rest of your lads arrived yesterday, Ruslan. For now, they're bunking with my air and ground crews."

"Any complaints?"

"Major Zelin did bitch a little about the selection of drinks at the O Club," Annenkov allowed.

Baryshev raised an eyebrow. "You have an officers' club here?"

"Only if you count a folding table with a bottle

of vodka and a supply of disposable plastic cups as a club."

"Ah, luxury," Imrekov said. "Back at our old fighter base at Syktyvkar, we had to share our cups. And they were made out of paper. Cheap paper."

"You were lucky to have that much, Oleg," Baryshev said with a grin. "In my days as a lowly junior pilot, we were only issued one drinking straw per regiment." Dumping the grin, he turned back to Annenkov. "How about our gear? Is everything in order?"

"No problems," Annenkov assured him. "My ordnance man, Filippov, reports he'll have your *Kiberneticheskiye Voyennyye Mashiny* fully reassembled and battle-ready by tomorrow morning."

"That's excellent news." Satisfied, Baryshev sat back. "Have we received the 'go' orders and mission assignments from Moscow?"

Annenkov shook his head. "Not yet. But it can't be long now. Major General Kurakin is pulling in all of our covert reconnaissance outfits. Once they get here, Captain Aristov's team will switch over to act as your local security element and ground transportation unit." Baryshev nodded his understanding.

"I do have one question, Ruslan," Annenkov said carefully. "Why only employ six of these combat robots in your unit? If *Shakh i Mat* is so important to the higher-ups in Moscow, why not send a larger assault force?"

"Do you have any idea of how much it costs to manufacture a KVM?" Baryshev asked quietly.

"Quite a bit, I would imagine. Perhaps the cost of a T-90 main battle tank? Or a little more?" Annenkov guessed.

"Try nearly six billion rubles, Yuri," Baryshev said flatly. "Each."

Annenkov felt his eyes pop open wide in amazement. *Six billion rubles?* For a single robotic war machine? *My God*, he thought. That was around one hundred million American dollars, which meant a KVM cost more than one of those fifth-generation Su-50 stealth fighters Baryshev and his wingman used to fly. Or two hundred of the Kh-35 cruise missiles arming his converted 737-200F cargo jet. "And they're worth that much?"

"Without question," the other man said. His pale eyes were infinitely colder now. "Only wait until my fighting machines go into action against the Americans. For years, their puppets and mercenaries have swaggered around the world, believing that no one else could ever develop this technology. Soon they will realize just how big a lie that was."

THE KREMLIN, MOSCOW
A short time later

For a long, uncomfortable moment, Gennadiy Gryzlov sat in silence, coolly observing the two men who'd just been ushered into his private office. As usual, Viktor Kazyanov, his long-suffering minister of state security, looked apprehensive. He was more a rabbit than a man, Gryzlov thought in contempt. Droplets of sweat already beaded the intelligence director's high forehead.

Vladimir Kurakin, the head of RKU, was evidently made of stronger stuff. As befitted a decorated special forces commander with years of combat experience, he met the president's hard-eyed gaze without flinching.

Gryzlov nodded politely to him and then turned his attention back to Kazyanov. "So, Viktor, from that uncontrollable quiver in those fat white hands of yours, I assume your efforts to find and capture the foreign spies who infiltrated the Twenty-Second Spetsnaz Brigade HQ have failed," he said. "As usual."

The minister of state security swallowed convulsively. "I am afraid so, Mr. President," he admitted, with clear reluctance. He moistened dry lips. "Without photographs or even decent descriptions of those who masqueraded as Colonel Zakharova and the accountant Solomin, our army and police units manning checkpoints on the highways and at airports and rail stations had too little to go on."

"So the criminals who murdered two of our soldiers and stole vital secrets have successfully escaped?" Gryzlov asked. He forced himself to speak calmly, almost as though he were asking the spy chief about the weather outside. Miserably, Kazyanov nodded. "And which of the various foreign intelligence services do your analysts believe committed this outrage?"

"Without more evidence, that is a difficult

question to answer," Kazyanov said carefully. "Ballistics analysis indicates that the weapon used to kill Captain Leonov and Sergeant Isayev was originally issued to an FSB assassination squad that disappeared without a trace in Thailand more than ten years ago. And unfortunately, nothing else we've found so far concretely ties this operation to any particular enemy country."

"And yet your analysts are paid to answer difficult questions, are they not?" Gryzlov asked with deceptive mildness.

"Yes, Mr. President," Kazyanov agreed hurriedly. He hesitated for a second or two and then went on. "Well . . . the consensus seems to be that it might have been the CIA—"

"Bullshit," Gryzlov snapped. "Are you really that stupid, Viktor? Do you genuinely believe the CIA would try something so audacious? Or authorize its agents to kill so mercilessly?" He shook his head in disgust. "Haven't you been paying attention to your own damned reports? The dickless cretins Barbeau put in charge of the CIA are far more interested in handing out rainbow-colored condoms at Langley gay-rights celebrations than in conducting high-risk operations like this one."

He stared coldly at Kazyanov, savoring the sudden rush of power as the bigger man physically wilted into his chair. "No, this was Martindale's doing. He's the only one out there ruthless enough to order this kind of 'wet work' on our soil."

Kurakin spoke up. "That would certainly explain those brief radar contacts made by the S-400 battalion at Feodosia."

"Precisely," Gryzlov said. "It was one of Martindale's damned stealth aircraft, probably the same STOL transport he used at Perun's Aerie. And it slipped through our whole air defense network without anyone laying a finger on it." His eyes were hooded. "I am getting very tired of watching our vaunted 'defenders of the Motherland' screw up time and time again." The corners of his mouth turned down. "Perhaps our radar crews, SAM units, and fighter pilots need another taste of the lash."

Neither Kazyanov nor Kurakin said anything to dispute him.

And they are wise not to, Gryzlov thought icily. Thanks to hacked acquisition and targeting software installed in Russia's most advanced SAM regiments, some of Martindale's Iron Wolf mercenaries had escaped his carefully laid trap at the Perun's Aerie cyberwar complex. And unable to trust his own weapons, he'd been forced to concede a draw to the American and his Polish paymaster, Piotr Wilk. Furious, he'd made sure that heads rolled.

The first of those to fall had been Colonel General Maksimov, once his own mentor at the Yuri Gagarin Military Air Academy. Maksimov had been forced to resign as head of the Aerospace Defense Force for "medical" reasons. When the general suffered a fatal stroke a few months later, Moscow gossips had darkly whispered the old man's death wasn't natural. Gryzlov considered it revealing that so many of his countrymen were willing to blame poison for a seizure actually triggered by deep personal shame and public humiliation. On the other hand, there'd been nothing natural about the sudden deaths of more than a dozen top software engineers in Nizhny Novgorod—unless, of course, you understood that taking a bullet in the back of the head was the natural and inevitable consequence of treason and incompetence.

For a few seconds, he pondered ordering another round of courts-martial and executions, starting with those lazy buffoons at the 22nd Guards Spetsnaz Brigade and eventually moving on to the blind, deaf, and dumb Su-27 fighter pilots who'd failed to intercept Martindale's stealth aircraft. Not yet, he decided. None of those he might punish were going anywhere. Let them sweat.

His decision made, Gryzlov looked up from his brief reverie with a scowl.

Kazyanov, who'd been caught mopping at his own brow with a handkerchief, froze. His face turned gray with fear.

"Get out, Viktor," Gryzlov said with a heavy sigh. Verbally abusing the other man was still mildly amusing, but the experience was beginning to pall. Sooner or later he was going to have to get rid of Kazyanov. And the minister of state security knew only too well that men in his position— with access to so many secrets—rarely lived long enough to enjoy retirement. Gryzlov made a mental note to have Kazyanov put under even closer surveillance. It would never do for poor, old Viktor to imagine he could successfully defect.

* * *

When the door closed behind Kazyanov, Gryzlov turned back to Kurakin.

"How badly has our security been compromised?" he asked bluntly.

"I've reviewed the files those two spies accessed," Kurakin said. "Whoever did this must now be aware of RKU's existence . . . and at least some of our capabilities." He shrugged. "If there were any doubt, cyber specialists from the FSB's Q Directorate detected in-depth probes of different commercial and governmental databases within twenty-four hours after the incident at Bataysk. But they were unable to trace those probes back to any identifiable source."

"Which really tells us all we need to know about who was responsible," Gryzlov said dryly. "Martindale's Scion operatives were poking around for more information about RKU."

"Yes, Mr. President." Kurakin nodded. He hesitated, knowing how little Russia's leader liked hearing unwelcome suggestions. "It might be best to delay implementing *Shakh i Mat* until we can build in more layers of operational secrecy. If Martindale or the Poles pass their information on to the Americans—"

"Checkmate will proceed on schedule," Gryzlov said, cutting him off with a sharp, decisive rap on his desk. "Whatever personnel files and equipment records were stolen from Bataysk could not have compromised our operational plans. Meanwhile, your forces are already in position. Delay now would only increase the risk of the Americans stumbling across some of our people by accident."

Again, Kurakin nodded. There was truth in the president's blunt assertion. While internal security in the United States was so lax as to be almost nonexistent, there was always the chance of one of his teams being caught in a routine traffic stop gone wrong or in some other slipup.

"Besides, Vladimir," Gryzlov continued with a smile. "The fact that Martindale knows he has a new Russian 'competitor' is essentially meaningless. Even if he somehow persuades Barbeau and others that he's telling the truth, what can they do?" He leaned back in his chair. "That is the beauty of our plan, is it not? We are co-opting the same tactic of plausible deniability so often used by the Americans to evade responsibility for Scion's own actions."

Privately, Kurakin suspected almost no one would swallow Gryzlov's claims of innocence once the Americans figured out what was really going on. Oh, he supposed that a few neutrals and a handful of the weaker Western-allied powers might be willing to choose a convenient lie over the inconvenient truth. But no major world player would buy the idea of a freelance, rogue Russian military corporation operating outside Moscow's command and control.

Still, he concluded, handling the inevitable diplomatic and military fallout from this operation would be a problem for the president to solve later. His particular and immediate task was simpler. His job was to make sure that RKU's attacks were structured to cause maximum confusion and to inflict as much damage as possible in a short period of time. The more confusion, the longer it would take the U.S. to pin this operation on Moscow. And the more damage his forces caused, the more difficult it would be for the Americans to retaliate effectively against the Motherland.

Kurakin came back to the present moment. Wisely or unwisely, President Gryzlov had made his decision: *Operatsiya Shakh i Mat* would proceed. Julius Caesar's comment on crossing the Rubicon, declaring war against Pompey and the Roman senate came to mind. *Alea iacta est.* The die is cast. So now, as a loyal soldier, he must do his best to make sure that die landed with the winning number faceup.

"Yes, Mr. President," he said simply.

"Good. I'm glad that's settled," Gryzlov said, sounding satisfied. "So now we can move on to the details. First, have your staff planners finally settled on a first target? Or are they still pissing around with their maps and briefing books?"

With an effort, Kurakin suppressed a quick flash of irritation. Selecting the most vulnerable and valuable targets from the wealth of information gathered by his covert recon groups was no easy matter in the first place. But it was child's play compared with the work required to develop coordinated movement and assault plans that made the most effective use of RKU's war robots—enabling them to arrive in striking distance in secret and then to escape undetected.

"We do have a recommendation, Mr. President,"

he said finally. "We propose launching Checkmate's first blow to cause maximum damage to our country's most dangerous enemy."

"Show me."

Kurakin pulled out his laptop and connected it to Gryzlov's ultrasecure private network. Completely independent of any Kremlin servers connected to the outside world, this network was designed to be almost impossible for hackers to penetrate. Only the president's most trusted subordinates were granted access or allowed to connect their own devices. Periodic sweeps by Q Directorate specialists checked for any signs of infiltration or hidden malware.

A map of the western United States appeared on the large LED screen set into Gryzlov's desk.

Kurakin tapped a key on his laptop. The map zoomed in, revealing a stretch of high desert in northern Nevada nestled in among several mountain ranges. A target icon blinked into existence on top of what looked like an airfield. "As you can see, there are only a few highways we can use to move our KVMs into range of this objective. But that same relative isolation ensures a significant delay before regular American military forces can react to our assault. By conducting simultaneous cruise-missile strikes at key choke points, we can further—"

"Permission denied," Gryzlov said quietly.

Startled, Kurakin looked away from the projected map. "Excuse me, Mr. President?"

"I know you're not deaf, Major General," the president said. "You heard me perfectly. This proposed target is off the table, at least for now."

"But *why*?"

"Because," Gryzlov said patiently, "if we play our cards right, the Americans themselves will take care of those troublemakers. We won't even have to lift a finger. Or fire a single missile."

For a moment, just a moment, Kurakin saw red. What the hell kind of manipulative game was the president playing with him? Only years of ingrained discipline prevented him from throwing a punch right into the younger man's smug face. That and the certainty that doing so would mean a painful and lingering death. Gennadiy Gryzlov was not a forgiving man.

With difficulty, he regained a small measure of control over his emotions. "I see," he said through gritted teeth. "Does this mean you've already chosen another target of your own, sir?"

"That's correct," Gryzlov agreed. He held up a hand in apology. "I'm sorry to have sprung this on you so suddenly, Vladimir. But we're being handed a golden opportunity . . . one we would be fools to ignore."

He tapped the slick surface of the computer built into his desk. Instantly, Kurakin's operational map disappeared. In its place, short clips from several recent American television news programs scrolled across the screen, accompanied by subtitles in Russian. When they ended, another map appeared—this one centered on the southeastern United States. A single red targeting icon blossomed on the map.

"*There's* your new first objective," Gryzlov said. He smiled, seeing Kurakin's face suddenly pale.

Devilish amusement danced in his eyes. "The Americans are busy making themselves look like idiots with this interminable political season of theirs. So why shouldn't we help make sure their presidential election campaign starts off with a bang, eh?"

CHAPTER 15

AIR FORCE ONE, **BARKSDALE AIR FORCE BASE, LOUISIANA**
Several days later

"**W**e're on final approach to Barksdale, Madam President," one of Stacy Anne Barbeau's uniformed military aides reported.

With a big, friendly smile, she looked up. "Why, thank you, Tommy. I appreciate the heads-up. I must have been lost in my reading."

Ostentatiously, she closed the thick briefing book she'd been pretending to study since flying out from Andrews Air Force Base outside Washington, D.C., more than two hours ago. Why the Pentagon brass thought she could possibly be interested in an assembly of boring background papers about the different units stationed at Barksdale was a mystery. Irritating though it was, there were certain niceties to be observed in her sometimes tense relationship with the U.S. military. Despite the big-ticket weapons projects and pay increases she'd rammed through Congress, too many officers and enlisted personnel disliked her administration and were hoping that Farrell would beat her in November.

The big 747-200B, designated a VC-25B in its military configuration, vibrated slightly as its landing gear came down and locked.

Barbeau leaned over in her luxurious big leather seat to look out the armored window. They were coming in low over the lush green woods and bayous of northwestern Louisiana. Off to the west, she could see the muddy brown waters of the Red River snaking back and forth between Shreveport and Bossier City.

Luke Cohen poked his head in through the open door to her onboard office. "We're all set. The press plane landed an hour ago. And our advance team has the good little boys and girls of the media safely corralled in a roped-off area. They've got great camera angles for your arrival, review of the troops, and speech—but they're set up just a little too far away for any awkward candid interviews with people on the base."

"Are any of them bitching about that?"

Her White House chief of staff shrugged. "A couple." He gave her a sly grin. "But our guys blamed it on the Air Force. The imperatives of national security, you know."

"Nice job," Barbeau said, pleased. The fact that Barksdale itself was closed to civilians was one of the pluses in what her staff was billing as an official inspection of "renewed American airpower" by the nation's commander in chief. The press could either parrot back the story she handed them on a platter . . . or nothing. "How's the weather shaping up?"

"It's hot and muggy as hell," Cohen said. "But the most recent forecast says it won't rain until much later, long after we're gone."

She nodded. Louisiana was her home state and oppressive temperatures and humidity were typical for this time of year. Fortunately, the same Botox injections that smoothed out her wrinkles and made her look years younger than her real age also kept her from sweating. That was just one more secret weapon in her political arsenal. While everyone around her looked about ready to melt, she would come across as cool, clean, and perfectly composed.

Air Force One touched down with barely a jolt and decelerated in a roar of reversed engines and brakes, slowing fast as it rolled down the air base's nearly twelve-thousand-foot-long runway. Cohen gripped the edge of the doorframe and rode easily with the motion.

Barbeau turned back to the window. Outside, she could see thousands of airmen and officers lined up at parade rest in neat ranks. Their blue dress uniforms made a nice contrast with the reddish-brown earth tones of the wide concrete apron. Twenty-four multirole stealth fighters of the U.S. Air Force's first operational F-35 Lightning II squadron were parked behind them. Next to the fighters were a half-dozen mammoth, dark gray B-52H Stratofortress strategic bombers, along with two swept-wing XB-1F Excaliburs.

She hid a frown. Those two Excaliburs, and the others deployed elsewhere, were old B-1B Lancers originally upgraded by Sky Masters as part of one of Patrick McLanahan's nutty private military schemes. Sure, she'd had the Air Force seize the XB-1F bombers for its own use as soon as she took office. Nevertheless, seeing them here was an unwelcome reminder that the U.S. armed forces were still too dependent on weapons and aircraft authorized by her old political rivals.

For nearly four years, Barbeau's administration had blocked Sky Masters from landing new Pentagon contracts, but the company limped along anyway—surviving on sales to the domestic market, foreign countries, and Martindale's Scion mercenaries. She gritted her teeth. It was high time that she shoved Sky Masters and its backers into the dustbin of aviation history. And with luck, today's big show would help make that happen by unveiling America's newest and most advanced long-range stealth bomber.

"Where's our B-21 Raider prototype?" she asked, still watching out the window. There, at the far end of the apron, she saw a light gray C-17 Globemaster III transport waiting off to the side. That plane had flown in ahead of *Air Force One*, ferrying the black SUVs and limousines that made up her presidential motorcade. There were no plans for her to drive anywhere on this trip, but the Secret Service always insisted on covering all possible bases.

"Orbiting a few miles away, out of sight," Cohen told her. "I confirmed that with our liaison to the contractor a couple of minutes ago."

"And the flight crew knows what to do?"

The New Yorker nodded. "As soon as we're parked and the Secret Service has cleared you to deplane, they'll start their approach. Everything's timed so that shiny new B-21 Raider will touch down just as you're being greeted by the base commander and his staff." He winked at her. "Those pictures are going to lead every newscast tonight, Madam President. They'll be on the front page of every newspaper tomorrow morning. Hell, they'll go viral on the Internet as soon as we upload them to the White House website and reporters post their own pics on social media."

Stacy Anne Barbeau smiled broadly. This taxpayer-funded kickoff for her presidential re-election campaign would be a day to remember.

INSIDE THE BASE PERIMETER
That same time

Accompanied by the soft whine of servos and actuators, a sleek, deadly-looking gray machine stalked through the woods and bayous east of Barksdale's runway. Shadows cast by magnolias, oak trees, and tall slash pines flowed across its elongated torso, eyeless spherical head, and thin, agile arms and legs. Despite the bulky weapons packs strapped to it, the robot moved with remarkable speed and stealth.

Quietly, it came to a placc where the trees grew closer together. Ahead, the ground sloped down very slightly into a tangle of ferns and thickets of switch cane. Knobby, thick-trunked bald cypresses rose out of a ribbon of stagnant, tea-colored water.

Suddenly the robot stopped moving. It crouched lower, nestling down among the undergrowth. Its antenna-studded head swiveled rapidly from side to side.

Inside the cockpit, KVM senior pilot Oleg Imrekov studied his displays. He was picking up a bright green thermal signature, man-sized and -shaped, a little over one hundred meters ahead—on the other side of this narrow stretch of bayou. Using a low-light visual sensor slaved to his robot's thermal imager, he zoomed in on the same spot.

He saw a young American soldier in camouflage fatigues standing next to a small, four-wheel all-terrain vehicle. Through a pair of binoculars, the soldier was peering up at a bird's nest in the branches of a tall pine tree farther down the bayou. By the twin stripes on his sleeve, he was an airman first class, and a unit patch identified him as a member of the 2nd Security Forces Squadron. Apart from a holstered 9mm pistol, the American was unarmed.

Imrekov opened a secure radio link. "*Prividenye* Lead, this is Two."

Colonel Baryshev replied immediately. His own combat robot was moving through the woods about five hundred meters north of his position. "*Specter Lead to Specter Two. Go ahead.*"

"I've encountered an American airman to my

front. He hasn't seen me yet, but there is no way I can go around him without being spotted."

"Is this man a sentry or a scout?" Baryshev asked, sounding concerned, and rightly so. Nothing in Kirill Aristov's reconnaissance reports had suggested they might run into enemy resistance along this concealed line of approach. If the Americans had scouts or observation posts deployed this far out from the runway, their assault could be easily compromised. It was essential that all six Russian KVMs reach the target without being detected.

"Neither," Imrekov said. "The American seems to be bird-watching. He may be one of their game wardens."

He heard the colonel bite down on a curse. Barksdale Air Force Base sprawled over more than twenty-two thousand acres. Some of that land was set aside as protected nature preserves. Monitoring the endangered plant and animal species on this huge base was the job of a very small force of airmen assigned as game wardens. And that made this sudden, unexpected meeting sheer bad luck.

"Can you silence the American before he raises an alarm?"

"I think so," Imrekov replied calmly.

"Then do it."

Obeying the commands he relayed through his neural link, Imrekov's KVM leaped to its feet and charged forward into the bayou, accelerating up with every long-legged stride. Stagnant, foul-smelling water splashed high across the robot's spindly legs.

Startled by the sudden explosion of noise, the young American airman spun toward the bayou. He dropped his binoculars, fumbling for the pistol holstered at his side. His eyes widened. "What the hell—"

Imrekov's machine burst out of the swamp in a spray of mud and torn vegetation. Before the airman could get a firm grip on his Beretta M9 pistol, the Russian KVM pilot leaned forward and batted him aside with one of the robot's large metal hands. With a muffled cry, the American went tumbling head over heels in a spray of blood and broken bone. He landed facedown in a clump of ferns and collapsed in an unmoving heap, clearly dead.

"Situation resolved satisfactorily," Imrekov radioed. "Specter Two is proceeding to target at best possible speed."

OVER SOUTHERN ARKANSAS
That same time

Regan Air Freight Flight 175 flew southeast at twenty-five thousand feet through blue skies marked by wisps of high, thin white cloud. According to its flight manifest, the 737-200F cargo jet was ferrying wind turbine components from Indianapolis to Dallas/Fort Worth International Airport. But instead of turbine blades and nacelles, sixteen Kh-35UE cruise missiles filled its cargo compartment, waiting silently on four track-mounted rotary launchers.

"Regan One-Seven-Five, Memphis Center," an air traffic controller said in Colonel Yuri Annenkov's headset, "contact Fort Worth Center on one-three-four-point-four-seven-five. Have a good day." They were leaving the airspace supervised by the FAA's Memphis Air Traffic Control Center and entering that monitored by its Fort Worth counterpart.

Annenkov clicked his mike. "One-three-four-point-four-seven-five for Regan One-Seven-Five. Thank you, Memphis." He waited while his copilot, Major Konstantin Uspensky, changed radio frequencies as directed. Then he keyed his mike again. "Fort Worth Center, Regan One-Seven-Five, level two-five-zero."

The voice of a new controller responded immediately, acknowledging that they were in his area of responsibility and that he had them on his radar screen. "Regan One-Seven-Five, roger."

Annenkov made sure he wasn't broadcasting over the radio and glanced at Uspensky. "Give me a position check."

His copilot toggled one of the multifunction cockpit displays added when this old Boeing air freighter was secretly converted into a cruise-missile carrier. A map appeared, showing their current position and projected course. A red dot pulsed rhythmically about twenty nautical miles ahead. "We're coming up on our preplanned launch coordinates, Colonel," he confirmed. "Three minutes out."

"Then let's run through the attack checklist," Annenkov said, summoning up his own digital copy with a quick tap. He read off the first item. "Confirm power to rotary launcher handling system."

"The handling system is live," Uspensky said, checking to make sure electrical power was flowing to the array of high-speed pulleys and hoists that would haul their rotary launchers along the rails built into the cargo deck floor.

"Bring the launchers online."

The copilot tapped controls on his MFD. Four lights on a schematic of the cargo compartment turned green. "Our rotary launchers are online and linked to the attack computer."

"Transfer our GPS coordinates to the computer and initialize the missile inertial guidance systems."

Uspensky obeyed, efficiently keying in the commands that fed their precisely calculated current position to the inertial navigation systems that would control the Kh-35s in flight. More green lights blossomed on his displays. This was a workaround to help reduce the small position errors inevitably accumulated by inertial systems during flight. More modern Kh-35 missiles included GLONASS receivers, which enabled them to obtain highly accurate satellite navigation data from Russia's equivalent of the U.S. global positioning system. But using those advanced missile variants would have made it easier to pin this attack on Moscow itself, rather than on someone else using Kh-35s covertly purchased on the international arms black market. "Guidance systems initialized."

"Confirm preselected target sets are down-loaded to the missiles," Annenkov ordered.

"All target sets are downloaded."

"Bring the missiles to full readiness."

Uspensky tapped more virtual controls on his display. He watched closely as data scrolled across the screen in response. "Radar altimeters are good. Turbofans are good. Self-destruct systems are good." He looked up. "All missiles are flight-ready, Colonel."

"Checklist complete," Annenkov said in satis-faction. "Time to launch position?"

"Thirty seconds."

Annenkov tightened his shoulder straps and donned an oxygen mask. Beside him, Uspensky did the same. He reached up to the overhead instrument panel and set the 737's pressuriza-tion control system to manual. He flipped two switches on the same panel. "Depressurizing the cargo deck."

The engine bleed valves feeding pressurized air to the jet's cargo deck closed tight. At the same time, outflow valves opened on the fuselage. Pressure on the cargo deck dropped fast, rapidly equalizing with that of the much thinner atmo-sphere at twenty-five thousand feet.

"Fifteen seconds," Uspensky reported, watch-ing their current position indicator close on the launch coordinates RKU's planners had selected for this mission.

Carefully but quickly, Annenkov entered an-other command on his MFD, temporarily trans-ferring control of the aircraft to their attack computer. He put his hands back on the yoke, but kept them relaxed.

"Five seconds."

At a precisely computed moment, the 737's enlarged forward cargo door unlatched and slid back along its fuselage. The twin-engine jet shuddered, rocked by increased turbulence.

"Commencing attack," Uspensky said tersely.

Smoothly, their first rotary launcher whirred into position at the open cargo door and started spinning, ejecting sky-gray cruise missiles out into the slipstream. As soon as all four of its missiles were away, the now-empty launcher swung toward the rear of the aircraft—replaced almost immediately with the next in line.

One by one, the sixteen Kh-35s dropped toward the distant earth. Their turbofan motors would not ignite until they reached their operational attack altitude, just ten to fifteen meters above the ground. No one saw them falling away from the 737. Between their camouflage paint and relatively small size, the missiles were effectively invisible to other aircraft in the area—all of which were separated laterally by at least five nautical miles and vertically by two thousand feet. The Kh-35s were also too small to show up on the civilian air-traffic-control radars monitoring this sector.

"Launch complete," Uspensky reported from his side of the cockpit. "No ordnance remaining."

The 737's forward cargo door slid shut and sealed. With Annenkov back at the controls, Regan Air Freight Flight 175 continued on its submitted flight plan toward Dallas/Fort Worth. To all outward appearances, it was again just one of the thousands of commercial jets operating in U.S. airspace.

INTERSTATE 20, NEAR HAUGHTON, LOUISIANA
Several minutes later

Louisiana state police sergeant Damon Benoit swung down out of his official Chevrolet Tahoe and started walking up the shoulder of Interstate 20 toward the blue Honda Odyssey minivan he'd just pulled over for speeding. The Honda had Texas plates.

Ah, how wonderful, he thought sarcastically. Yet another family from the Dallas or Fort Worth suburbs heading off on vacation and too rushed to obey the traffic laws of their neighboring state. He sighed, already imagining the harassed-looking driver's embarrassed apologies and pleas for mercy.

Suddenly a finned gray cylinder blurred overhead with an earsplitting howl. It was flying so low that it barely cleared the tops of the trees lining both sides of the divided highway. Startled, Benoit dove for the ground, instinctively clawing for the Glock 22 pistol at his side. His campaign hat flew off, blew into the road, and disappeared under the wheels of an eastbound Toyota Camry.

More missiles slashed through the sky in rapid succession, all heading southwest. Along the highway, shocked drivers gawked up through their windshields at the shapes streaking through the air just above them . . . and then just as abruptly slammed on their brakes, frantically swerving to avoid colliding with other cars and trucks. Tires squealed and horns blared in all directions.

Swearing out loud, Benoit scrambled to his feet, turned, and sprinted back toward his patrol SUV and its radio.

CHAPTER 16

BARKSDALE AIR FORCE BASE, LOUISIANA
That same time

"**A**nd so, my fellow Americans, this nation will stay the course of peace through strength *and* common sense! While I am president, we will never entangle ourselves in petty overseas squabbles that are none of our business. But at the same time, America will be powerful enough to deter any aggression against our vital national interests. That is why I am committed to rebuilding our neglected military, especially the Air Force I've loved and admired all my life. And as new and ever-more-advanced aircraft, like our spectacular F-35 Lightning II stealth fighters and the incredible B-21 Raider parked behind me, roll off our production lines in growing numbers, the whole world will see that *I* mean business!" President Stacy Anne Barbeau promised in a clear, determined voice. She paused, allowing the huge crowd of U.S. Air Force personnel ranked below her dais to clap for a few seconds.

Behind the broad smile she displayed for the TV cameras focused on her, she kept a firm hold on a growing feeling of irritation. Despite the guaranteed applause lines her White House speechwriters had sprinkled throughout this address, rousing genuine fervor from this bunch was proving almost impossible. She wasn't drawing the wild whoops and cheers she'd expected. They were polite, but not enthusiastic. Her only consolation was that most of the media would focus its reporting on the good stuff. *Today is all about the visuals, Stacy*, she reminded herself—all about the images of shiny new warplanes, flags fluttering, gorgeously uniformed bands playing, with her front and center as the nation's tough, plainspoken commander in chief.

Before the tepid applause could fade into embarrassing silence, Barbeau made a big show of shushing the crowd. "Thank you! Thank you so much," she said with grace and tremendous warmth. Sincerity was one of the first things she'd learned to fake when she'd picked out politics as her path to the top. "And so together, we're going to—"

And then a missile screamed in low across the runway, ripping past the crowded dais at more than five hundred knots. It slammed straight into the base of the ten-story-tall control tower and exploded. A burst of searing white light flared for a millisecond, followed by a roiling cloud of orange-and-red flame.

For what seemed an eternity but couldn't really have been much more than a second, Barbeau stood frozen, rooted to her podium in utter disbelief. Then one of her Secret Service agents hurtled across the dais. He knocked her flat and covered her with his body. "*Stay down! Stay down!*" he screamed.

More missiles shrieked past, veering off to strike different targets. One after another, Barksdale's communications center, hangars, machine shops, and fuel storage areas went up in towering columns of smoke, flame, and falling debris. The ground rocked. As the missiles detonated, the noise was so loud that each separate blast struck with the force of a physical blow. Across the wide concrete apron, airmen and reporters and White House staffers scattered frantically in all directions, seeking cover.

With their weapons out and aimed in all directions, Secret Service agents formed a human phalanx around Barbeau as she lay prone, still winded and gasping for air. Special Agent in Charge Rafael Díaz leaned over and yelled loud enough for her to hear over the high-pitched howl of incoming missiles and deafening, bone-rattling explosions. "We're getting you out of here, Madam President! Right *now*!" Without waiting for a reply, Díaz whirled around to his nearby agents. "Get the Beast moving! Let's go! Let's go!"

Painfully, Barbeau turned her head, blearily peering through the crouched huddle of agents who were shielding her from flying fragments and falling debris. Just a few yards away, her big black fifteen-thousand-pound limousine, nick-named the "Beast," started rolling forward from its assigned station. Agents leaped off the dais and yanked the car's rear door open using coded taps on hidden sensor panels. With their sole prior-ity being to remove the president from immediate danger as quickly as possible, two agents uncer-emoniously grabbed her by the arms and hustled her bodily toward the moving car. Without paus-ing, they pushed her through the open door and onto the limo's plush rear seat. One agent leaped in behind her as the other agent slammed the solid, eight-inch-thick door shut.

Then, with all four tires squealing across the pavement, the Beast took off. Its powerful V-8 turbo engine labored under tons of armor plat-ing, bulletproof glass, communications gear, and defensive systems. As it accelerated, the limousine barreled straight through a mob of panic-stricken journalists and camera crews scrambling to get out of its way. Muffled *thumps* and screams showed that not all of them succeeded.

The Secret Service agent who'd piled in before the door was shut squirmed around on the seat and stared back through the rear window. "Jesus Christ!" he exclaimed. "What the hell *are* those things?"

"Specter Lead to all Specter units," Colonel Ruslan Baryshev radioed from inside the cockpit of his KVM. "Attack. Repeat, attack."

Gleeful acknowledgments poured through his headset. But he was already in motion—sending his war robot lunging out of the forest lining the east side of Barksdale's long runway. His battle computer silhouetted the two dozen American F-35 stealth fighters lined up wingtip to wingtip on the apron, identifying them as priority targets. They were more than a thousand meters away.

Closing the distance at more than seventy kilometers an hour, Baryshev raised his 30mm autocannon and opened fire on the run. Multiple armor-piercing, high-explosive rounds hammered the distant fighters. Hit repeatedly, the F-35s disappeared behind a rippling curtain of smoke and fire. Jagged fragments of wings, canopies, and fuselages cartwheeled away out of the smoke. American airmen caught in the path of his bullets vaporized, blown apart into bits of flesh and shattered bone.

The other KVMs were shooting, too—pounding the XB-1F Excaliburs and the just-landed B-21 Raider prototype with their own autocannons and the Israeli-made Spike antitank missiles. Plane after plane down the flight line exploded. "This is a turkey shoot!" Imrekov yelled exultantly over their secure link. "We've caught the Americans with their pants down! They can't touch us!"

With a harsh laugh, Baryshev shifted his aim, zeroing in on one of the mammoth B-52H bombers parked next to the fighters. Bigger than the single-engine, multirole F-35s, the Stratofortress absorbed several direct hits before slewing sideways, wrecked and cloaked in dancing orange flames and oily black smoke.

Panting, Barbeau hauled herself upright in the limo's rear seat as it raced away at sixty miles an hour. She turned to look back at the nightmarish scene behind them. Her bruised ribs sent pain sleeting through her brain like white-hot, stiletto-sharp needles. For a moment, she thought she would vomit.

Then her vision cleared.

There, out of the thick billowing clouds of smoke, several tall spindly metal shapes appeared, moving with eerie precision and terrifying grace. The weapons they carried spat fire and death—slaughtering everyone in their path and destroying stationary aircraft with contemptuous ease.

Barbeau's eyes widened in horror. She knew only too well what those creatures were.

An antitank missile launched by one of the robots streaked across the path of the speeding limousine. Trailing smoke and fire, it slammed into the fuselage of *Air Force One* and exploded.

"Pop smoke! Pop smoke!" the Secret Service agent next to her screamed into the intercom.

Whummp. Whummp. Whummp.

Three multispectrum infrared smoke grenades triggered by the driver exploded around the Beast. In a fraction of a second, billowing white clouds blotted out Barbeau's view of the two-legged war machines that were systematically destroying Barksdale Air Force Base. Terrified almost out of her wits and desperately trying to tell herself that what she'd seen with her own eyes could *not* possibly be real, she sat frozen, staring back into the swirling veil of protective smoke as her limousine sped away toward safety.

Through his neural link, Imrekov "felt" several rifle-caliber rounds smack into his KVM's rear composite armor. They ricocheted off. *No damage*, his computer reported. *Hostiles at six o'clock*.

Irked, he whirled through a half circle. There, half hidden by the blazing wreckage of the American president's 747 jetliner, his sensors showed several airmen lying prone on the pavement. They were shooting at him with M4 carbines and pistols. *That is brave, but very, very foolish*, he thought. *And it will be fatal*.

Grinning cruelly, Imrekov raised his 30mm autocannon. It fired once and then fell silent. *Cannon ammunition expended*, the KVM told him. He'd used up all of his rounds destroying the enemy fighters and bombers they'd caught on the ground. "*Der'mo*," he growled. "Shit."

So be it. He would handle this the old-fashioned way.

Imrekov sprinted toward the enemy soldiers who were shooting at him. More 5.56mm rounds spanged off his robot's armor. He ignored the hits and ran on, closing fast.

At the last moment, the tiny group of Americans scrambled to their feet and tried to fall back. But it was too late. His KVM burst into their midst and blurred into lethal motion—lashing out with its robotic hands and feet. Airmen went flying in every direction, felled by powerful blows that crushed rib cages and shattered skulls.

Exhilarated by the ease with which he'd slaughtered his enemies, Imrekov crouched down among their mangled corpses, employing his passive and active sensors to scan for more targets to kill. To his intense annoyance, he could not find any.

The American air base was a sea of devastation. Buildings hit by Kh-35 warheads were smoldering heaps of broken concrete and twisted steel. Curtains of fire rippled high above destroyed fuel storage tanks. Wrecked aircraft and torn corpses littered the field.

Baryshev's exultant voice broke into his thoughts. *"Specter Lead to all Specter units. Mission complete. Disengage and withdraw to the rally point."*

Brought back to the present, Imrekov replied, "Two copies, Lead. Disengaging." He brought the KVM back to its feet and moved off across the runway, joining the other RKU war machines as they broke off and headed for the woods.

Captain Paul Fraser skidded around the corner of a burning, bomb-ravaged building. Scorching waves of heat washed over him. Gasping, the Air Force captain raced on and broke out into the open. There, across the pad, he saw his HH-60G Pave Hawk search-and-rescue helicopter. His co-pilot, Seth Hahn, already had the bird spooling up. His crew had been on standby in case anything went wrong during the president's visit.

Responding to a massive surprise missile and ground attack hadn't been very high up on their briefed list of possible missions. But as far as Fraser could see, his Pave Hawk was the only flyable aircraft left at Barksdale. Which made it imperative that they get in the air and at least try to track the bastards who'd nailed the base.

He pulled himself up into the cockpit and dropped into his seat. Hahn tossed him his headset and he plugged in. "All set?"

"We're set!" his copilot assured him. "The engines and flight controls look solid."

"Gunners ready," the two crewmen in back reported. They were already manning the HH-60G's two 7.62mm miniguns.

Rapidly, Fraser ran through an extremely abbreviated takeoff checklist. The moment he finished, he throttled up to full power and took them into the air—climbing as fast as possible. They needed to break clear of the smoke and turbulence created by fires burning everywhere across the base.

A minute later, the Pave Hawk clattered over Barksdale's runway, heading east at sixty knots. Sitting in the left-hand seat, Hahn peered down at the display he'd set to show images captured by their nose-mounted forward-looking infrared camera. "Contact with multiple thermal sources! Some sort of legged machines. Big suckers. Maybe twice human-sized. Maybe more. They're moving east through the woods and bayous about five klicks ahead."

"Speed?" Fraser asked.

"Damned fast," his copilot said, sounding surprised. "Whatever those things are, they're clocking at up to forty miles an hour. And that's cross-country. None of them are using the roads or trails in this part of the reservation."

"You're shitting me," Fraser said. He looked ahead through the windscreen. All he could see was a solid green canopy of trees and more trees. What kind of machines could move so fast right through the heart of that swampy, overgrown forest? And where the hell were they headed?

Enemy helicopter closing fast, Colonel Baryshev's computer reported. He frowned, seeing the icon appear on his display. It was unfortunate that the Americans had been able to react so rapidly. This deep in the forest, his robot's weapons would be of little use against an airborne target. He needed to find a better position. Through his neural link, the KVM highlighted a small clearing not far away. It was the site of a mothballed oil and gas well, one of the dozens scattered across this part of Louisiana.

He splashed across a shallow bayou in a spray of muddy water and pounded through the woods at high speed, leaving a trail of broken branches and flattened undergrowth. On the run, he detached an American-made Stinger surface-to-air missile from one of his weapons packs.

Baryshev broke out into the clearing and swiveled around to face the oncoming helicopter. It was very close now . . . no more than a few hundred meters away and little more than a couple of hundred meters above the forest canopy. A harsh buzz sounded in his headset. The Stinger's infrared seeker had locked on.

He fired.

The missile streaked skyward in a plume of flame and white exhaust. Only a second later, before its crew could trigger their countermeasures, the Stinger exploded just below the helicopter's main rotor. Trailing smoke and torn pieces of rotor blade, the Pave Hawk tumbled out of the sky and crashed into the woods.

Baryshev started moving again, heading for the rally point secured by Kirill Aristov and his Spetsnaz troops. Once there, his KVMs would be loaded back aboard three FXR Trucking semi-trailer trucks that had been specially converted to hide them. Then Aristov and his "truckers" would simply drive away, blending in with local traffic. And the Americans would be left without any clues as to where the enemy who'd just blasted Barksdale Air Force Base to hell had vanished.

CHAPTER 17

With his chin tucked against his chest and his hands up to protect his face, Brad McLanahan closed in to make an attack. Quick as lightning, his opponent lashed out with a straight punch aimed at his chin. He parried it and riposted—only to find himself striking at empty air as she danced away out of reach.

"You are slow today, Brad," Nadia Rozek said with a grin. There was a challenging gleam in her eye. She'd backed away across the padded practice mat and now stood balancing easily on the balls of her feet, obviously ready to react to any new move he made. This close to the dinner hour, they had the Iron Wolf gym all to themselves.

"Maybe you're just hellaciously fast," he countered. Then he grinned back at her. "Or maybe this is part of my cunning plan to lure you in closer."

"For what? A kiss?"

"Well, either that . . . or a good shot at a couple of elbow strikes and a quick leg sweep," Brad allowed.

Nadia dropped back into a fighting stance. "Well, then, come and take your best shot," she taunted.

They closed with each other again and exchanged a rapid-fire flurry of blows, kicks, and parries delivered with stunning speed and precision. Each of them landed hits that could have been disabling if it hadn't been for their protective sparring gear. Shaking off the pain, they broke contact a second time and fell back to their respective corners.

"Captain McLanahan! Major Rozek!" Brad heard someone call.

He glanced toward the voice, keeping a wary eye on Nadia with his peripheral vision. In the past, she'd proved all too willing to throw a sucker punch or three or four at distracted opponents. "All is fair in love, war, and Krav Maga," was the excuse she'd gleefully offered.

Mike Knapp, one of Iron Wolf's recon troopers, stood in the door looking worried. "What's up, Sergeant?" Brad asked.

"Captain Schofield wants you both in the communications center, pronto," Knapp said. "Somebody just whacked an Air Force base back in the States."

An hour later, Brad, Nadia, and Macomber gathered in the squadron's briefing room to go over what they'd learned. Polish president Piotr Wilk and Martindale were connected by a secure video link to Warsaw.

Brad kicked things off by replaying the most comprehensive of the breathless news flashes currently flooding the world's airwaves and every corner of cyberspace. The others sat in silence, grimly focused as they watched Stacy Anne Barbeau's visit to Barksdale Air Force Base turn from a public-relations triumph into a full-fledged national security disaster in the blink of an eye.

Near the end of the short news report, he tapped a control, freezing an image on their wall-sized screen. Through their link to Warsaw, the same picture could be seen by Piotr Wilk and Martindale. It showed a scene of horrific destruction, a vast expanse of concrete strewn with wrecked and burning aircraft and dead or dying U.S. Air Force personnel.

"This bit of footage of the attack on Barksdale was shot by one of the local TV news crews assigned to cover President Barbeau's appearance on the base," he said. "The rest of the ladies and gentlemen of the press ran for cover when the first missiles started screaming in."

"Can't say as I blame them," Macomber grunted. "They don't wear the uniform. And TV ratings aren't worth getting killed for."

Brad nodded. "No kidding." He shrugged. "Nevertheless, we're lucky these guys were either too gutsy or too dumb to bail out. Because otherwise, we'd be operating pretty much in the dark—relying on shaky eyewitness testimony about what just happened."

"Operating in the dark about what?" Nadia Rozek asked carefully. This was the first time she'd seen these pictures. While Brad tried to make sense out of the reports cascading in, she'd been busy arranging this secure link to Warsaw and contacting Wilk and Martindale. She indicated the screen. "Isn't what happened obvious? Someone, almost certainly the Russians, fired a large number of cruise missiles into that air base."

"Sure." Brad nodded. "But that's only part of the story. From what I can figure, those missiles were all aimed at fixed targets. At stuff like the control tower and hangars and other key facilities. They weren't fired at the F-35s, B-52s, and other aircraft parked out on the apron for Barbeau's dog and pony show."

"That would make sense," his father agreed. "Buildings don't move. Aircraft can. Setting up a coordinated cruise-missile strike like this one takes time. Why take even the slightest chance that your warheads will detonate over empty stretches of concrete when you can guarantee hits on fixed installations?"

Martindale's face frowned from one corner of the screen. "Okay, what am I missing here?" he asked. "If it wasn't Russian missiles, then what wiped out all of our planes?"

"Machines like this," Brad said quietly. He leaned forward and tapped the video controls to zoom in, allowing the others to take a closer look at what he'd found while reviewing these images. Though blurry, the picture showed a dull gray human-shaped robot outlined against the distant woods in the background. It was carrying what appeared to be a large machine gun or autocannon in its hands. Weapons of other kinds studded its long torso.

"*Mój Boże!* My God!" Piotr Wilk said, almost too low to be heard.

Macomber sat staring at the screen for a long, painful moment. His jaw was set. Then he glanced at Patrick McLanahan. "You were right, General. Charlie Turlock and I fucked up at Perun's Aerie. Somehow, we left enough pieces behind for that son of a bitch Gryzlov to build his own CIDs."

"We all walked into that ambush, Whack," Brad told him with a rueful look. "It wasn't your fault."

"My son's right, Colonel," the older McLanahan said. Through the visor of his life-support helmet, the lines on his face deepened. "Sooner or later, the Russians were bound to develop this technology. Exactly how they managed it is no longer important. What matters now is that we come up with a plan to handle what used to be our worst-case scenario."

Slowly, Wilk nodded. His face was troubled. "That is indeed the issue, General. And I must admit that I am not sure of our best course of action in the face of this surprise attack."

Caught off guard by the Polish leader's unexpected hesitation, Brad glanced around the table at Nadia, Whack, and his father and then turned to face Wilk and Martindale squarely. "With respect, Mr. President, I would think our first step is pretty doggone clear," he said carefully. "We've got to deploy a CID-equipped Iron Wolf team to the U.S.—and as quickly as possible."

He leaned forward, intent on making his point. "We all know what these robots can do. Under most circumstances, there's no way conventionally equipped U.S. troops, let alone any state or local cops, can tangle with the Russian equivalent of CIDs and survive, let alone win. Not if Gryzlov's guys can operate covertly and strike at will . . . which sure as hell seems to be what he's got in mind."

"Yes, that is true. But we have to consider the possibility that a campaign of terror aimed at your country might not be *all* Gennadiy Gryzlov has planned," Wilk said.

Brad frowned. "Meaning what, exactly?"

"This may be a feint," the other man said. "The Russians could be attempting to lure the Iron Wolf Squadron's combat robots out of position before launching a new onslaught against Poland and the rest of our allies." He sighed. "Even without the services of its best Spetsnaz units, Russia's armed forces still substantially outnumber ours. Your CIDs are the key to our defenses. Moscow knows that. Which is why sending your machines half the world away might be exactly what the enemy is counting on."

"So we're supposed to just sit here on our asses

while Gryzlov wipes the floor with the U.S.?" Macomber snapped. "Look, I've got no great affinity for Stacy Anne Barbeau and the assholes she has running things, but that sure as hell doesn't mean I don't love my country . . . or that I don't care what happens to it. Most of the people the Russians killed a couple of hours ago used to be my brothers- and sisters-in-arms. And I will be damned if I sit back and do nothing."

"I'm sure that is not President Wilk's intent, Colonel," Martindale said cautiously. His eyes were watchful. "But he is right to urge caution until we get a better read on the situation . . . and a clearer sense of Gryzlov's intentions." He shook his head. "Besides, what can a single Iron Wolf team accomplish? Given the sheer size of the continental United States and the staggering number of potential targets, we have no realistic way to predict where the Russians might strike next. Without better intelligence, haring off into the wild blue yonder would be unwise."

Macomber snorted angrily.

"I'm not proposing some wild-eyed stab in the dark," Brad said flatly, working hard to sound calmer than he felt and defuse the tension. Whack could have been a lot more diplomatic, but fundamentally he was right. There was no way the Americans in the Iron Wolf Squadron could stand by and do nothing—not with their homeland under direct enemy assault. Which made it his job to persuade Wilk and Martindale to take them off the leash. "If you think about it logically, there's at least one site that *has* to be pretty high up on Gryzlov's list."

"Very well, I'm open to the possibility that I've missed something obvious," the head of Scion said with a wry half smile. "By all means, enlighten me."

Oh, man, Brad thought, gritting his teeth, *Martindale is so lucky that he isn't sitting across the table from me right now.* You couldn't actually punch someone through a high-definition video link, which was too darned bad. And from the tight-lipped expression on Nadia's face, he'd bet she was thinking along the same lines.

"The Russians are bound to hit Battle Mountain," he said quietly. "And if they're smart, they'll do it soon."

On the screen, he saw Piotr Wilk sit up straighter. "You believe Gryzlov will try to destroy the Sky Masters facilities there?" he asked.

"Yes, sir," Brad said. "Right now, we're almost totally dependent on the flow of CID upgrades, aircraft, drones, weapons, and sensors from Sky Masters. They're the core of our current technological superiority over Russia."

"A superiority that is already in serious jeopardy now that Gryzlov has his own combat robots," his father said somberly.

Brad nodded. "Yep." He looked pointedly at both Wilk and Martindale. "If we sit back and let the Russians destroy the labs, production facilities, and aircraft storage hangars at Battle Mountain, it's not going to matter how many CIDs we have holding down the fort here in Poland or the rest of Eastern and central Europe—not in the long run, anyway."

"Ah, jeez," Macomber said grimly. "The kid's right. Without the shiny Buck Rogers–style gizmos Sky Masters supplies, we'd be in a world of hurt." He turned to Wilk. "You said it yourself. We're already heavily outnumbered. If we lose our qualitative edge over the Russians, it's all over." Slowly, the Polish president nodded in agreement.

Frowning in concentration, Martindale stroked his chin. "And if you're wrong and Gryzlov has other plans?" he asked after a moment.

"Then we recalibrate," Brad said. "At a minimum, if we have a team already on the ground in the States, we cut our reaction time significantly."

There was a long pause while the two older men in Warsaw silently considered what he'd said. Then Wilk nodded again, coming to a decision. "What do you propose, Captain McLanahan?"

"That we fly three Iron Wolf Squadron CIDs and a recon team to Nevada," Brad told him.

"Openly?"

"No, sir. We'll use the XCV-62 Ranger stealth transport to insert our force covertly."

"You don't trust the goodwill of Stacy Anne Barbeau?" Martindale asked dryly.

Brad shook his head. "Not so much as an inch."

Everyone else nodded their understanding and agreement. For three long years Barbeau had stabbed them in the back every chance she got— even going so far as to send in a U.S. Special Forces team on a failed raid to sabotage the Iron

Wolf Squadron's base and then ordering American F-35s to shoot down the survivors of a desperate raid on Russian missile bases. There was no percentage in giving her another opportunity to take a shot at them, especially since they knew she desperately wanted to get her own hands on CID technology.

"Who will you assign to pilot the combat robots in this force?" Wilk asked.

"I'll fly the XCV-62 in myself," Brad said. "And then once we're on the ground, I'll take one of the CIDs." He turned to Macomber. "I figure you'll want to run one of the others, Whack."

"Damn straight," the bigger man agreed.

"And *I* will pilot the third Iron Wolf machine," Nadia Rozek said in a firm voice that clearly indicated she would brook no argument.

"This isn't exactly your fight, Major," Martindale pointed out. "If things go wrong and this force gets nailed by the U.S. authorities, it's going to be tough enough for any American-born member of Iron Wolf. It would be a lot worse for a Polish national—"

"Major Rozek is right, Mr. Martindale," Piotr Wilk interrupted. "Your people have sacrificed much to help defend my country's freedoms. Now it is our turn. Poland will stay true to its friends." His eyes crinkled in a sudden smile. "Also, I suspect the good major would probably mutiny if I commanded her to remain behind."

"'Mutiny' is a harsh word, Mr. President," Nadia said demurely. She smiled back at him. "I think I would prefer to characterize my probable

response to such an ill-advised order as an 'unauthorized exercise of personal initiative.'"

"You see?" Wilk said to Martindale with an
amused look. "The matter is completely out of my
hands."

CHAPTER 18

DALLAS/FORT WORTH INTERNATIONAL AIRPORT
That same time

While two Texas Air National Guard F-16C Falcon fighters that had been hurriedly scrambled from Joint Base San Antonio–Lackland orbited overhead, *Marine One* came in low over the suburbs north and west of Dallas. Rotors beating, the twin-engine Sikorsky VH-92A helicopter flared in fast and landed just outside a huge 270,000-square-foot American Airlines maintenance hangar at the Dallas/Fort Worth International Airport. The hangar doors were open, revealing a four-engine E-4B National Airborne Operations Center jet aircraft waiting inside.

Inside *Marine One*, President Stacy Anne Barbeau stared out through the square window next to her seat. She could see a composite force made up of Air Force personnel, National Guard troops, Regular Army soldiers airlifted in from Fort Hood, and airport police officers streaming out of the hangar. They spread out across the tarmac to form a perimeter around her helicopter.

The head of her Secret Service detail, Rafael Díaz, came back from talking to the Marine Corps pilots up front. They'd flown her here after an emergency pickup from one of the greens on the Fox Run Golf Course just outside Barksdale. "We'll open the forward door just as soon as you're ready to move, Madam President," he said.

Barbeau nodded shakily. Every bone in her body felt bruised and sore. And every time she closed her eyes, even for a few seconds, she saw images of those robots . . . those brutal killing machines . . . come striding out of the woods and then turn toward her. She gulped, swallowing down another wave of fear and nausea that seemed to come crawling up her throat.

Beside her, Luke Cohen unbuckled his seat belt and then reached over to do the same thing for her. "We need to go, boss," he murmured. In his ripped suit jacket and torn pants, the White House chief of staff looked as battered as she felt. Like most of her senior staff, he'd been hustled away from the attack in another of the armored SUVs belonging to her presidential motorcade. A few of her aides were still missing—probably left among the dead and wounded heaped across the burning air base.

Supported by Cohen's arm, Barbeau staggered upright. More Secret Service agents formed up around them. "Tempest is in motion," Díaz said into his radio, using her assigned Secret Service code name. "Let's make this transfer fast and clean, people."

Marine One's forward door opened. Hot air swirled inside, mixed with the tang of jet fuel.

Surrounded by Díaz and the other agents, Barbeau and Cohen hurried down the steps and out across the tarmac toward the waiting E-4B. The big jet was one of several Boeing 747-200s converted into strategic command and control aircraft. Designed to remain aloft for at least a week with constant air-to-air refueling, they were intended to serve as mobile, survivable command posts for ranking U.S. military and government officials, especially the president, in the event of a serious national emergency.

One of the E-4B's crewmen motioned them toward the forward crew entrance, up a ladder near the aircraft's nose. He saluted Barbeau. "What are your orders, Madam President?"

"Get this goddamned plane in the air ASAP," she snapped. She didn't want to spend another minute longer than she had to on the ground. If there was another attack by those murderous combat robots, this hangar was a deathtrap . . . no matter how many soldiers, airmen, and airport cops were posted on guard.

They helped her up the metal stairs and into the plane, and then up another short flight of steps to the E-4B's main deck. From there it was just a few feet to the small, utilitarian office suite reserved for the National Command Authority. The aircraft's cockpit was directly overhead, up on the modified 747's flight deck.

Gratefully, Barbeau dropped into one of the suite's big chairs. She fastened her seat belt with trembling hands and then laid them flat on the desk in front of her—battling the urge to scream and swear at her staff to move faster as they scurried aboard and found seats.

Outside, the aircraft's four huge General Electric turbofan engines started spooling up.

Ten minutes later, they were airborne and climbing fast toward a cruising altitude of more than forty thousand feet. A uniformed Air Force officer, one of the battle staff permanently assigned to this command center, entered the compartment. "We've established secure links to Admiral Firestone and the NSC, Madam President."

"Patch them through to here," Barbeau ordered.

"Yes, ma'am," he replied, leaning past her to flip several switches on the wall-mounted communications control panel above her desk. Its central video screen flickered to life, showing Firestone, the short, stocky chairman of the Joint Chiefs of Staff, in his office at the Pentagon and Ed Rauch in the White House Situation Room.

She picked up one of the white secure phones; Cohen took the other. Barbeau took a deep breath. She knew that it was vital that she come across to these men as calm and in command. "Brief me on the situation," she said tersely.

"We are now at DEFCON Three," Admiral Firestone reported. "And we are ready to go to DEFCON Two on your order."

Barbeau shook her head. "Let's hold off on that for now, Admiral," she said. Moving to DEFCON Two would significantly ratchet up the readiness level of the entire U.S. military—especially its remaining nuclear-armed and nuclear-capable air and naval forces. But it would also put the U.S. just two steps away from signaling a move to all-out nuclear war. She wasn't ready just yet to take such a drastic measure, not without more information.

Ed Rauch spoke up. "The vice president is on his way to Site-R, Madam President." Site-R was an underground alternate command and communications center at the Raven Rock Military Complex in Pennsylvania, not far north of Camp David. "He and his staff should be there in thirty minutes or less."

Barbeau concealed a sneer. She'd chosen Raymond Summers, a former governor of Ohio, as her vice president for purely political reasons during her first presidential campaign. She'd counted on him to swing his home state's electoral votes into her column. But that had turned out to be the absolute limit of his usefulness. Aside from an aptitude for glad-handing and spouting meaningless, folksy-sounding one-liners, Ray Summers had no real discernible leadership skills that she could detect. *God help the United States if that fatuous moron ever lands in the Oval Office*, she thought bitterly.

"There haven't been any other raids against our bases here or overseas," Rauch continued. "And we see no indications of any additional overt offensive moves by the Russians or by the People's

Republic of China. In fact, there are no signs that their conventional or nuclear forces are even moving to higher states of readiness."

Barbeau felt cold. "You're sure about that?" she demanded.

"So far, yes," her national security adviser said. "Satellite imagery and NSA signals intercepts haven't picked up any evidence of movement out of garrison by their major ground forces. The same thing goes for their warships and combat aircraft. At this point, all we're detecting are routine air and sea patrols."

My God, Barbeau thought in dawning horror. Her suspicions about the attack on Barksdale, wild as they had seemed to her at first, were being confirmed. After all, why would the Russians or the Chinese blow up an American air base and then stop there? It didn't make any strategic or political sense for Moscow or Beijing to commit an outright act of war against the U.S. and then sit back on their hands—leaving their own troops, ships, and planes completely vulnerable to any counterstrike. Nobody but a fool or a madman would do something that dumb. And while neither Gennadiy Gryzlov nor Zhou Qiang, his Chinese counterpart, was especially stable, she couldn't see either of them taking that kind of risk.

With an effort, she regained her focus. "What are your recommendations, Admiral?" she asked Firestone.

"Even if we hold at DEFCON Three for now, I strongly recommend moving elements of the fleet to sea, as a precautionary measure," the chairman of the Joint Chiefs said. "Especially our ballistic missile submarines." He grimaced. "Now that we've lost more of our long-range B-52 and XB-1F strategic bombers, those boomers represent most of what's left of our deterrent force."

"Absolutely not," Barbeau said quickly. "If Gryzlov and Zhou aren't putting their own military forces in motion, the last thing I want to do is trigger a dangerous round of escalation and counterescalation. We simply cannot afford to stumble into another pointless confrontation with the Russians or the Chinese."

Which was probably just what the crazy bastard who'd orchestrated the strike on Barksdale Air Force Base hoped for, she realized abruptly.

"But we're already under attack, Madam President," Rauch protested.

She glared at him. "Tell me something I don't damn well know, Dr. Rauch! I was standing right *there* when we got nailed. Remember?" That shut him up. Barbeau scowled. "It's time to face the facts, gentlemen. We were *not* attacked by Moscow. Or by Beijing."

"Then who—" Rauch wondered.

"It was that scumbag Martindale," she said. "And his mercenary Iron Wolf Squadron." She saw the disbelief on her national security adviser's narrow, pallid face. Angrily, she snapped, "I *saw* his damned CIDs shooting the hell out of our planes. Those robots were there—as big as Death itself." She gripped the secure phone tighter. She was *not* going to allow the dread those memories conjured up to show on her face or in her voice. Not in front of these men. Instead, she channeled her fear into fury. Her voice cut like a knife. "Do you know of anyone else out there with Cybernetic Infantry Devices *besides* Martindale's Iron Wolf thugs, Ed?"

On the screen, Rauch visibly flinched. "No, ma'am," he admitted.

"I didn't think so," Barbeau said, not bothering to hide her scorn. "And the cruise-missile strike that kicked the attack off is more proof of who's responsible—as if we needed any." She turned back to Firestone. "Do the Russians or the Chinese have any long-range stealth bombers, Admiral? Bombers that could have launched those missiles and evaded our radar?"

The chairman of the Joint Chiefs shook his head. "No, Madam President." He looked thoughtful. "Both Moscow and Beijing are working hard to develop long-range stealth aircraft, but they're not there yet."

"Which leaves Martindale," Barbeau said coldly. "And thanks to Sky Masters, he has a whole slew of manned and unmanned stealthy aircraft in his arsenal. And plenty of missiles to go with them." She gritted her teeth. "Only now instead of using those weapons against the Russians, he's turned them against *us*."

Rauch frowned. "I can't see what former president Martindale could hope to gain by destroying Barksdale," he said cautiously. "It's an act of treason. One we cannot possibly overlook or forgive. Why would he take that chance?"

"That's because you don't understand how Martindale thinks," Barbeau retorted. "He's always been a game player . . . and he sees people and countries as pieces he can move around on his chessboard. Well, by wrecking those B-52s, our B-21 prototype, and our first operational F-35 fighter squadron, he's just wiped out a sizable fraction of our frontline strategic and tactical airpower, right? So, with them gone, now what are we going to do?"

"I'm not sure," her national security adviser admitted. He shook his head. "We can replace the fighter aircraft we lost in a few weeks, but working up another group of F-35 pilots and ground crews will take months. And rebuilding our bomber force will take years . . . especially now that we've lost the B-21 Raider prototype."

"Exactly." Barbeau nodded. "Which is why I can tell you what Martindale's plan is, Dr. Rauch. He wants us so desperate that we're forced to fall back on the super-high-tech, gee-whiz weapons produced by his pals at Sky Masters."

"But you'll never buy into that idea," Rauch pointed out.

"No kidding," she snapped. "Which is why Martindale wants me dead or run out of office by that prick J. D. Farrell. Either way he wins."

For the first time since boarding the E-4B, Luke Cohen ventured an opinion. He cleared his throat. "I can see where he might have been hoping to kill you, but . . ." His voice trailed off uncertainly.

"Go on, Luke," Barbeau said, irritably waving him on. "What's eating at you?"

"It's just that whether or not Martindale had a hand in what happened today, this attack is going to backfire on him big-time . . . and on Farrell, too," her chief of staff said. "You're bound to get a huge boost in the polls from this. People always rally around the flag in times of national crisis."

"Sure they do," she agreed bluntly. "And if the election were going to be held in the next couple of weeks, I'd be sitting pretty." Then her eyes hardened. "But November's too far off. Any polling bounce I get will fade over time. And it will fade even faster once Farrell and his surrogates start pounding away on us for screwing up so badly."

Cohen looked blank.

"Oh, for God's sake, figure it out, Luke," Barbeau said in exasperation. "Everybody in the fucking world just saw my strategic rearmament program go up in highly publicized flames. And whose bright idea was it to mass so many of our remaining bombers and our best stealth fighters in one vulnerable spot . . . as part of a political show?" She felt her mouth twist into an ugly smile. "Tell me, how popular was General Short on Oahu once the bombs stopped falling?"

"Pearl Harbor," Rauch murmured, suddenly catching her historical reference.

She nodded. The stories her father, a career Air Force officer, had told her when she was young had sunk deep. Before the Japanese sneak attack on Pearl Harbor, Lieutenant General Walter C. Short, who commanded the U.S. Army's defenses in the Hawaiian Islands, had ordered all of his fighter planes and bombers parked wingtip to wingtip—so that they could be more easily defended against saboteurs. That made them sitting ducks when Japanese Zeros came slashing in on strafing runs.

The parallels were unpleasantly close.

CHAPTER 19

IRON WOLF FLIGHT LINE, POWIDZ, POLAND
A short time later

Brad McLanahan finished entering his flight plan into the XCV-62 Ranger's main navigation computer. Then, methodically, he started clicking through a series of digital maps, checking and rechecking his work. Sometimes prepping for a mission took more time and effort than the flight itself. In this case, that wasn't true. He was facing a grueling, eleven-thousand-nautical-mile, one-way trip. Even with all the automation built into the Ranger's flight controls and several planned refueling and crew rest stops, he knew he was going to be pushing his endurance to its limits. When you threw in their need to avoid detection by radars and air patrols over several different countries—Algeria, Morocco, Colombia, Mexico, and, finally, the United States itself—the full magnitude of the challenge came into focus.

At last, satisfied that he'd caught and corrected

all the obvious and not-so-obvious flaws, he pushed a virtual "key" on his MFD. *"Mission plan accepted,"* the computer acknowledged. *"Minimum flight safety and fuel parameters met."*

Brad glanced across the cockpit at Nadia Rozek. The beautiful, dark-haired Polish special forces officer had her head down, studying her own displays. One of them showed a map of the North Atlantic. Colored icons indicated their best estimates of the positions of a number of Western and Russian naval task forces, including a U.S. Navy carrier group operating off America's Eastern Seaboard. Circles of varying diameters showed radar ranges and the airspace within reach of routine combat air patrols for each group of warships. The circles moved and changed size and shape often, reflecting the flight path of E-2C Hawkeye radar planes on patrol.

As Brad's copilot and systems operator, she was steadily working her way through Scion's most recent intelligence on any air surveillance radars or other threats they might encounter along their planned route. At first he thought she was completely focused, so intent on her task that she was entirely unaware of his admiring gaze. Then he noticed the faint smile hovering at the corner of her lips.

Nope, he thought with inward amusement. The day he caught her off guard would be a first. She had more natural situational awareness than anyone he'd ever met, including Whack Macomber and his dad.

"I'm going to check on the rest of our gear," Brad said. "Need anything?"

Nadia shook her head. "Not just yet, thank you." Her faint smile deepened. "But I may want a foot rub or a massage later."

"I'll pass the word to our flight attendant," he promised.

"My God, that's not Colonel Macomber, is it?" she said, pretending to sound worried.

Brad chuckled. "Nah, he's just a passenger." He jerked a thumb at himself. "I guess I'm it, ma'am. Since I'm already the designated pilot, cook, bottle washer, and all-around, general-purpose gofer on this aircraft, what's one more tough job?"

With a theatrical sigh of relief, Nadia got back to work.

Still smiling, Brad opened the hatch and slid down the Ranger's crew ladder. He dropped lightly onto the hangar floor. Crews were working in every corner of the large bomb-resistant shelter the Iron Wolf Squadron used to prep its aircraft and CIDs for missions.

Technicians and mechanics swarmed over the XCV-62, making sure its avionics, engines, and other systems were in tip-top condition. They were devoting special care to the four Rolls-Royce Tay 620-15 turbofan engines buried in the wing's upper surface. This was likely to be a long-duration mission and Brad and his team would be operating out of rough, improvised landing strips the whole time. Losing an engine to avoidable mechanical failure was not an acceptable risk.

He walked around the Ranger, making his own visual inspection. The STOL transport was around the size of a Gulfstream 450 business jet.

It was big enough to carry two-plus tons of cargo or around twelve to sixteen passengers. Between its batwing configuration and the special radar-absorbent material coating its surfaces, the aircraft had a remarkably low radar cross section. While the Ranger wasn't in the same stealth league as an F-22 Raptor, which had the radar signature of a marble when viewed head-on, it was close to that of the B-2A Spirit bomber.

The aircraft's rear ramp was down. Brad squatted down beside the ramp, taking a good look inside the troop compartment. It was overcrowded, packed from floor to ceiling with equipment, weapons, ammunition, CID batteries and fuel cells, and other spare parts. The three combat robots he, Nadia, and Macomber would pilot were secured to bulkheads. They were powered down, seemingly lifeless. Six uncomfortable-looking web seats in two rows of three each filled the remaining space—providing cramped accommodations for Macomber and a five-man Iron Wolf recon team commanded by Captain Ian Schofield.

"Not a lot of legroom, is there?" a cheerful voice said.

Unhurriedly, Brad rose, dusted off his flight suit, and turned toward Schofield. The Canadian had served in his country's special operations regiment before joining Scion and the Iron Wolf Squadron. His teeth gleamed white in a face weathered by years spent outdoors in all climates and seasons.

"Afraid not," Brad agreed, with a note of apology. "If I said you guys were going to be packed in like sardines, you could sue me for overly optimistic false advertising." Then he matched the other man's wry smile. "But think of it like this, if we hit turbulence, you'll never know it . . . because you'll be jammed in too tight to move so much as an inch."

Schofield laughed ruefully. "There is that."

"We will be landing to refuel and grab some quick shut-eye at a few places along the way, so you and your men can at least get out and stretch your legs," Brad promised.

"Ah, and these landing sites of yours would be an easy stroll away from various tourist hot spots, no doubt," Schofield said dryly.

"Well, not exactly," Brad admitted. "Martindale has Scion teams out setting up improvised airstrips and refueling points in the western Sahara, somewhere in the middle of the Colombian jungle, and the Chihuahuan desert in northern Mexico."

Schofield's easy grin flashed again. "You see? I knew there'd be lots of nightlife for my lads to enjoy on this little jaunt."

"Pardon me?"

"Nightlife as in bugs, spiders, snakes, and other slithering creatures, Captain McLanahan," the Canadian explained patiently. "The stuff of jungles and deserts, though not perhaps of pleasant dreams."

Brad shook his head in mock pain. "Ouch. You were *this* close to making me feel sorry for you, Ian." He checked his watch. "You'd best go round up your troops. We take off in thirty minutes."

OFFICE OF THE PRESIDENT, BELWEDER PALACE, WARSAW, POLAND
That same time

Polish president Piotr Wilk fought to control his temper as he listened to Stacy Anne Barbeau's wild, almost unhinged accusations. The American president's normally honey-sweet voice was full of dark rage. Although her image was grainy, distorted by the need to bounce encrypted signals from her orbiting E-4B command and control aircraft through multiple communications satellites, he could tell that same anger contorted her usually smooth features.

"What in God's name were you thinking, you stupid son of a bitch?" she snarled at him. "Are you looking for a war with the United States? Because I can assure you that is what's headed your way if you turned a blind eye to this massacre committed by Martindale and his mercenary soldiers!"

"And I can assure *you*, Madam President, that *no one* from Scion or from the Iron Wolf Squadron played any part in that monstrous attack on your country," Wilk said, choosing his English language words with care and precision. "I know those men and women. Whatever their political or policy disagreements with your administration, they are all patriots. Every one of them. None would harm their homeland or its armed forces. If you doubt that—"

"Oh, spare me the sentimental bullshit," Barbeau ground out through gritted teeth. "Patriots don't fight for profit. And they certainly don't do so at the orders of a foreign government like yours, Wilk." She leaned closer to the camera, an action that only magnified the ugly look of fury plastered on her face. "You Poles hired a bunch of stone-cold killers because you were scared of the Russians. I warned you that was a dangerous move at the time. Well, fine. What's done is done. But what made you think you could control thugs like that forever? Because now it looks to me as though Martindale's dropped you right in the shit."

Wilk shook his head. "You are overlooking the obvious, Madam President."

"Like what?" she snapped.

"At my urging, former president Martindale contacted you some days ago to go over intelligence reports indicating that Gennadiy Gryzlov was organizing a deniable, covert mercenary force of his own." Wilk set his jaw. "Unfortunately, now we see what he had planned. That is why I worry that this Russian attack on your air base is only the beginning of a much bigger and even more deadly clandestine war."

Barbeau snorted. "Nice try. But no sale."

"What do you—"

"Martindale's robots," she said flatly. "His precious CIDs. They were there. I saw them. Hell, we've got pictures of them, shooting up our planes and our people. Too bad your so-called warning didn't include any mention of the Russians building their own war robots. Since we all know that kind of technology is way beyond Moscow's reach, I guess you both figured that would be one lie I wouldn't swallow."

Wilk winced. "At the time, we had no hard evidence that the Russians were building their own cybernetic war machines. Their appearance at Barksdale Air Force Base was as much a surprise to us as it was to you. We now suspect that Gryzlov was able to reverse-engineer CID technology from components captured when two of our machines were destroyed in action more than a year ago."

"How wonderfully *convenient*," Barbeau said with a cold edge to her voice. "So, then, Mr. President, can you prove any of that? Or am I just supposed to bob my head and grin while Martindale screws me over for his own political ends and financial gain and then walks away clean?"

For a moment, he could only stare back at her in dismay. Was the American president really so blind? So caught up in dark paranoid dreams that she believed political rivals would be willing to commit treason to throw her out of office?

"Yeah, that's what I thought," she said dismissively. After a moment's thought, she shrugged her shoulders. "Okay, so here's how we're going to play this, Piotr: You say the Russians did this? With some mysterious new force of war robots? Fine. Then you give me your solemn assurance as Poland's commander in chief, right now, with no 'ifs, ands, or buts,' that *all* of Martindale's robots are still stationed in Polish territory or elsewhere in your piss-ass alliance."

Frowning, Wilk glanced at the clock on his office wall. Brad and his team should still be on the ground, though only for another few minutes. He hesitated slightly, reluctant to sacrifice his personal honor in this way. Then he steeled himself. He'd sworn to defend his country and its freedom. If doing so required him to mince words to avoid confirming this woman's obsessive fears, so be it. "You have my assurance, Madam President. All of the Iron Wolf Squadron's CIDs are currently deployed in Poland."

"Good." Barbeau smiled unpleasantly. "Now that we're on the same page, you'd better goddamned well make sure your hired killers stay put." Her voice took on an even harder tone. "Because, if it turns out that you've lied to me . . . and those damned machines *are* operating inside this country, I promise you that my government will hold Poland and its allies directly responsible for an act of war committed against us . . . an act of war committed on our own soil."

With that, she broke their connection.

Wilk looked away from the screen. His eyes met those of Kevin Martindale, who'd been sitting quietly in a chair listening to Barbeau's tirade. "This is very, very bad. If any of our people are caught or killed now . . ." He let the thought trail off.

Somberly, Martindale nodded. "We're damned if they are, and probably damned in any case. If we abort the mission, we give Gryzlov free rein to wreak havoc inside the United States." His expression was bleak. "And if we don't, and Brad and his team are spotted and identified, there's a serious risk Barbeau might go off half-cocked. Which would pretty much guarantee that Poland gets crushed between the world's two most powerful nations."

CHAPTER 20

**ABOARD THE E-4B NATIONAL AIRBORNE
OPERATIONS CENTER, SOMEWHERE OVER
THE UNITED STATES**
That same time

Barbeau swiveled in her chair to look at Luke Cohen. Her chief of staff had changed out of his torn and singed clothes, donning an Air Force flight suit that was at least a couple of inches too small for his lanky frame. "Well?"

"Wilk was lying."

She nodded. "Through his teeth. Dithering like that when I asked him to confirm the locations of those robots was the tell. So there's our confirmation . . . we were hit by Iron Wolf CIDs." She frowned. "The circle I can't square is why Wilk would take a risk like this. Why allow his paid soldiers to attack us? Let's say their plan worked perfectly and I'd been killed. Even a buffoon like Ray Summers would have to retaliate against Poland big-time once he took the oath of office. Wilk has everything to lose and nothing to gain from letting Martindale run wild."

"Maybe the Poles really are as much in the dark about this as we are," Cohen suggested. "That would explain a lot."

"You think those Iron Wolf mercs have gone totally off the reservation?" Barbeau asked. "That they're acting without Warsaw's approval?"

Cohen nodded.

"Then why not just admit that right off the bat?"

"Figure it like this: You go out and buy a big mean pit bull as a guard dog. And then one day, the damn dog breaks out of your yard, runs off, and mauls some kid to death. And when a cop shows up at your door, you say . . . ?"

"That's not my dog, Officer," Barbeau said automatically.

"Exactly. That may not be the smartest reaction, but it's natural."

She pondered that. All along, she'd been sure that Piotr Wilk would someday learn, the hard way, what the head of Scion was really like. She'd certainly never bought the notion that Martindale would genuinely subordinate his own will to that of anyone else. Why would he take orders from some rinky-dink leader like Poland's president? His ego was too big. Right from the beginning, the former American president would have seen Wilk and his country as tools to be used and then cast aside when necessary.

Barbeau grimaced. It was a good enough working theory, but she was getting tired of operating on the basis of half-formed and maybe half-baked guesses.

"Okay, so it's possible the Poles were blindsided by this like we were. But something else still bugs me," Cohen went on slowly. The tall New Yorker looked down at his lap, deliberately not meeting her eyes—which was a sure sign that he was about to say something he was afraid might piss her off.

She sighed. "Go on, Luke. I won't bite."

Cohen forced a nervous half smile. "I understand what you're saying about Martindale and how he wants someone like Farrell in the White House who'll do things more his way."

"Not to mention letting Scion and Sky Masters shove their snouts in a trough full of juicy, big-money Pentagon contracts," she muttered.

"Yes, Madam President." Distractedly, Cohen ran his hands through his disheveled hair. "But what I don't get is why Martindale would do something so obvious." He dropped his hands back into his lap. "I mean, why not use Scion's capabilities for something slicker? Say, like sabotaging that B-21 prototype instead? Making sure our fancy new bomber crashed right in front of the TV cameras would have done more political damage to your campaign—without nearly as much fallout."

Barbeau considered that. *Jesus*, she thought, *Cohen is right*. Something about this just didn't fit. Martindale might be a sneaky, ruthless, corrupt son of a bitch, but he'd also always been a clever, calculating son of a bitch. Screwing around with the B-21's avionics or even bribing its crew to fake an in-flight emergency would have been a lot easier and safer stunt for him to pull. The kind of pulverizing, direct, all-out assault that hammered Barksdale into smoldering ruins wasn't his style.

In fact, it was more like something that swaggering, shoot-from-the-hip, militaristic cowboy Patrick McLanahan would have thought was brilliant. But McLanahan was dead . . .

She shivered suddenly, caught up in a memory that was three years old but that still had the power to give her nightmares. To persuade Gennadiy Gryzlov that the U.S. wasn't covertly supporting Poland in its war with Russia, she'd ordered Army Rangers and Air Force special operations commandos to assault the Iron Wolf base. Their orders were to stop the mercenaries from carrying out a bombing raid on Russian missile bases near Kaliningrad.

But the assault failed. And then the lethal-looking combat robot piloted by McLanahan had looked straight into a camera carried by one of her captured soldiers . . . looked straight at *her*. "You are a traitor to your country, Barbeau," the machine had growled in its menacing, electronically synthesized voice. "If we get out of this alive, I'll make you pay. I promise."

Barbeau had believed him. That was one of the reasons, besides Gryzlov's threats that he would launch a wider war, that had prompted her to order American F-35s to shoot down every Iron Wolf plane that survived the attack on Kaliningrad. She'd been determined to make sure that Patrick McLanahan really was dead this time. It was the only way she could think of to stop him from fulfilling the terrifying promise he'd made. Her pilots had obeyed their orders—blowing the last two Iron Wolf XF-111 SuperVarks out of the sky.

No one had heard anything from the retired Air Force general since then.

Until now, maybe, she thought in growing horror. Could McLanahan somehow have survived . . . again? It seemed impossible. For all his skills, he had been a man, as mortal as any other human being. He wasn't a machine. *No,* she thought desperately, *Patrick McLanahan is dead.* He had to be dead. Because otherwise, he'd be coming for her—

Involuntarily, Barbeau's hands tightened on her chair's armrests. Her face felt numb, as though it were carved from stone.

"Madam President?" Cohen said uncertainly. He looked worried.

She forced herself to let go of the chair. "I need you to get in touch with Ed Rauch right away," she said. Her voice sounded strange in her own ears, as if it was coming from millions of miles away. "Tell him I want the NSA and the other agencies to reexamine *every* piece of intelligence that led them to conclude Patrick McLanahan was killed when his XF-111 went down over Poland three years ago."

Her chief of staff stared back at her. "Do you think—?"

"I don't know what to think!" Barbeau countered harshly. "But if there's a chance . . . any chance at all . . . that psychotic bastard is still alive, I need to know about it!"

RKU SECURITY DETACHMENT, TX-151 LOOP W, NEAR TEXARKANA, TEXAS
A short time later

Perched high in the cab of his FXR Trucking–registered eighteen-wheeler, Kirill Aristov checked his side-view mirror. He could make out the unit's two other big rigs stuck in the traffic jammed up behind him. They were all separated by at least ten to fifteen other vehicles, which made it less obvious that they were traveling in a convoy. *Not that any of us are going much of anywhere right now,* the former Spetsnaz captain thought irritably. A long line of cars and trucks bottlenecked this stretch of single-lane highway looping around Texarkana. They were stopped dead.

Up ahead, maybe a mile or so, he could see what was causing the holdup. Flashing red-and-blue lights showed where police, ambulance, and fire crews were working to clear a serious accident that had blocked the highway.

"Specter Lead to Checkmate One, what's going on up there? Why are we stopped? Is there a mechanical problem with your vehicle?" Colonel Ruslan Baryshev asked suddenly through Aristov's headphones. They'd rigged up an intercom between the truck's cab and the trailer it was hauling—enabling communication with the pilots of the two KVM robots hidden aboard.

"We're fine, Colonel," Aristov assured the other man. "We're just stuck in traffic. The local

American authorities are clearing a wreck ahead of us. Once they're finished, we'll be moving again."

"Are you sure that isn't a security checkpoint set up by the American military or spy services to hunt for us?" Baryshev snapped. *"This so-called accident could be a ruse."*

Aristov exchanged glances with Nikolai Dobrynin in the passenger seat. The other veteran Spetsnaz trooper rolled his eyes. The captain shrugged his own shoulders in a wordless reply. Their passengers were still jumpy. Baryshev and his KVM pilots seemed to be taking a long time to come down off the adrenaline high they'd experienced during their attack on the American Air Force base.

"We're already more than one hundred and twenty kilometers from Barksdale, sir," Aristov said patiently. "That's well beyond the zone of any likely search. The Americans would have to deploy thousands of soldiers and police to cover all the possible roads and highways this far out. And they simply do not have that kind of manpower available to them."

"Let us hope you are right, Aristov," the colonel replied. *"Stay alert. If you are wrong and there are American police or military units blocking our path, my machines will eliminate them."* And the intercom went dead.

Dobrynin shook his head. "Those guys are a little too kill-happy for my comfort, Captain. If it's all the same to you, I'd rather make it to Dallas without having their robots burst out of those trailers and start shooting up the whole highway."

"That makes two of us." Aristov saw the traffic ahead of him starting to inch forward. He reached down to put the big rig in gear. "Let's hope they calm down once we reach the warehouse and get them out of those metal suits."

THE KREMLIN, MOSCOW
A few hours later

Gennadiy Gryzlov prowled back and forth across his office like a caged animal. From time to time, he paused to check the newscasts streaming across the screen of his smartphone. But never for very long. After the first deeply satisfying images of burning aircraft and dead Americans, no new information had emerged. Instead, journalists around the world were busy doing what they always did in times of crisis—replaying the same tired video clips, indulging in pointless speculation, and interviewing the usual groups of "experts," none of whom could shed any useful light on events.

He was getting tired of waiting. In his view, patience was a virtue desirable in underlings, not for those with real power. A soft chime sounded from his phone. He stabbed the answer button icon. "Yes?"

"Mr. Kurakin has arrived, Mr. President," his long-suffering private secretary, Ivan Ulanov, announced. "By your orders, I have not logged his arrival."

"Good," Gryzlov approved. Now that things

were heating up, it was time to make sure there were no obvious connections between Russia's head of state and Vladimir Kurakin's "private" military company. "Send him in."

He spun on his heel and sat down at his desk while Ulanov ushered the head of RKU into the office. A curt nod sent his secretary scurrying back to his post. He waited only long enough for the door to close before demanding, "Well?"

"Our attacks were completely successful," Kurakin reported. It was clear that he was enormously relieved. From the moment Gryzlov set Stacy Anne Barbeau's political rally at Barksdale Air Force Base as *Shakh i Mat*'s first target, he had been focused on the dangers involved in carrying out a military operation that could easily kill or wound America's national leader—even if only by accident.

"Spare me the standard briefing boilerplate, Vladimir." Gryzlov nodded the other man toward a chair. "I want solid numbers."

"Yes, sir." Kurakin pulled out his own smartphone. He opened up several files. "From satellite photos, my analysts estimate that fourteen of our Kh-35 missiles hit their assigned targets."

"And the other two?"

"One detonated prematurely seconds before impact," Kurakin said. "The other appears to have crashed in the swamps east of the air base, probably due to an engine or avionics failure of some kind."

"So the Americans will find it?"

"Eventually," Kurakin agreed. He shrugged his

shoulders. "But even then, the wreckage shouldn't lead their investigators anywhere."

Gryzlov nodded. Besides Russia, at least eight other countries around the world used the same subsonic cruise missiles. Many of them were building their own versions of the Kh-35 under license or reverse-engineering their own designs. No one would be shocked by the possibility that some of them had filtered out onto the international arms black market. As an added precaution, the missile components shipped covertly to Annenkov and his men had been thoroughly "sanitized"—stripped of any identifying serial numbers. That would certainly arouse suspicion, but it would also delay any investigation.

"Has your 737 returned to its base?" Gryzlov asked.

"It landed in Utah an hour ago," Kurakin confirmed. "Annenkov made his scheduled stop at Dallas/Fort Worth and then continued on as planned without any delay." He smiled thinly. "In the circumstances, the local airport officials were only too glad to expedite the departure of as many aircraft as possible."

"I can imagine," Gryzlov said dryly. News of the attack had caused the American FAA to temporarily ground or reroute all passenger and cargo flights scheduled to pass anywhere within a couple of hundred miles of Barksdale. Naturally, the effects had rippled across the entire United States, spreading havoc as connecting flights were canceled or delayed. With eastbound passenger jets

and air freighters stacking up at their gates and on
their runways, Dallas/Fort Worth's managers had
no interest in holding up planes headed in other
directions.

He leaned forward. "What about your ground
units? What's their status?"

"The trucks carrying Baryshev's KVMs and
Aristov's covering force have reached our safe
house in Dallas," Kurakin continued. "Again,
without incident."

Like the sites Aristov's teams had set up in several other places across the U.S., the Dallas secure
site was a warehouse nominally owned by FXR
Trucking. Most were located on the outskirts of
cities and large towns—in busy industrial parks
where no one would be surprised by trucks and
other vehicles coming and going at all hours of the
day and night. As far as FXR's American corporate executives were concerned, these warehouses
now belonged to yet another fledgling subsidiary
funded by the company's new owners. Employees
who once worked in those warehouses had either
been transferred to other facilities or laid off with
generous severance packages.

"Very good," Gryzlov said. "Now, how much
damage did your war machines inflict?"

Kurakin smiled more broadly. "More than my
planners' most optimistic hopes. For once, the
American media is not exaggerating. Colonel
Baryshev's robots destroyed every single military
aircraft on the ground at Barksdale."

"All of them?"

"Yes, Mr. President," Kurakin said proudly. "Including *Air Force One*."

Gryzlov felt a huge, answering smile of his own spread across his face. With one blow, he'd further ravaged the already weakened American strategic bomber force and wiped out an entire squadron of its most advanced stealth fighters. Best of all, there was no indication that Barbeau or her advisers had any idea that Russia was responsible for this attack.

To his surprise, the American president hadn't even raised the alert status of her forces beyond DEFCON Three. In fact, there were no signs of any unusual activity by ground, air, or naval units deployed outside the continental United States. It was a very different story at military bases on U.S. soil. Satellite imagery and signals intercepts all showed that they were on high alert, with fighters and early-warning aircraft aloft on patrol. Their combat squadrons and other air units were being dispersed to alternate fields. Army units had been deployed to nearby military bases and high-value government buildings, and reserve and National Guard units had been activated.

The picture those facts painted was clear. The Americans did not know they had been attacked by a foreign power. They were taking purely defensive measures, not preparing to conduct a retaliatory strike against an identified aggressor. Which meant that Gryzlov's plan, in all its cunning permutations, was unfolding just as he had intended.

"Do you have any idea of how many casualties you caused?" Gryzlov asked.

"No precise numbers," Kurakin said. He shrugged. "I don't think even the Americans have an exact count yet. But they were substantial. My best guess would be that we killed or badly wounded several hundred of the enemy, including many of their best pilots."

"*Molodets!* Well done," Gryzlov told Kurakin, openly delighted. For years, the Americans and their hirelings had battered Russia and its allies, often without paying any significant price. Exacting a measure of revenge for those years of pain and humiliation was incredibly satisfying. Knowing that this was only the beginning was even better. "I'd have you convey my personal congratulations directly to RKU's troops and pilots, Vladimir." He grinned. "Except, of course, that might imply I have some knowledge of your criminal and *wholly* unauthorized actions."

"I can't imagine what you're referring to, Mr. President," Kurakin agreed with an answering smile of his own. "After all, I was never here."

Gryzlov nodded approvingly. "Of course not." His eyes hardened. "So, when do you plan to strike your next target?"

"My forces can be ready to strike again within twenty-four hours," Kurakin promised.

The Russian president held up a hand. "Not so fast," he said with a sly smile. "*Pospeshish'—lyudéy nasmeshish',*" he continued, quoting an old proverb. "'If you hurry, you'll just make others laugh.' Give the Americans a little time to work themselves into a frenzy, eh? Let them sit and wonder and fret about what's going on while they exhaust their pilots and policemen with fruitless searches and patrols. Then, once they begin to relax, *that* will be the time to hit them hard again."

CHAPTER 21

THE GOVERNOR'S MANSION, AUSTIN, TEXAS
That same time

"While the White House will not confirm it, informed sources close to the president tell CNN that she is currently aboard one of the nation's airborne command centers—and that she is directly coordinating the federal government's response to this vicious terrorist attack against the United States. Her likely opponent in the fall, Governor Farrell, remains huddled in his mansion, meeting with political advisers—"

With a snort, John Dalton Farrell turned off the television in his book-lined office. He turned to the group of men and women gathered around the antique oak ranch table set in the middle of the modest-sized room. "Well, there you have it, folks." He gave them a lopsided grin. "Apparently, *we're* the ones cowering in a corner, while Stacy Anne Barbeau heroically leads the fight . . . from inside a heavily guarded airplane flying around at forty thousand feet."

"Jesus," one of them murmured. "Those bastards in the media aren't even pretending to be unbiased anymore. That so-called news report might as well be a full-on Barbeau campaign commercial."

Farrell shrugged. "No one ever said this would be easy, did they?" Seeing their glum faces, he deliberately struck a dramatic pose. "Was it over when the Germans bombed Pearl Harbor? Hell no!"

His senior campaign staffers groaned. Sure, their boss's love for occasionally quoting old movies like *Animal House* was endearing. But they couldn't help worrying that a hostile press would hear about him joking like this and use what he said, out of context, to paint him as an uneducated moron.

Farrell relented. "Okay, so the press hates my guts and worships the ground Stacy Anne treads on. Well, we knew that going in. Nothing's changed, except that now we need to figure out *exactly* what I'm going to say about this terrorist attack on Barksdale Air Force Base and, it sure looks like, against the president herself."

They nodded. The boilerplate condemnation the campaign had released earlier was good enough as far as it went, but they needed something more concrete. Except for his criticisms of Barbeau's weakness toward the Russians and the crony defense contracts she doled out to big contributors, most of the governor's focus had been on domestic policy. Today's horrific assault on a major American military installation was guaranteed

to shift public attention to national security and
defense policy—which was, traditionally, a boon
for any Oval Office incumbent.

"You think they were really trying to kill her?"
Sara Patel asked skeptically. The University of
Chicago–educated daughter of Indian immigrants,
she was Farrell's top aide for trade policy.

"You saw the videos," he said. "There were one
heck of a lot of bullets and missiles flying around
out there at Barksdale. If whoever hit us there
wasn't really trying to kill President Barbeau,
they sure as shit made it look that way."

Slowly, she nodded.

"Well, crap, Governor, if these terrorists were
actually gunning for her, it's too bad they missed,"
Michael Dowell said with a cynical laugh. Dowell,
short and wiry with the build and aggressive atti-
tude of a welterweight boxer, was an acknowledged
expert on banking regulation and small-business
formation. "It would have saved us a few hundred
million in projected campaign spending."

He fell abruptly silent when Farrell turned an
icy glare on him. "Stacy Anne Barbeau is still our
president and this nation's commander in chief,
Mike," the powerfully built Texan said coldly.
"You may not like it. Hell, *I* don't like it. Which
is why I plan to beat her like a dirty rug come
November. But in the meantime, *everyone* in this
room will show the proper respect due her office.
Is that under*stood*?"

Dowell stared at the table for a moment and
then quietly agreed. "Yes, Governor."

"Good," Farrell growled. He looked around the crowded room. "And we will make damn sure we don't fall into the trap of siding, even rhetorically, with the assholes who've just killed and wounded so many of America's brave soldiers and airmen. Is that clear enough for y'all?"

They nodded quickly, with murmured, embarrassed-sounding assents.

For a moment longer, Farrell stared them down. These were good people, he knew. Smart people. But like a lot of smart people, sometimes they lost sight of the forest for the trees. For all her many faults and manifest failings, Stacy Anne Barbeau was still a fellow American. Yes, he was in this campaign to win, but he wasn't in it to lose his soul along the way.

Suddenly his smartphone started playing music, indicating that he was receiving an incoming call. He stared down at it in surprise. Not only had he set the phone to vibrate, but that snippet of Aaron Copland's *Billy the Kid* was *not* the ringtone he had set. To his wife's occasional dismay, he was more of a country-and-western fan. Which meant someone had hacked the device. In and of itself, that wasn't a crisis. Unlike a lot of people, Farrell used his smartphone sparingly, and never for anything seriously confidential. His aides sometimes joked that if their boss had his way, he'd still be transacting official business by telegram and mounted courier.

For a brief moment, he considered handing the problem off to his security people, but then his natural curiosity got the better of him. Whoever was responsible had gone to a lot of time and trouble to set this up. Why not find out who?

Farrell looked up at his advisers with an apologetic look. "If y'all don't mind, I think I need to take this in private. Let's take a short break and come back at this in ten minutes."

Once they'd filed out clutching their array of briefing books and personal laptops, he swiped a callused finger across the smartphone's screen to accept this mysterious call. But instead of connecting, his swipe activated software hidden deep inside its operating system. Rows of random-seeming numbers and symbols flowed across the screen and then vanished. LEVEL FIVE ENCRYPTION PROGRAM ACTIVE, LINK FULLY SECURE appeared in their place—followed immediately by the live video picture of a man with longish gray hair and a neatly trimmed gray beard. He looked back from the screen with a hint of amusement.

Farrell raised an eyebrow. "And here I'd thought your reputation for pulling technological rabbits out of the hat was somewhat exaggerated, Mr. President. I guess I was wrong about that."

"I apologize for this unexpected intrusion, Governor," Martindale said, though without sounding very sorry. "But since President Barbeau seems determined to make the same foolish mistakes over and over again, I need to brief you on what Piotr Wilk and I believe is actually happening."

WOLF SIX-TWO, OVER THE NAVAJO NATION RESERVATION, ARIZONA
The next night

Two hundred and seventy nautical miles and thirty-six minutes after crossing into U.S. airspace roughly halfway between El Paso and Nogales, the XCV-62 Ranger zoomed low over high alpine forests, sharp-edged canyons, and cliffs. Against a night sky speckled with thousands of stars and the softly glowing band of the Milky Way, the Iron Wolf stealth aircraft was nothing more than a dark shadow rippling across a pitch-black landscape empty of any man-made light.

Brad McLanahan pulled his stick gently to the left, banking to follow the glowing navigation cues on his HUD. A jagged pillar of rock slid past outside the right side of the cockpit and then vanished astern. Without his input, the XCV-62 pitched up slightly, streaked over a low rise, and then descended again before leveling off just two hundred feet above the ground. They were relying on the Ranger's digital terrain-following system to keep them safe even at 450 knots. Using detailed digitized maps stored in the aircraft's computers and repeated short bursts from its radar altimeter, the DTF system allowed feats of long-distance, low-altitude flying that would be almost impossible for any unaided human pilot.

"AN/APY-2 Pulse-Doppler radar still active. Bear-

ing now four o'clock. Estimated range is one hundred and fifty miles," their computer reported. *"Detection probability at this altitude remains virtually nil."*

In the Ranger's right-hand seat, Major Nadia Rozek leaned forward. She checked a menu on her threat-warning display, watching as the computer compared the signature of the radar emissions it was picking up against its database. "That is the same E-3 Sentry we saw earlier," she told him.

Brad nodded tightly, keeping his eyes on his HUD. "Yeah, they must be circling over Kirtland AFB outside of Albuquerque. There's a huge underground nuclear weapons storage complex on the base. Nobody there wants to get blindsided by another cruise-missile attack."

Even before the XCV-62 crossed the U.S. border from Mexico, they'd started picking up the emissions of several E-3 Sentry AWACS aircraft deployed to cover the Air Force bases in Arizona, New Mexico, and Texas. Each of the modified Boeing 707s had a thirty-foot diameter rotating radar dome mounted atop its fuselage. Their radars could scan huge volumes of airspace—spotting nonstealth targets out as far as two-hundred-plus miles. And where those radar warning planes were, he knew pairs of F-16 and F-15 fighters were bound to be orbiting also—ready to intercept any unidentified aircraft the Sentries detected.

Slipping through this airborne web without setting off alarms meant flying an intricately plotted course at extremely low altitude, using the rugged terrain so prevalent in the American southwest to mask their passage wherever possible. So far they'd been fortunate. The Air Force had deployed its limited number of AWACS aircraft pretty much as Brad had predicted. There were gaps in effective radar coverage they could exploit.

Following the cues on his HUD, he banked left again, harder this time. With his left hand, he pushed the throttles forward a scooch, adding power to the engines to keep his airspeed up through this tighter turn. Then he leveled out again and reduced power, decreasing their thermal signature.

They were flying northwest now, headed directly into the badlands of Utah's Grand Staircase–Escalante National Monument. Once the Ranger broke free of that labyrinth of canyons, cliffs, and soaring buttes and mesas, they should have a straight shot to Battle Mountain in northern Nevada.

Three hundred fifty nautical miles farther on, the Iron Wolf stealth transport swooped low over a jagged ridge and dropped back down into a wide, lifeless valley. Brad peered through his HUD. More high ground spread across the horizon. Seen through their forward-looking night-vision cameras, those steep, rocky slopes took on a green-hued glow. Nevada was the most mountainous state in the Union, with over a hundred and fifty named ranges, and thirty separate peaks that soared more than eleven thousand feet into the air.

He blinked away a droplet of sweat. His flight suit was soaked. Even with all of their advanced avionic and navigation systems, this prolonged nap-of-the-earth flight was imposing a serious strain on both his mind and his body.

"Not much longer now, Brad," Nadia said quietly, offering him some encouragement.

He forced a tired grin.

"Caution, S-band multifunction phased array radar detected at ten o'clock. Range approximately forty miles," the Ranger's computer reported. *"Evaluated as Sky Masters ARGUS-Five. Detection probability low, but rising."*

That was the advanced "civilian-grade" radar sited at McLanahan Industrial Airport. One of Jon Masters's last designs, it was almost as capable as some of the U.S. military's top-end radar systems . . . and at a fraction of the cost.

"Nice to see that our friends are awake," Brad muttered.

"Can you blame them?" Nadia said. "By now, Dr. Noble and the others at Sky Masters must know the Russians have their own combat robots. They are wise to take precautions against unexpected and unwelcome visitors."

He shook his head. "No, I can't blame them. But the fact they've got that big-ass radar powered up this late is going to make things a little trickier."

"Perhaps Martindale should have warned them we were coming."

"Too risky," Brad countered. "It's unlikely that the feds or the Russians have penetrated Sky Masters communications, but if either of them has . . ." He let the thought trail off.

Nadia sighed. "It would be a very bad day for us."

"Yep. So the name of the game tonight is still How Not to Be Seen." He thought for a moment. "Bring up NavPlan Two."

"Understood. Going to NavPlan Two." Nadia pulled up her navigation display. Deftly, she entered commands instructing their computer to switch to one of the several alternate flight plans Brad had plotted before leaving Poland.

Their cues on his HUD shifted immediately. Brad tugged the stick to the right, pulling the Ranger into a tight turn toward the north. This new course would take them around the outer edge of that ARGUS-Five radar's detection envelope. Once they put the concealing mass of the Sheep Creek Range between them and the Sky Masters–operated airport, they could safely swing back south. Land-based radars could not see "through" higher ground.

"*New S-band Doppler radar detected at eleven o'clock*," the computer said suddenly. "*Signal strength increasing.*"

That was the kicker, Brad knew. Evading the Sky Masters ARGUS-Five meant flying almost straight into the zone of another radar, this one sited high up in the Sheep Creek Range's jumble of high plateaus, rounded rises, and boulder-strewn washes. The good news was that this new radar was one of the U.S. Weather Service's NEXRAD stations. And that gave them a chance to spoof it without being noticed.

"Activate SPEAR," he told Nadia. "Target that S-band Doppler weather radar."

Her fingers danced across one of her MFDs, bringing their ALQ-293 Self-Protection Electronically Agile Reaction system online. SPEAR transmitted carefully tailored signals on the same frequencies used by radars hunting for their XCV-62. By altering the timing of pulses returned to a potentially hostile radar, it could trick that radar into thinking the Ranger was somewhere else in the sky . . . or even render it effectively invisible. "SPEAR is engaged," she said. "Matching frequencies."

Crossing his fingers mentally, Brad held his course north. Since the primary mission of the WSR-88D radars in the NEXRAD network was weather tracking, they were highly automated. Plus, any meteorologist who was up so late keeping tabs on this particular radar should be paying more attention to cold fronts, thunderstorms, and the like than to a single tiny blip that quickly faded off his or her screen.

"NEXRAD radar now at ten o'clock. Range thirty miles."

Nice theory, McLanahan, Brad thought, trying not to hold his breath. Now to see if it matched reality. They were almost broadside to that radar now, without any terrain between them high enough to provide cover. If they were going to get pinged, this was the time. Seconds passed, each seeming longer than the last while the Ranger streaked on, flying low over the arid Nevada desert.

"No detection," Nadia said finally with mingled relief and satisfaction. "SPEAR has control over that radar. It can't see us!"

"Copy that." Brad tweaked his stick again, following the steering cues on his HUD as they slid left a few degrees and then kept moving. "Starting our final turn toward the LZ."

The XCV-62 banked slightly, starting a long, curving turn that would bring them back around to the southwest—coming in along the spine of the Sheep Creek Range. The aircraft's nose pitched up, climbing to stay above the fast-approaching high ground. Brad started throttling back, slowly shedding airspeed.

Beside him, Nadia had her eyes fixed on a computer-generated map. "We are three minutes out from the landing zone," she told him.

"No visual yet," Brad said tightly. They were roughly fourteen nautical miles out from the straight stretch of little-used dirt road he'd picked out earlier from satellite imagery as a possible place to land. It was still hidden in among the rugged hills and gullies ahead of them. "DTF disengaged," he said, toggling a control on his stick that turned off the Ranger's terrain-following system. He pulled back slightly, gaining more altitude to take a look at their planned LZ. Their airspeed dropped to three hundred knots.

Abruptly, a cursor blinked into existence on his HUD. "There it is."

"Ninety seconds out." Nadia slaved one of her MFDs to their forward-looking passive sensors and zoomed in her view. "The LZ appears clear. I am not picking up any unidentified thermal contacts."

Brad nodded. Except for occasional hikers, no

one spent much time this high up in the Sheep
Creek Range. Through his HUD, he could see
the dirt road rolling away into the distance. It was
a thin, bright green line against the darker green
of the surrounding plateau. Using another control on his stick, he selected a touch-down point.
Instantly, the Ranger's navigation system updated
his steering cues. "We're go for landing."

"Sixty seconds out." Nadia tapped a key, alert-
ing their passengers in the troop compartment
that they were making their final approach.

Brad entered a quick command on one of his
own MFDs. "Configuring for a short-field rough
landing." Then he throttled back some more. The
Iron Wolf aircraft slid lower.

The muffled roar from the Ranger's four turbofan engines diminished fast. As their airspeed
dropped, hydraulics whined shrilly. Computer-
directed control surfaces opened along the trailing edge of the wing, providing more lift. The
XCV-62's nose gear and twin wing-mounted bo-
gies swung down and locked in position.

The dirt road, with a glowing line drawn across it
to mark Brad's desired touch-down point, loomed
ahead through the windscreen, growing larger
quickly as they descended. They came in low over
the road, thundering along just feet above the
ground. His left hand hovered over the throttles.

One hundred yards. Fifty yards. Twenty-five yards.
The computer-drawn touch-down marker was suddenly a fiery green blaze across his whole HUD.

"Landing . . . *now*," he said decisively. With a

smooth motion, he chopped the throttles back almost all the way.

The Iron Wolf stealth transport dropped out of the sky. It touched down with a sharp jolt—shaking and rattling hard as it bounded down the rutted dirt road. Plumes of dust and sand kicked loose by its passage drifted away on a light breeze. Quickly, Brad reversed thrust, gradually bringing them to a full stop about a thousand feet from where the Ranger's landing gear first kissed the earth.

For a moment, he sat still, breathing hard. Then he grinned over at Nadia. "Well, check off one more successful landing in this crate. Or, depending on how you look at it, one more narrowly avoided crash."

She made a show of peering out both sides of the cockpit and then looked back at him with a crooked smile of her own. "Since the aircraft *does* seem to be in one piece, I suppose your more optimistic appraisal is warranted." She turned more serious. "Now what?"

"Now we drop the ramp and have Captain Schofield and his merry band of scouts guide us to a somewhat less conspicuous position a little off this road. Before the sun comes up, we need to be out of sight, especially from the air."

Thirty minutes later, the Ranger was parked near the opening of a draw lined with sagebrush just east of the dirt road they'd used as an improvised landing strip. Schofield and one of his men were draping Scion-designed camouflage netting across the aircraft to shield it from visual, thermal, or radar detection. The rest were hard at work smoothing out the tracks left by the aircraft's gear when it taxied into this hiding place.

Inside the cockpit, Nadia opened a com window on her display and typed in a short message reporting their safe arrival. Their computer automatically encrypted, compressed, and transmitted her message via satellite.

An icon flashed within seconds, signaling an acknowledgment and urgent message. "It's from Martindale," she said to Brad and Whack Macomber. Her brow furrowed as she read through the decoded message. "He urges us to exercise extreme caution. We are to avoid detection by U.S. authorities at all costs." With an exasperated sigh, she glanced up at the two Americans. "Apparently your President Barbeau is more than half convinced that *we* are the ones responsible for destroying your country's bomber base."

"This just gets better and better," Macomber growled. "How the fuck are we supposed to smack down a raid on Sky Masters without being spotted? I don't care how nifty-keen these Mod IV CIDs are. All the fricking camo systems in the world won't hide a rail-gun shot or autocannon fire."

"Oh, once that happens, we won't have to hide any longer, Colonel," Nadia said with forced good cheer. "It's simple. When the Russians do attack, we kill them. Then we show their wrecked machines and mangled corpses to your government." She shrugged. "That should be proof enough, even for a shortsighted cretin like your president. And then we can all go home without all this sneaking around." That drew a reluctant, rare laugh from Macomber.

Brad joined in, glad that Nadia could still shake Whack out of his occasional fits of gloom. Inwardly, though, he couldn't shake a nagging worry of his own. What had appeared an obvious course of action back in Poland seemed a lot less obvious now that they were here on the ground deep inside the States.

Sure, realistically, he and the others had no way to hunt down the covert forces Gennadiy Gryzlov was using to attack the U.S. There were too many possible hiding places and America was just too big a country. All of which made stationing their CIDs on overwatch near Battle Mountain the only rational play. Viewed logically, Sky Masters had to be a high-priority target for the Russians. Now that Moscow had its own combat robots, the high-tech weapons and other equipment developed by Sky Masters were sure to be the key to survival for Poland, its allies, and the United States itself.

They were essentially employing the same tactics used by big-game hunters when setting out to bag a tiger in the trackless jungle. Instead of beating around futilely in the bush, the idea was to stake out a live goat as bait . . . and then lie in wait until the hungry big cat came prowling into your rifle sights. Well, Sky Masters was their bait.

But what if the tiger had other prey in mind?

That was the worry Brad couldn't shake. What if he'd misread Gryzlov's plans? Then what?

CHAPTER 22

RKU SECURE SITE, DALLAS, TEXAS
That same time

Unhurriedly, Kirill Aristov sauntered along the withered grass strip lining the north side of Irving Avenue. His hands were buried in his pockets. He came to the corner of a small side street and paused, looking around in all directions as if making sure it was safe to cross. Under the crumpled brim of an oil-stained baseball cap, his eyes were watchful. A few cars and trucks drove past in both directions along the wide, six-lane avenue, but no one seemed to be paying any real attention to him.

His lips thinned. After all, why should they? This late at night, the only people wandering out on the streets were either drunk or crazy or homeless, or most likely all three in combination.

Satisfied that he was clear, Aristov strolled on up the narrower side street. Halfway down the block, he came to a padlocked chain-link gate. A rusting sign wired to the gate warned passersby that this was an FXR Trucking facility and that trespassers would be prosecuted. "Or right now, quite probably shot and killed," he murmured to himself.

He dug a key out of his jeans pocket, unlocked the gate, pulled it open just far enough to squeeze through, and then relocked the gate behind him. With only three tractor-trailers backed up against a single, slab-sided steel warehouse, the lot looked almost empty—especially when compared to those of the dozen other much-busier trucking companies and freight lines operating out of this run-down industrial neighborhood.

Over time, Aristov supposed this lack of activity might strike FXR's rivals as odd. Fortunately, he and his men, along with Baryshev's war robots, would be gone long before anyone got too curious. After one last slow look around to make sure no one was watching, he crossed the parking lot to the warehouse, rapped twice on a door, and then went straight in.

With a curt nod, Pavel Larionov slid his pistol back out of sight. The former Spetsnaz sergeant sat back down behind a solid metal desk that faced the door. A bank of TV monitors showed grainy images captured by low-light security cameras set up at various points outside the warehouse. "Any trouble?" he asked.

"None," Aristov said. He'd gone out earlier to walk around the neighboring area, looking for any signs that they were drawing unwelcome attention—either from the Dallas police or from America's domestic spy agency, the FBI. He'd figured that it would be a lot harder to hide a law enforcement surveillance operation now that things were quieting down outside. And he'd been right. The panel vans and unmarked cars favored by the police and the FBI would have stood out like lions among alley cats on those nearly empty streets. They were still safely hidden here.

Nikolai Dobrynin met him just inside the main warehouse area. "We've received a new warning order from Moscow. General Kurakin wants us to hit our next scheduled target in forty-eight hours."

Aristov looked past him to where several men stood grouped around a folding card table. The KVM pilots were studying maps while their leader, Colonel Baryshev, ran through yet another proposed attack plan. "Do they know about this additional delay?"

Dobrynin nodded.

Aristov frowned. Baryshev and his pilots should be grabbing some sack time right now. What were they doing awake this late—especially after learning they wouldn't be going into action for two more nights? If any of them had slept for more than a couple of hours after reaching this secure site, he'd missed it. Quietly, he said as much to Dobrynin.

"I've asked about that. Baryshev and his men claim they don't need much sleep," the other man said carefully. "Apparently, they're taking it in turns to spend some time plugged into those war robots of theirs."

"For what purpose?"

Dobrynin lowered his voice. "Those machines

include advanced medical diagnostics and health maintenance systems. While they're hooked up, these guys filter out the fatigue toxins from their bloodstreams. Plus, they can juice up on different hormones and neurotransmitters."

"So Baryshev and the rest of his KVM pilots are screwing around with their brain and body chemistry in order to go without sleep?" Aristov frowned. "Does that sound like a good idea to you?"

The other man shrugged. "In combat, maybe. But outside of an emergency situation? Hell no." He looked at his team leader with a worried expression. "Should we report this to Moscow?"

"Without more evidence this behavior is causing a problem?" Aristov said slowly. Reluctantly, he shook his head. "No. The colonel and his men have been trained on these war robots. We haven't. They must know what they're doing."

"I hope so." Dobrynin sounded unconvinced.

Aristov clapped him gently on the shoulder. "That makes two of us, Nikolai." His eyes hardened. "Which is why we're going to keep a very close eye on them from now on. Just to make sure."

BATTLE MOUNTAIN, NEVADA
Several hours later

Rubbing at bleary eyes that felt like they'd been sandpapered, Hunter "Boomer" Noble slid behind the wheel of his Lincoln luxury sedan, hit its push-button ignition, and then bit down on a ferocious yawn. *Do not start that or you'll never stop*, he thought tiredly. Instead, he ordered, "Open the pod-bay doors, Hal."

The integrated voice-command system he'd set up to control the lights, air-conditioning, and other electronics in the house he was renting instantly obeyed. With a low rumble, the garage door rolled up—revealing a row of large, two-story homes across the street. With the sun still below the eastern horizon, lights showed behind only a few windows.

Carefully, Boomer backed out of the garage, down his driveway, and out onto the empty street. No other cars were in sight. Naturally. His neighbors were mostly up-and-coming executives working for some of the other tech companies lured to Battle Mountain by Sky Masters' presence and subcontracts. But not even the eagerest beaver among them made a habit of heading to the office at this ungodly hour. That was a "pleasure" reserved for top-level Sky Masters executives and engineers since the bolt-from-the-blue sneak attack on Barksdale Air Force Base.

He put the Lincoln in gear and drove off. Behind him, his garage door rolled back down and locked automatically.

Boomer rolled through the nearest stop sign and took a left onto a bigger street that would take him to Interstate 80. Suddenly his headlights picked out a man wearing jeans, hiking boots, and a hooded maroon MIT sweatshirt standing right in the middle of the road—apparently trying to thumb a ride.

"Oh, man, you have *got* to be kidding me," he snarled under his breath. Now they were getting guys to bum rides in his suburban neighborhood, and practically in the middle of the night? This was the kind of crap that people moved out of places like Las Vegas or San Francisco to escape. What was next? Upscale panhandlers trying to rustle spare change for a round of golf at the local public course?

Still grousing out loud to himself, Boomer started to pull around the would-be hitchhiker. Then he saw the crude, hand-lettered sign the other man held up. It read, WILL WORK FOR FOOD FOR MY WOLF.

"Ah, hell," he muttered, with almost resigned incredulity. "And here I thought today would be boring." Scowling, he jammed on his brakes, bringing the big Lincoln to a full stop next to the hitchhiker. Silent now, he waited while the other man popped open the passenger door, climbed in, and flipped back the hood of his sweatshirt.

"Well, this is just great," Boomer said with a wry smile. "So Bradley James McLanahan has come to call. With all the hell breaking loose in the world, I should have figured you'd be dropping by to visit your old pal Hunter Noble and his Sky Masters hangar full of super-duper, high-tech wonder planes."

"Nice to see you, too," Brad replied with a lopsided grin. "Hope I didn't startle you too much." He shrugged. "I'd have picked a less cloak-and-dagger way to get in touch, but I'm not supposed

to be in the States at all, let alone here in Battle
Mountain."

Boomer snorted. "No kidding. If there's anyone else in the world who's more *non grata* as a
persona, with both the feds and the Russians, than
you and your Iron Wolf compadres, I'd be very
surprised." He raised an eyebrow. "Which makes
me curious as to just how far you're planning to
ride with me this morning."

"All the way to your office," Brad said simply.
"I need to brief you on some developments and
I'd rather not do it outside a secure environment."

"Yeah, see, there's the problem," Boomer told
him with a frown. "Our corporate security guys
have gotten a lot twitchier since someone kicked
the crap out of Barksdale. They aren't exactly going to let you come waltzing through the gate,
even on my say-so."

In response, the younger man unzipped his
sweatshirt. A Sky Masters ID card was clipped to
his shirt pocket. Made out in the name of someone named Michael Kelly, it showed a recent
photo of Brad wearing a coat and tie and it looked
completely genuine. Not only that, but the ID indicated that he was a "special projects engineer"
for Sky Masters' aerospace unit—the same outfit
headed up by one Dr. Hunter Noble, Ph.D.

Boomer stared at it for a long second. Then he
shook his head in disgust. "Don't tell me . . . that
shiny new ID of yours is already planted in our
personnel system, too, right?"

"Yep."

Boomer let out a breath. "How the hell did Martindale—?" Then he stopped himself and just held up a hand, with a deep, frustrated sigh. "Never mind, I really do *not* want to know."

He grimaced. Every time the former U.S. president and current head of Scion pulled one of these spooky stunts, Sky Masters security people scrambled around like maniacs trying to plug whatever gaps he'd found in their systems. Martindale was one of the company's best customers, despite Stacy Anne Barbeau's efforts to close off their sales to him, so this was more like a game than anything more serious. But it was still a game Boomer was getting tired of losing.

"Mind telling me what you're up to?" he asked finally.

"Right now?" Brad offered him a seriously shit-eating grin. "I'm going to grab a little shut-eye on the way into work. I put in a couple of incredibly long days just getting here, you know." With that, he reclined the Lincoln's comfortable leather passenger seat and closed his eyes.

Idly contemplating whether his neighbors would really mind so much finding a corpse sprawled across one of their nice, neat streets when they woke up, Boomer took his foot off the brake and drove on toward Sky Masters.

Brad looked around Boomer's cluttered office while the other man sat down and fired up his office computer. Stacks of aircraft manuals, binders crammed full of engine specifications and test results, and printouts of other scientific and engineering data occupied almost every flat surface. Detailed models of every aircraft and spacecraft Hunter Noble had ever flown lined the shelves behind him.

He nodded at one of them, a 1:64th-scale version of the sleek, single-stage-to-orbit S-19 Midnight spaceplane. It was a cutaway model, showing the S-19's revolutionary triple-hybrid engines, which could transform from air-breathing supersonic turbofan engines to hypersonic ramjets to pure rocket engines. "Getting any flight time these days?"

Boomer looked up from his computer and followed Brad's gesture. "On the S-19s?" With a sour look, he shook his head. "Zero. Zip. Nada. All of our spaceplanes are mothballed for now. Stacy Anne Barbeau is allergic to orbital operations, especially by anything with the Sky Masters logo on the side."

"What's her excuse? Too expensive?" Brad asked.

"Nope, it's not that," Boomer replied. "She's all about spending taxpayer money . . . but only as long as the money stays well inside the earth's atmosphere."

"And ends up in the pockets of contractors who back her politically?" Brad guessed.

Boomer snorted. "I hate to hear someone so young sounding so cynical."

"Especially when I'm right?"

"Well, yeah," Boomer admitted. He rocked back in his chair. "But I bet you didn't come all this way to Nevada just to talk politics." His eyes narrowed. "And I really hope you weren't planning to *acquire* another one of the X-planes we've got stashed out in Hangar Five. Because I can tell you that's a total nonstarter, in the current circumstances."

Brad shook his head, hiding a grin. Though he would never probably confess it openly, it was pretty clear that Boomer hated the idea of letting any of the highly advanced prototypes stored here at Battle Mountain slip through his fingers. Most of them were the products of the late Jon Masters's irreplaceable genius. Every one of them was literally one of a kind. They incorporated revolutionary technologies and design concepts that might someday be applied to new aviation projects. Watching any of those experimental aircraft fly off into danger with the Iron Wolf Squadron or some other Scion covert outfit must be like seeing one of your kids ride a tricycle out into traffic.

"Your X-planes are safe from my nefarious clutches . . . this time," Brad promised, holding up three fingers. "Scout's honor."

"Okay, so why am I not feeling hugely relieved to hear that?" Boomer asked quietly. He leaned forward again. "Look, if you're not here to snag a new plane, why the hell *are* you here?"

Brad lowered his hand. The other man was right. It was past time to get serious. "I've got a team of three CIDs parked up in the hills just north of here," he said flatly. "Because we think the Russians are likely to hit Sky Masters next." Quickly, he outlined his reasoning.

When he was done, Boomer sighed. "Yeah, that

all makes sense. I wish it didn't." He forced a tired smile. "But other people around here see the situation the same way you do. I know the possibility of a Russian attack against us has been on my mind ever since I saw the pictures out of Barksdale. And it sure explains a lot of the weird shit we've been doing over the past couple of days."

"Like what?"

"Richter's had all of us—all of his top people— working like dogs to secretly transfer all of our CID-related materials, components, and software to hidden storage facilities off-site," Boomer explained. "By the time we're finished, which should be in the next couple of days, you could walk in here and never realize that Sky Masters had anything to do with those machines."

Brad felt himself relax slightly. Learning that Jason Richter, Sky Masters' chief executive officer, was on the ball was a relief. Even though the Russians already had their own combat robots, it was a safe bet that their war machines were not quite as advanced as the Cybernetic Infantry Devices built and continually upgraded by Richter and his cybernetic engineers. But given Russia's enormous resources, it was also probable that Gryzlov's robot force now had numerical superiority over the Iron Wolf Squadron. Which meant that allowing the Russians to attain technological parity using information they captured at Battle Mountain would be catastrophic.

Unfortunately, though, CID technology was only the tip of the iceberg.

"What about everything else?" he asked. "All

of your X-planes, UAVs, advanced weapons, and sensors. Are you dispersing them, too?"

Boomer shook his head gloomily. "No can do," he said. "The feds have their guys keeping close tabs on the airport. And more FBI types are arriving all the time. It's getting so crowded that the trench-coat-and-fedora boys are practically tripping over each other outside our main gate. Right now, I can't fly anything bigger than a quadcopter toy without setting off alarms from here to Washington, D.C."

Brad thought about that. "Are you sure all of these new arrivals are FBI agents?" he asked. If Gryzlov *was* planning a raid on Sky Masters soon, he was bound to have a recon team deployed to scout the company's Battle Mountain facilities.

"Hell no," Boomer said, shaking his head. "We've got spies hanging off us like fleas on a mangy old dog. Exactly who works for whom is anyone's guess." He looked hard at Brad. "Which kind of raises the question of how you're proposing to set up a defensive perimeter to protect us without getting tagged yourselves."

"That's a definite problem," Brad acknowledged. "The camouflage systems on our CIDs are fantastic, but we can't run them for more than a few hours without draining our battery power. So with federal agents . . . and maybe Gryzlov's people . . . crawling all over Battle Mountain, the best I can do is post my CIDs high up in the Sheep Creek Range. That way our sensors and computers will have a shot at spotting any incoming missile or ground attack."

"And then what?"

"Then we'll come running," Brad said.

Boomer sighed. "No offense, kid, but I'm sensing a heck of a lot of 'ifs' and 'maybes' and 'hope so's' in this plan of yours." He looked out his window. "How close do you figure you can post your robots without being detected?"

"About six miles away," Brad said reluctantly.

"Which means it'll take your CIDs at least ten minutes to get here if the balloon goes up," Boomer pointed out grimly. "The problem being that it took less than ten minutes for the Russians to wipe Barksdale off the map."

Brad nodded again, even more reluctantly this time. "Which is why it might be a smart idea to move your people away from Battle Mountain until this is over."

"Because burned-out buildings can be replaced more easily than good scientists and engineers?" Boomer suggested. He shrugged his shoulders. "Helen Kaddiri, Richter, and I have already hashed that possibility out. And it's not going to fly."

"Why not?"

"Can you imagine what our brilliant president, Stacy Anne Barbeau, would think if she heard we were closing up shop here? Given her long-standing deep regard and admiration for Martindale, your dad, and Sky Masters, I mean?" Boomer asked dryly.

Brad winced. "She'd think you were guilty as hell and hoping to get out of Dodge ahead of the posse."

"Exactly," Boomer replied. "Which is why we're

just going to sit here going about our normal business like the good little boys and girls that we are." His face was a lot darker than his tone.

Slowly, Brad nodded in agreement. The prospect of using friends as bait for Gryzlov's mercenaries was looking more unpalatable than ever. No matter how quickly his Iron Wolf team reacted, a lot of good people were likely to die.

CHAPTER 23

STRATEGIC COMMAND BUNKER, WRIGHT-PATTERSON AIR FORCE BASE, DAYTON, OHIO
Later that day

President Stacy Anne Barbeau took her seat at the conference table with a sense of relief. For the first time in nearly forty-eight hours, she was back on solid ground. This briefing room was situated on the lowest of five levels in the new Strategic Command bunker buried deep below the surface of Wright-Patterson Air Force Base. It shared the same overbright LED lighting and drab institutional carpet and paint scheme found aboard the E-4B . . . but at least it wasn't in constant motion and at the mercy of high-altitude winds and turbulence. Or in danger from some mercenary-piloted stealth aircraft or air-to-air missile.

Far from it, in fact.

This secure bunker had been built at tremendous expense to replace its predecessor, destroyed along with the rest of Offutt Air Force Base in a Russian nuclear-armed cruise-missile attack more than a decade ago. It was housed inside a thick cube of steel, which was, in turn, encased in solid concrete, the bunker's command, intelligence analysis, and communications facilities designed to ride out a full-scale nuclear war. In short, she was safer here from a missile or bombing attack than anywhere else in the United States.

Barbeau caught the eye of Colonel Daniel Kim, the Air Force officer in charge of security for the facility. "Have those Ohio National Guard armored units arrived yet?" she demanded.

Kim nodded confidently. "Yes, Madam President. The heavy tank transporters carrying Charlie and Delta companies from the Hundred and Forty-Fifth Armored Regiment rolled through Gate 15A an hour ago." He checked the digital clock displayed beneath one of the large LED wall screens that lined the briefing room. "Their twenty-eight M1A1 main battle tanks should be fully deployed within the next fifty minutes."

Barbeau nodded, satisfied by this news. Not even those Iron Wolf CIDs could fight their way through two full companies of armor mounting 120mm guns. Sharply, she rapped her knuckles on the table. "Enough chitchat, people. I need answers, and I need them *now*."

The assembly of high-ranking civilian and military officials she'd summoned to this gathering abruptly fell silent. Apart from Luke Cohen and Ed Rauch and Admiral Firestone, chairman of the Joint Chiefs, most of them were ranking deputies and senior staffers in the various federal agencies and departments essential to national security— the CIA, NSA, FBI, the Defense Department, Homeland Security, State, and the Department of Justice. These were the men and women who could make things happen.

Luke Cohen hunched forward in his seat. He'd changed into fresh clothes flown out from D.C. on the same plane that ferried Rauch and the others to Wright-Patterson. Only the dark circles under his eyes showed the ordeal he'd been through. He cleared his throat nervously. "Uh, Madam President? We're getting some pretty pointed queries from Congress. Both the Speaker of the House and the Senate majority leader are asking when you plan to return to the White House."

Barbeau's lips thinned. "Not anytime soon. The White House is too vulnerable, too exposed to attack. We'd have to evacuate half the city to set up a defensive perimeter solid enough to stop an attack like the one that smashed Barksdale. And it doesn't make sense to tie down the huge numbers of troops and combat aircraft a defense of that magnitude would require."

She saw Admiral Firestone and some of the other Defense Department types nodding sagely in agreement. *How nice*, she thought tartly. It was always an added plus when concern for her own personal safety meshed so closely with military common sense.

Cohen looked even unhappier. "We could take some serious political damage if you stay off the public stage much longer," he warned. "People get kind of nervous when they start thinking that the nation's commander in chief is running scared."

"Maybe so," Barbeau snapped, feeling her temper flare. "But I'd sure as hell rather be a *lame* duck than a *dead* duck!" Angrily, she glared at her chief of staff. "And it's *your* job, Luke, honey, to convince the American people that I'm acting in the interests of national security . . . and not to save my own skin. So you do your goddamned job, or I'll find someone else who can. Do you understand me?"

Miserably, he nodded.

She swung her icy gaze toward Rauch. To his credit, her national security adviser didn't flinch. Working for her administration must be toughening the little man up. She'd put him in charge of coordinating the federal investigation into what they were still calling a terrorist attack on Barksdale Air Force Base. "What have you got for me, Ed?"

"Info on one of the cruise missiles used to hit us," he said quietly. "We think either the engine or the guidance package failed, which is why it crashed into a bayou about two miles east of the runway."

"Let's see it."

Rauch tapped the screen of his laptop, opening a file and sending the images it contained to one of the briefing room's video screens. Photos blossomed on the LED display, showing the mud-smeared, crumpled gray fuselage and fins of what was unmistakably a missile. Shots showing the wreckage being loaded into a sling beneath one of the Air Force's Pave Hawk helicopters gave a sense of scale.

"Have our people been able to identify this weapon?" Barbeau asked.

"Yes, Madam President," Rauch said carefully. "The wreckage has been examined by specialists from both the Air Force and the intelligence community. There's no question that what you're looking at is a Kh-35UE short-range, subsonic cruise missile." He brought up another image, this one a file photo showing an intact version of the same missile. "It's a Russian design, comparable to our own Navy's Harpoons. And like the Harpoon, these missiles can be fired by a wide range of platforms—by fixed-wing aircraft, helicopters, ships, and ground-based launchers. In fact, some analysts have nicknamed the Kh-35 the 'Harpoonski' because they're so similar."

Barbeau narrowed her eyes in annoyance. "Dr. Rauch, are you telling me this *was* a Russian attack after all?"

He shook his head. "Not with any certainty." Seeing her confusion, he explained. "The Russians have been selling export versions of the Kh-35 around the world for decades. Plus, several countries—some of them with governments that are extremely unstable and corrupt—build their own copies under license."

"Which means there's no way to tell how many of these missiles have made their way onto the black market," she realized.

"Correct," Rauch agreed. "And since we can't find the usual serial numbers on any of the components in this missile, that's probably what we're looking at. Certainly, there's no doubt that whoever sold these weapons doesn't want them traced back to the source."

Admiral Firestone stirred in his seat. "That applies to the Russians, too," he pointed out. "They'd have just as much interest in sanitizing any Kh-35s transferred from their own arsenals."

"Yes, sir," Rauch agreed. "Which is why I want our interagency scientific groups to examine different methods we might use to narrow down the provenance of these weapons—perhaps by analyzing the kerosene fuel blend we found in that wrecked missile's engine or by studying the precise chemical composition of its warhead."

"That's a hell of a tall order, Ed," one of the CIA officers objected. "Without other intact Kh-35s from known sources to use as controls, how can we possibly draw any reliable conclusions from—"

Barbeau felt her eyes glazing over as the discussion spiraled off into a long and highly technical debate. Instead, while her advisers wrangled, she sat wrapped in her own thoughts, wrestling with an array of contradictory evidence and wild speculation. It would be a typical Martindale move to use Russian-designed missiles to muddy the waters, she fumed. Was the raid on Barksdale his doing after all—part of some insane scheme to lure the U.S. into an open confrontation with Gennadiy Gryzlov? If so, it might explain why he'd opted for an all-out deadly attack instead of simply trying to embarrass her politically by sabotaging the B-21 Raider prototype.

But if Martindale was trying to spark a war between the U.S. and Russia, why use a weapons system, the CIDs, that pointed the finger right back at himself?

Unless, Barbeau thought, *the Poles were right after all*. If the Russians had their own combat robots—

Impatiently, she dismissed that thought as even crazier than all the others. Top U.S. government weapons labs had repeatedly failed to replicate the cybernetics and engineering breakthroughs needed to build new CIDs. How could the Russians, who were so far behind the U.S. in those same technologies, have suddenly leapfrogged past them? The idea that Moscow could achieve so many separate technological breakthroughs by simply scooping up a few broken and burned-out pieces off a battlefield was ludicrous.

If that weren't enough, the idea that this was a Russian operation didn't square with any diplomatic or political reality Barbeau could see. Why would Gennadiy Gryzlov order an attack that could easily have killed her? She certainly wasn't his ally, but she also worked hard to avoid any unnecessary confrontation with Russia . . . and she'd paid a significant political price for her restraint. Why on earth would the Russian leader risk handing the presidency to John Dalton Farrell? The Texan was another unreconstructed cold warrior, a would-be Ronald Reagan. For crying out loud, he was already colluding with two of Moscow's most determined enemies, Piotr Wilk and Kevin Martindale. How could Gryzlov possibly see clearing Farrell's path to the Oval Office as being in his country's best interest?

No, she thought coldly, when faced with two or three improbable scenarios, it didn't make any sense to choose the one that was the nuttiest of them all. Which left Martindale . . . or Patrick McLanahan, if he was still alive somehow. They were the only two men in the world who controlled a force of stealth aircraft *and* combat robots. She made a mental note to push Rauch to crack the whip on the intelligence experts tasked with reexamining the evidence of McLanahan's death over Poland three years before.

"Oh, that's just great," Barbeau heard Luke Cohen mutter from beside her. Her chief of staff was staring down at an e-mail he'd just received on his smartphone.

"*More* trouble, Luke?" she asked pointedly.

He nodded. "Farrell has just requested a detailed intelligence briefing on this situation."

Barbeau frowned. By custom, presidential candidates didn't receive access to classified intelligence information until after their party formally nominated them at its national convention. In Farrell's case, that wouldn't be for some weeks yet. "On what grounds?"

"His argument is that the severity of the crisis confronting the nation warrants moving the regular timetable up."

"Not a chance," Barbeau said icily, not even bothering to waste time thinking it through. Her suspicions were now fully aroused. If the Texas governor was a political stalking-horse for Mar-

tindale and his hard-line allies, every scrap of secret intelligence they gave him would end up in
enemy hands. And even if she were wrong about
his role in this mess, there was no doubt that
Farrell or his operatives would find ways to leak
any damaging or embarrassing information they
learned. After all, she knew that was exactly what
she would do if she were in his place.

"But, he'll go running to the press—"

"Let him whine," Barbeau snapped. "You tell
J. D. Farrell for me that the United States has
just one president at a time. And right now, that's
me." She folded her arms across her chest. "This
is *my* watch, not his. For now, he can go peddle
his Texas he-man political bullshit to the rubes
while I'm doing the hard work to keep this country safe."

IRON WOLF FORCE, IN THE SHEEP CREEK RANGE, NORTH OF BATTLE MOUNTAIN, NEVADA
The next day

Brad McLanahan squatted down next to Captain
Ian Schofield. The Canadian lay prone at the very
edge of the camouflage netting that sheltered
their encampment and protected the XCV-62
Ranger from prying eyes. Even under its welcome
shade, the very air was so hot and so bone-dry
that it seemed determined to suck every drop of
moisture from their mouths and eyes.

Schofield lowered the binoculars he'd been

using to survey their surroundings. Under the
scorching rays of the sun, the high desert plateau
seemed utterly lifeless. Nothing seemed to move
except for the heat waves dancing above a barren
landscape of sagebrush, wind-eroded rock, and
bare, sunbaked dirt. "You know," he said reflectively, "I really should stop volunteering for missions in the less salubrious parts of the globe."

Brad moistened his cracked lips and managed
a painful grin. "Hey, show a little respect, Ian.
Battle Mountain is my home turf. Summers here
aren't usually so bad." Then he shrugged. "Well,
as long as you've got air conditioning, anyway. Or
at least an ice chest full of cold drinks."

"All of which are in extremely short supply just
now," Schofield pointed out.

"Yeah, there *is* that." Brad sighed. "Water is the
big problem, isn't it?"

The Canadian nodded. "It is. We have plenty
of food." He smiled wryly. "None of it especially
gourmet, to be sure. But water is bulky, and in
this heat, we all need to drink a fair amount." He
sat up. "With reasonable rationing, we can maintain our position here for another four or five
days. After that, we'll need a resupply mission. Or
we'll have to leave."

Brad nodded. There was no way Scion could fly
in more supplies to them—not covertly, anyway.
The Ranger was their only stealth STOL aircraft. The stealth-modified PZL SW-4 helicopter
they'd used to fly Sam Kerr and her fellow agents
out of Russia was thousands of miles away. Knowing Martindale, he was sure there were other

Scion-operated aircraft and helicopters based in the U.S., but nothing that could land here without setting off a lot of alarms.

"Any news from the OP?" Schofield asked.

Using their CIDs, Brad, Nadia, and Macomber were taking it in turns to man an observation post they'd established high up on the slopes overlooking Battle Mountain. The position they'd selected gave their passive sensors a clear field of view over every likely avenue of approach to the Sky Masters complex around the airport.

"Well, Colonel Macomber says he's pretty sure he's tagged every FBI surveillance team based in or around Battle Mountain. My friend Boomer was right. There are a lot of them . . . and they're not being real subtle. The feds have two-man teams parked right outside every gate and at key vantage points that give them a good view of the airport."

Schofield frowned. "What about others?"

"Like the Russians?" Brad shook his head with a frown. "Nothing so far. Which means either they're not here at all, or—"

"They're very, very good," the other man finished for him. He shrugged. "I've studied the personnel records those Scion agents you rescued snatched from Bataysk. The Spetsnaz troops who hired on with Gryzlov's mercenary force are top class."

"As good as your guys?" Brad asked seriously.

Schofield smiled. "Perish the thought." Then he shrugged his shoulders again. "But good enough to give us some trouble in a fair fight? Probably so."

"Great."

"If it's any consolation, I don't think I could work any of my men into position outside Sky Masters without your CIDs spotting us," Schofield said firmly. "The terrain is too open. Between your thermal and audio sensors, and those advanced motion-detection algorithms programmed into your computers, I doubt a field mouse could sneak up to the perimeter fence without being spotted, let alone a man."

Brad sighed. "Let's hope you're right." He rose to his feet. "Speaking of which, it's my turn on sentry duty." He chuckled. "The last time I checked, Whack was so bored that he was starting to place bets with himself on how many big rigs he'd count per hour driving along Interstate 80."

CHAPTER 24

NEAR U.S. AIR FORCE PLANT 4,
FORT WORTH, TEXAS
Later that night

Kirill Aristov cranked the wheel of his big rig, turning off the West I-820 frontage road and into the empty lot of a large discount furniture warehouse. He pulled around the back of the store and parked alongside two other FXR Trucking–registered tractor-trailers already there.

When he clambered down out of the cab, the first thing that struck him was the silence. Apart from insects chittering in the nearby woods and the occasional soft *whoosh* of a truck or car speeding past on the highway, everything was quiet.

Pavel Larionov stepped out of the shadows to greet him. "We're secure here, Captain. I've got Yumashev and Popov posted to keep an eye on the road."

"Good work." Aristov heard footsteps crunch across gravel and turned to see Dobrynin and

Mitkin, the other members of his six-man security team, emerging from the woods. Both men were armed with Heckler & Koch MP7 submachine guns. Just over sixteen inches long with the stock collapsed, the compact weapons fired 4.6mm copper-plated solid steel rounds that could penetrate body armor at up to two hundred meters. MP7s equipped the special forces of more than twenty countries, including the Vatican's Swiss Guard.

Dobrynin gave him a thumbs-up sign. "We scouted all the way to the edge of the woods. No problems. If they stay away from the shoreline, the colonel's KVMs should have a clear shot straight to their objective."

Aristov nodded. They were not far from a winding cove that led out onto Lake Worth, which was a man-made reservoir and recreational waterway on the northwestern edge of Fort Worth. Although a number of private homes and boat docks lined this cove, a thick belt of scrub oaks and underbrush farther inland offered a concealed way past them. Decisively, he jerked a thumb toward the three trucks. "Okay, then let's get Baryshev and his robots outside and send them on their way."

Moving with practiced efficiency, the four former Spetsnaz soldiers unlatched the doors on the back of each of the three semitrailers and hauled them open. More quick work propped open the package- and box-studded false fronts that concealed the compartments hidden inside.

One after another, Colonel Baryshev's six combat robots spooled up with a low, ominous *whir*. They came smoothly to their feet, bending at the torso to clear the trailer ceilings. The *Kiberneticheskiye Voyennyye Mashiny* straightened up once they were outside—towering over Aristov and his men. Each carried an arsenal of heavy weapons, mostly 30mm autocannons and antitank guided missiles, in their hands and stowed in packs slung across their torsos.

Unable to shake off a feeling of primitive dread, the former Spetsnaz captain stared up at them. Everything about these machines exuded inhuman precision and lethality. Nervously, he made his report.

An antenna-studded head swiveled noiselessly in his direction. "Understood, Captain," an emotionless, electronically synthesized voice said. "Guard this position until we return."

Without waiting for an acknowledgment, the six Russian war machines swung away and stalked off into the woods—heading southeast toward a bright orange glow visible above the treetops. Those lights marked the location of U.S. Air Force Plant 4, a sprawling aircraft assembly facility. Almost ten thousand people were employed there, working in shifts around the clock, to build America's top-of-the-line F-35 Lightning II stealth fighters. Sixteen aircraft assembly stations and a wing manufacturing plant were all housed inside one enormous, nearly mile-long building at the heart of the giant complex.

* * *

Minutes later, Colonel Ruslan Baryshev hunched low near the edge of a tangle of scrub oaks and brush. He was only a few hundred meters west of the F-35 assembly building. Five green blips on his tactical display showed the other KVMs. They were concealed close by in the same scraggly patch of woods, awaiting his final attack orders.

He concentrated, using his neural interface with the robot's computer to see more of the composite imagery obtained by its passive sensors. Two red dots, evaluated as hostile, blinked into existence on his display. They were positioned just off the two-lane road leading to the American aircraft plant.

Baryshev zoomed in on them, using a night-vision camera. He saw a white Tarrant County sheriff's patrol cruiser parked next to a desert-camouflaged U.S. Army National Guard Humvee. The Humvee carried a 40mm grenade launcher in a 360-degree traversable mount. Several soldiers had dismounted from their armored vehicle to man an improvised roadblock. A couple of them were smoking cigarettes. One was chugging a bottle of water. All of them looked bored and tired.

He smiled thinly. Originally, he'd questioned Moscow's orders to delay this next attack—arguing that only an unrelenting clandestine offensive would knock the Americans off balance and keep them there. Now he could see that prolonging the interval between their terror operations was yielding dividends. Every experienced commander knew how difficult it was to keep troops fully alert as hours and then days passed without action.

Situation update, his computer reported coolly. *Communications intercepts have pinpointed additional enemy patrols and defensive positions.*

Baryshev widened his sensor fields again, seeing more red icons appear at various points around the aircraft plant's seven-kilometer-long perimeter. Radio chatter between the different American posts and mobile units had enabled his robot's systems to identify more of the police cars and army vehicles deployed to defend this facility. He sneered. The defenders were too few in number, too poorly equipped, and too widely dispersed to offer any significant opposition to his attack force.

Instead, he turned his attention to the local National Guard armory, not far south of his current position. It was a cluster of one- and two-story buildings—offices, maintenance and equipment sheds, and living quarters—and two vehicle parks crammed with dozens of trucks, Humvees, mine-clearing vehicles, and MRAP troop carriers. "Evaluate this facility," he ordered the computer.

Thermal signatures indicate up to one hundred personnel currently deployed at the enemy base, it reported. *Motion-capture analysis confirms that most are asleep or resting. Three armed vehicles and two infantry squads are on alert status.*

Those National Guard troops were not much of a threat, Baryshev knew. Only the heavy machine guns and grenade launchers mounted on their

Humvees presented any real danger to his KVMs. On the other hand, there was no point in running any unnecessary risks. *Besides*, he thought, yielding to a sudden predatory impulse, *why not try to kill as many Americans as possible?* If nothing else, running up the casualty totals would spread even more terror and anguish among Russia's enemies.

He opened a secure channel to one of his robot pilots, Major Viktor Zelin. "Specter Lead to Specter Three."

"Three," the former Su-34 fighter-bomber pilot's laconic voice replied.

"On my order, you will destroy the American National Guard base on our flank." With a quick flick of a finger, Baryshev opened a data link to Zelin's robot and uploaded his computer's intelligence evaluation and target analysis. "Leave no survivors."

"Data received," the major said a second later. He sounded happier now. *"I will comply. Three, standing by."*

Satisfied that his subordinate knew what to do, Baryshev turned his attention back to the improvised roadblock up ahead. He opened another channel. "Lead to Two. You take that police car. I will destroy the enemy armored vehicle."

"Affirmative, Lead!" KVM senior pilot Oleg Imrekov radioed back. His former wingman sounded keyed up and impatient, eager for action.

Baryshev felt his own pulse accelerating. A targeting icon blinked into existence, highlighting the Humvee parked four hundred meters away. He raised his 30mm autocannon, selecting armor-piercing ammunition. He took a deep breath, savoring the fierce sense of anticipation rising in his mind—sweeping away any lingering doubts or hesitation. It was the same feeling of exultation, of near omniscience, he experienced when hurling his Su-50 fighter into a whirling, close-range dogfight, only now multiplied tenfold. "Specter Lead to all Specter units," he snapped. "Execute attack as ordered!"

Immediately he opened fire.

Tungsten-steel alloy slugs tore through the Humvee's side armor and blew out the other side in a spray of molten metal. Its bullet-resistant windows shattered. The gunner manning the grenade launcher was killed instantly by a 30mm round that cut him in half. The soldiers who'd been manning the roadblock crumpled, either hit by cannon fire or shredded by jagged shards of armor spalling off the wrecked Humvee.

Baryshev ordered his robot to its feet and dashed out of the woods—sprinting fast straight up the road. Smoke from the Tarrant County sheriff's car that had been ripped apart by Imrekov's shells curled across the scene, momentarily blotting out the carnage on his visual sensors.

His tactical display showed four more KVMs following him toward the brightly lit F-35 assembly plant up ahead. The icon representing Major Zelin's machine moved at right angles, closing in on the National Guard armory he'd been ordered to destroy. Flashes lit the sky to the south as the former Su-34 pilot started firing antitank missiles into buildings at close range.

Baryshev broke past the shattered American roadblock's jumble of burning vehicles and dead men and kept going. He bounded high in the air, clearing two fences topped with razor wire, and thudded down on a low berm in a spray of torn earth and grass. Still on the move, he slung his autocannon and rearmed with one of the three Israeli-made Spike antitank missiles he carried. Thanks to his neural interface, he was aware of everything going on in all directions. Behind him, the four other KVMs assigned to this part of the mission fanned out across the assembly-plant complex.

As he crested the shallow berm, he saw a startled security guard come running around the corner of a nearby building. The heavyset American skidded to a halt when he saw the tall gray war robot lunging toward him out of the darkness. His mouth fell open in horror. Without pausing, Baryshev swatted him away in a grisly fog of splintered bone and blood.

The Russian laughed aloud, seized suddenly by the feeling of being a god striding majestically through a sea of confusion and panic among mere mortals—dealing out death and destruction with every step. Through his radio links, he could hear Imrekov, Zelin, and the others echoing his jubilant shouts.

ATGM targets selected, his computer reported calmly. New aim points appeared before Baryshev's eyes. Without thinking, he fired at the closest. The small missile streaked low across the ground, slammed into the long aircraft assembly building, and punched through its thin steel wall. The missile's high-explosive fragmentation warhead exploded deep inside. Flames boiled back out through the ragged hole it had torn. Through his robot's hyperacute audio pickups, he could hear screams and shrieks echoing from inside the building.

F-35 assembly station severely damaged, the KVM's battle computer judged.

More explosions erupted down the length of the huge structure as the rest of his force opened fire using their own shoulder-launched antitank missiles. The high-pitched yells of the American technicians and engineers trapped inside amid a hail of fire and shrapnel were continuous now, creating an uncanny, discordant symphony of agony and terror that he found electrifying.

Baryshev dropped the smoking launch tube and yanked a fresh weapon from one of his weapons packs. Exultantly, he aimed and fired a second time. And then again, using his last missile.

Discarding the launch tube, he drew his autocannon. *Loading preselected mix of armor-piercing and incendiary ammunition*, the computer said calmly. Sighting along the torn and smoking building, he squeezed the trigger and fired repeatedly—sending 30mm round after round ripping through the battered structure.

WHANG. WHANG. WHANG. WHANG.

Razor-edged steel fragments whistled away through the night air. More flashes erupted inside the assembly plant, followed by billowing clouds of gray-and-black smoke. Hot spots bloomed in his thermal sensors, each showing a new fire ignited amid the heaps of debris strewn across a formerly pristine factory floor.

Baryshev's autocannon fell silent. *All ammunition expended*, his computer reported. *Mission damage parameters achieved. Recommend immediate tactical withdrawal.*

For a split second, he felt the urge to press on, using his KVM's powerful metal hands to tear open the F-35 assembly plant's walls and continue his rampage. But then, reluctantly, he allowed reason to regain its grip over his mind. "Specter Lead to all Specter units," he radioed. "It's time to go. Withdraw to rally point Alpha. Repeat, head for rally point Alpha."

One by one, the other pilots acknowledged. Baryshev could hear the strain in their voices, as if they, too, were fighting the temptation to override his orders and continue their killing spree. But like the disciplined warriors they were, they obeyed.

He took one last look at the shattered building. Flames crackled in dozens of places now, feeding on paint, splintered wood, and superheated carbon-fiber fragments. He grinned triumphantly. Between the evident damage to expensive, virtually irreplaceable machinery and the terrible losses they'd inflicted on the plant's skilled workforce, it was clear that America's F-35 stealth-fighter production line would be out of commission for many months.

Laughing again, Baryshev turned and sprinted away into the darkness.

By the time the Americans could organize any kind of effective pursuit or search, he and his robots would be safely hidden again . . . concealed in the Dallas FXR Trucking warehouse right under their noses. And then, once the heat died down, Aristov and his men could ferry them on to their next assigned objective.

CHAPTER 25

STRATEGIC COMMAND BUNKER, WRIGHT-PATTERSON AIR FORCE BASE

A few hours later

National Security Adviser Edward Rauch tugged at his tie, loosening it while he clicked through to the next image in his situation update. His forehead and palms felt damp. Despite a climate-control system that continuously recirculated air scrubbed of all possible radioactive, chemical, or biological contaminants, the atmosphere in the lower-level briefing room tasted stale and felt unpleasantly warm. And while it might only be his imagination, he could swear that he could smell the stomach-churning traces of lubricating oils and acrid cleaning solvents wafting sporadically out of the bunker's air vents.

Or, it might just be that I hate being the bearer of never-ending bad tidings, he thought gloomily, seeing the look of barely suppressed fury on President Stacy Anne Barbeau's face. Like the Red

Queen in *Alice in Wonderland*, she seemed on the verge of snarling, "Off with his head!" For the thousandth time since joining her administration, he wondered what had possessed him to yield so easily to ambition. It was one thing to write learned papers about the ins and outs of high-level statecraft and national security policy. It was quite another to learn, from harsh personal experience, that serving in the White House—at least under this president—meant stumbling through a maze of narrow political calculations and even more narrow-minded bureaucratic rivalries.

"Jesus," Barbeau said softly, staring up at the picture he'd selected.

Taken only hours after the terrorist attack, it showed the interior of U.S. Air Force Plant 4. Scorched and melted heaps of wreckage were only barely recognizable as the remains of F-35 Lightning II fuselages, tail assemblies, and wings. The vast assembly floor was a jumble of mangled machinery, equipment hoists, ladders, and work platforms. Tarp-covered bodies were strewn in every direction.

With obvious difficulty, she turned her gaze away from the image of so much death and destruction. "Is this as bad as it looks?"

Rauch nodded. "Every single one of the sixteen F-35s that were being assembled is a total write-off. Even more wing and fuselage components that were waiting their turn on the line were destroyed. Of the aircraft assembly stations themselves, our best estimate is that more than half will have to be rebuilt from scratch. The rest suffered so much damage that it will take weeks, maybe months, before we can get them back into operation."

"Wonderful," Barbeau muttered. Her jaw tightened. "How long will the Fort Worth plant be out of commission?"

"At least four months." Rauch sighed. "But that's the contractor's optimistic assessment. My personal bet is that it'll require a lot more time to get that fighter assembly line up and running again. And ramping back up to full production will take even longer—at least another twelve to eighteen months."

Barbeau frowned. "Why so long? If it's a question of money to buy and build more machinery and tools, we should be able to slide an emergency appropriation through Congress toot-sweet."

"It's not just a question of replacing damaged or destroyed equipment," Admiral Firestone explained. The chairman of the Joint Chiefs looked haggard. Like Rauch, he'd been up all night trying to piece together more details about the attack. "In some ways, the horrible losses we took among the plant's workforce are our biggest problem. The F-35 is an incredibly complex aircraft. Key components are manufactured by contractors in nine separate countries. Assembling each of these fifth-generation warplanes requires tens of thousands of hours of work by highly trained and skilled technicians."

Rauch nodded, grateful for the other man's intercession. The president had an unfortunate habit of focusing her anger narrowly, trying to fix the blame for everything that went wrong on a single person or cause. Anything that spread her irritation more widely was welcome. "From the numbers I've seen, well over a thousand people inside that plant were killed or very badly wounded. That represents close to half of those who were on shift. Training that many replacement workers is going to require a tremendous investment of money *and* time." He shrugged his shoulders. "And that's not counting the skilled people we're likely to lose going forward."

"Lose how?" Barbeau demanded.

"We can expect a pretty big fraction of the workforce to walk away," Rauch pointed out delicately. "Yes, these are good-paying jobs and the people there are deeply patriotic, but all the money and patriotism in the world aren't enough to compensate for the risk of being killed or maimed in another attack by these terrorists and their war robots and missiles."

"Then we guarantee their damn safety!" Barbeau snapped. "Tell the commander down at Fort Hood that I want heavy armor from the First Cavalry Division deployed north. And have him rustle up some of the air defense units he's got in the garrison there, too."

With obvious reluctance, Admiral Firestone shook his head. "Ringing what's left of that aircraft plant with troops and tanks might reassure the surviving workers, Madam President. But it won't solve our bigger problem. We can't possibly station Army units around every defense industry facility and military base that might be a target for these terrorists." He spread his hands apologetically. "We just don't have enough troops or equipment. We'd have to reintroduce the draft and radically increase the size of the armed forces even to come close."

"I am getting awfully tired of you people telling me what *cannot* be done," Barbeau said. There was a dangerous edge to her voice. "I think it's high time I started hearing some solutions to this mess . . . instead of more pathetic hand-wringing."

Rauch winced. There was no doubt about it: She was sharpening up her ax. Hastily, he said, "There are two other F-35 assembly plants. One in Italy, at Cameri, northeast of Turin. The Italians are turning out F-35As and the short-takeoff/vertical-landing F-35B version for themselves and for the Dutch. And the Japanese have a plant at Nagoya to assemble their own fighters. As a stopgap measure, we could ask for the delivery of some of the production from those two factories to our own Air Force squadrons."

"No," Barbeau said flatly. She scowled. "It's bad enough that so many of my shortsighted predecessors farmed out so much of the production work for F-35 components to foreign companies. But I'll be damned if I let the American people see me going begging, hat in hand, to the Europeans or the Japanese for a few spare fighters . . . fighters that we designed in the first place!"

For "people" read "voters," Rauch thought wearily. Somehow, the realization that the president would prefer to see the Air Force go without its own chosen top-of-the-line multirole fighter longer than necessary rather than risk her standing in the polls didn't come as much of a shock as it should have.

"What I want from you *gentlemen* is a plan to track down and destroy these terrorists before they hit us again," Barbeau said acidly. "So far, everything I've heard here today is the equivalent of rearranging the deck chairs on the goddamn *Titanic*."

In for a penny, in for a date with the headsman, Rauch decided. A few months ago he would have seen the prospect of being fired—especially for telling the truth—as the worst thing that could happen to him. Now that possibility was beginning to look considerably more appealing. "Unfortunately, we're no closer to being able to formulate a plan to do so than we were yesterday, Madam President," he said, not bothering to sugarcoat his assessment. "None of the police roadblocks thrown up around the Dallas/Fort Worth Metroplex have stopped any plausible suspects so far. Nor were any unidentified aircraft picked up on radar either before *or* after the attack. Without a better idea of just who we're fighting and how they're evading our efforts to find them, we are inherently limited to purely reactive and defensive measures."

To his surprise, the chairman of the Joint Chiefs nodded in agreement. "Dr. Rauch is quite correct. While these enemy war machines, the CIDs, are obviously dangerous opponents, I'm confident that our conventional forces—our armor, artillery, and airpower—could whip them in a stand-up fight. But to do that, we have to pin this enemy force down in a fixed location . . . or at least intercept them on the way to or from a target."

"The very fact that these damned machines keep appearing and disappearing so quickly and easily is a key piece of the evidence pointing straight at that bastard Martindale . . . or at least his Scion mercenaries," Barbeau said through clenched teeth. "Thanks to those money-grubbing cretins at Sky Masters, they're the ones with advanced stealth aircraft, remember?"

Rauch saw no point in replying to that. Even if the president's fixation on Scion was justified—and it was, at least as long as you only focused on known technological capabilities without considering rational motives—it didn't get them any closer to figuring out a way to find their elusive enemies.

Luke Cohen couldn't stay quiet any longer. In a cracked and urgent voice, the White House chief of staff broke into the discussion. "For God's sake, this is all just spinning our wheels here. We have to *do* something. And fast. Or we're screwed."

Barbeau whipped around on him. "Oh, by all means, do feel free to give us the benefit of your wisdom, Luke," she said with venom dripping from every word. "I'm sure Dr. Rauch, the admiral, and I have all missed some perfectly obvious course of action."

Helplessly, the lanky New Yorker shrugged. "I'm not saying that, Madam President. But we both know you pay me mostly to keep tabs on politics, right?"

"Go on," Barbeau said coldly. Her mantra had

always been: Policy followed politics. If you were operating from a position of political strength, you could eventually shove through any piece of policy, whether good or bad. But if you were seen as politically damaged, you were finished . . . because Washington was a town that revered popularity and despised weakness.

"Look, what happened at Barksdale was terrible. But from a political point of view, seeing the bad guys walk all over us again down in Fort Worth is going to be a lot worse," Cohen said rapidly. "We got a little bump in our numbers at first. But the polls are already starting to skew fast in Farrell's direction—even with the press playing it pretty much our way."

"And why is that?" Barbeau demanded.

Cohen swallowed hard. "I put in a call to our campaign people before this meeting," he said. "They've been running focus groups with swing voters, the folks who've been hard for either campaign to lock down so far. But the longer this situation drags on, the more they see you as weak and even afraid . . . hiding out here while the bad guys whack our troops and factories at will."

Despite himself, Rauch felt a new surge of respect—both for Cohen for daring to tell his boss something so unpalatable . . . and for the focus-group swing voters who seemed to have figured her out.

Obviously pushed to the brink and beyond, Barbeau slammed a hand down on the table. "Enough!" She fought to regain her composure for a moment and then went on in a quieter voice: "You want action, Luke? You want a big show for the low-information bozos who're buying Farrell's BS? Well, so be it." She pushed back her chair and stood up. "In fact, this is something I should have done a long, long time ago."

Icily, she turned toward Firestone. "Admiral, my understanding is that the Insurrection Act of 1807, as amended in 2006, gives me the authority to deploy the armed forces for the purpose of maintaining law and order on U.S. soil."

Warily, he nodded. "That's correct, Madam President. At least, in certain limited conditions. For example, you can use regular troops or the National Guard to restore order and enforce the law in cases where a terrorist attack makes it impossible for the local authorities to handle the situation."

"Very well," Barbeau continued coolly. "As your commander in chief, I now declare those conditions met."

"Yes, ma'am," Firestone agreed slowly. "That is your prerogative." He seemed to sit up straighter in his chair. "May I ask what you intend?"

Listening while she outlined her plan, Rauch felt his eyes widening in disbelief.

IRON WOLF FORCE, IN THE MOUNTAINS NORTH OF BATTLE MOUNTAIN, NEVADA
Later that day

Stripped down to shorts and a T-shirt, Brad McLanahan lounged in the pilot's seat of the

XCV-62 Ranger. Even with the shade provided by
the camouflage netting draped across the aircraft,
the cockpit was uncomfortably hot, though more
bake oven than steam room, because the air was
so dry. Since they couldn't afford to run down the
fuel cells in their auxiliary power unit, cooling the
aircraft's interior spaces was out of the question.
They were operating on minimal power, drawing just enough juice to run the Ranger's secure
satellite communications system and some of its
computers.

He finished reading the message from his father, typed in a short acknowledgment, and hit
the send button on his MFD. It beeped once,
confirming that his reply had been uploaded and
transmitted to Poland.

Besides trying to figure out how Gryzlov's
mercenaries were hiding their movements, the
older McLanahan had been riding herd on a
group of Scion weapons analysts and cybernetics experts. They were tasked with preparing
quick-and-dirty intelligence assessments of Russia's new combat robots. Knowing how important any information—even of the sketchiest and
most speculative kind—was to the Iron Wolf CID
team lying in wait outside Sky Masters, his father
had been sending them updates on a regular basis.

Brad sat back, thinking through the tactical
implications of what he'd just read. Like the rest,
this most recent assessment was long on guesswork and short on confirmed facts, but it was all
they were going to get . . . at least until he and
the others met Gryzlov's machines in combat.

Figuring out tactics that would give them a shot at winning that first fight was a daunting task. Sure, the battle simulations they'd run through back in the spring gave him a rough framework to work with. But those sims had been purely hypothetical. And tactics and maneuvers that worked well in the computer could fail miserably against actual machines whose speed, agility, armament, armor, and sensors varied significantly from their imaginary digital counterparts.

Ideally, they'd have been able to run through a new series of mock battles—this time against computer-generated enemies whose capabilities more closely matched those of the real-world Russian robots. He snorted. *Yeah, Brad,* he told himself, *and in an ideal world you also wouldn't be sitting sweating your ass off in this cockpit under the high desert sun.* In the here and now, they were just going to have to suck it up and do their best.

"Wolf Two to Base Camp." Major Nadia Rozek's voice sounded in his headset. *"I am just outside the perimeter. Request clearance to enter."*

"Copy that, Wolf Two," Ian Schofield replied. *"You're clear to come on in."*

Smiling, Brad yanked off his headset and climbed down through the open hatch. This was what he'd been waiting for. Since relieving him shortly before dawn, Nadia had been on watch at their observation post overlooking Battle Mountain. Now it was Whack's turn to keep an eye on things . . . which meant this was another of those all-too-brief periods when he and Nadia were both in the same place at the same time.

Outside the Ranger, the air was even hotter.

Schofield and Mike Knapp, a former sergeant in the U.S. Special Forces, had already rolled back a section of the camouflage net. Sunlight, impossibly bright after the dim cockpit, streamed through the opening.

Brad squinted against the brightness. A patch of the clear blue sky and sagebrush-strewn high desert plateau outside shimmered strangely, almost as though it were some kind of weird, moving mirage.

And then, accompanied by a faint *whir* from its actuators and hydraulics, Nadia's Cybernetic Infantry Device was inside the shelter—apparently appearing out of thin air when she shut down the robot's chameleon camouflage system. The two Iron Wolf recon troopers dragged the net back into place behind her.

The CID came to a halt and crouched down. A hatch on its back cycled open. Nadia swung herself out and dropped easily to the ground. After a quick, friendly nod to the other two men, she walked over to Brad with a big, heartfelt smile. She was already unzipping her black flight suit, revealing a skintight gray tank top and khaki shorts. Brad's pulse quickened a bit. For the moment, she looked completely cool and comfortable. And, as always, incredibly alluring . . . at least to anyone who wasn't scared of her physical prowess and intellect.

Climate control was one of the few good things about pulling a duty stint inside one of the robots here, he decided. If you had to isolate yourself from the human race inside a machine for an eight-hour stretch, at least you got air conditioning.

"Nice to see you, Major Rozek," he said gravely. "Anything new down in the world?"

With equal gravity, she shook her head. "Nothing, Captain McLanahan. Even the FBI agents sound bored to death when they report to each other over the radio."

Brad couldn't help wincing. "Yeah, well, after learning what happened in Fort Worth last night, I'm starting to think the Russians aren't coming after all." Though he tried hard to keep his tone level, he knew she would be able to sense both his frustration and the nagging fear that he'd taken them on a wild-goose chase. Certainly, every day that passed without any sign of hostile activity made that seem more and more likely. "This stake-out operation could be a total waste of our time and resources."

"I do not agree." Nadia looked thoughtful. "Your reasoning was sound. And while our enemies clearly are not operating on the precise time-table you predicted, they still have every incentive to destroy Sky Masters. Unless they wreck the Battle Mountain labs and production facilities, all the Russians will have done is make the high-tech weapons Dr. Noble and his colleagues are developing even more valuable to your country—and to mine."

"Maybe so." He frowned. "But I can't help worrying about the fact that Gryzlov really seems to enjoy putting together complicated plans—the kind where he sets up a series of moves he can use to achieve very different objectives . . . depending on how we react."

"Like the fork tactic in chess," Nadia said slowly. "Where a single piece threatens two or more defending chessmen simultaneously. So that no matter how the defender reacts, he will lose something of value."

Brad nodded.

"You may be right," she agreed. "But even then, the defender still has a choice of which piece to sacrifice. And since Sky Masters and the weapons and equipment it provides are beyond price, we *must* protect it. Gryzlov is not a fool. He knows this as well as we do. Which is why you should consider the possibility that last night's attack may have been at least partly intended to draw our force away from this place."

"You're assuming that the Russians know we're here," Brad objected.

Nadia shrugged. "As I said, Gryzlov is not a fool. He, more than anyone in the world, understands and fears what the Iron Wolf Squadron can do. You must look at this from his perspective: If we *are* deployed to protect Battle Mountain, he loses nothing by trying to lure us out of position. And if our CIDs are *not* here after all, he loses nothing by attacking other, equally vulnerable targets first."

"Frankly, trying to think like that son of a bitch makes my head spin."

She smiled wryly. "Well, you Americans do talk a lot about 'wheels within wheels.'"

Almost against his will, Brad laughed. "Okay, I

give. We won't slink away with our tail between our legs just yet. We'll hold here awhile longer . . . at least until our water runs out."

Nadia raised an eyebrow suggestively. "And in the meantime?" Silent laughter danced in her big blue-gray eyes. "How *do* you suggest that we occupy our time, Captain McLanahan?"

"Well, I—" Brad felt a lot hotter all of a sudden. To his chagrin, he noticed Schofield and Knapp studiously pretending to look in every other direction but at them. *Oh, just great*, he thought. Nadia had decided to push all his buttons right when they were about as likely to get some much-desired privacy as a guy who never bought a ticket was to win the lottery.

Then, suddenly, an idea percolated into his overheated mind. He almost gave it away by grinning back at her, but instead he forced himself to look virtuous—donning the air of eager, dedicated determination used by junior officers everywhere to bullshit their superiors. He carefully avoided Mike Knapp's eyes. Sergeants always seemed immune to the "look."

Brad nodded toward the Ranger. "Well, Major, I suggest we work some more on tactics we might use against the enemy's robots."

For just a moment, Nadia seemed surprised. "Really?"

"Yes, ma'am," he said forthrightly. "Scion intelligence just sent us another classified assessment on those Russian machines. And I really think you should read it for yourself."

"I see," she said carefully. "Yes, perhaps I should."

Brad saw one corner of her mouth twitch upward. He maintained his own devoutly serious expression with the greatest difficulty.

Once they were alone in the Ranger's cramped and darkened cockpit, Nadia squirmed across and took the copilot's seat. She offered him a challenging stare. "Do you actually believe that incredibly transparent ploy of yours fooled any of our comrades?"

"What ploy?" Brad asked innocently. *Two can play the "wheels within wheels" game*, he thought. He reached over and brought one of her multifunction displays to life. The intelligence summary his father had sent flashed on-screen. "I was being perfectly serious. The Scion team really did send a new report. And you do really need to see it."

"Oh," she said, sounding surprised. With a tiny frown, she leaned forward and started reading. Her eyes narrowed in concentration. "So your father's analysts are now confident that these Russian robots are smaller than our own CIDs?"

He nodded. "Yeah. But not by much." Careful scrutiny of every piece of footage shot during the Barksdale attack had finally given Scion's photo interpreters enough separate data points to peg the height of Gryzlov's machines at a little over ten feet. "What that size differential means in terms of relative combat endurance, speed, and agility is anyone's guess, though."

"They seemed fast enough in those videos," Nadia pointed out.

"That they did," Brad agreed. "Our guys clocked at least one moving at more than seventy klicks per hour. But what's not clear is how long the Russians can operate at speeds that high without draining their batteries and fuel cells."

"It would be safest to assume their endurance is comparable to ours," she said seriously. "Since they are using technology they stole from us, that is probable." Her mouth turned down. "Which means we must count on these enemy robots being our equal in every important respect."

Brad shook his head. "Not quite, fortunately." He pointed to the conclusions listed at the bottom of the report. "For example, the Russians don't seem to have our rail-gun technology. At least not yet."

"For that I am grateful," Nadia said somberly.

Brad nodded. No armor in the world could stand up to a rail-gun slug if it scored a solid hit. On the other hand, he wasn't sure how effective their own CID rail guns would be in a dogfight with other combat robots. The weapons were deadly against tracked and wheeled armored vehicles, aircraft, and fixed fortifications . . . but their relatively slow rate of fire might be a handicap against smaller, far more agile machines. "The better news is that the Russians don't have anything comparable to our thermal and chameleon camouflage systems. Which gives us a decent shot at pulling off an ambush under the right circumstances."

"Gryzlov's pilots could have stripped their camouflage equipment off before launching that attack," Nadia said stubbornly. "As we did before the raid on Perun's Aerie."

"My dad's team has pretty much ruled out that

possibility," Brad said. "Our people studied highly magnified imagery of the different sections of those robots. And they couldn't find any attachment points for additional gear or systems."

"So then, how best do we fight them?" she asked. Her eyes were half closed in thought.

"Well, see, that's where I think the two of us should thoroughly explore different tactical concepts," Brad said, unable to stop himself from grinning. "While we have some private time together, I mean."

Nadia must have heard the eager note in his voice, because she looked up quickly with a lopsided smile of her own. "And just which tactic do you propose we explore first?" she challenged.

"Close-quarters action," he said cheerfully. "Really close." And with that, he leaned over, picked her up, and put her down on his lap. Her lips parted and he kissed her deeply.

Coming up for air, he asked, "So what's your view on my plan, Major Rozek?"

She smiled back at him. "Well," she said reflectively, "I don't know how well it would work against the Russians, but I like the way this is shaping up so far."

CHAPTER 26

IRON WOLF OBSERVATION POST, NORTH OF BATTLE MOUNTAIN, NEVADA
The next morning

Cushioned by his CID's haptic interface and feeling blessedly cool, Brad McLanahan let his mind roam free. He grinned to himself, remembering the expression of surprise and eagerness on Nadia's face when he'd pulled her onto his lap yesterday afternoon. Idly, he wondered if they would ever be able to look at the Ranger's cockpit in quite the same way again. In the background of his pleasant daydream, routine reports from the robot's array of passive sensors scrolled through his drifting consciousness—but there was nothing among them that he needed to handle.

And then, suddenly, there was.

Sky Masters ARGUS-Five signal characteristics have changed, the CID's computer told him. *The radar has switched to tracking mode.*

He jolted back to full awareness. Switching

from general air-search mode to tracking mode meant the advanced radar sited at McLanahan Industrial Airport had detected one or more airborne contacts that its human operators wanted more data on and fast. Whatever had spooked them must still be too far away to register on his thermal or visual sensors.

Without waiting any longer, Brad readied his rail gun. It whined shrilly, powering up. If there were Russian cruise missiles heading this way, he would do his best to engage and destroy as many of them as he could. He opened a secure channel to their base camp. "Wolf One to Two and Three. Believe unidentified airborne contacts inbound. I am preparing to engage if necessary."

It sure would be nice to be able to open a data link to that Sky Masters radar, he thought pensively. Seeing what the ARGUS-Five was "seeing" would probably answer a lot of his questions. But doing that risked giving away his position to the FBI or the Russians if either of them had hacked their way inside the Battle Mountain facility's electronic systems. As it was, he was operating half blind—forced to rely entirely on whatever he could pick up with his passive sensors.

With the CID's camouflage systems running, Brad was effectively invisible to visual or IR detection. And his current position hidden in among a jumble of solid boulders and brush offered good protection against radar. Unfortunately, activating his own radar would light him up just as surely as if he sent his robot dancing downslope and into town.

"*Wolf One, this is Two. Whack and I are suiting up,*" Nadia radioed back. "*We should be operational in less than two minutes. We will move toward your position at top speed.*"

"Copy that, Wolf Two," he replied.

Dozens of icons suddenly blinked into existence across his tactical display. *Forty-plus IR contacts inbound from the east at low altitude,* the computer reported. *Range twenty-plus miles, but closing. Four contacts at six-hundred-plus knots. Remainder at one hundred fifty knots. Negative identification at this range.*

Brad frowned. What the hell was this? One thing was sure. Whatever was happening *wasn't* a Kh-35 cruise-missile attack. Those four fast movers out there were flying faster than the Russian-designed missile's maximum speed. And no missile ever made stayed in the air at just a hundred and fifty knots. Were Gryzlov's mercenaries using a mix of high-speed and slower drones?

Through his neural link, he ordered the CID computer to lock on to the four fast targets. He swung the rail gun up, following the aiming cues on his display. There, off to the east, low above a wide stretch of flat, almost featureless valley, red boxes silhouetted four green, brightly glowing shapes streaking toward Battle Mountain at more than six hundred knots. At that altitude, with all the heat haze, his thermal sensors still couldn't get a firm fix on their identity and type. His finger settled gently on the trigger.

And then two separate wavelengths of microwaves washed across his robot. The neural link translated the sensations into something like the gentle flick of a dog's tail across his face coupled with fingernails scratching across his head. *Warning, warning*, his computer reported. *New active airborne radars detected. One evaluated as AN/APY-2 Pulse Doppler E-3 Sentry AWACS. The other is a Ku-band agile active frequency signal. Probable identification is an E-8 JSTARS AN/APY-7. No detection threat from the AWACS. JSTARS detection probability currently very low.* New icons appeared on his display, showing the two radar planes orbiting sixty miles east—*behind* the wave of oncoming bogeys.

Swallowing hard, Brad took his finger off the rail-gun trigger. There was no way the Russians had a Sentry-type airborne warning and control aircraft aloft over the United States. Nor could they have a JSTARS, a Joint Surveillance and Attack Radar System plane of their own. The powerful phased-array radar aboard a JSTARS aircraft, a modified 707-300 designated as an E-8C by the Air Force, could scan up to nineteen thousand square miles of terrain—hunting for hostile ground vehicles and low-flying helicopters.

He keyed his com link to the other CIDs. "Wolf Two and Three. Hold your position! Repeat, hold your position! Do *not* move out from under the camouflage. These aren't Gryzlov's guys. They're ours."

Christ, Brad thought, *I almost fired on friendly aircraft.* The realization of how close he'd come to killing fellow Americans was chilling. He fought to control a sudden tremor in his hands.

Quickly, he ducked lower, further reducing his CID's radar signature. That JSTARS plane high overhead was designed to pinpoint enemy tanks, artillery pieces, and armored personnel carriers. It should have a hard time spotting something as relatively small as his robot, especially if he stayed still. But there was no percentage in taking any unnecessary risks. After the massacre at Barksdale Air Force Base and then the attack on that F-35 assembly plant at Fort Worth, his fellow countrymen were probably just about as trigger-happy as he obviously was.

The four fast movers he'd locked on to earlier, now clearly identifiable as F-16C Falcon fighters, screamed low past his mountaintop position, spreading out across the airport and the neighboring Sky Masters complex. A cloud of white-hot magnesium flares trailed behind them, mixed with thousands of tiny Mylar strips of antiradar chaff. He frowned. Why in God's name were those pilots taking precautions against a missile launch? Did they think the Russian combat robots were already here?

The F-16s peeled away in fighting pairs, going vertical. Sunlight glinted off their clear bubble canopies as they climbed higher—soaring fifteen thousand feet in twenty seconds. Once at high altitude, all four fighters leveled off and started orbiting in slower, lazy circles.

Behind them came an aerial armada. Flanked by shark-nosed AH-64D Apache helicopter gunships, a cloud of dozens of UH-60 Black Hawk troop carriers and large CH-47 Chinook heavy-lift helicopters clattered low across the desert floor . . . heading straight toward the airport and Sky Masters. From his hiding place high on the slopes above them, Brad watched, transfixed by what he was seeing. This had to be the better part of a whole U.S. Army combat aviation brigade, he realized. It was an enormous show of force, especially at a time when the army, like all the other U.S. armed services, was already stretched thin.

Accelerating suddenly, the Apache gunships broke away from the main formation. They fanned out, swinging wide to take up station at various points several hundred feet above the Sky Masters complex. Bristling with Hellfire antitank missiles, Hydra 70 2.75-inch, fin-stabilized rockets, and 30mm M230 chain guns, they hovered threateningly in midair.

Once the gunships were in position, the slower Black Hawks swooped lower still—flaring in to land on the airport tarmac and in the wide-open spaces between hangars, office buildings, machine shops, labs, and warehouses. Squads of heavily armed infantry poured out of the grounded helicopters. They were accompanied by groups of journalists and camera crews wearing body armor and helmets over their civilian clothes.

Directed by their officers and NCOs, the soldiers deployed fast across the compound. Some units fanned out to surround key buildings. Others stormed inside with their weapons at the ready.

Grim-faced now, Brad reopened his radio link. "Wolf One to Two and Three. You know how we thought this situation was already pretty bad?

Well, believe it or not, but I'm pretty sure things just got a heck of a lot worse."

OFFICE OF JASON RICHTER, SKY MASTERS AEROSPACE, INC.
That same time

With his hands clasped firmly on the back of his head, Hunter Noble walked into the spacious corner office. At the sight of the two other top Sky Masters executives already inside, he stopped dead in his tracks. "Oh, man," he said over his shoulder to the soldier behind him. "This is so unfair. You *cannot* sling me in here with these hard-core lifers. I'm too damned pretty. They'll carve me up."

The middle-aged noncom only rolled his eyes. "Very funny, Doc. I'll make sure I catch your comedy club act the next time I'm in town. Now get over with those people and keep your mouth shut until the colonel gets here." He prodded Boomer ahead with the barrel of his M4 carbine.

"Tough crowd today." Boomer sighed. He moved farther into the room to join the others.

Jason Richter, a retired U.S. Army colonel and now the company's chief executive officer, sat in one of the chairs in front of his own desk. The tall, athletic man's face was carefully blank, empty of all obvious emotion. Sky Masters' president, Dr. Helen Kaddiri, sat next to him. She wore an expensive dark gray business suit. Her very long black hair was tied back in an intricate knot at the nape of her neck. Her dark eyes were watchful. They were being held at gunpoint by four stern-looking young soldiers wearing the ivy-leaf shoulder sleeve patch of the 4th Infantry Division from Fort Carson, Colorado.

The troops stiffened to attention when a trim, efficient-looking lieutenant colonel strode into the office. The name tape on his uniform read STRANG. "At ease," he snapped. He motioned for them to lower their weapons. "These people aren't going to cause us any trouble." He turned to Boomer and the others. "Are you?"

"We have no intention of violently resisting this illegal action, if that's what you mean, Colonel," Helen Kaddiri said carefully. Her lips were pursed. "But I fully expect our lawyers to file a series of vigorous legal challenges to this unwarranted trespass on our property. And to our arrests."

The Army officer shook his head with a fractional smile. "You're not under arrest, Dr. Kaddiri. At least not yet." He shrugged his shoulders. "For the moment, the president, acting under the authority granted her by the Insurrection Act, is placing you and your entire staff in protective custody—pending further investigation. The same goes for your corporate facilities and other property."

"On what grounds?" Richter asked bluntly.

"Suspicion of possible involvement in terrorist actions against the United States," the other man replied.

Boomer snorted. "That's crazy! Barbeau's lost her freaking mind."

"I am not here to debate the issue," the lieutenant colonel said, without batting an eye. "Now, with respect, I need you all on your feet and moving outside." He checked his watch. "I've got helicopters waiting to fly you and all of your people out of here."

Gracefully, Helen Kaddiri rose from her chair, a movement echoed by Jason Richter. "Fly us to where, exactly?"

"A safe location."

Richter shook his head. "You're making a very big mistake, Colonel Strang."

TEMPORARY DETENTION CAMP, MOUNTAIN HOME AIR FORCE BASE, NEAR MOUNTAIN HOME, IDAHO
A short time later

Squinting against the sun, Hunter Noble jumped down out of the just-landed Black Hawk helicopter and strolled out from under its still-turning rotors. He straightened up and turned to take a look around. At least twenty UH-60 troop carriers sat on a wide concrete apron. Armed Air Force and Army security personnel surrounded clumps of frightened Sky Masters employees as they scrambled out of the helicopters—shepherding them toward a tent city being erected by sweating soldiers next to the base motor pool. Coils of razor wire surrounded the half-finished camp.

"What do you think, Boomer?" Jason Richter

asked quietly. The Sky Masters CEO had come up beside him.

Boomer shook his head, staring at the flat, featureless landscape beyond the base perimeter. It stretched on for miles and miles and more damned miles. Far off, along the northern horizon, he could barely make out a few darker shapes that might be foothills of the Sawtooth Range, an offshoot of the Rocky Mountains.

"I think this sucks," he said finally. He jerked a thumb toward the tents. "I bet there's no cable. And no pool. Hell, I bet even the Wi-Fi is as slow as molasses." He folded his arms stubbornly. "In fact, I'm so pissed off that I am seriously considering voting against our good pal Stacy Anne come November."

Richter gave him a pained half smile. "That's not quite what I meant, but I take your point."

"Okay, more seriously, I'd say we're being herded into an out-and-out prison camp. Not that I ever bought the good Colonel Strang's line of bullshit about putting us in 'protective custody.'"

"Yeah, that was a pretty glaring bit of fiction," Richter agreed. "I suppose calling it that serves Barbeau's legal purposes, but the ground truth is pretty clear. We're in the bag—at least until the courts or Congress can spring us." His eyes narrowed. "But I don't think locking us up is all she's got in mind."

Puzzled, Boomer turned to stare at him. "Say again?"

Richter nodded toward a group of camouflaged shapes visible in the distance beyond the flight line. "Take a good, hard look over there and tell me what you see."

Boomer did as he was asked. His own eyes widened in surprise. "Jesus, those are M1A1 Abrams tanks. And Bradley fighting vehicles."

"And Paladin self-propelled howitzers," Richter pointed out quietly.

"What the hell's up with that?" Boomer wondered. He grimaced. "Except for you and maybe me, nobody else at Sky Masters is exactly he-man fighting material. The Army doesn't need that kind of heavy-duty firepower to keep a bunch of engineers and scientists in line."

"No, they don't," Richter agreed. His jaw tightened. "Which is why I'm reasonably sure we're more than just prisoners or detainees."

"Then what are we?"

"We're bait, Dr. Noble," the other man said. "A nice, shiny lure dangling on a hook."

CHAPTER 27

**IRON WOLF FORCE, NORTH OF
BATTLE MOUNTAIN**
A short time later

Brad watched the four F-16s break off their patrol orbit over Battle Mountain and fly back east. The fighters passed high over another wave of helicopters ferrying in more troops and equipment from the 4th Infantry Division. He frowned. There were already at least two full infantry battalions deployed around the Sky Masters facility and they were fortifying their perimeter—digging fighting positions and building sandbagged bunkers for machine guns, mortars, and Javelin antitank missile teams. This was no snatch-and-grab raid. This was a full-fledged military occupation.

JSTARS and AWACS radars are no longer active, his computer reported suddenly. *Aircraft departing this area of operations.*

The two icons representing the E-3 Sentry and E-8C JSTARS were heading north-northeast, in the same direction taken by the Black Hawks and Chinook helicopters packed full of Sky Masters scientists and engineers, he realized. Which meant they were probably bound for Mountain Home Air Force Base, too. The southern Idaho base was the only military installation the helicopters could have had the fuel to reach.

What Barbeau thought she was accomplishing with this sudden show of force was a puzzle for later, Brad decided. Right now, the JSTARS departure gave him the freedom to head back to the Ranger without the risk of being detected. "Wolf One to Wolf Two and Three," he radioed. "Returning to base."

"*Two copies*," he heard Nadia say. "*I will pass the word to Captain Schofield.*"

"Thanks, Two," Brad said. "And look, we need to talk to Poland as soon as I get back, with full audio and visuals . . . if we can swing it."

"*Three here,*" Whack Macomber said gruffly over the same circuit. "*We've already reported the situation to Martindale and Wilk. What more do you want? Besides, a direct audio and video connection via satellite is gonna suck up a shitload of bandwidth . . . which means the chances of detection go up exponentially.*"

Patiently, Brad replied. "Understood, Whack. But I think it's worth the risk now that President Barbeau just tipped the chessboard over. We're going to have to rethink our whole strategy. Text-messaging back and forth isn't going to cut it."

Over the radio link, Macomber grunted. "*I suppose not, Wolf One. I'll pass your request on to our high-and-mighty lords and masters. Three out.*"

A private communication from Nadia on a separate channel caught Brad's eye. *"Fear not. I will make sure the grumpy colonel is persuasive.* Kocham cię. *I love you."*

Thirty minutes later, safely concealed under their camouflage netting, he opened his CID's hatch and climbed down out of the robot.

Nadia and Macomber were waiting at the foot of the XCV-62's ladder. "We're all set," the colonel said tersely. "Warsaw and Powidz are standing by. And I've patched the signal through to the troop compartment so that Schofield and his guys can listen in. Hope you knights of the air and metal don't mind, but I figured our poor, unfortunate ground pounders deserve to know how fucked we are in real time."

Brad hid a smile. In his heart, Whack remained the quintessential foot soldier. Though he was a superb CID pilot, the big, powerfully built man retained the attitudes he'd developed over years of service in the U.S. Air Force Special Operations Command. Machines were either transport, fire support, or trouble for the real fighters—the tough men and women who closed with and destroyed the enemy up close and personal . . . without anything more than bullet-resistant body armor to protect them. To this day, Macomber never really felt comfortable inside one of the robots. "When those fricking computers get done meshing with my nervous system," he'd sometimes growl, "who's really in charge? Me? Or the damn machine?"

Instead, Brad contented himself with politely gesturing Nadia and Macomber up the ladder ahead of him.

With three people crammed inside, it was hard to move around inside the Ranger's small cockpit without banging into each other or some of the instruments. Brad settled into his pilot's seat, carefully ignoring the way Nadia's face flushed a little when she remembered the last time they'd been here together. Bright-eyed now, she clambered back into the right-hand copilot's position while the colonel squeezed himself awkwardly into the narrow space behind their seats.

Brad tapped his MFD, bringing it live. Nadia did the same with hers. A menu appeared on their screens: SECURE SATELLITE COM LINK READY.

"Initiate satellite link," he ordered quietly.

"*Link open*," the Ranger's computer said in a calm female voice.

Instantly, three familiar faces looked back at them from the big displays. Martindale and Piotr Wilk were in the Polish president's private office in Warsaw. Patrick McLanahan, recognizable through his LEAF's clear visor, was at the squadron HQ in Powidz. Because their signals were being simultaneously encrypted and then bounced through several different communications satellites, the images were grainy and slightly distorted. There was also a slight, but noticeable lag between video and audio, which added a herkyjerky quality to the conversation.

"Go ahead, Wolf Force," Wilk said with a nod. "What is your situation?"

"Not great," Brad admitted. "Barbeau is still flying troops in to Battle Mountain. Plus, I saw a number of civilians arriving in the most recent helicopter lift."

"Those are probably intelligence and technical experts," his father said. "My guess is DARPA, the CIA, and a whole alphabet soup of federal agencies are starting to dig around in Sky Masters' databases. This is the chance they've been waiting for to ferret out a lot of the company's closely held secrets—especially those concerning the construction of Cybernetic Infantry Devices."

"Which they won't find," Brad pointed out. "From what Boomer told me, all of the CID-related components and data are safely hidden away somewhere off-site."

Martindale frowned. "Unfortunately, that only ends up making Sky Masters appear even more guilty. It will look as though the company anticipated this forceful U.S. government reaction and took preemptive measures to hide its involvement in the recent attacks."

"Swell," Whack muttered. "So our guys do the right thing and it ends up feeding Barbeau's paranoid fantasies."

"That's about the size of it, Colonel," the Scion chief said. His mouth twisted into a frown. "Although now that the Russians have their own war robots, it might have been better if Richter and his people had simply left their CID files and materials in place for the U.S. authorities to find."

Brad saw his father stir. "Not in a million years," Patrick McLanahan said flatly. "The federal government has a shitty record of keeping really valuable secrets. Anything the CIA, DARPA, and the rest scooped up would end up in Gryzlov's hands sooner or later. And right now, our rail guns and camouflage gear may be the only edge Brad and the other CID pilots have over the Russians."

Piotr Wilk shrugged. "The point is moot, anyway. Short of extracting the location of those secrets from its Sky Masters prisoners, your government will not be able to lay its hands on this technology. At the moment, our first priority must be to decide our next course of action." He looked straight into the screen. "Captain McLanahan, can you fly your aircraft out of there without being detected?"

"Negative, Mr. President. At least not yet," Brad said without hesitation. "The JSTARS and AWACS planes are gone, but there's still way too much U.S. military air and vehicle traffic in this area. Even if we could dodge radar detection, the Ranger's not invisible. Some pilot or ground observer would be bound to spot us using the good old-fashioned Mark I eyeball. And then we'd be toast. Between the F-15E Strike Eagles based at Mountain Home and the Aggressor Squadron F-16s flying out of Nellis, we wouldn't make it a hundred miles before being either shot down or forced to land."

He glanced outside the cockpit windows. Even

seen through their camo net, the daytime sky was still blindingly bright. "That all changes once the sun goes down. As soon as it gets seriously dark, we should be able to make a break for it . . . but not a moment sooner."

"Which leaves open the question of precisely where you should go, once it is safe to fly," Wilk said slowly.

Martindale sighed. "That's an easily answered question, Piotr. We have to pull Brad's team out of the U.S. and get them back to Poland. At this point, it's the only sensible option we've got left." He looked tired. "Risking an Iron Wolf unit to protect Sky Masters and its secrets from Gryzlov's mercenaries was a reasonable gamble. But now Barbeau has preempted that mission. Staying longer in the States, even if I manage to scratch up a new covert base out in the boonies somewhere, only increases the odds of someone spotting our CIDs or the Ranger stealth aircraft . . . either of which would confirm all of Stacy Anne's darker suspicions about our involvement in this mess."

Brad opened his mouth to object, but Nadia beat him to it.

"On the contrary, Mr. Martindale, we are *not* simply going to run home like frightened children," the Polish Special Forces officer said with unconcealed disgust. She eyed Martindale's static-distorted image with cold contempt. "The situation here remains the same. Without the combat power represented by our Iron Wolf machines, your country is effectively defenseless against Gryzlov's forces."

"The major's right," Macomber said. "There's no way those Russians are going to let themselves get sucked into a stand-up fight where our Army and Air Force can use tanks and precision-guided missiles against their robots. They're not that dumb."

"Ambushes happen, Colonel," Martindale retorted. "You, of all people, ought to know that."

Brad held his breath, waiting for Whack to explode in fury. Hitting him like that with a reminder of the disaster that killed Charlie Turlock was a very low blow.

But the big man surprised him by staying calm, on the outside at least. "The Russian cyberwar complex at Perun's Aerie was a point-source objective," Macomber said frostily. "It was also a setup from the beginning. And the bad guys knew right where we had to be in order to destroy it. But Gryzlov's mercs aren't limited the way we were. They can go after any of dozens of potential targets. There's no way the Pentagon can assign enough forces to picket all of them."

Exasperated, Martindale threw up his hands. "That's precisely my point! You can't fight someone you can't find! If the combined air and ground forces of the United States, the FBI, the state, and local police can't track down these Russians, what in God's name do you really think one Iron Wolf aircraft, three CIDs, and a handful of dismounted scouts can accomplish?"

"Drawing a bead on the enemy is the core of this problem," Patrick McLanahan agreed quietly. "We know that Gryzlov has figured out ways to move his robots and missiles around the U.S. without anyone seeing them. Once we crack the code on *how* he's doing that, we ought to be able to find his mercenaries . . . and finish them. But we can't do that unless we already have a team in reasonable striking range."

"Which rules out trying to fight this war from Poland," Brad argued. "Our base at Powidz is a minimum of twenty hours' flying time from just about anywhere in the States—unless, of course, we decide to just barrel straight through the North American Air Defense Identification Zone—"

"Which would break the record on stupid," Macomber interjected. "Especially with Barbeau's itchy finger on the trigger."

"Yeah, no kidding," Brad said, glancing over his shoulder with a quick, humorless smile. He faced the screen again. "So there's the dilemma. We can't hope to hit Gryzlov's forces without actionable intelligence. But by the time we could get back here from Poland, any intelligence we picked up would be stone-cold . . . and almost certainly useless."

After a moment's thought, Wilk nodded, accepting his reasoning. He turned to Martindale. "Brad and the others are right, Kevin. As are you about the dangers involved. But we have no other acceptable choice. Unless we can prove that the Russians are behind these raids, using their own war machines, Poland is in grave danger. The longer our enemies operate unchecked and undetected on American soil, the higher the risk that President Barbeau will publicly accuse Scion and the Iron Wolf Squadron of these crimes—and demand that I hand you over for punishment." He sighed. "Refusing such an ultimatum would risk a disastrous war against both of the world's strongest powers. But accepting it would effectively disarm us in the face of Gryzlov's next inevitable aggression."

"Our American friends would call that a no-win scenario," Nadia murmured.

Wilk nodded again. "Which is why we cannot back away now. We must press on. No other honorable course is available to us."

Brad saw his father smile approvingly. "'He either fears his fate too much, or his deserts are small, who dares not put it to the touch, to win or lose it all!'" the older McLanahan quoted.

"Very nice," Martindale said sourly. "Of course, the guy who said that, the Earl of Montrose, fought for the Royalists during the English Civil War. And they lost." Then, plainly almost against his will, he shrugged his shoulders. "But at least *I* know when to stick to my guns and when to yield . . . at least to my friends. I'll see what the Scion operatives I have positioned in the U.S. can rig up." He looked at Brad. "What do you need most?"

"Besides a secure landing site somewhere within a thousand miles or so?" Brad ticked off their requirements on his fingers. "Jet fuel, first. By the time we land, our tanks will be almost dry. And more drinking water. We're down to about two or three days' supply."

Martindale stared at him. "You're almost out of water?" He scowled. "Are you telling me that you and I would have been having pretty much this *same* conversation in a couple of days . . . no matter what boneheaded move Stacy Anne Barbeau pulled?"

"I try never to deal in hypotheticals," Brad said virtuously. Out of the corner of his eye, he caught Nadia stifling a grin.

"I bet you don't," Martindale snorted. He shook his head. "Never mind. Stay put. Stay hidden. I'll get in touch as soon as I have somewhere else for you to fly."

THE KREMLIN, MOSCOW
That same time

The big-screen monitor in Gennadiy Gryzlov's office was tuned to one of the more excitable American cable news networks. Though their reports were often inaccurate and hopelessly one-sided, its anchors did an excellent job of conveying the conventional wisdom of Washington, D.C.'s political and chattering classes. And in some ways, that was more useful than anything else to Russia's youthful, aggressive leader. For the pure raw facts, he had the reports of his own intelligence services. But facts were of limited use when you were trying to understand an enemy's mind-set and psychology.

Images of attack helicopters and troop carriers clattering low over a rugged desert landscape filled the screen. They were replaced by action shots of American soldiers fanning out at the double across a large complex of office buildings, windowless machine shops and engineering labs, and huge aircraft hangars. More pictures followed, showing troops marching crowds of bewildered-looking civilians out of those same buildings at gunpoint. "While it appears there was no significant resistance at the Sky Masters Nevada facility, anonymous White House and Pentagon sources credit this success both to President Barbeau's decision to use overwhelming force and to the complete surprise achieved by the brave soldiers and airmen involved in this high-stakes raid. Administration spokesmen stress that although no formal charges have yet been filed, federal law enforcement and intelligence officials are only at the beginning stages of this important investigation. In the meantime, the suspects seized by troops from the Fourth Infantry Division remain locked up in what is termed 'protective custody' at an undisclosed location—"

Shaking his head in delighted disbelief, Gryzlov muted the monitor. He turned to Vladimir Kurakin with an exultant, predatory grin. "Astounding, eh? That overstuffed, oversexed cow Barbeau has done half our work for us! And she's done it out of sheer malice and seemingly invincible stupidity."

Cautiously, Kurakin nodded. "Yes, Mr. President."

Gryzlov heard the hesitation in his voice. "You still think we should have attacked Sky Masters ourselves?" he asked. "Using your KVMs and Annenkov's cruise missiles?"

The other man shrugged. "I only worry that its scientists and engineers are still alive."

"And dead men and women build no robots and stealth aircraft?" Gryzlov suggested dryly. He shook his head. "Don't fret, Vladimir. Trust me, what Barbeau has done today will inflict almost as much damage on Sky Masters in the end." He waved a hand at the screen, which was still showing video clips of heavily armed infantrymen kicking open doors and searching buildings. "Pictures like that are racing around the world at light speed. After this humiliation, where will Sky Masters find the money to design, test, and manufacture its expensive weapons and aircraft? Who will risk investing in such a company? For that matter, how many of those scientists and engineers you worry about will dare to go back to work at Battle Mountain once they're released?"

He wagged a finger in mock reproof at Kurakin. "No, hitting Sky Masters with your robots and missiles would have put Russian fingerprints all over this operation. After all, why would the Iron Wolf mercenaries attack their own arms supplier? Not even Martindale is that crazy. Instead, we've managed to trick the Americans into waging war against their own best and brightest weapons designers! What could possibly be more satisfying?"

"I see," Kurakin said slowly. "I'm afraid that I have been focused more on operational considerations than on the broader political implications. You have my apologies, Mr. President."

With a self-satisfied air, Gryzlov waved his

apology away. "No matter. You were right to let me look after the big picture." He looked more carefully at the other man, noting his pained expression. "You still look as though you're chewing lemons, Vladimir. What's eating at you now?"

"Only the thought that this might be the best possible moment to withdraw our forces," Kurakin suggested with some reluctance. "They've been lucky so far. They can't be lucky forever. But if we bring them home now, before any of our men are caught or killed, the Americans will be left with no one to blame but Poland's own mercenaries."

Briefly taken aback, Gryzlov stared at him for a long, unpleasant moment. Nothing in the other man's military record had suggested he was a coward or a fool—or even one of those overcautious commanders afraid to spend men's lives to achieve a decisive victory. For an instant, he considered explaining his deeper political and strategic objectives in launching this clandestine war. But then he thought better of the impulse. Looked at rationally, Kurakin and his men and machines were nothing more than tools, weapons to be expended as he saw fit. And one did not waste time explaining higher strategy to a rifle bullet or a bomb.

Instead, he snorted. "You give our enemies too much credibility. Right now, the Americans are too busy chasing their own tails to think straight. So this is the time to close in and hit them even harder. Russia has years of humiliating defeats to avenge, Kurakin. This is not the moment to turn tail and run!"

CHAPTER 28

WOLF SIX-TWO, IN THE BIGHORN NATIONAL FOREST, WYOMING
Later that night

The XCV-62 Ranger cleared the crest of a steep forested ridge with a couple of hundred feet to spare and dove down the other side, almost skimming the treetops at just over two hundred knots. Another ridge soared black against the night sky just half a mile away. Immediately the navigation cues on Brad McLanahan's HUD spiked right.

He banked sharply, rolling to follow the cues, and then leveled out. The Iron Wolf aircraft arrowed northeast down a narrow valley between the two higher elevations, following the trace of a gravel road. Ahead, the road dropped toward a dry streambed marked "Fool Creek" on their maps.

"We're less than two minutes out," Nadia said from her copilot's position. She had her eyes firmly fixed on her navigation display. "We have a green light from the Scion ground crew."

"Copy that," Brad said tightly. "Hang tight." He leaned forward and tapped a key that activated preset landing commands he'd entered earlier. Hydraulics whined as the Ranger configured itself for another very short, rough-field landing. Control surfaces opened to their maximum extent, providing extra lift they sorely needed. This high up in the Wyoming mountains, the air was already pretty thin. "Gear coming down."

There were a series of muffled thumps below the cockpit. A slowly blinking icon on his HUD turned solid green. Their ride got bumpier right away as drag increased. "Gear down and locked."

They crossed the dry streambed and climbed again, following the ground as it rose toward the even-steeper wooded slopes of Dry Fork East. Brad fed in a little more power to keep up his airspeed.

Not far ahead, he saw a smaller dirt road branch off to the northwest. It paralleled another winding stream, this one full of water flowing downhill toward a distant junction with a larger river. Its name appeared as a small tag on his HUD. "Nice," he muttered ironically. "What a great omen."

He banked left, turning to follow this new road. On their right, Dry Fork East towered another couple of thousand feet above them—a dark mass studded with fir and spruce trees and large bare patches of loose weathered scree. The ground below the ridge was mostly open, a mixture of high alpine grassland and sagebrush.

"An omen? Why?" Nadia asked, sounding puzzled.

"Because we're going to be landing upslope from a tributary of the Little Bighorn River," Brad explained. "And just about fifty miles north of here is where George Armstrong Custer and the Seventh Cavalry stumbled into a bazillion Sioux warriors and wound up dead."

"Then if we are going to play cowboys and Indians, I want to be the Indians," Nadia said with a laugh.

He felt a tight smile flash across his face.

Through his HUD, he could see a small campsite just off the dirt road, which was little more than a trail now. Besides a couple of tents, there were two parked trucks, both with U.S. Forest Service markings. One was a fuel tanker.

The touch-down point the Ranger's computer had selected blinked insistently in his HUD. He pushed a button on his stick, confirming the selection. It went solid, slashing across the trail no more than a few hundred feet beyond the trucks. Not much more than a thousand feet up the trail, a stand of tall fir trees blocked the far end of their projected landing zone.

Brad felt his mouth go dry. He was going to have to set this crate down right on the mark. There was no room for error.

Now! He pulled the throttles way back.

The Ranger slid down out of the sky. They dropped onto the rough, brush-strewn ground, bounced back up in the air a few feet, and then came back down with a jolt that rattled his teeth and threw him forward against his straps. The trees ahead loomed ever bigger as the plane roared along the gently inclined slope. Brad reversed thrust as much as he dared. He couldn't risk skidding out of control if they hit loose gravel or dirt.

They slewed to a halt just a few yards short of the first trees.

Relieved, Brad fed a little power to the engines and swung the Iron Wolf aircraft through a tight, 180-degree. The Scion fuel tanker disguised as a Forest Service vehicle was already rolling toward them. He and Nadia got busy, working with practiced teamwork to shut down their avionics and engines.

Whack Macomber's deep voice rumbled through his headset. "Where the hell did those guys come from?" Like the others strapped in the crowded troop compartment, he was watching a video feed from the Ranger's cameras.

"Apparently, there's a Scion sleeper cell operating out of a hangar at the Casper-Natrona County International Airport," Brad told him. "Since we would have been a mite conspicuous landing there, this was the next best alternative."

"Martindale's got a fricking sleeper cell in Wyoming?" Macomber snorted. "Guarding against what? Another Indian uprising?"

"I don't know, Whack," Brad said. He winked at Nadia. "I didn't ask—"

"And he didn't tell," the big man said in disgust. "Yeah, I get it. Seriously, though, kid, sometimes that guy creeps me out."

Silently, Brad agreed. Part of him understood the former president's habit of secrecy and his dogged determination to compartmentalize key information—keeping as much as possible about his various covert activities on a strictly need-to-know basis. Throughout recent history, loose lips had sunk far too many important American covert operations. But there were also moments—far too many for Brad's comfort—when it seemed that Martindale kept most of his secrets simply because he craved the feeling of being the smartest man in any room.

On the other hand, Brad reminded himself, the Scion chief had again come through in the clutch. This new improvised airstrip might be a long way from anywhere that mattered, but at least they were still in the U.S.—ready to act if only they could figure where Gryzlov's forces were hiding . . . or where they planned to strike next.

RKU FLIGHT OPERATIONS CENTER, NEAR MOAB, UTAH
That same time

Colonel Yuri Annenkov and his copilot, Major Konstantin Uspensky, entered the missile assembly area at the back of the crowded warehouse. Technicians were busy at several of the workbenches, systematically disassembling a new shipment of desktop computers.

Annenkov found Andrej Filippov, his ordnance specialist, hunched over an open Kh-35 fuselage. The short, balding man didn't look up at their approach. He was completely focused on carefully plugging a new component into place in the section of the missile dedicated to its navigation systems. The two pilots waited quietly until he finished, stripped off his latex gloves, and turned to face them.

"We're just configuring the weapons for your next attack," Filippov said. Gently, he patted the cruise missile. "Moscow approved my request for the use of our new jam-resistant GLONASS receivers on this mission."

Annenkov snorted. "I imagine General Kurakin was not particularly happy about that." Upgrading their Kh-35s to receive in-flight course corrections from the GLONASS constellation of space-based navigation satellites measurably increased the odds of someone figuring out that Russia itself was hip-deep in this clandestine war.

"Not especially," Filippov agreed. He shrugged. "But it was either that or find a different set of targets. There was simply no other way to resolve the technical and tactical problems involved."

Annenkov and Uspenksy both nodded. To avoid detection on launch for this mission, their missiles would have to fly a long, complicated, and extremely precise path through very rough terrain. Relying on inertial navigation was a nonstarter. Too many seemingly small errors would inevitably accumulate throughout the flight—resulting not only in a large number of catastrophic crashes en route, but also in the likelihood of any surviving missiles missing their targets by dozens of meters.

"Even with satellite navigation, how many hits

can we really count on scoring?" Uspensky asked bluntly. "By now the Americans must have GPS and GLONASS jammers deployed around all of their key military installations. Once they realize there are missiles inbound, they'll bring those jammers online fast."

"We will probably lose a few weapons to jamming-induced guidance errors," Filippov said, with equal frankness. "Our upgraded GLONASS receivers are untested under combat conditions. On the other hand, the American jamming systems are almost equally untested. Without more data, the range of likely outcomes is difficult to accurately calculate." For a few seconds, his narrow face took on a detached expression, almost as though he were running through a number of different scenarios in his mind. Then he shrugged his shoulders again. "Reaction time is the key, Major. Deny the enemy time to act and you greatly reduce the effectiveness of his defenses. So long as you achieve tactical surprise, your missiles will kill many Americans."

10TH SPECIAL FORCES GROUP A-TEAM, IN THE SHEEP CREEK RANGE, NORTH OF BATTLE MOUNTAIN, NEVADA
The next day

Team Sergeant Casimir "Kaz" Ostrowski stopped for a short breather. He squatted down on his haunches and took a quick sip from his Camelbak

hydration pack. Out of long habit, he glanced left
and right, checking the alignment of the other
Green Berets in this extended skirmish line. They
were all separated by at least fifteen meters.

He frowned. Dispersed this way as they scouted
across the high desert plateau, their twelve-man
A-team was screwed if it made contact with an enemy force—but it was also the only formation that
would let them cover their assigned patrol territory in any vaguely reasonable amount of time.

When he'd asked what they were looking for,
their CO, Captain Michaelson, had at first only
said, "Robots, Kaz. Big nasty killer robots."

Pressed for more details, the captain had finally
relented far enough to tell him that some of the
4th Infantry Division's brass had already had the
jitters—imagining the hell that would break loose
if the same kind of war machines that blew the
shit out of Barksdale and that Fort Worth aircraft
factory came charging down off the high ground
above Battle Mountain to attack them. Then,
earlier today, when a helicopter pilot ferrying
supplies into the occupied Sky Masters complex
reported that she'd thought she'd seen "something
weird" up in the Sheep Creek Range . . . well, that
was enough to set off alarms all the way back to
Fort Carson.

And so here Ostrowski and his teammates
were, humping across a desiccated landscape apparently empty of everything but sand, sagebrush,
rocks, and more rocks. They had been sweeping
north, following the line of a little-used trail, for
hours. It hadn't taken them very long to figure

out that the Army helicopter pilot's "something weird" was nothing more than a heap of boulders that maybe looked a little like a giant man lying prone—if, that is, you squinted at it with one eye closed and had a really overactive imagination.

Unfortunately, Captain Michaelson had decided that today he was a firm believer in turning a dumb-ass, rookie pilot's mistake into a useful training and endurance exercise. Which was why they were doggedly plodding deeper into this sunbaked wasteland instead of turning back to hitch a nice, relaxing helo ride out.

"Getting old, Kaz?" the captain's voice crackled through his tactical headset. "No offense, Team Sergeant, but you seem a little slow today."

"Just conserving my energy, Captain," Ostrowski retorted. "Because I figure I could be stuck carrying your exhausted, eager-beaver ass back down this mother of a big, damn hill come sundown."

Michaelson laughed. "I appreciate you keeping my welfare in mind, Sergeant."

Yeah, I bet you do, Ostrowski thought sardonically. In most respects, the captain was a top-notch officer, but he had his weaknesses. Showing off for the battalion commander was one of them. Hence his decision to volunteer them for this grueling recon so that he could demonstrate his team's physical fitness and devotion to duty.

Scowling, the Green Beret noncom got back to his feet and started on again, pushing his pace a little to catch up with the others. He was working his way through a withered clump of sagebrush about fifty meters east of the trail they were following when he spotted his very own "something weird."

Ostrowski swung out of line to check it out. He frowned. What he saw looked a little like someone had taken a huge divot out of the hard-packed sand with a golf club . . . only it would have to be a golf club that was maybe twice the height of a man. Almost immediately he spotted another, almost identical, big divot in the ground, offset from the other, and nearly two meters farther on. More of them were visible in a line heading away to the north. Turning around, he could see the same strange marks vanishing off into the distance.

Jesus, the sergeant thought, feeling suddenly cold despite the scorching heat. Those were tracks. But they weren't tracks made by any kind of animal he'd ever encountered. Whatever had made them moved on two legs . . . and based on the stride length, the fucking thing had to be at least twelve feet tall.

"Captain!" Ostrowski said urgently into his throat mike. "Remember those big nasty killer robots you were talking about? Well, sir . . . I think we've found them!"

CHAPTER 29

**STRATEGIC COMMAND BUNKER,
WRIGHT-PATTERSON AIR FORCE BASE**
A short time later

Stacy Anne Barbeau finished skimming the hurriedly transmitted report and tossed it across the conference table to Rauch. "So I was right all along," she snapped. "Take a look at *that*! A special forces patrol found tracks made by those goddamned CIDs a few miles north of Battle Mountain. And not only that, they just spotted the marks left by the landing gear of some type of unknown aircraft along a dirt road in the same general area. Their best guess is that it took off sometime in the last twenty-four hours." She raised a triumphant eyebrow. "And yet, not a single civilian or military radar anywhere around picked up so much as a blip from this mystery plane. Which makes it what, Dr. Rauch?"

He sighed. "A stealth aircraft, Madam President."

"A stealth aircraft," she confirmed coldly. She saw his reluctance to draw the obvious conclusion from the facts and shook her head in frustration. What more did her national security adviser need to convince him that her instincts were on target? A signed confession from Kevin Martindale and Piotr Wilk, for Christ's sake? "Open your eyes, Ed. Those Scion and Iron Wolf mercenaries are the ones who've been kicking the crap out of us. Why else would they have a stealth plane and their killing machines secretly based near Sky Masters?"

"I've read Captain Michaelson's report myself," Rauch said with a frown. "And so far, what he and his men have found doesn't seem like much. Just a spot where one relatively small aircraft might have been concealed under camouflage netting— plus what appear to be tracks made by one or more Cybernetic Infantry Devices coming and going from an outcrop overlooking the Battle Mountain area." He shook his head. "But without finding evidence of stockpiles of ammunition, missiles, food, water, and fuel, I don't see how this site could possibly have served as a genuine base of operations for the attacks we've experienced."

Barbeau took a deep breath, willing herself not to lose control over her temper. In the current political climate, with rumors circulating that her administration was in complete disarray, she could not afford to unceremoniously dump Rauch, no matter how tempting it was. "Then our scouts will just have to keep on looking, *won't* they?" she said scathingly.

"There's another consideration," he said. "If Scion is behind these raids against us, why didn't those CIDs attack our soldiers when they overran the Sky Masters complex?"

For an otherwise intelligent man, Ed Rauch could be astonishingly stupid, she decided. "Because they were overmatched and they knew it," she said flatly. "Those robots may be tough, but they're not invincible. Put enough firepower against them and they'll go down." Inwardly, she felt vindicated. Except for poor, panicky Luke Cohen, her other advisers had thought she was overreacting when she'd ordered the use of overwhelming military force at Battle Mountain. Well, if she'd listened to the naysayers and relied on sending in a few FBI agents and the local sheriffs to serve a federal warrant, yesterday's operation against Sky Masters would have had a very different ending.

One of her aides rapped gingerly on the conference room door. "Excuse me, Madam President, but Admiral Caldwell has arrived. Security has cleared him through and he's on his way down from the surface now."

Caldwell? The head of the National Security Agency was coming here in person? What was so important that he couldn't report by secure link? Barbeau turned a questioning look toward Rauch.

"The admiral's people have finished the investigation you ordered into the circumstances surrounding Lieutenant General McLanahan's death over Poland three years ago," he said.

"So what did they learn?" she demanded. "Did

we kill him? Is that lunatic son of a bitch finally dead?"

Rauch looked back at her without any discernible expression. "I don't know," he said coolly. "Given the strict need-to-know classification level on that entire . . . *episode* . . . the admiral thought it wiser to brief you first in person rather than risk disseminating the information through regular channels."

Barbeau didn't much like his tone. Learning that she'd ordered American F-35 pilots flying covertly over Poland to shoot down the last survivors of a desperate Iron Wolf bombing mission hadn't gone over very well with her military and national security team. Imposing a total security blackout on the incident was the only way she'd kept word of what she'd done from leaking to the press and the broader American public. She bristled at the memory of their unspoken but evident disgust and disapproval. Presidents were paid to make the hard decisions, not to pussyfoot around. What was she supposed to have done with Gryzlov screaming his head off for vengeance? Allowed Patrick McLanahan and Kevin Martindale to drag her into an unwinnable war against the Russians? No, she thought resolutely. It had been far better to order the deaths of a handful of hired Iron Wolf mercenaries than to risk countless innocent American military and civilian lives.

Fortunately for Rauch, Admiral Caldwell arrived before she had quite decided whether or not to ream him out for his implied criticism. He hurried in, accompanied only by a single aide carrying a laptop case.

As was his custom, the NSA chief wore a nondescript civilian suit. Anyone seeing him out of context would have taken him for a typical dull, middle-grade government bureaucrat. But Caldwell's almost painfully ordinary features hid a brain of remarkable power. Since being detailed to the National Security Agency as a young naval officer, he'd risen steadily through its ranks on pure merit and technical brilliance. He was also completely apolitical, seemingly intent only on the business of providing the best possible intelligence to whichever administration was in power.

Barbeau nodded toward an empty chair. "Take a seat, Admiral," she snapped, unable to conceal the strain she felt. With an effort, she regained enough composure to offer him the semblance of a smile. "I gather you have some news for me?"

"Yes, ma'am." Caldwell opened the laptop computer his aide handed him. "To answer the question you posed, my analysts dug through every piece of information we had concerning the two XF-111 SuperVarks our F-35 pilots shot down—everything from satellite photos of the crash sites to recordings of radar imagery and radio intercepts."

"And?"

The head of the NSA pulled up an audio file on the laptop. "The key piece of intelligence proved to be this last-second radio call from the last Iron Wolf aircraft just before we fired on it." He tapped a key, opening the file.

"Unknown aircraft, this is McLanahan!" a horrified voice yelled, through a rush of static. *"Break off your attack! We're friendlies! Repeat, friendlies!"* The recording broke off abruptly.

Perplexed, Barbeau looked at the admiral. "I don't get it," she said. "How is that supposed to be important? We already knew McLanahan was aboard that plane when it went down. The real question is whether or not he survived the crash, isn't it?"

Caldwell shook his head. "Your premise is incorrect, Madam President," he said quietly.

"Don't screw around with me, Admiral," she warned.

"Comparing voiceprints of this radio intercept with previous recordings proves that retired lieutenant general McLanahan was *not* the pilot of that XF-111," he explained. "It was his son, Bradley James McLanahan."

"Oh shit," Rauch muttered.

Barbeau felt the blood drain from her face. Patrick McLanahan was alive after all. "Oh, my God," she stammered. "We killed his son. And now that psychotic bastard is coming for me. Just like he promised he would." She swung toward her stunned national security adviser. "That's what this is all about, Dr. Rauch! Revenge. Pure and simple. McLanahan wants me dead. And after his goons missed me at Barksdale, he's going for the next best thing—wrecking my reelection campaign."

She felt cold dread ripple down her spine.

"Christ, once I'm out of office, I'll be a sitting duck. No matter how many Secret Service agents I have protecting me, those goddamned CIDs of his will cut right through them to rip my heart out!"

"But General McLanahan's son is not dead," Caldwell interjected. "Intelligence reports from a number of sources confirm that he's on active service with the Iron Wolf Squadron."

Angrily, Barbeau waved the reminder aside. "It doesn't matter. The McLanahan kid is a total nonentity," she said forcefully. "His father's the real threat. He's always been able to round up rabid followers to execute his insane plans." She shuddered. "Now we know what's going on. Martindale and the Poles must have lost their control over him. He's gone completely rogue."

Rauch swallowed hard. "That is possible," he admitted. "In fact, there is one more piece of data that may lend credibility to your hypothesis."

"Go on," she rapped out through gritted teeth.

"The two F-35 pilots who carried out your orders over Poland were present at Barksdale Air Force Base when it was attacked," he said slowly.

"So?"

"They were both killed," Rauch said.

She stared back at him, feeling suddenly nauseous. "Get out," she snarled. She jerked her head toward the door, including Admiral Caldwell and his aide in the gesture. "All of you! Get out now!"

For a long, terrible moment after they left, Stacy Anne Barbeau sat in silence, staring into nothingness with a worn and haggard face.

OUTSIDE AT&T STADIUM,
ARLINGTON, TEXAS
That same time

With the monumental glass, steel, concrete, and fabric structure of Cowboys Stadium rising nearly three hundred feet in the air behind him, John Dalton Farrell strode confidently down the walk toward the spot where his campaign staff had set up microphones and a podium. Reporters jostled each other in front of the podium—angling for the best shot at gaining his recognition during what was described as a brief "press availability."

Through the massive stadium's open retractable roof, he could hear the muffled rattle of drums and the keening sound of bagpipes as the last honor guards and bands marched slowly away. Apart from the normal sounds of traffic, an almost unearthly hush had fallen across the area. It was almost as if every one of the hundred thousand people who had attended this public memorial service were holding their breath in a spontaneous moment of silence for the National Guard troops, law enforcement officers, and F-35 assembly-plant workers who'd been killed at Fort Worth.

Farrell stepped up to the microphones and nodded gravely to the assembled members of the media. "I won't be making a prepared statement this afternoon, ladies and gentlemen," he told them quietly. He nodded back toward the stadium. "The memory of the brave men and women we've honored here today deserves more than canned political double-talk." The crow's-feet around his eyes deepened as he shot them a quick, self-mocking smile. "Which means I'll do my level best to just give you straight answers to your questions."

That opened the floodgates.

Over the braying din of dozens of journalists all trying to talk over each other, he picked out one, Lyndy Vance. His staff had privately dubbed the blond-haired CNN reporter "the Inquisitor." They called her that because she always seemed more interested in accusing Farrell of some heinous personal fault or failing than in seeking genuine insight into what he proposed to do as president.

"Go ahead, Lyndy," he said into the mike, pointing at her.

Behind the crowd of reporters, Farrell saw Sara Patel and Mike Dowell cringe. He hid a grin. They could never understand why he so often gave this particular reporter the first crack at him. He'd tried explaining that it was precisely because her questions were so obviously biased that it worked in his favor—especially with undecided voters—but they couldn't seem to wrap their heads around the concept. In his view, most people had enough common sense to pick up on someone playing "gotcha" games instead of asking fair questions.

True to form, Lyndy Vance didn't disappoint him. "What was the real point of this big public show of yours, Governor?" she said, with cool cynicism dripping from every syllable. "Was it part of a deliberate political strategy to make President Barbeau look bad?"

"Not at all, Ms. Vance," Farrell replied calmly. "Yes, the president was invited to be here today. But I think every decent American understands that she has more than enough on her plate in dealing with this crisis. She is our commander in chief. And given the security risks, it would have been foolish for her to further expose herself to a possible terrorist attack."

While every word of what he said was literally true, he could almost hear his long-departed mother's voice telling him, *You are so going to hell for that fib, John D.* No matter how you sliced it, and intentionally or not, his public appearances contrasted sharply with Stacy Anne Barbeau's continuing refusal to leave the heavily guarded confines of Wright-Patterson. Her terse, tough-sounding televised speeches full of vague promises to "destroy those attacking our beloved country" were no substitute for a demonstrated willingness to share some of the risks run by others.

"You're seriously claiming you won't criticize President Barbeau for not showing up at this memorial service?" another journalist chimed in with open disbelief.

"That's not a claim. That's a cold hard fact," Farrell shot back. "I will never criticize the president for acting sensibly." He showed his teeth in a slashing half smile. "Especially since she does it so rarely." Then he shrugged. "I will, however, gladly dispute some of those *anonymous* administration sources y'all are so fond of quoting."

"About what?" a third reporter asked.

"Poland is *not* our enemy," he said bluntly. "Nor are the brave men and women volunteers in the Iron Wolf Squadron who are risking their lives to help the Poles and their allies stay free and independent. And whoever is out there telling you anything different is full of bull crap."

Lyndy Vance raised a skeptical eyebrow. "Then just who *is* responsible for these terrorist attacks?" she asked. "Metal men from Mars?"

"Since the president refuses to provide me with access to national security intelligence, all I can do is speculate, Lyndy," Farrell said. "But if I were a betting man . . . and I *am* a betting man, my money would be on Russia. And on its cruel, vengeful, and often reckless leader—Gennadiy Gryzlov."

That drew pained stares from many of the press. Most of them had long since stopped writing glowing stories about Russia's "charismatic" young president, but that didn't mean they liked hearing what they considered to be worn-out, old-fashioned Cold War–style boilerplate served up this way.

One of them sneered openly. "Oh, come on, Governor. You're clutching at straws. Every military expert we talk to comes back to one basic fact: The Poles and the mercenaries they pay are the only ones in the world with the kind of war robots that have been attacking us."

"Last time I looked, there were a whole lot

of *experts* around who've turned out to be dead wrong about a whole lot of things," Farrell said dryly. "For example, I earned a couple of billion dollars pumping oil and gas the *experts* said didn't exist." As he'd expected, that little sally drew some laughs—albeit reluctant ones. "Weapons aren't magic talismans," he went on more seriously. "They're devices made by men, pure and simple. And what one man can make, another man can copy . . . or steal."

In the short silence that followed, Farrell saw Sara Patel tap her watch significantly. He nodded slightly and turned back to the reporters. "Now, folks, you're going to have to excuse me, but I need to wrap this up."

Undeterred, Lyndy Vance got in one more shot. "Is the line your staff has been feeding us about your plans for the next couple of weeks accurate? Or just spin?"

"What line is that?" Farrell asked.

"That you're going to take some time off the campaign trail? That you're retreating to that Texas Hill Country ranch of yours for the next few days?"

Farrell nodded. "It is, Lyndy." He shrugged. "Partly, it's to avoid further politicizing events in this time of crisis. As you've noted, it might be unfair of me to continue campaigning while the president is locked away, unable to respond in kind. But mostly, I want some quiet time to put serious meat-and-bone on the reform proposals I'm taking to the American people in November." He shrugged. "My office in Austin will keep you apprised of any important developments, but I don't expect there'll be much to report before the convention. Now, after that, you'd best buckle up tight . . . because I plan to hit the campaign trail running hard. There's no prize for second place when it comes to the White House, and I am in this race to *win*."

CHAPTER 30

That same time

Regan Air Flight 281 cruised south-southwest through the night sky over Southern California. Flying from its base near Moab, Utah, it approached the border near Mexicali, Mexico.

"Regan Air 281, radar services terminated, contact Tijuana TCA on one-one-niner-point-five, good evening," the Southern California terminal radar controller radioed.

"One-one-niner-point-five, Regan 281, roger, good evening," the pilot aboard Regan Air 281 responded.

The controller checked the flight information strip—the flight was dead on time and course, as reported to U.S. Customs and Border Protection. He picked up his telephone and hit a button for a direct-connection line.

"CBP, Lewis," came the reply a moment later,

all for the benefit of the digital memory system recording every word.

"Simpson at SOCAL," the controller replied. "Regan 281 is right on time and course as filed."

"Copy. Thanks," and the line went dead. Both operators were off the hook now—Regan Air 281 had flown exactly where and when they said it was going to, and now it was Mexico's target. Big, privately chartered cargo jets flying into Mexico at night always raised suspicion, but Regan Air had filed all the proper paperwork with both the U.S. and Mexican authorities and had been exactly where and when they said they'd be, and they were flying *away* from the United States, so it was someone else's concern now. It was again suspicious that the flight didn't land at the first port of entry airport at General Rodríguez International in Tijuana: Flights inbound to the U.S. were required to land at the first port of entry after crossing the border and were not permitted to fly past any port of entry. But Mexico was different . . . and again, it was not CBP's or SOCAL's problem any longer.

Regan Air 281 proceeded south to San Felipe and its small nontowered regional airport for its customs inspection. The small detachment of *federales* and the *commandante* had already been paid off, so when they boarded the plane they relaxed in the 737's six-seat passenger section forward of the walled-off cargo section, enjoyed a cigar and some *cerveza*, waited the proper amount of time that it might take for an inspection, then departed.

After refueling, the plane took off and headed back west-northwest, and then entered a timing orbit ninety kilometers from San Felipe—on the other side of the ten-thousand-foot-high *Picacho del Diablo*, Devil's Peak.

Inside the cockpit, Colonel Yuri Annenkov and Major Konstantin Uspensky were busy working their way through their attack checklist. "All four rotary launchers are online," Uspensky said from the copilot's seat. "They are linked to our attack computer."

Annenkov nodded. "Activate the Kh-35 satellite navigation systems."

While waiting for his copilot to finish this step, he took a quick look outside. Off to their left, the whole horizon glowed. From this altitude, even more than 250 kilometers away, the lights of Los Angeles, San Diego, Tijuana, Mexicali, and the sprawling suburbs around those cities were visible—reflecting off the clouds above coastal mountain ranges. Ahead, the sky blazed with stars strewn across an infinite ink-black backdrop. Distant blinking lights showed dozens of other commercial airliners and cargo jets crisscrossing the region at high altitude. The view truly was quite beautiful, he thought dispassionately. And, to the naked eye, enormously peaceful.

But those appearances were deceiving. Far off to the northwest, well out to sea, the Americans had one of their Navy E-2C Hawkeye airborne early-warning planes flying a fuel-saving racetrack pattern while they conducted training for naval reserve crews and kept watch over the approaches to this area. The Russians had detected emissions from its APS-145 radar several minutes ago. Fortunately, their converted 737 was still just outside the range where the American AEW aircraft could spot the Kh-35 cruise missiles they were about to launch. If one of the Navy's newer E-2D Advanced Hawkeyes had been on station instead, Annenkov knew they would have had to abort this attack. But those planes, with their incredibly powerful solid-state AN/APY-9 radars, were fully committed to service aboard active-duty U.S. Navy aircraft carriers. And fortunately, for the purposes of tonight's mission, the carriers were far out to sea—safe from attack.

The Russian pilot shrugged. True, getting the chance to sink an American aircraft carrier would have been glorious. On the other hand, if a carrier had been in port, this whole mission would have been effectively impossible in the first place. It was the old military conundrum. High-value targets generally had the strongest possible defenses. In an all-out war, that might not have mattered. But their job tonight was to strike from concealment and live to fight another day.

"Sixteen green lights," Uspensky said, sounding satisfied. "The cross-check with our own navigation fix is complete. All missiles are receiving accurate GLONASS navigation data."

"Very good," Annenkov said, equally pleased. He trusted Filippov's missile assembly work, but he was also well aware that every new piece of technology added yet another potential failure source to any weapon. Computer cards could malfunction for any number of reasons. Power and data cables might be jarred loose by sloppy handling or even turbulence. And without functioning satellite navigation capability, there was no way any of their missiles could possibly come near tonight's chosen targets—let alone actually score hits.

"Downloading preprogrammed attack profiles to the missiles," his copilot continued, selecting new virtual controls on his display. More lights went green. "Attack profiles are locked in."

Annenkov double-checked him on his own display and then ordered, "Bring all missiles to full readiness."

Uspensky entered more commands into his computer. He checked off reports as they flowed across his display. "All Kh-35 radar altimeters are online. Their turbofans are ready. All self-destruct systems are live."

"Confirm that every Gran-KE radar seeker is disabled," the colonel said.

His copilot brought up another schematic. "All radar homers are disabled," he reported.

That was perhaps the most ironic part of this planned attack, Annenkov realized. Since their Kh-35s were originally intended for use against enemy ships on the high seas, their advanced on-board radar seekers were optimized for use against moving targets. Which meant relying on them tonight would have been a catastrophic mistake.

Satisfied that their cruise missiles were ready for launch, Annenkov and Uspensky donned their oxygen masks, depressurized the 737's cargo deck, and transferred flight control to their attack computer.

Turbulence increased as the jet's forward door slid open. Launcher after launcher rolled into position at the door, ejected its four attached missiles and swung away to make room for the next in line. In less than a minute, all sixteen Kh-35s were safely away—plummeting silently through the night sky toward San Diego.

Ten to fifteen meters above the ground, each cruise missile's motor ignited. One after another, the sixteen missiles streaked northwest above scattered clumps of cholla and yucca cactus, desert saltbush, and other scrub brush. Their speed increased steadily, peaking at close to a thousand kilometers an hour.

Thirteen minutes after launch, the Kh-35s screamed low over the low hills southwest of Tijuana. Panicked by the shrill howl of their jet engines, thousands of migratory shorebirds fluttered upward in dense, swirling clouds. One Russian cruise missile raced straight through a maddened flock of gulls, slammed head-on into several of the screeching seabirds, and wobbled out the other side in a cloud of scorched feathers and pulverized bits of flesh. Its turbofan motor fell silent. Shedding shattered pieces of fan blades, it veered away just above the surface of the water and then exploded in midair. The rest of the Kh-35s flew on, still heading northwest.

Thirty seconds later, the first missile executed

a sharp course change, turning almost due east. One by one, the remaining fourteen followed suit. They were paralleling the rugged slopes of the San Miguel Mountains, which straddled the U.S.-Mexico border. Nearing a narrow canyon between two sheer masses of high ground, the Kh-35s jinked again—swinging back a little to the west-northwest.

Now deep in the jumble of mountains and high-rises of San Diego, the missiles steered an increasingly complicated course. For kilometer after kilometer, they swerved to the east or west around peaks and hilltops, climbing just high enough to clear buildings and hills. Between the radar shadows cast by surrounding elevations and their extremely low altitude, they were still effectively undetectable by the U.S. Navy E-2C Hawkeye orbiting off the coast.

The GLONASS satellite navigation card inside one of the Kh-35s abruptly failed. Although the missile's inertial guidance system tried to take over, integration drift—the accumulation of small errors by its accelerometers and gyroscopes over the past several minutes of flight—led its tiny onboard computer astray. Thinking itself still several hundred meters behind on the flight plan, the missile flew right through a programmed way point and crashed into the southern flank of the San Miguel Mountains. Twisted shards of burning wreckage sprayed across a wide area, igniting small fires that quickly guttered out among the mountain's rugged boulder fields and widely scattered tufts of cactus and brush.

The surviving fourteen cruise missiles came on—streaking west toward San Diego at high speed.

SUN KING THREE-ONE, E-2C HAWKEYE 2000, OFF THE CALIFORNIA COAST
That same time

"Hey, that's weird," U.S. Navy Lieutenant (junior grade) Carly de Mello said suddenly. The short, perky brunette, only a couple of years out of Annapolis, was the Hawkeye's radar officer, the most junior of the three equipment operators seated in the crowded compartment behind the turboprop's cockpit.

Her boss, Lieutenant Tim Layton, frowned. "Show me," he snapped. As the combat-information-center officer, he occupied the middle crew position—seated squarely between the E-2C's radar officer and its aircraft control officer.

"I may be picking up bogeys out in the mountains east of San Diego, south of Los Alpine and I-8," de Mello said. With deft fingers, she used keyboard commands and her trackball to "hook," or select, the new contacts on her big center display. "But they keep disappearing on me."

Following along on his own display, Layton saw a succession of dots blink briefly into existence during a radar sweep and then vanish again. His eyes narrowed in concentration as he invoked his radar-masking tool. Immediately sections of the map layered below their radar imagery showed areas where terrain would block their APS-145 radar. More contacts appeared during the next sweep . . . and disappeared as soon as they crossed into those terrain-masked places. A text box showed their estimated course, speed, and altitude.

Without hesitating, he mashed his transmit button and said excitedly, *"Broadsword, Broadsword, Sun King Three-One, quail, quail, quail! Multiple high-speed targets inbound bearing zero-eight-two, one-three miles, speed five hundred, on the deck!"*

"What the hell, Layton?" the pilot shouted on the intercom. *"This is a training mission! You just radioed an actual hostile missile report to the damned command post!"*

"That's because *I've got actual missiles in the air,* heading right for the Navy piers!"

"Oh shit," de Mello muttered. "This is so *not* good."

Silently, Layton agreed with her. While everything the Hawkeye's radar saw was being simultaneously fed through the Cooperative Engagement Capability data link to all Navy ships and installations in the region, the speed of those incoming missiles gave the defenders less than two minutes to react. That wouldn't have been an insurmountable problem if the fleet were at sea—able to employ every component of its layered defenses from Standard medium- and long-range antiair missiles to its Phalanx Close-In Weapon System 20mm automatic cannons and

Nulka missile decoys. Unfortunately, though, a substantial number of the Pacific Fleet's warships, including several *Ticonderoga*-class cruisers and *Arleigh Burke*–class destroyers, were tied up along the piers . . . held at anchor by President Barbeau's direct orders.

COMBAT INFORMATION CENTER, CG-53 USS *MOBILE BAY*, PIER 3, NAVAL BASE SAN DIEGO
That same time

Commander Dennis Ninomiya hurried into the dim, blue-tinted CIC. No one commented on the fact that the cruiser's normally unflustered and wholly unflappable executive officer looked out of breath. The klaxons blaring in every compartment as *Mobile Bay* came to Condition I, general quarters signaled this was no ordinary drill. "Status report!" he snapped.

"Missiles inbound, XO!" Brian Thorson, the young lieutenant assigned as tactical action officer for this watch, said, sounding rattled. He pointed to the large screen echoing radar data transmitted by the E-2C Hawkeye offshore. Red icons showed cruise missiles arrowing closer—screaming in just above the rooftops of San Diego's hilly, densely populated suburbs. The leader was just over one minute out, with thirteen others trailing after it at several second intervals. "By their flight profile, they're probably Kh-35s."

"Shit," Ninomiya cursed. Whoever had smacked

Barksdale Air Force Base a few days ago was now coming after them. He took a closer look at the screen. More icons showed civilian aircraft, including passenger jets on approach to San Diego International, all over the local sky. The airport was less than five miles northwest of their berth. Even if they could bring the ship's antiair missiles online in time, there was no way they could fire. In this cluttered air environment, the odds of knocking down a friendly airliner by accident were far too high. Which left his cruiser and the other ships tied up in port largely dependent on passive defenses. "Activate electronic and passive countermeasures only—no kinetics, repeat, no Sea Sparrows or Sea-Whiz." "Sea-Whiz," or Phalanx CIWS, was a radar-guided 20mm cannon designed to protect a vessel from incoming missiles out to a range of about a mile—fractions of a second before impact. "Close-in" was a polite way to put it: "Last prayer" might be a better description. "Tell Lindbergh Tower and SOCAL Approach to clear the Class Bravo airspace *now*, air defense emergency. As soon as the Class Bravo is clear, activate all defenses and countermeasures. Status of the port defenses?"

"Port defenses activated when we got the warning from the AWACS, sir," Thorson reported. The port defenses consisted of a variety of electronic jammers that could shut down GPS signals and a missile's active guidance, but those were a last-ditch effort. Nervously, he shrugged his shoulders. "Missiles still inbound, sir. Five miles."

Damn, *Mobile Bay*'s XO thought grimly. Without satellite navigation systems there was no way those missiles could have flown undetected through the mountain ranges east of the port. So why weren't the high-powered jamming systems the Navy had deployed to spoof GPS and GLONASS receivers working? Had the enemy missiles already shifted to their final radar-homing attack mode? "Where are my . . . ?"

At that instant, the tactical action officer shouted, "Decoys away, decoys away!" Once launched, the Australian-designed *Nulka* rockets—the very word *nulka* was an Aboriginal term for "be quick"—could hover in midair. As they slid downrange from their parent ship, they emitted precisely tailored signals that simulated the signature of a larger vessel, seducing radar-guided missiles off target.

"Quails Four, Six, Seven, Nine, and Thirteen departing observed course!" one of the CIC operators said abruptly.

Staring back at the big tactical display, Ninomiya saw five of the fourteen incoming missiles veer away in several different directions. For a few more seconds, they kept flying, streaking low over San Diego's suburbs at close to the speed of sound. But then, in quick succession, the five Kh-35s disappeared off the screen—replaced by fast-fading radar blooms of smoke, flame, and falling debris.

"Our satnav jammers worked!" Ninomiya said exultantly . . . and then felt his exultation vanish when he realized what had just happened. Each of the five missiles decoyed off course had plowed into neighborhoods packed with single-family homes, apartment complexes, schools, churches, and shopping centers.

"Permission to release CIWS to automatic mode?" the lieutenant asked.

Appalled, Ninomiya snapped, "Permission denied." From the ship's position along the pier, only one of *Mobile Bay*'s two 20mm Phalanx Close-in Weapons Systems could bear on the nine missiles still racing toward the harbor. But if he allowed the computer-controlled, six-barrel Vulcan cannon to fire, it would be shooting right into the heart of San Diego—spewing hundreds of armor-piercing tungsten penetrator rounds per second toward multistory apartment buildings and houses built on rising ground. The civilian death toll would be horrendous.

On the screen, the inbound Kh-35s were spreading out. Course tracks showed they were targeted on several of the moored ships—including *Mobile Bay*. They were close now, only a few seconds away. "Oh, Jesus," Ninomiya muttered, suddenly praying that officers aboard the other ships in port would decide to risk the collateral damage and open fire.

"We're gonna get hit!" one of the ratings shouted.

Ninomiya's nerve broke. He swung toward Thorson. "Belay that last order! Release batteri—"

And then it was too late.

The first cruise missile slammed into the cruiser's port side—ripping an enormous hole as it punched through hull plating and a thin layer of

Kevlar armor designed only to protect against fragments and small arms. Its high-explosive shaped charge warhead went off deep inside the ship . . . right outside the combat information center.

Neither Commander Dennis Ninomiya nor any of the other officers and sailors inside the CIC had time to react before a wave of fire and razor-edged metal washed across the compartment and killed them all.

HURRICANE ONE FIVE, HH-60H SEAHAWK HELICOPTER, OVER NAVAL BASE SAN DIEGO
A short time later

Peering down at the wrecked and burning ships lining the waterfront, U.S. Navy captain Blair Pollock felt sick. Three missiles had hit *Mobile Bay*—gutting her from stem to stern. Only the top of her superstructure and triangular mainmast were still visible, poking up out of the oil-stained water. Blackened corpses bobbed alongside the pier. At Pier Four, damage control teams were trying to put out a roaring, fuel-fed fire aboard the *San Antonio*–class amphibious ship USS *New Orleans*. More thick black smoke boiled away from the splinter-torn side of USS *Dewey*, an *Arleigh Burke*–class destroyer. In all, seven of the nine surviving Kh-35s had slammed into ships moored alongside San Diego's piers. Hundreds of officers and men were dead or maimed and burned.

Inland, more fires were burning. Huge plumes

of smoke soared hundreds of feet in the air, fed by
flames consuming homes and businesses in different neighborhoods. Most of the damage came
from the five missiles that had lost guidance and
crashed well short of the waterfront. But in the
last seconds, the tactical action officer aboard
another of the *Ticonderoga*-class cruisers, USS
Lake Erie, had opened fire with her Phalanx guns.
They'd knocked down the two missiles headed
her way . . . but hundreds of stray 20mm rounds
had also shredded homes and businesses across
a four-block-wide swath of the Paradise Village
neighborhood just across the 805 Freeway. Early
reports flooding in from hospitals and triage centers suggested civilian casualties could easily be
higher than those suffered by the Navy.

Intellectually, Pollock knew this wasn't as bad
as Pearl Harbor. The vast majority of the Pacific
Fleet's surface warfare ships were still afloat and
undamaged. Nor had any serious damage been
inflicted on its vital shore installations. But the
knowledge was cold comfort in the face of so
much death and suffering.

CHAPTER 31

IN THE ALTAMONT HILLS, NEAR LIVERMORE, NORTHERN CALIFORNIA
That same time

Kirill Aristov lay prone along the crest of the hill, scanning the barren slopes to the west through his night-vision binoculars. He ignored the deep *whump-whump-whump* coming from the row of 140-meter-tall wind turbines built along the service road just behind him. About five kilometers away, fires lit the night sky. Several buildings on the Sandia National Laboratories' Livermore campus were burning—set ablaze by antitank missiles and incendiary cannon rounds.

Nikolai Dobrynin scuttled up beside him and dropped to one knee. "Any sign of Baryshev and the others yet?" Aristov shook his head. "What the hell are they waiting for?" Dobrynin hissed.

Two police helicopters appeared out of the night, clattering toward the burning lab complex. Their green and red navigation lights strobed

rhythmically. Dazzling white spotlights probed
at the ground, hunting for the attackers. Suddenly there were two blinding flashes from near
one of the shattered buildings. Trailing bright
plumes of exhaust, two surface-to-air missiles
streaked skyward—already guiding on the helicopters. Explosions lit the night as the shoulder-
launched SAMs detonated. Enveloped in flames,
both helicopters spun down out of control and
smacked into the ground. Shards of torn metal
and shattered Plexiglas pinwheeled away from
each crash site.

"That, I think," Aristov said coolly. Now that
they'd disposed of the threat of aerial surveillance,
he could see six big human-shaped machines
sprinting out of the wrecked American science
complex. The KVMs were moving at more than
sixty kilometers per hour, covering ground with
every long-legged stride as they climbed into the
hills. He lowered the binoculars and looked at
Dobrynin. "The colonel's robots are on the way
now. They'll be here in a couple of minutes. Is
everything on our end set?"

The other man nodded. "Our guys are standing by to load the trucks."

Aristov got to his feet and stuffed his binoculars into a backpack. Their three converted
tractor-trailers were parked at points along the
deserted service road. Once they had Baryshev's
war machines safely aboard, it was a short thirty-
kilometer drive through the Altamont Pass to
another safe warehouse. This one was located on
the outskirts of the town of Tracy. By the time

the Americans could respond in force to this new attack, both the RKU security team and the colonel's KVM unit would be well hidden.

With Dobrynin, he waited at the crest of the hill.

When the tall gray war machines drew near, they slowed down. Five stalked silently past the two former Spetsnaz officers, moving on toward the parked trucks. The sixth KVM stopped a few meters away. Its antenna-studded head swiveled toward them. "Any problems, Captain Aristov?" a cold, synthesized voice asked.

"No, Colonel," Aristov replied. Then he noticed the dark smears of blood streaked across the robot's torso and limbs. His voice faltered. "Good God, what happened down there?"

"Oh, this?" the machine asked, holding out a large, metal-fingered hand that appeared to be coated in dried blood and torn human skin. "After I expended all of my ammunition, some of the American scientists and engineers were still alive. They tried to hide in one of their labs. So I liquidated them at close quarters." For a moment, the KVM appeared to reflect. Then it said, "The exercise was very . . . *satisfying*. In fact, we may be able to conserve our limited ammunition supplies by employing similar tactics on a bigger scale in the future. I will have to consider this option more closely."

Without waiting for a response, the robot turned away and strode off into the darkness.

Aristov stared after the KVM in horror. He fought down an urge to vomit.

"*Nu ohuet teper.* Okay, we are fucked," he heard Dobrynin whisper. "Whatever that *thing* is now, I don't think much of it is really Colonel Baryshev. Not any longer. What the hell have these guys done to themselves?"

IRON WOLF SQUADRON HEADQUARTERS, POWIDZ, POLAND
A short time later

Patrick McLanahan closed his eyes, accessing the wireless computer links built into his LEAF. Most of the exoskeleton's computers and machinery were devoted solely to keeping his crippled body alive, but the system retained a small fraction of the neural-interface capability employed by Cybernetic Infantry Devices. It gave him the ability to assimilate and analyze large amounts of data in a fraction of the time it would have taken an unassisted human brain.

Ordinarily, he significantly restricted his use of this ability—fearing that it might trigger the same sense of profound, debilitating isolation and mental instability he'd suffered while forced to exist entirely inside one of the robots. But the news from the United States was bad and growing worse with every passing hour. Unless he somehow worked out how the Russians were conducting this secret war of cruise-missile strikes and war machine raids, his son's Iron Wolf combat team might as well be based on the dark side of the moon for all the good that it could do.

Without information that would allow them to hit Gryzlov's forces, Kevin Martindale was right, he thought grimly. Right now, Brad and the others were simply hostages to fortune. If they were caught or even spotted by forces loyal to Barbeau, the repercussions would be almost unimaginable. Poland was not his native country, but the years he'd spent in its service had taught him to admire its proud, fiercely independent people.

A wry smile creased Patrick's worn, lined face. Okay, perhaps not to the same extent as his son, who was plainly head over heels in love with Nadia Rozek. Still, seeing the Poles crushed between a hostile America duped by Gryzlov's machinations and Moscow's tank and motorized rifle divisions was not something he could accept. So even if rapidly analyzing their painstakingly accumulated fragments of intelligence required him to risk a bit of his regained sanity, it was worth trying, he decided.

He was pretty sure that spending more time working through the demonstrated powers and tactics employed by the Russian war robots was a dead end. Scion analysts had already milked every pixel of video footage and piece of eyewitness testimony for whatever information they contained. But while they now had a much clearer grasp of what the enemy's machines could do in battle, they were still no closer to understanding *how* those robots avoided detection before they conducted their raids. There were simply too many hypothetical ways to do that—ranging from shipping the war machines as separate components and reassembling them before every attack to using trucks or other large vehicles to move them around.

Which left the cruise-missile attacks conducted by Gryzlov's mercenaries. Patrick strongly suspected that the clues he needed to crack their operational patterns wide open were buried somewhere in all the bits and pieces of evidence gathered in the two different strikes—the first on Barksdale Air Force Base and now the second, on the Pacific Fleet's San Diego piers.

Seeing what he could deduce from the fact that they'd used versions of Russia's Kh-35 subsonic cruise missiles in both attacks was his first step. Knowing the maximum range for those weapons—around 160 nautical miles—at least narrowed down the locations of possible launch sites. Reacting to his mental commands, his computer pulled up maps of both the southwestern and southeastern United States, pinpointed Barksdale AFB and Naval Base San Diego, and then drew circles with a radius of 160 miles around each site. Of course, "narrowing down" was a relative concept, Patrick decided dryly, since each of those highlighted zones contained rather more than 100,000 square miles. He could shave that somewhat for the raid on San Diego, since the Navy's E-2C Hawkeye would have easily detected any launch off the California coast. But even erasing the areas within its effective radar coverage still left a vast region of rough, almost uninhabited deserts and mountains stretching from the Mojave southward deep into Mexico.

Bring up all available video and recorded radar footage from each missile strike, he mentally ordered.

Downloaded through his neural link, the imagery scrolled through his mind at high speed. Okay, Patrick thought, reviewing what he'd observed, each attack involved a salvo of between fourteen and sixteen missiles. And those missiles were fired in rapid succession, with no more than four seconds between each launch. So what did that tell him?

For one thing, it almost certainly ruled out the use of any land-based missile system, he realized suddenly. The Russians did have mobile coastal defense batteries equipped with Kh-35s. But each Bal-E battery contained up to eleven specialized vehicles—including self-propelled command and control centers, launchers, and reloading machines. He strongly doubted Gryzlov's mercenaries could hope to move that much equipment along the nation's roads and highways without raising eyebrows somewhere . . . even if it were possible to believably disguise the launchers and command vehicles as something more innocent.

Nor could they hope to fire the Kh-35s from the ground undetected. The add-on boosters required to accelerate those missiles to attack speed from the ground generated huge plumes of flame and smoke. Maybe you could get away with a stunt like that out somewhere deep in the Mojave Desert, he thought. But not in Louisiana, Mississippi,

Arkansas, Oklahoma, or Texas—the five states within possible striking range of Barksdale. Rural or not, there were too many people living and working in those places for anyone to have missed seeing a torrent of fire climbing skyward that would have made the biggest county Fourth of July fireworks display look like kids shooting off a couple of bottle rockets.

He sat up straighter, hearing the servos in the exoskeleton that supported his body whine softly. That left only one realistic option: The Russians were launching their cruise missiles by air. But how exactly?

Quickly, he called up more data. Like the U.S., Moscow didn't have many long-range bombers left, no more than a handful each of their sleek Tu-22M-3 Backfires, turboprop-powered Tu-95 Bears, and supersonic Tu-160 Blackjacks. Both the Backfire and the Blackjack maxed out at eight Kh-35 cruise missiles apiece, so a sortie would require two aircraft. And while a single Tu-95 did have the necessary payload capacity, it was impossible to imagine even one of the big, slow-flying Bears successfully penetrating so far into U.S.-monitored airspace without being picked up on civilian and military radars. In fact, none of the Russian bombers were stealthy by any stretch of the imagination. There was just no conceivable flight profile that would let any of them hit either target and escape detection.

Which meant Gryzlov's forces were flying in plain sight, Patrick thought coldly. They had to be using a civilian aircraft—one converted to launch cruise missiles. What was more, it had to be a good-sized plane, one with multiple engines and plenty of payload capacity. Jerry-rigging Cessnas or Gulfstream business jets to carry a couple of missiles each wouldn't cut it. And since there was no way the Russians could hope to hang sixteen Kh-35s off the fuselage and wings of any commercial jet without raising all kinds of unanswerable questions, they must have modified their attack plane to carry its weapons internally.

He nodded to himself. No other possibility fit all the known facts. Besides, this wasn't even a new idea. Way back during the Carter administration, there had been a lot of talk about converting Boeing 747 Jumbo Jets to launch up to fifty Tomahawk cruise missiles as a cheaper alternative to the B-1 Lancer bomber program. He doubted the Russians were using anything as big as a 747 for their clandestine air campaign. If they had, they'd be salvoing a hell of a lot more than sixteen of those Kh-35s in every attack. No, based on the number of missiles they were launching, Gryzlov's pilots were probably flying a converted twin-engine jet—something like a Boeing 737 or an Airbus 300 or 320.

But that still left a hell of a lot of possibilities. Between Boeing and Airbus alone, well over twenty-two thousand of those planes were still flying worldwide. And more than two thousand commercial cargo flights crisscrossed U.S. airspace on any given day. Was there any way he could winnow out the single kernel of wheat he wanted from all that chaff? For a few moments more, he contemplated the problem—raising possible approaches and as rapidly discarding them.

And then, with the sudden zigzag streak of lightning-like inspiration, he saw the answer.

Access Federal Aviation Administration flight plan and air-traffic-control databases, Patrick told his computer through the LEAF's neural link.

Access achieved, it reported. If ever a collection of circuit boards and software could sound smug, this one did. Years ago, while he was still president, Kevin Martindale had made sure he could covertly gain entry to most of the federal government's computer networks—using carefully concealed back doors written into their operating systems' software. He'd justified his actions to those in his inner circle by arguing he needed a way to bypass elements of the cumbersome federal bureaucracy during a crisis. Now that Martindale headed Scion, of course, those same hidden back doors allowed his intelligence analysts and field operatives to roam practically at will through the mountains of information routinely collected and squirreled away by a host of different government agencies and departments. The FAA, for example, kept recordings of everything its air traffic controllers saw on radar and said over the radio or telephone for forty-five days.

With the assurance of long practice, Patrick began sorting through thousands of filed flight plans and air-traffic-control radio contacts—ruthlessly discarding anything but that pertaining to commercial aircraft transiting the critical zone centered on Barksdale Air Force Base within thirty minutes of the time the first Kh-35 missile exploded. Given the enormous volume of airspace it contained, he still wound up with a list of dozens of different planes that could have been in the right place at the right time to carry out a missile launch.

While that was a measurable advance over their prior state of complete ignorance—usually abbreviated as NFC, for "no fucking clue," on internal Scion reports—it was still insufficient. But now, solely because the Russians had carried out a second cruise-missile strike, he should be able to winnow that list down even further.

Unfortunately, when he ran the same kind of search focused on the possible launch zones for the Kh-35s that had hammered the Pacific Fleet, he drew a blank. Oh, there were plenty of cargo aircraft flying through U.S. airspace or bound for Mexico during the half hour or so before the cruise missiles were detected . . . but none of them matched those on his list from the attack against Barksdale.

Patrick frowned, deep in thought. Had he gotten this wrong? Was he missing something obvious?

Of course he was, he realized suddenly. He'd committed a classic error of intelligence analysis—relying on assumptions that were too narrowly focused. *Expand my time parameter*, he ordered. *Retrieve all available information for flights through the highlighted regions for up to six hours before the attack.*

Within milliseconds, the computer did as he asked. His list of suspect aircraft expanded almost exponentially. *Take one step forward and end up two steps back*, Patrick thought dryly. So now it was time to take a running jump.

Now, he thought, *cross-check this list of planes against those observed flying through the Barksdale missile launch zone.*

Only one plane appeared on both lists.

"Gotcha," Patrick growled, looking at the tail number assigned to a 737-200F cargo jet owned by a company called Regan Air Freight. To make sure, he activated another of Scion's concealed software back doors to enter the databases of SENEAM, *Servicios a la Navegación en el Espacio Aéreo Mexicano*—the Mexican government's equivalent of the U.S. Federal Aviation Administration.

After clearing American airspace, the Regan Air plane had landed at San Felipe. In and of itself, that wasn't too big a black mark—big planes usually landed in Tijuana, and light planes landed in San Felipe, but either was legal. But then, barely an hour later, it had taken off again, this time heading deeper into the mountains running down the spine of the Baja peninsula. And there, right around the time those missiles could have been launched toward San Diego, radar data from the Mexican station at Puerto Peñasco Sonora showed the 737-200 orbiting over the Baja hinterlands . . . just close enough to the U.S. naval base to carry out a maximum-range strike. And it had the payload capacity to carry the number of Russian cruise missiles used in each attack.

Bingo, Patrick thought. The crew of that aircraft had the means and the opportunity to hit both Barksdale and San Diego. Their motivation, whether Russian patriotism or mercenary greed, was unimportant. Still using his LEAF's interface, he opened a secure channel to Martindale in Warsaw.

The older man answered right away. "What is it, General?" Quickly, Patrick filled him in on what he'd discovered. "Regan Air Freight? Yes, I see the significance," Martindale said grimly. "I'll see what my people can learn about this corporation. And as fast as possible."

Patrick heard the strain in his voice. "What's happened?" he asked.

"Gryzlov's combat robots just destroyed a number of research labs at Sandia's Livermore campus," Martindale said. "Including one the administration funded to try to replicate Jason Richter's work on Cybernetic Infantry Devices."

"Oh shit," Patrick growled. "I can't think of anything more likely to convince Stacy Anne Barbeau that we're gunning for her."

"Nor can I," Martindale agreed. "Which is undoubtedly Gryzlov's plan." He sighed. "We never had much time to stop him before this spirals out of control, General. Now we have even less."

CHAPTER 32

Brad McLanahan listened closely to his father's explanation of how the Russians were concealing their cruise-missile attacks. "So they're flying this converted 737 out of a private field in Utah?" he asked. "Is that the base for their air-launched strikes?"

The retired general nodded. Because they had a good, secure satellite link, his image was only slightly distorted on their cockpit displays. "The pattern is pretty clear . . . at least now that we know what we're looking for. My guess, based on the flight plans and filed manifests I've examined, is that they've been ferrying in missiles, or, more likely, missile components, from overseas for weeks."

Nadia leaned forward. She appeared wholly focused, like a bird of prey circling on the hunt.

"Is it possible that this Moab facility is also the command and control center for Gryzlov's robot forces?"

"I doubt it," the older McLanahan replied. He shrugged. "Though it might serve as a logistical hub for their robots, since they can fly in equipment, spare parts, and ammunition through the field. But even that isn't certain."

"Yeah, Gryzlov may be crazy, but he's not stupid," Whack Macomber said roughly. "Running both elements of his clandestine operation out of the same location would be way too risky."

Nadia scowled. "So we could destroy the air base in Utah and still end up no closer to being able to eliminate the primary threat, these Russian fighting machines?"

Brad looked at her. "At least now we know how they're avoiding detection," he pointed out. He turned to the image of Kevin Martindale on the screen. "Right, Mr. Martindale?"

The gray-haired man nodded. "Quite so, Captain McLanahan." He shrugged. "Your father's discovery that an aircraft owned by Regan Air Freight had been converted into a cruise-missile carrier was the break we needed. There is no way an otherwise legitimate corporation like this air cargo company would lend itself to a Russian covert operation—"

"Unless Moscow controls it from the inside," Brad finished.

Somewhat nettled by the interruption, Martindale nodded tersely. "Exactly. My operatives have only begun digging, but it seems likely that

Russia—or possibly Gryzlov himself in his private capacity—now owns a controlling interest in both Regan Air and a ground-based freight hauler, FXR Trucking. Their original owner, a Canadian billionaire named Francis Xavier Regan, sold his personal stake in both companies to an international consortium of banks and investment firms several months ago." He smiled thinly, without humor. "My guess would be this purported consortium is nothing more than a group of straw buyers, a front for Gennadiy Gryzlov."

"Has anyone contacted this man Regan to learn more about what he knows?" Nadia asked.

"The thought had occurred to me, Major Rozek," Martindale said quietly. "Unfortunately, Regan vanished somewhere in the North Atlantic—along with his seventy-five-meter-long sailing yacht and its entire crew—a few days after finalizing the sale."

Macomber snorted. "Gee, isn't that just fricking convenient?"

"Yeah, there's the Gennadiy Gryzlov we all know and hate," Brad agreed. "Leaving a trail of death and disappearances wherever he goes."

Polish president Piotr Wilk frowned. "The only reason the Russians would want to own a trucking company would be to transport men and supplies . . . and their war robots . . . inconspicuously."

Patrick McLanahan nodded. "Using big rigs as a means of covert movement was one of the possibilities my analysts zeroed in on a while back, Mr. President."

"And yet you say this gets us no closer to

finding Gryzlov's action teams?" Wilk asked. "Even though we now know how to identify the vehicles his men are using?"

Martindale shrugged his shoulders. "It's a variation of the needle-in-a-haystack problem, Piotr. There are more than two million tractor-trailers operating on U.S. roads and highways. Of those, FXR Trucking owns hundreds in its own right and leases or rents thousands more. And that's not counting the tens of thousands of independent drivers it hires for single deliveries or short-term contracts. Virtually any of those big rigs might be the ones the Russians are using to transport their war robots and support units."

"Then why not narrow down that field by using the same method General McLanahan employed to identify their cruise-missile aircraft?" Wilk argued.

"By correlating the movements of FXR-owned or -leased trucks near the areas the Russians have already attacked?" Wilk nodded. "Because no one really tracks trucks or cars in the United States," Patrick explained. "Short of a driver getting a speeding ticket or being involved in an accident, there's no real reason for any government—state, local, or federal—to pay much attention . . . or keep any records."

Brad frowned. "What about toll roads and bridges, Dad? Most of them are automated now, right? They use license-plate readers or electronic passes to keep tabs on who owes what. Can't you hack into their databases?"

His father smiled. "Not a bad idea. Unfortunately, there aren't that many toll roads *or* bridges in any of the areas the Russians have hit so far."

"But there are a lot of interstate highways, all of them toll-free," Brad realized disgustedly.

"And the same goes for state roads and county roads and surface streets," the older McLanahan finished with a wry smile. He shrugged. "The same problem applies to the idea of cracking into Gryzlov's movements by checking which trucks supposedly delivered loads to cities or towns near Barksdale AFB, Fort Worth, or the Livermore labs . . . or even to destinations that would take them past those places. No one gives a damn what particular routes a truck driver uses. All they care about is whether the goods get to where they're supposed to go on time."

The predatory gleam in Nadia's eyes sharpened. "If it is truly impossible to track these vehicles, then we should come at this problem from the other direction."

Martindale looked puzzled. "And what direction is that, Major?"

"Despite their robots, Gryzlov's men themselves are not machines," she explained. "And like all men, they must eat and sleep and bathe and sh—"

"Yeah, we get the picture," Brad said hastily.

She grinned at him. "So then, we know the Russians must have places to rest and recuperate between operations, yes?"

Brad nodded and saw his father, Wilk, and Martindale doing the same. "And to hide out in while the heat dies down," he agreed. "Which would explain why none of the police roadblocks and checkpoints thrown up around the sites they've attacked have ever turned up anything suspicious."

Macomber stirred. "Well, they're sure as hell not hiding out in a Motel 6 or a Travelodge. Truckers on a job don't hang out parked in one motel lot for days on end. That'd draw way too much unwelcome attention—especially around places that just got blown to hell and gone."

"But I bet this FXR outfit owns a bunch of buildings," Brad said slowly.

Martindale nodded. "Public records show that the company has a very large number of warehouses and operating and maintenance centers. They're spread throughout the U.S., Canada, and Mexico."

"Just frigging wonderful." Macomber grimaced. "Gryzlov's bought himself a whole transportation and logistics network for his goddamned private war."

"So it would seem, Colonel," Martindale said, sounding pained. "And that doesn't count any additional facilities his agents or front companies might have bought or leased before his forces went into action." He sighed. "If this were a Scion operation, that's certainly what I would have done."

"He sure seems to be using your playbook," Brad agreed somberly. He glanced at Nadia and then at the others. "Which doesn't really get us much further. I guess we could narrow down where the Russians probably *were* by checking into what FXR owns around Dallas/Fort Worth or Shreveport, but that wouldn't get us any closer to figuring out where they are *now* . . . or where they're going to strike next."

Nadia swung toward him in sudden excitement. "That is not quite so!" she said quickly. "Since Gryzlov's robots smashed your national laboratory in California only a few hours ago, it is likely they are still concealed somewhere not far away. Gryzlov has made a mistake. He has extended himself out too far."

On the screen, Brad saw his father's eyes take on a distant look and suddenly realized the older man must be using his LEAF's built-in links to access various databases. He hoped Nadia wouldn't notice. His father's earlier brush with madness while forced to exist inside a Cybernetic Infantry Device still frightened her. She would not welcome any sign that he might be slipping back into that twilight digital world.

In a matter of seconds, Patrick's eyes snapped back into focus. "FXR Trucking owns three separate warehouse and maintenance facilities within a fifty-mile radius of Livermore, California," he said flatly. "There are two more within a hundred miles."

"You see!" Nadia said elatedly. "Now we know where to hunt!"

Martindale stared at her. "You're not seriously proposing to fly the Ranger straight into a region that is currently crawling with U.S. military units and federal law enforcement agents, are you? Because I don't give a rat's ass how good a pilot Brad is, there's no way you could pull off a stunt like that."

Sadly, Wilk shook his head. "Kevin is right, Major. The risk is far too great. Even if you could somehow arrive without being detected, Captain Schofield's scouts would have to investigate at least five separate sites . . . and all without being noticed themselves. By either the Russians or the Americans." He turned his gaze to Brad. "What would happen if your countrymen saw your aircraft? Or spotted Schofield's men conducting a covert reconnaissance?"

Brad thought about that. He winced. "We'd trigger an immediate and very violent reaction," he admitted. "And it would be aimed at us, not at Gryzlov's men."

"There is another problem," his father said gravely. "From what I can tell, almost all of FXR's facilities are located in or very near cities and sizable towns. Even if you got lucky and zeroed in on the Russian's current operating base, any fight against them would turn ugly very quickly."

Macomber swore suddenly under his breath. "Ah, damn, the general's right." Tight-lipped now, he glared at them. "If we tangle with Gryzlov's robots anywhere around civilians, there's going to be a hell of a lot of collateral damage." He shook his head. "You ever figure out just how many cars, school buses, houses, and apartment buildings even a single rail-gun round moving at Mach 5 could blow through?" he asked. "A shitload . . . that's how many!"

Brad stared back at him, seeing what could happen in his mind's eye. A battle between rival combat robots in an urban setting would inevitably result in horrific destruction. Innocent men, women, and children would be slaughtered by the scores and hundreds. "Oh, my God," he murmured.

"God's got nothing to do with it," Macomber growled. He shook his head. "Look, I want to smash those fucking Russian robots to bits as much as anyone else here, but I did *not* sign on with this outfit to participate in any massacres."

Nadia's shoulders slumped, all the fire seemingly gone out of her. "Then what do you propose, Whack?" she asked softly. "Do we just sit here in safety while the Russians destroy your country from within—and blame it all on us?"

There was silence for a long moment.

"We could pass what we know and suspect to the American government," Wilk suggested at last.

Martindale shook his head. "I'm afraid Barbeau is too hostile to me, the Iron Wolf Squadron, and Poland in general to pay much attention to anything we tell her." He frowned. "Even if we could somehow get through to her, word of what we'd learned would probably leak . . . either to the press or directly to Russian agents. And Gryzlov would just pull the plug on his operations before the FBI or the U.S. military got close. He'd call his forces home and clear away any evidence that might pin these attacks on him, instead of on us."

"And then we'd end up looking like the Iron Wolves who cried 'wolf,'" Brad said bitterly.

"Something like that." Martindale looked

beaten down. "So we're still stuck at square one. Unless we can catch Gryzlov's robots out of hiding and in the open where you can safely engage them, we have no good options."

Brad gritted his teeth. Like Nadia, he was tired of sitting idle while the enemy acted with impunity. How could they continue doing nothing, especially now that they had ripped at least a small hole in the *maskirova*, the cloak of deception, Russia was using to conceal its clandestine operations? What they needed was some way to tear that hole open wider.

He stirred suddenly, feeling the first faint glimmering of a plan starting to take shape in his mind. Admittedly, it bore no real resemblance to the kinds of "perfect war plans" so popular with armchair generals . . . but then again, real war was always messy and chaotic. Waiting for the chance to employ some tactic or strategy that looked perfect on paper only conceded the initiative to your enemy. That was what they'd been doing since Gryzlov's first attack . . . and it was obviously a dead end.

When he said as much out loud, Martindale shrugged. "Maybe so, Brad. But what's your alternative?"

"We stop pussyfooting around. We hit the concealed Russian air base at Moab," Brad said flatly. "The way I see it, Gryzlov has been controlling the tempo of this secret war from the get-go. Everything that's happening is following his script. We need to change that. We have to rattle his teeth so hard that we knock him off his preset plan. Because once he's forced to start improvising, he's more likely to start making mistakes—mistakes we can exploit."

"Yes!" he heard Nadia crow. Macomber and his father both nodded their agreement.

Martindale frowned. "I understand the impulse to do something," he said slowly. "But an attack on his base in Utah could easily backfire. What if it only convinces Gryzlov to withdraw the rest of his men and machines—leaving us worse off than we are now?"

Wilk nodded reluctantly.

"He won't back off," Brad said confidently. "Not if he's sure that *we* were the ones who took a whack at him . . . instead of the U.S. government. It'll be like waving a red cape in front of a bull. Gennadiy Gryzlov's not going to turn tail and run from a small Iron Wolf unit. Not when he has a stronger force of his own combat robots."

"Sure," Macomber agreed. "Just how do you plan to let that Russian SOB know we were the ones who kicked him in the 'nads? Put out a press release? Or are you thinking about inviting a fucking CNN camera crew on a ride-along?"

"Not exactly," Brad said. "But we will need to shake up our standard Iron Wolf operating procedure a little."

"You mean the one where we storm in, blow the shit out of everything and everyone, and then book like bats out of hell?" the bigger man asked.

"Yep," Brad agreed, with a boyish grin. "That would be the one."

THE KREMLIN, MOSCOW
That same time

Gryzlov glowered at Vladimir Kurakin. "You can't be serious! You actually believe this superstitious nonsense? That long-duration service in our *Kiberneticheskiye Voyennyye Mashiny* is inflicting psychological damage on their pilots?"

"Captain Aristov's most recent reports do concern me," Kurakin admitted. "The way he describes Colonel Baryshev and the others behaving is not . . . normal."

"Normal?" Gryzlov scoffed. "Compared to what? How many other men have ever been given the chance to operate machines of such power?" He eyed the other man with open amusement. "Because the colonel and his men are extremely aggressive and eager to kill using their KVMs, you think that is somehow evidence of madness?" He smiled. "Have you ever really studied the way successful fighter pilots think, Vladimir? Because I can assure you that what Aristov describes is really nothing out of the ordinary. Good combat pilots are hunters whose prey is other men. Without the killer instinct, they are nothing."

Kurakin looked unconvinced.

Gryzlov's smile thinned. "Tell me . . . has this so-called psychological impairment you discern threatened the success of any mission?"

"No, sir," the other man admitted.

"Then stop worrying," Gryzlov ordered. "And tell Aristov to quit pissing himself just because better men are proving they have more guts than he does."

For a moment, he thought Kurakin would argue with him. But the RKU chief only subsided with a tired nod. *Too bad*, Gryzlov thought coldly. He would have relished a confrontation, if only as a change of pace. But like so many others in his inner circle, the former special forces general was showing himself when pushed to be more lapdog than mastiff. Idly, he wondered what it said about the quality of his subordinates that Daria Titeneva was more of a man where it counted than any of the rest of them.

CHAPTER 33

Wolf One, the Cybernetic Infantry Device piloted by Brad McLanahan, stood motionless two hundred meters east of the chain-link, razor-wire-topped fence that surrounded this private airport. The CID's chameleon camouflage mirrored the soaring, faintly moonlit sandstone cliffs at its back, rendering it virtually invisible to the naked eye. The twelve-foot-tall machine was equally undetectable by IR sensors, since the thermal adaptive tiles coating its skin currently matched the precise heat signatures of the surrounding scrub, rock, and sand.

Two slowly pulsing green dots on Brad's tactical display showed the positions of the other Iron Wolf robots in his combat team. Nadia and Whack Macomber were stationed about two kilometers east of the airport. Like his, their machines

were using an array of passive sensors to probe
the Regan Air facility—sharing every scrap of information the three of them amassed over secure
data links.

He felt uneasy, all too aware that they were
pressed for time . . . which denied the chance to
make a really thorough reconnaissance. He and
Nadia hadn't been able to fly the Ranger into yet
another improvised landing strip on a high mesa
south of the Arches National Park until well after
nightfall. Covering the intervening miles had required slow and painstaking movement across the
rocky Moab highlands and then down onto the
valley floor. And whatever happened here, they
had to return to the XCV-62 and get her back in
the air well before sunrise. All of which meant
they had only a limited window of opportunity in
which to strike.

Seen from the outside, this Russian-controlled
airfield wasn't much to look at, Brad decided. Just
a couple of prefabricated metal buildings, a portable trailer, a handful of fuel trucks and cargo
loaders, and the twin-engine Regan Air Freight
737-200F itself. Arc lights rigged to allow crews
to work at night illuminated the cargo jet and the
concrete apron around it.

His computer highlighted the trailer. *Active
satellite communications link detected*, it reported.
*Additional electronic emissions indicate this building is
the current flight operations control center.*

He scanned along the perimeter fence. Apart
from a linked network of IR-capable cameras,
there were no other obvious defenses or sensors—

no minefields, motion detectors, or even trip-wire-triggered flares. Nor could he spot any signs of bunkers or dug-in heavy weapons. Overall, it looked as though the Russians had opted for discretion over airtight security.

Across the runway to the west, a locked gate and guard shack blocked road access to the airport. Two men, wearing tan-and-blue uniforms that identified them as Regan Air security personnel, were posted at the gate. One had a pistol holstered at his waist. The other carried a shotgun.

Brad tagged the two guards on his display for the others. "Not exactly heavy-duty firepower," he radioed. "Those guys at the gate look pretty much like standard-issue rent-a-cops to me."

"That's just a little show for the locals," Whack replied. "But take a gander at the fellas prowling out there away from those lights. If you were wondering what happened to those Spetsnaz veterans Gryzlov hired away from his own army, I'd say we just found at least four of them."

Brad zoomed in on the four men walking obvious sentry beats in the darkness well beyond the parked cargo jet. He was close enough for his night-vision cameras to pick up enormous amounts of detail. All four of them wore body armor, tactical radios, and night-vision gear. Two carried unfamiliar-looking assault rifles. *Israeli-made Galil ACE 53 7.62mm weapons*, his computer reported. The other two cradled standard-issue, military-grade M4 carbines. But each of them also had a disposable AT-4 84mm antitank rocket launcher slung over his shoulder. Bits of encrypted transmissions intercepted by his CID showed the four heavily armed guards were in frequent communication with each other, the gate shack, and the flight operations trailer. "You've got a point there, Whack," he said over their secure circuit. "They're loaded for bear." He grinned. "Or maybe wolves like us. And they're definitely pros."

Nadia cut in. "What is the point of those guards?" she wondered. "Even assuming there are more Spetsnaz personnel currently off duty, they are still far too few in number to repel a determined military assault."

"They're not posted to fight off the U.S. Army," Brad said. "My bet is their primary mission is providing security against possible intruders or spies. Plus, even a small Spetsnaz force like that could sure put a world of hurt on the cops and county sheriffs if local law enforcement got too curious and came calling."

"Maybe so," Nadia said, sounding both unconvinced and uncharacteristically worried. "But the possibility also exists that they are support troops for one or more of the Russian combat robots. I do not believe that Gryzlov would leave this base so exposed."

"From his perspective, this facility's security rests on its secrecy," Brad pointed out. "Aside from the cruise-missile-carrying 737 parked out on that apron, his war robots are his primary offensive striking power. Committing any of them to a static defensive role here would be a waste of resources."

Macomber intervened. "He's right, Major Rozek.

Anyway, if there were robots deployed here, we'd have picked up their thermal signatures by now."

"They could be powered down," she argued. "Or our intelligence might be wrong. And if the Russians do have their own camouflage systems . . ." Her voice trailed off for a moment. "Wolf One," she said formally. "I recommend we alter the plan. We should all assault simultaneously in order to overwhelm any such hidden forces."

Inside his CID's darkened cockpit, Brad nodded to himself, suddenly understanding why Nadia seemed so nervous. She hated watching him take risks while she waited in relative safety. "Negative, Wolf Two. You and Whack will cover me while I make the hit." He cleared his throat. "Now, if you spot anything big and metal with arms and legs coming my way, you have my permission to shoot the hell out of it without hesitation. Otherwise, though, this is strictly a one-man show." He felt a wry smile cross his face. "With the emphasis on *show*."

"Copy that," Macomber said.

Nadia sighed. "Very well. But I do not like this."

Movement alert, Brad's computer reported suddenly. *Increased activity at target facility*. Across the runway, he saw men in grease-stained coveralls opening big doors on one of the prefab buildings. His sensors showed rows of tarp-shrouded shapes inside a brightly lit interior. *Chemical sniffers detect traces of kerosene fuels and high-explosive compounds*, the computer told him. *Analysis suggests those are Kh-35 cruise missiles*.

While he watched, one of the cargo loaders

roared to life and trundled toward the weapons storage building. Lights blinked on inside the Boeing 737's cockpit. Its big forward door whirred open—spilling more light out onto the airport apron. Inside the cargo compartment, he could see more ground crewmen working on some kind of machine. Abruptly, he recognized what it was: a rotary missile launcher, very similar to those used on the XB-1F Excalibur bombers he'd flown with his father. And those technicians were prepping the launcher to receive new missiles.

His eyes narrowed. They'd arrived just in time. The Russians were getting ready to launch another strike.

RKU FLIGHT OPERATIONS CONTROL CENTER
That same time

Colonel Yuri Annenkov typed in a quick acknowledgment of Moscow's most recent attack order, watched while the computer encrypted it, and then hit the send key. The machine beeped once shrilly as it transmitted his reply through their satellite link. He donned his radio headset and keyed the mike to speak to his copilot. Uspensky was already in the cockpit of their aircraft, running through preflight checks.

"Did those new missile target coordinates come through the link clean, Konstantin?" he asked.

"Yes, sir," Uspensky replied. "The attack computer confirms all target sets received." He sounded puzzled. "What I don't understand is why we're hitting a school in New Orleans. What is so militarily significant about Tulane University and its law school?"

"This is a political target, not a military one," Annenkov explained, hiding his own feelings. After all, orders were orders. "Tulane is where the American president Barbeau received her education. Moscow believes damaging the campus will throw her further off balance and negatively affect her mental state."

Uspensky snorted. "General Kurakin is getting a bit too fancy for my tastes, Colonel."

Privately, Annenkov agreed, though he was equally sure Kurakin was not the one who'd made the ultimate decision to hit a civilian university for purely political and psychological reasons. That was more President Gryzlov's style. "It's a mission, Konstantin," he said finally. "Where the missiles fly isn't really our concern, is it?"

"I suppose not," the other man agreed, though without much conviction. "See you in a few minutes?"

Annenkov nodded. "Yes. Get the bird warmed up for me. I'll be there as soon as Filippov and his men start loading the Kh-35s. Pilot out."

He pulled off the headset and glanced across the crowded trailer. A bank of five monitors displayed live feeds from the cameras set up around the airport. One showed ground crewmen carefully hoisting a cruise missile into position on the cargo loader. In another, angled to cover the 737 and its surroundings, he could see Filippov and two of his technicians fussing with one of their rotary launchers. He smiled. Like all good specialists, the former Russian Air Force ordnance officer was a stickler—striving to make sure the weapons and machines under his care performed perfectly when put to the test.

The remaining three TV monitors were the province of his security team. They were set to show images from the IR-capable cameras covering the airport perimeter fence. "How does it look out there tonight?" he asked. "Anything stirring?"

The officer on duty shook his head without taking his eyes off the screens. "Not a peep, Colonel." He sounded vaguely disappointed. "Not even a few nosy teenagers to scare off. I guess the word got around."

Annenkov chuckled. So far, the biggest challenge his security personnel had faced was breaking up illegal, underage drinking parties—gatherings the Americans called keggers—outside the airport grounds. He supposed that was quite a comedown for a group of battle-hardened Spetsnaz and GRU veterans.

He turned away.

"*Kakogo cherta?* What the hell? Where did *that* come from?" the other man said in sudden surprise. "Is that machine one of ours?"

Annenkov spun back to stare at the monitor he was pointing at. It showed a huge, manlike shape bristling with weapons charging out of the darkness beyond the perimeter fence. For a fraction of a second, he froze, caught completely off guard. Then trained instincts kicked in and he recovered. "No!" he snapped. "Sound the alarm! And transmit those images to Moscow! Tell them we're under attack by the Iron Wolves!"

THE PERIMETER FENCE
That same time

Brad McLanahan ran straight toward the airport, speeding up fast. Through his CID's audio pick-ups, he could hear klaxons blaring across the lit compound. More indicators blinked across his tactical display as his computer intercepted frantic radio calls from the Spetsnaz guards on duty. A pulsing dot appeared on the portable trailer the Russians were using for flight ops. *Secure satellite transmission detected*, the CID reported.

Someone in there has good reflexes, he noted approvingly. Without slowing down, he smashed straight through the chain-link fence. Pieces of torn and twisted metal flew away across the concrete apron.

Threat icons flashed into Brad's consciousness. Two flared bright red, signaling an immediate high-priority danger. There, off in the darkness, the two Spetsnaz guards armed with antitank rockets were desperately trying to draw a bead on his quick-moving robot. A solid hit from one of those high-explosive warheads would tear right through his composite armor. *Not tonight, guys,* he thought coolly. He swiveled on the run and opened fire on them first with his 40mm grenade launcher.

Two dazzling flashes lit the night. He caught a brief glimpse of shrapnel-torn bodies tumbling to the ground.

Several pistol and 7.62mm rifle rounds slammed into his side and ricocheted off. *Minor damage to torso camouflage plates and thermal tiles*, the CID told him. He whirled toward the Russian soldiers who were shooting at him. Three, including the two uniformed gate guards, were out in the open. A fourth had taken cover behind a cargo loader.

Brad triggered a short burst from his autocannon. The guards charging toward him simply blew apart, hit in the center of mass by 25mm high-explosive rounds. His next burst tore across the cargo loader—ripping through thin-skinned cruise missiles. Burning kerosene fuel sprayed across the Spetsnaz trooper hiding behind them and set him alight.

He moved on, heading across the apron toward the two metal buildings. The biggest was the brightly lit weapons storage shed. Men wearing T-shirts and shorts scrambled out of the other prefab structure, which seemed to be the living quarters for the Russians based here. Several of them were armed. They saw him coming and started shooting.

Bad decision, Brad thought. And quick as his thought, he fired back. Amid screams, dead and dying Russians toppled in all directions.

Now it was time to wreck those buildings.

He switched back to using his grenade launcher. But against targets of that size, he needed something with a much bigger bang than his regular 40mm HE rounds. *Load thermobaric grenades*, he ordered his CID. They should do the trick. Each contained two small explosive charges and a container of flammable, highly toxic fuel. When the first charge detonated, it punctured the container, spraying a mist of dispersed fuel. And then, when the second charge exploded a fraction of a second later, it ignited the drifting fuel cloud.

Icons flashed across Brad's display as the computer selected aim points calculated to do the maximum possible damage. One after another, he pumped three grenades into each building.

Huge explosions lit them up from the inside. The temperature at each detonation point soared instantly to more than four thousand degrees Fahrenheit—briefly igniting the surrounding air. Hit by powerful shock waves, metal walls buckled. Both buildings collapsed inward in a smoldering tangle of broken steel frames and joists and warped and burning aluminum siding and roof panels. Even at a safe distance, his sensors recorded a stunning wave of heat wash across the CID's armor. Anyone still inside the buildings would have either been incinerated by the blast, suffocated by the follow-on shock waves, or crushed by falling debris.

"Oh, subtle, kid," Macomber radioed. "Real subtle. I bet people could hear those explosions twenty miles from here."

"Wait . . . you mean I was supposed to do this

quiet-like?" Brad said, taking refuge in gallows humor. He paused. "Oops. My bad. Sorry about that, Wolf Three." Striding away from the burning buildings, he slid the grenade launcher back into one of his weapons packs.

He moved back across the airport grounds. A pulsing dot centered on the flight operations trailer showed that someone inside was still in touch with Moscow via satellite. "Wolf Two, any luck hacking into that transmission?"

"Wait one," Nadia replied tersely, sounding intensely absorbed in her task. CIDs had enormous computing power and electronic warfare capabilities. The higher-grade encryption used for secure e-mails was beyond the reach of anything less powerful than the supercomputers used by America's NSA and the UK's Government Communications Headquarters at Cheltenham. But the time imperatives of live, two-way voice and picture communication denied the application of those more rigorous methods. So, in theory, she should be able to break past the digital encryption protecting this Russian satellite phone transmission. Now it was time to find if real-world practice matched academic theory.

Brad closed in on the Boeing 737-200F cargo jet still parked out on the apron. Its forward door was just sliding shut. Puffs of exhaust from the aircraft's two engines indicated that the pilot was trying for an emergency start. Which made him brave, Brad guessed, but very low on common sense.

He checked the ammunition remaining for his autocannon. He still had plenty of rounds left. Fire discipline was the key to fighting effectively inside one of the Iron Wolf combat robots. Caught up in the false sensation of superhuman power and invulnerability that came with piloting one of the machines, it was all too easy to get carried away and fire wildly—expending rounds unnecessarily. Hundreds of hours of simulator practice and real-world experience, coupled with rigorous mental control, were required to resist this temptation.

Load 1:1 mix of armor-piercing and incendiary ammunition, he ordered.

Machinery whirred and clicked, detaching the autocannon's current belt of HE ammo and replacing it with a new one configured to his specifications. *Weapon ready*, the CID reported.

With one smooth, economical motion Brad raised the 25mm autocannon and sighted toward the cargo jet. *C'mon*, he mentally urged its crew, *bail out of that crate*. There was no way the converted 737 could possibly escape. He waited long enough for anyone watching to know he was deliberately holding his fire. "Cut your engines and come out!" he ordered. The CID's translation software turned his spoken words into Russian.

More seconds ticked by without any visible response.

"This ain't a damned tea party, Brad," Macomber growled over the radio. "And stupidity carries its own price tag. So nail that plane!"

"Copy that, Wolf Three," he said, with a sigh. He pulled the autocannon through an arc, squeezing the trigger again and again and again.

WHANG. WHANG. WHANG. WHANG.

More than a dozen 25mm rounds hit the enemy aircraft—shredding it from nose to tail. Its cockpit windows exploded, blown inward. Shards of torn fuselage spun into the air. Rivulets of flame from burning fuel and hydraulic fluid rippled across the 737's punctured skin. Oily black smoke billowed away from the wrecked cargo jet, thickening as the fires his incendiary rounds had set took hold.

Feeling sick at heart, Brad turned away. He didn't mind killing men who could fight back. But this felt more like murder, even though he'd given the crew inside that plane at least a brief chance to surrender.

"I have broken into their satellite connection," Nadia said suddenly. "They are in contact with RKU headquarters in Moscow. And they have reported they are under attack by an Iron Wolf combat robot."

"Did they send any images from their security cameras?" Brad asked. He reloaded his autocannon.

"Beautiful pictures," she confirmed, sounding gleeful. "You look quite terrifying!"

Macomber broke in. "Let's finish this, Wolf One. If we don't book out of here in the next few minutes, we're gonna have a very up-close and personal encounter with the sheriff's department."

Without hesitating any longer, he opened fire on the flight operations trailer. Armor-piercing rounds ripped through its thin walls and exploded out the other side—destroying everything and everyone in their path. Fires fed by smashed furniture and short-circuiting electronics glowed orange in the wreckage. On his CID's display, the pulsing dot showing a live transmission to Russia vanished as the signal cut off.

Brad whirled away from the airport and loped east out into the desert, heading to join the other two Iron Wolf combat robots. Behind him, flames crackled noisily—spreading fast through the ruins of Gennadiy Gryzlov's covert air base.

CHAPTER 34

RAZDAN-1 ELECTRO-OPTICAL SURVEILLANCE SATELLITE, IN SUN-SYNCHRONOUS LOW EARTH ORBIT
A short time later

Russia's most advanced spy satellite orbited several hundred kilometers above the cloud-flecked globe—circling the world once every hundred minutes at nearly twenty-seven thousand kilometers per hour. As it crossed the terminator into darkness over the central Pacific, new commands reached its onboard computer. In response, its telescope rotated slightly, focusing on a different sliver of the earth spinning past far below.

Fourteen minutes later, the Razdan-1 satellite came into visual range of the new target its masters wanted investigated. Over the next few seconds, high-resolution digital cameras took several extremely detailed infrared pictures of a very small area of the United States. A high-speed radio antenna instantly relayed the images to Moscow through Russia's Meridian satellite military communications network.

THE KREMLIN, MOSCOW
A short time later

Russian president Gennadiy Gryzlov's face contorted in anger as he studied the satellite pictures on his monitor. Even without the benefit of detailed analysis by the military's photo interpretation experts, it was clear that RKU's Utah base had been completely destroyed—along with its converted 737-200F cruise-missile carrier. He looked up at Vladimir Kurakin. "Were there any survivors for the Americans to interrogate?" he demanded.

"None," the other man said. His face was pale and set. "As a security precaution when we established the Moab facility, the FSB's Q Directorate hacked into the communications networks of all the local law enforcement and emergency services agencies. Our intercepts of police and ambulance service calls make it clear the Americans found no one left alive at the scene. Only mangled and burned corpses."

Gryzlov nodded, feeling his anger subside. "So at least the Poles and their mercenaries did us one small favor." One side of his mouth twitched upward in a wry, half smile. "That was kind of them."

Kurakin stared back at him in disbelief. "I just lost nearly fifty of my best airmen, special forces operatives, and ordnance technicians, Mr. President," he said stiffly. "I find it very difficult to see anything positive in this catastrophe."

"Casualties are an inescapable consequence of war," Gryzlov retorted. He shrugged his shoulders. "A few men killed and a single aircraft destroyed? Weighed against the damage your operations have already inflicted on the Americans, that's nothing . . . a mere fleabite."

Kurakin's jaw tightened. But he stayed silent.

"From the beginning, we both knew basing an aircraft inside the United States was a high-risk venture," the Russian president continued coolly. "Losing it is an unfortunate occurrence, but nothing more than that."

Kurakin's nostrils flared. "*Unfortunate?*" he growled. "That is not the word I would choose . . . sir."

Gryzlov eyed him closely. The man he'd selected to command his mercenaries had served him loyally thus far. Was that time coming to an end? He hoped not. Replacing the former Spetsnaz general now—so close to the culmination of this secret war—would be difficult. No, he decided, it would be better to ride this faltering horse awhile longer, to death if need be, rather than waste valuable time looking for a new mount.

With a swift flick of his finger, he dismissed the satellite photos from his monitor. "Never mind, Vladimir. We don't have time to waste on minor setbacks. Now that we've lost the ability to launch more cruise-missile strikes, we need to recalibrate your operations."

"Recalibrate my operations?" Kurakin said, clearly taken by surprise. "You intend to continue this war? Even now?"

"Of course." Gryzlov raised an eyebrow. "What else do you propose?"

"That we withdraw Baryshev's KVM unit and their security team!" the other man replied forcefully. "And as soon as possible. The Iron Wolf attack that destroyed Colonel Annenkov and his entire unit proves that the Poles and Scion have penetrated our operational security. Baryshev's robots are vulnerable."

"Your fears are irrational," Gryzlov said coldly. "You saw the pictures from the security cameras at Moab. Your base was destroyed by a single Iron Wolf machine. Correct?"

Kurakin grimaced. "Yes."

"You see what that implies, of course?"

"That just one of the enemy robots was available," Kurakin guessed.

Gryzlov nodded approvingly. "Exactly. The Poles must be too afraid to risk more of their foreign soldiers and machines in operations inside the United States." He shrugged again. "I don't see one lone Iron Wolf robot as a serious threat to our remaining forces . . . or to our plans. It would only be easy prey for our own KVMs."

"But the Poles *could* pass on what they've learned to President Barbeau," Kurakin warned.

"And what is that?" Gryzlov said. "Nothing beyond supposition and guesswork. Nothing in the wreckage of your Utah base ties directly back to us."

"The Americans are sure to dig deeper into the

new owners of Regan Air Freight and FXR Trucking," Kurakin argued.

Gryzlov laughed, remembering the contingency arrangements he'd made with Willem Daeniker, the utterly mercenary and thoroughly amoral Swiss banker who'd been his go-between with Francis Xavier Regan and then with the managers of both companies. Gryzlov had sent a text message activating those emergency measures as soon as he'd received the first word of the Iron Wolf raid on RKU's airbase. "Oh, I earnestly hope the Americans do conduct a thorough investigation, Vladimir," he said cheerfully. "What they would learn would be most . . . instructive.

"Let me make this plain to you," Gryzlov continued bluntly. "So long as it is likely that Barbeau and her advisers are still in the dark about our involvement, Operation Checkmate will proceed."

Reluctantly, Kurakin nodded. "Very well, Mr. President. But I must tell you that our options going forward are increasingly narrow—especially now that we've lost our cruise-missile aircraft."

"Why is that?"

"Because the Americans are learning from their earlier mistakes," the RKU chief explained. "Their warships and submarines are putting to sea, where Colonel Baryshev's robots cannot touch them. And their air and ground forces are mostly dispersed to heavily defended bases. Our KVMs could probably overrun one of those military installations . . . but not without being detected, tracked, and, ultimately, run to ground and destroyed."

Gryzlov frowned. "Then we go after more of their armaments factories and weapons labs. Like that F-35 assembly plant and the cybernetics lab we just hit. The Americans don't have enough troops or planes to defend every possible target against our robots."

"They don't," Kurakin agreed heavily. "But they do have enough drones."

"What?"

"The Americans are bringing more and more of their long- and medium-duration drones home from overseas," the RKU chief explained. "Counting their operational MQ-1 Predators, MQ-1C Gray Eagles, MQ-9 Reapers, RQ-7 Shadows, and RQ-4 Global Hawks, that's a fleet of a thousand unmanned aircraft. Most of them were once committed to hunting for terrorists, but it's clear that homeland defense now takes a much higher priority."

"Drones!" Gryzlov jeered. "Why should our KVMs fear them? Most of them don't even carry weapons."

"The Americans don't need weapons," Kurakin said. "They need information." He shrugged his shoulders. "A single real-time image showing Colonel Baryshev's machines loading or unloading from Aristov's trucks would blow our whole operation sky-high."

"Then we will turn our forces in another direction," Gryzlov said coolly. "We will strike something the Americans do not expect. Something political."

What Kurakin and the others had never understood was that his overall concept for *Shakh i Mat*, for Operation Checkmate, had always entailed a three-pronged assault on the United States— striking first at its military power and defense industries . . . and then, later, nearer to its presidential election, taking aim directly at its political stability. But now that America's armed forces and factories were too well protected, it was obvious that the time had come to go straight for the throat.

Still smiling, Gryzlov gave Kurakin his new target.

The other man turned even paler. "But, Mr. President, that would be—"

"An act of war?" Gryzlov said mildly. His eyes were ice-cold. "What did you think we were doing here, Vladimir? Playing a game? What is one more dead American, among so many others?"

Kurakin's face froze for a long moment. At last, he dipped his head, acknowledging the instructions he'd been given. "Your orders will be obeyed," he said carefully. "But I strongly recommend that Aristov and his team be allowed to conduct a thorough reconnaissance before Baryshev's war machines attack. Given the consequences of any failure, we cannot risk encountering anything unexpected."

Blithely, Gryzlov agreed. "If you strike the king, you must kill the king." His expression grew even more callous. "And of course, the same rule applies even when you strike at the king-in-waiting."

CHAPTER 35

STRATEGIC COMMAND BUNKER, WRIGHT-PATTERSON AIR FORCE BASE

Early the next morning

Suppressing a massive yawn, national security adviser Edward Rauch rubbed hard at his tired eyes. He'd already been up for more than twenty-four hours—ever since the incredible reports that someone had just blown up a private airport in Utah first hit his desk. One of the many downsides of Barbeau's refusal to delegate her power was the workload she placed on the shoulders of the handful of subordinates she did trust.

Rauch took a sip of the coffee some enlisted man had brought him . . . when? Hours ago, by the stale, cold taste. Grimacing, he shoved the mostly empty paper cup into his wastebasket. Didn't the Air Force give its combat pilots and bomber crews stimulants? He vaguely remembered reading an article about something called modafinil. It was supposed to be nonaddictive and incredibly effective. Maybe he should see if the bunker medical staff could find some of the pills for him.

"Jesus, you look like hell, Ed," Stacy Anne Barbeau said with some relish, barging into his tiny office without knocking. Luke Cohen tagged along behind her. From the dark shadows under his eyes to the way his shoulders sagged, the White House chief of staff didn't appear to be in much better shape than Rauch was.

Of the three of them, only the president seemed reasonably awake and rested—though she was unnaturally bright-eyed, with a brittle, false smile plastered across her once-attractive face. Ever since she'd learned that Patrick McLanahan was still alive, Barbeau had been teetering on the edge of panic.

She took the chair across from Rauch. "Well?" she demanded. "Brief me. What the hell happened at this Podunk airport out in the middle of nowhere?" Her lips twisted into an even uglier, phonier smile. "I'm guessing this wasn't some weird Mormon missionary send-off gone wrong."

"No, ma'am," Rauch said shortly. "Based on reports from Air Force specialists, there's no doubt that it was the operating base for those cruise-missile attacks against both Barksdale and San Diego. They've already identified dozens of Kh-35 missiles in the wreckage." He shrugged. "There never was a stealth bomber attacking us. We were hit by what looked like an ordinary commercial jet flying right out in the open."

Barbeau scowled, clearly unhappy with his

dismissive tone. She'd invested considerable time and presidential clout in badgering the Air Force and Navy to deploy their limited numbers of air surveillance aircraft to spot a Scion-piloted stealth plane. "So who was flying that plane, Doctor?" she snapped. "And manning this secret base?"

"We don't know," he admitted. "Not yet."

"Well, why the hell not?" she growled. "I've seen the pictures. There are dead bodies scattered all over that damned place. Don't any of your freaking specialists know how to run a few fingerprints through the FBI database?"

To his surprise, Rauch discovered that he was able to ignore her jab. "Many of the corpses were very badly burned," he said evenly. "But the site investigation team has been able to run fingerprint checks against a number of federal databases, including the Pentagon and the FBI."

"And?"

"Well, there's the dog that didn't bark in the night, Madam President."

Barbeau glowered at him. "Spare me the fucking Sherlock Holmes references, Ed," she said tiredly.

"So far, we haven't been able to identify any of the bodies," he explained. "Which is not what I would have expected . . . if this really was a Scion or Iron Wolf Squadron operation."

The president's jaw tightened. "How so?"

"Most of the men and women working for Scion and Iron Wolf are prior-service U.S. military and intelligence agency personnel," he explained. "Which means their biometric data is on file with the Department of Defense and other federal agencies. So we should have been able to put names to some of those corpses. But whoever these men were, their records aren't in any of our databases."

Barbeau nodded grimly. "Well, that makes it obvious. McLanahan must have recruited his own hired guns for this operation. Probably a bunch of right-wing Ukrainian neo-Nazis. And maybe a few Polish ex-special-forces troops and pilots he managed to brainwash."

Rauch stared at her. "McLanahan?"

"Who else?" she demanded. "Don't you get it, Ed? That was Patrick McLanahan's air base."

Carefully, he asked, "If that was the general's base, then who destroyed it?"

Barbeau laughed harshly. "That playboy prick Martindale and his Polish piggybank, Piotr Wilk. They know McLanahan and his fanatics are out of control," she went on. Her voice shook slightly. "By now, Wilk and Martindale must be going frantic trying to stop that lunatic's crusade for revenge against me before it's too late." Beneath her makeup, her face turned pale. "Christ, don't you get it? These assholes are fighting a civil war against each other . . . and they're doing it on our soil, with no concern about who gets killed in the cross fire!"

Rauch forced himself to consider her theory—as wild as it sounded. It did match up with some of the few facts they possessed. Special forces teams dispatched to Moab had found tracks of one of the lethal combat robots in and around the wrecked airport. That strongly suggested the attack *had* been an Iron Wolf and Scion operation. Unless, of course, the Russians really did have their own war robots after all, as Poland claimed? But he'd tried approaching the Poles through various diplomatic and military back channels . . . hoping to see their evidence—only to learn that they didn't have anything solid yet. "Proving any of this may come down to figuring out who really owns Regan Air Freight, Madam President," he said cautiously.

"What does Murchison say?" Barbeau snapped. Sara Murchison was the former federal prosecutor who headed the FBI. Like Rauch, she was one of those the president viewed as reasonably competent.

"Director Murchison has had agents all over the company's Indianapolis headquarters ever since we identified that burned-out cargo jet," Rauch told her. "From their first reports, Regan Air's management appears as much in the dark about this as we are. Apparently, that converted 737 belonged to the company's new owners."

Barbeau pounced. "New owners?"

He nodded. "The founder sold out to some kind of international consortium a few months ago . . . right before he disappeared. The CIA and the NSA are digging into this syndicate now— trying to sniff out who's behind the money. Plus, the CIA and the FBI have agents on the way to Zurich to investigate a Swiss investment banker, a man named Willem Daeniker, who seems to have pulled the whole deal together."

"It's Martindale," Barbeau said decisively. "He's

behind this guy Daeniker, mark my words. This is his MO, for God's sake. He runs his illegal ops through a network of shell companies and dummy corporations. Well, now that penchant for secrecy and double-dealing has come around to bite him in the ass. McLanahan got his fingers into the Regan Air pie and he's been using the company and its resources for his own whacked-out ends."

Luke Cohen stirred in his chair. "How much of this can I tell the press, on background?" he asked.

"Not a damn thing!" Barbeau snapped at her chief of staff. "Do you think I want Joe Q. Public to know that all of this death and destruction is part of a madman's revenge plot aimed at *me* personally? How the hell is that supposed to help my reelection campaign?"

Sheepishly, Cohen shrugged in a wordless apology. "There's already all kinds of wild speculation about what happened in Utah," he pointed out. "If we don't get out in front of the story somehow, we're going to look really bad."

Rauch gazed at him, scarcely able to conceal the contempt he felt. The United States was under continuing attack . . . and the White House chief of staff's first concern was how events might affect his boss's poll numbers? Then again, he decided, seeing the anxiety on Barbeau's face, Cohen was only reflecting her own deepest priorities—which were her personal safety and her continued hold on political power . . . and in that very definite order.

"Okay, Luke," she said finally. "*On* the record,

you deny all the rumors. If any question cuts a little close to the truth, you fall back on the old 'I cannot comment on ongoing intelligence or military operations' drill, right?"

Cohen nodded sagely. "And *off* the record?"

"Off the record, you find some of our go-to people, say from the *Times* or the *Post* or the cable news networks," Barbeau continued. "And then you do a little tap dance for them. Talk about how there's no possible way you could ever confirm the rumors that a top-secret U.S. Special Operations Force attacked and destroyed some of the 'terrorists' at this Moab facility. Get it?"

Cohen nodded. "Nice."

Barbeau allowed a small smile to cross her lips. "Push any line that feeds the narrative showing me as a tough, active commander in chief tracking down America's enemies." Her smile turned feral. "Especially while that macho jackass, J. D. Farrell, is off playing cowboy at his luxury Texas ranch."

Rauch felt anger bubbling up inside. He understood the ways in which raw power politics drove the president a lot better now than he had when he first joined her administration. But it was an ugly process. And it was getting uglier by the hour. "Maybe we ought to focus more on our real plans to handle this crisis," he suggested quietly. "As opposed to Mr. Cohen's schemes to send the media haring off in the wrong direction."

Barbeau eyed him curiously. "What new plans do you suppose we need, Dr. Rauch? Now that we know what this is really all about—my death or defeat in November—my course of action is obvious. I'm going to stay here and wait for Martindale to finish off his lunatic protégé." She shrugged. "After all, he has the inside knowledge and the high-tech war machines needed to do the job. Whereas we quite clearly do not."

"Assuming former president Martindale succeeds, what then?" Rauch asked, hardly able to believe the depth of cynicism and pure self-interest he was hearing. Even if the president's theory was correct, thousands of American soldiers, sailors, airmen, and civilians were dying . . . killed in what she perceived as a fratricidal struggle between rival groups of Scion and Iron Wolf mercenaries. A commander in chief should have the best interests of the country in mind. Hiding underground and doing nothing while good people were killed should be unthinkable. But it seemed the president could think only of herself.

Barbeau smiled more genuinely this time. "As soon as Patrick McLanahan is dead, really dead this time, we'll go to the Poles with what we know and give them a choice: Cough up Martindale and his Iron Wolf thugs . . . or face the full force of an enraged American people demanding revenge. Piotr Wilk may be stubborn, but he's not suicidal. If it comes down to a choice between his country's continued survival and the lives and freedom of a few hired killers, he'll make the smart call."

An hour later, Rauch passed through a pair of guarded doors at the Strategic Command Bunker's surface level. Acting far more casual than he felt inside, he strolled across a parking lot toward the neighboring golf course. He blinked back tears against the harsh glare of the sun. The air smelled fresh, free of the faint, acrid traces of chemicals that always seemed to linger in the bunker's recirculated atmosphere. He was nerving himself up to act on the resolution he'd made earlier.

Morally, there was no real choice at all, Rauch knew. From a career perspective, what he contemplated was suicide. But doing nothing would make him no better than Cohen or the president herself. Sighing, he took out his personal smartphone and entered a number. Obtaining it had required pulling strings with a lot of old think-tank colleagues and former friends.

His finger hovered indecisively over the icon that would initiate a call. Once he pushed that icon, there really was no going back. He'd been forced to leave a trail a mile wide to get to this point. There would be no way to dodge Barbeau's fury if this leaked out.

Closing his eyes, Rauch tapped the call icon and brought the phone to his ear. It rang twice and then a deep, resonant voice, familiar from a hundred press conferences and speeches answered. "Yes? Who is this?"

"Governor Farrell, my name is Edward Rauch and I'm President Barbeau's national security adviser," he said simply. "The reason I'm calling is that we've learned certain things that I believe you need to know about—"

CHAPTER 36

IRON WOLF FORCE, IN THE BIGHORN NATIONAL FOREST, WYOMING
That night

Brad McLanahan stepped out from under the camouflage netting hiding their aircraft, joining Nadia Rozek and Whack Macomber on the shallow grassy slope. Ian Schofield and his four recon troopers were nowhere in sight—which undoubtedly meant they were lurking somewhere close by in cover, ready to respond to any attack.

Nadia and Macomber stood looking up into the starlit sky, listening to the faint clatter of a helicopter growing louder as it drew closer. Both had their personal weapons out and ready. "You can all stand easy," he said, raising his voice to be sure Schofield heard him, too. "That's one of ours. Or one of Martindale's, anyway. The recognition code they radioed checks out."

With a shrug, Nadia slid her 9mm Walther P99 pistol back into her shoulder holster. Whack did the same with his M1911A1 .45 Colt. "Any word on what this is about?" he asked.

"No idea," Brad said shortly. "We're not due for a resupply mission."

"Additional supplies would arrive by road anyway," Nadia pointed out. Her lips thinned. "Sending in a helicopter like this is very conspicuous. It risks giving away our position."

Shrugging, Brad pointed out, "Campers that hear the noise will probably write it off as a Forest Service aircraft up looking for poachers. Or flying on fire watch." Privately, he crossed his fingers. With half the U.S. Air Force probably tasked with hunting for them, they couldn't count on staying concealed here for much longer. But it would be nice to fly out because they had somewhere else to go . . . and not because their cover was blown.

The sound of the helicopter's twin engines ramped up suddenly as a black shape without any visible navigation lights swept low overhead. It slowed down and spun through a half circle, flaring in to land not far away. Its rotor wash sent dead grass and dust flying.

Through eyes narrowed against the rotor-blown debris, Brad identified the helicopter's type. It was a Bell 429 Global Ranger. Blessed with a fairly long range and able to carry up to six passengers plus a pilot, the helicopter was a favorite with police forces and emergency medical evacuation services. This one, painted entirely in black, belonged to Scion.

His eyes opened wider as he recognized the two men who climbed down out of the helicopter's

passenger compartment. One, with longish gray
hair and neatly trimmed gray beard, was Kevin
Martindale. The other, moving a touch awkwardly
in his cumbersome exoskeleton and life-support
backpack, was his father, retired lieutenant general Patrick McLanahan.

Brad and the others moved to meet them.

Smiling broadly through his helmet's clear visor, his father gave him a quick hug, did the same
for Nadia, and then vigorously shook Macomber's
hand. In contrast, Martindale greeted them with
a rueful nod.

"Jesus, Dad," Brad said, "I'm really glad to see
you. But how the heck did you get here?"

The older McLanahan shrugged. "By one of
Mr. Martindale's private jets to a little, out-of-the-way airport in Saskatchewan first. That helicopter brought us the rest of the way." His teeth
flashed white in the darkness. "Breaking quite a
few FAA and Customs regulations in the process,
of course."

"No shit," Macomber interjected. He looked
the two new arrivals up and down with a critical eye. "Which makes me wonder why on God's
green earth you two decided to risk this little
jaunt? Hell, Mr. Martindale, you have a huge
bull's-eye painted on your back by that bitch
Stacy Anne Barbeau. I haven't checked the FBI
list lately, but my guess is that you're Public Enemy Number One."

"Not quite," Martindale said with a forced
grin. "Since the president now knows that the
general here is most definitely alive and *not* dead,

I've apparently been demoted to Public Enemy Number Two."

Brad stared at them.

His father nodded. "It seems I've been resurrected, son."

"Does Gryzlov know this?" Nadia demanded. She looked deeply worried. And with reason, since the Russian president hated the older McLanahan for killing his own father in a retaliatory bombing raid years ago—a hatred that sometimes carried him far beyond the point of sanity. In the not-so-distant past, Gennadiy Gryzlov had even been willing to threaten all-out nuclear war with both the United States and Poland to avenge himself on the general.

"Not yet," Martindale assured her. "From what we know, the news is still closely confined to Barbeau's innermost circle."

The implications of that flashed through Brad's mind. If Martindale had learned something only a few people close to the president knew, that must mean he now had a source on the inside—a *very* highly placed source.

His father saw the look of realization on his face and nodded slightly. "Loose lips, son," he cautioned.

Sink ships, Brad remembered. He closed his mouth.

"Which makes this stunt even dumber," Macomber argued. "If you've got something to discuss with us, why not stick to secure video links?"

"Ordinarily, I'd agree with you," Martindale said with a wry glance at Patrick McLanahan.

"But the general here thinks otherwise. And, as you undoubtedly know, he can be a very persuasive man."

Macomber looked interested. "Really?" He turned to Brad's father. "So, what did you do? Pull a gun on him?"

"No guns were involved," Martindale said primly. "He simply pointed out—correctly, I fear—that the situation is now so critical that the two of us can no longer afford to stay safely removed from the action."

Brad felt cold. "What's changed?" he asked. "By wiping out that air base, we reduced Gryzlov's striking power and drastically narrowed his options, right? How is that a bad thing?"

"It's not," his father said quickly. "What has changed is our appreciation of how far out in left field President Barbeau's preconceptions and prejudices have led her." Quickly, he outlined her belief that everything happening was part of a covert war between himself and Martindale . . . a war supposedly aimed on his part at either killing her or driving her from office. And her consequent determination to sit back and do nothing while they fought it out.

"Christ, she's just as nuts as Gryzlov," Brad said in disgust.

"Barbeau may be strategically blind, cowardly, and wholly self-absorbed, but she is not clinically insane," Martindale disagreed. Then he shrugged. "Though in this particular case, I suppose that may well be a difference without much real-world significance."

Nadia frowned. "But when your FBI learns that the Russians now own Regan Air Freight, won't that open her eyes to the truth?"

"Unfortunately, that's not likely to happen anytime soon. And certainly not in time for it to matter," Patrick McLanahan said.

"Why not?"

Martindale smiled wryly. "Because Gennadiy Gryzlov turns out not to be a complete fool, Major Rozek. At least not in this case. You see, we've managed to identify his go-between, a Swiss investment banker named Willem Daeniker. By now, I've no doubt the FBI has the same information."

"So?" Nadia asked. "How is this a problem?"

"It's a problem because this man Daeniker very conspicuously flew to Warsaw yesterday evening," Martindale explained. "And now he's vanished without a trace. None of my operatives or those of your country's internal security agency have been able to pick up his trail."

Brad swore softly. "So when the FBI starts checking up on him . . ."

"It'll look very likely that Daeniker was working for Mr. Martindale. Or the Polish government. Or both of them," his father finished for him.

"Sucks when your enemy has a plan," Macomber commented sourly. He shook his head. "Okay, then it's basically down to just us and the Russians—and whoever's unlucky enough to get caught between us."

"Looks that way," Patrick agreed.

"Sitting around here on our asses isn't going to

pull those enemy war robots off their next planned target," Macomber said. "We've got Gryzlov's attention now. So I figure we should get out there and wriggle around. Let's make them come to us for a change."

"Use your team as bait, you mean?" Martindale asked.

Macomber shrugged. "Well, yeah."

"If we show ourselves openly, all we do is confirm all of Barbeau's insinuations," Brad pointed out, though he did so unwillingly. Everything told him they were running out of time and options. "We'd play right into her hands."

His father nodded. "That might still be worth it, if it lured the Russians out into the open. But it won't. For all his many sordid sins and faults, Gennadiy Gryzlov isn't stupid. He won't send his robots into an obvious trap . . . not unless the potential payoff is a lot higher than anything we can believably offer."

"And maybe not even then," Martindale commented. "Barbeau's clearly had the same idea. She didn't dump all of Sky Masters' top engineers and scientists into that detention camp up in Idaho just for show. She's using them as bait of her own."

"For us, though," Brad said. "Not for Gryzlov." He shrugged. "She must have thought we'd try to rescue Boomer and the others on our own."

"In this case, her motivations don't matter," Martindale said. "Nor does the worm on the hook have any say over which particular fish tries to swallow it. What matters is that Gryzlov has so far passed up what would be a golden opportunity to slaughter some of America's topflight aircraft and weapons designers . . . because it's so plainly a trap."

"I do not believe that you and General McLanahan came all this way to recite yet another litany of what we cannot or must not do," Nadia said evenly. Her eyes flashed a warning. "Or am I wrong about that?"

Patrick smiled. "You're not wrong." The exoskeleton supporting him whirred as he shrugged his shoulders. "Whack's idea of setting a trap isn't that far off base. It's picking the spot that will be difficult. The only sure way to ambush Gryzlov's robots is to figure out their next target in advance . . . in time to position your CIDs to nail them."

Macomber snorted. "Hell, General, thanks for sharing that brilliant tactical insight. Got any others for us? Like 'friendly fire, isn't'? or 'the easy way is always mined'?" He grunted when Nadia drove a sharp elbow into his side.

Brad hid a grin. Nadia's tolerance for sarcasm, except for her own, was sometimes severely limited. He stepped between the two of them. "I think there's a little more to my dad's thinking than that, Whack."

"There is." Patrick nodded. "Or at least I hope so, anyway." He looked at them all. "What we need to do is get inside Gryzlov's mind. He may be orchestrating this war through that private mercenary outfit he's created, but it's still a one-man show. When it comes down to it, he has the final say on where those robots will strike next."

"Maybe so. But I've been batting about point-zero-zero-zero when it comes to figuring out what that asshole plans," Brad said unhappily. "I was the one who was sure he'd hit Sky Masters next, remember?" He knew his voice showed his frustration.

"And we all agreed with you," Nadia reminded him. She took his hand in hers, offering what solace she could in front of the others. "It was a reasonable deduction."

His father nodded sympathetically. "What Winston Churchill once said about Russia goes double for Gennadiy Gryzlov. 'I cannot forecast to you the action of Russia. It is a riddle wrapped in a mystery inside an enigma.'"

Nadia swung back to the older McLanahan. "But that is not the end of what Churchill said, is it?" she said suddenly.

"No, Major Rozek," he agreed. "Though it is the part of the quote that most people remember, even if it was just the setup for the punch line. The rest goes like this: 'But perhaps there is a key. That key is Russian national interest.'"

Brad shrugged. "Sure, Dad. But Gryzlov sees anything that weakens the U.S. as being in Russia's national interest. So that doesn't narrow things down much."

"Actually, it does," Martindale said. "But only if you look beyond the purely military aspect of his operations."

"Just fricking great. Here comes the lecture on politics," Macomber said, rolling his eyes.

"I'll try to make it painless, Colonel," Martindale assured him dryly. "Even if doing so means using small words. The concept is fairly simple as it is. Gryzlov's secret war has definitely damaged our country's armed forces. But it also threatens Stacy Anne Barbeau's reelection campaign by making her look weak and ineffectual. And that is very definitely *not* in Russia's best interest."

"Because if she loses, Gryzlov will face a much tougher American president," Brad realized.

Martindale nodded. "I've talked to Governor Farrell several times now. His reputation as a militaristic hard-liner has been greatly exaggerated by the press. But there is no doubt that he holds a much more realistic view of Russia and its leaders than President Barbeau."

Nadia looked at him. "But will she lose the election?"

"Nothing is certain in politics, Major. But I've watched a lot of campaigns in my life . . . and I know when the people on the inside are getting desperate. And that's what I see happening to Stacy Anne's outfit." Martindale shook his head. "Take, for example, this phony story she's peddling about a secret U.S. Special Operations Force that supposedly blasted the airport at Moab. Even if she gets a short-term boost in her poll numbers, it won't last long. You can't keep secrets like that, not in this day and age. Too many people know the truth. Before too long, someone inside the Pentagon or SOCOM itself is almost sure to leak that the story is false. And then, as soon as Gryzlov's robots launch another attack, she'll end up worse off politically than she was before."

"There's also the factor that the Russians are

running out of military and economic targets they can hit safely," Patrick said. "Our base defenses have been hardened. Our warships are mostly at sea, out of reach now that you've blown their cruise-missile aircraft to bits. Plus, the Air Force has finally gotten smart. They're flying surveillance drones over our defense plants and weapons labs."

Nadia frowned. "Their war robots could still go after other civilian targets. Anything from shopping malls to major sporting events . . . and everything in between."

"To create more terror?" Martindale asked. She nodded. "That is certainly possible. But again, attacks aimed at striking terror into the American people will only make Barbeau's defeat in November more likely."

"But do the Russians understand this?"

"In my experience," Martindale replied, "the Russians have a very firm grasp of American politics, especially where it touches on their interests." With a rueful look, he continued. "Certainly, Moscow's higher echelons understand us a lot better than a great many people in Washington understand the Russians."

Brad considered that. "So you think Gryzlov will go after a political target next."

His father nodded firmly. "It's his next logical move." His voice was level. "And given the situation right now, there is effectively only one vital American political target left for him to strike."

Brad began to see where Martindale and his father were going. So far, Gryzlov's covert operations had achieved significant tactical victories. But those same victories were damaging his own strategic goals by boosting the odds that Stacy Anne Barbeau would lose to Farrell—the last man the Russian leader could expect to dance to his tune. And while Gryzlov *wasn't* a moron . . . he *was* ruthless, violent, and willing to run enormous risks to achieve his desired ends. Which meant—

"Oh shit," he muttered. "You think the Russians are going to kill Governor Farrell."

Martindale nodded grimly. "His murder would set off a political firestorm."

"But won't his party simply nominate another candidate?" Nadia asked.

"There would be nothing simple about it," Martindale said tersely. "Farrell was the only one genuinely positioned to give Barbeau a run for her money in November. With him gone, his party will divide into a dozen warring factions. I don't see any of the other possible contenders beating her."

"Especially not if she can blame his death on us," Brad said slowly.

His father nodded. "Which is why we need to find your team a new operating base considerably farther south. And why Mr. Martindale and I need to borrow Captain Schofield and his scouts right away."

CHAPTER 37

That same time

Inside the old warehouse, Kirill Aristov fought to control the dread he felt when he stared up at the metal war machine looming over him. When his security team first joined up with Colonel Baryshev and his lethal KVMs, his fears had been largely irrational—the natural unease of a human suddenly confronted by faceless machines that moved like men, but that were exponentially more powerful. Now, though, he had all too many real reasons to be afraid of them. With every passing day, the pilots inside those combat robots seemed to merge more and more with their automatons. It was as though they were purging themselves of almost every ordinary human emotion, retaining only those that would serve in battle . . . fury, bloodlust, and the will to dominate.

"You have your new vehicle," Baryshev's cold, electronically synthesized voice said. "So take your reconnaissance team and do your job, Captain."

"My *men* and I have just finished a twenty-four-hour drive across half of America," Aristov said, trying to stay calm. "We need to rest first. As soon as it gets dark tomorrow, we'll move out."

"You waste valuable time. I find that . . . unacceptable." Servos whined as the machine flexed its metal hands.

Aristov resisted the urge to turn and run. If Baryshev decided to kill him, he was already as good as dead. He forced himself not to show any emotion. "General Kurakin's orders are very clear. This is an extremely sensitive target—one with enormous political significance. We cannot risk making any mistakes."

"I have read Moscow's intelligence files myself," the robot retorted. "I see nothing to fear."

"Moscow's intelligence may already be out-of-date, Colonel," Aristov said. Looking for other reasons to justify obeying their superior's demands for caution, he seized on the first one that came to mind . . . as unlikely as it seemed. "Remember, an Iron Wolf war machine destroyed Annenkov and the others without any warning."

The KVM's antenna-studded head inclined toward him. "Do you believe the Poles have deployed some of their Cybernetic Infantry Devices to protect this target?" In the cool, outwardly detached tones of its artificial voice there was suddenly a definite undercurrent of . . . eagerness. "Confronting such an enemy would be the ultimate test of our strength and power."

"I don't know," Aristov said slowly, choosing his words with care. The last thing he could afford to do was trigger this eerie meld of man and machine's increasingly aggressive instincts. If they snapped, he suspected Baryshev and the others were quite likely to charge out of the warehouse, rushing north to conduct an immediate attack on their own—despite the fact that covering the ninety-odd kilometers would only drain their batteries and fuel cells . . . and trigger an immediate counterattack by the alerted American Army and Air Force. "That's why my team and I need to get in as close as possible and conduct a detailed reconnaissance. If the Poles and their mercenaries are there, we'll find them for you. And then you can destroy them."

The KVM seemed to ponder that for a moment. "Very well," it said at last. "We will wait here." It straightened up to its full height. "But do not dawdle, little man. Complete your task quickly and efficiently and report your findings immediately. My patience is not unlimited."

OUTSIDE J. D. FARRELL'S RANCH, IN THE HILL COUNTRY, NEAR SISTERDALE, TEXAS
The next day

Former U.S. Special Forces and Iron Wolf Squadron sergeant Andrew Davis kept his chestnut mare to a slow walk as he rode through a rolling landscape of scrub oaks and cedar trees, brush, low-growing prickly-pear cacti, and limestone rocks and boulders. He was following a trail that meandered along a streambed, which was mostly dry at this time of the year. Rounded and flat-topped hills rose on all sides, sometimes with slopes that were open grassland, but that were more often thickly wooded.

In his cowboy hat, jeans, and boots, with a scabbarded Ruger Mini-14 Ranch Rifle strapped to his saddle, Davis looked more like a ranch hand out for a Sunday horseback ride than the chief of Governor John Dalton Farrell's security detail. And that, of course, was exactly the impression he wanted to convey. While he lazed along, apparently half dozing in the high, dry heat of a Texas Hill Country summer day, his eyes were busy probing the apparently uninhabited countryside—checking for anything out of place.

At a spot where two narrow, chalk white trails crossed, he guided his horse to the right and climbed up out of the low ground paralleling the streambed. A gentle breeze riffled through the long brown grass on the slope ahead. Near the top of a shallow, boulder-studded rise, he noticed an empty beer bottle perched upright on a flat rock off to the side of the trail. Squinting against the sunlight, he made out the label . . . Moosehead Lager from Canada.

Davis hid a smile. Subtlety was apparently not in season. He reined in and dismounted. His mare whinnied softly, apparently made uneasy by something unseen. "Easy, girl," he murmured. "Nothing to be worried about."

After glancing around the seemingly empty countryside around him, he perched on the sun-warmed rock, right beside the beer bottle. "It sure is nice *not* seeing you, Captain," he said aloud, with a chuckle. "I always do appreciate the invisibility of a genuine special ops professional at work."

From the middle of a clump of tall grass next to the boulder, Ian Schofield laughed softly. "I appreciate the compliment, Sergeant. I hope you'll forgive my not getting up to shake your hand . . . but I spent quite a lot of time arranging this ghillie suit just so."

Davis refrained from looking in the direction of his former commander's voice. In all honesty, he was impressed. He'd thought Schofield was concealed in the bushes on the other side of the trail. Ghillie suits, first invented by Scottish gamekeepers to avoid scaring off game by allowing hunters to fade into their surroundings, had been in military use for more than a century. Usually handcrafted by the snipers and scouts who relied on them, the suits were covered in bits of fabric, twine, burlap, and local foliage. When worn by an expert, a good suit could render a man lying motionless effectively invisible at a distance . . . and nearly so at close range, if he was in decent cover.

"Then I figure this isn't a social call," he said.

"Shouldn't you have said, 'I reckon'?" Schofield asked curiously. "As a Texan deep in the heart of his home country, I mean?"

Davis grinned. "That's only in the movies, Captain." His smile faded. "Anyhow, I'm guessing you're paying us a visit because there's trouble on the way."

"Quite probably," Schofield said. "In fact, I rather suspect you'll soon have a few unwelcome guests prowling around your perimeter, looking for weak spots where they can infiltrate. In fact, they could easily be here already, which is why I decided not to come trotting up to the main gate."

Davis pulled at his jaw. "Wouldn't surprise me much," he agreed. He shrugged. "See, the governor's ranch is a mighty big piece of rugged, empty country—close to four thousand acres, with around eight miles of fence line. That gives anyone interested in poking his nose where it ain't welcome a hell of a lot of possible approaches."

"You can't possibly guard that much territory," Schofield said. "Not with the size of Governor Farrell's current security detail."

"Nope," Davis said. "I'd need a full infantry battalion to lock the ranch down completely."

"And yet you don't seem all that worried, Sergeant," Schofield said with a trace of humor in his voice. "Which either means you have a plan or you're a fool. And I know you're not a fool."

"Maybe not," Davis allowed. "Truth is . . . I don't have to secure the whole ranch. There's only so many vantage points that would be useful to a spy or an assassin. As you can imagine, we keep a real close eye on those spots . . . both in person and with the help of some handy Sky Masters–designed surveillance gizmos." Doggedly, he tugged the brim of his cowboy hat a little lower and folded his arms.

"Trust me, Captain. No one's getting close enough to the big house to put the governor on camera or in the sights of a rifle. Not on *my* watch."

"I don't doubt that for a minute, Sergeant," Schofield assured him.

Mollified, Davis nodded. "Now, with that taken as gospel, and since I'm *not* dumb, I'd be more than happy to accept any assistance you'd care to offer."

Schofield cleared his throat. "Ah, well, there's the rub, I fear," he said apologetically. "You see, I'm not here to help you plug any gaps in your security. I'm here to persuade you to leave one open."

THE RANCH HOUSE
That same time

While listening to Kevin Martindale over his smartphone, John Dalton Farrell slowly got up. When this call came in, he'd been sprawled back in a big easy chair with his feet up on a coffee table—trying to make up his mind about which of several, inch-thick briefing books he wanted to tackle next. Frowning, he moved over to one of the big picture windows looking out across the ranch. Ordinarily, he found the view of green, wooded hills and the wide-open sky restful. Now, though, it felt more like he was surveying an alien country, one that might be full of lurking dangers and hidden menace.

"How sure of this are you?" he asked, when the other man finished explaining why he'd called.

"I'm not *sure* of anything, Governor," Martindale answered. "But I learned a long time ago to follow where the evidence leads—no matter how improbable the ultimate destination seems at first. In this case, everything I know about Gennadiy Gryzlov's worldview, ambitions, and behavioral patterns, along with the capabilities demonstrated by his combat robots, leads to one conclusion: He plans to kill you."

Farrell's jaw tightened. "A foreign government assassinating an American presidential candidate? There's no way Stacy Anne Barbeau could overlook something like that."

"No, she couldn't," Martindale agreed. "But given her present state of mind, she's far more likely to blame your murder on this supposed 'civil war' between General McLanahan and myself."

"Leaving the Russians in the clear," Farrell said bluntly. "And this country in political chaos. And Poland and its allies basically up shit creek." He turned away from the window. "Even setting aside my natural care and concern for my own damn skin, that's a seriously crappy outcome."

"I agree," Martindale told him. "Which is why we need to act to avoid that outcome."

Listening to the other man outline Scion's plan, Farrell glanced around the room, seeing the much-loved and unpretentious comfortable furniture, favorite books, and mementos he'd spent half a lifetime acquiring. When Martindale finished, he sighed. "Okay, I'm in." He snorted. "But if I end up dead, I want it on record that this was a really stupid idea."

"If you get killed, Governor," Martindale said simply, "you'll have plenty of company."

CHAPTER 38

SAN ANTONIO, TEXAS
Late that night

Standing at a scarred, oil-stained workbench inside the warehouse, Dobrynin scrutinized the grainy, green-tinged night-vision pictures relayed by Aristov's reconnaissance team. So far, what his commander was seeing closely matched the intelligence reports they'd studied. There were only a handful of uniformed police officers stationed around Farrell's rambling, stone-walled ranch house and its outbuildings. Their pistols and shotguns wouldn't be much use against Russia's war robots.

He frowned down at his laptop.

Still, it had proved surprisingly difficult for Aristov to reach a concealed position on one of the wooded hills overlooking the American politician's compound. Several of the most promising infiltration routes had been blocked by watchful guards or electronic surveillance gear. During the weeks their RKU unit had spent traveling the U.S. to scout possible targets, they'd never had so much trouble getting a man in close. Dobrynin was bothered by the disconnect between such tight outer security on the one hand and this apparent sloppiness so close to Farrell's country house on the other. But what could explain the seeming inconsistency?

"Enough time has been lost," a cold machine voice said over his shoulder. "Get your vehicles ready. We must be on the move to the Farrell ranch in the next ten minutes."

Taken by surprise, Dobrynin jerked upright. He'd been so preoccupied that he hadn't even heard the huge KVM come up right behind him. With his heart pounding so loudly that he was sure the machine's sensitive audio sensors could hear it, he turned around. "Excuse me, Colonel?"

"Don't play games with me," Baryshev said bluntly. "I've given you an order. Now obey it."

Dobrynin stared up at the robot. "But we haven't finished our reconnaissance yet."

"Further spying is unnecessary." The machine stepped closer, crowding him back against the workbench. "Already, Aristov has thrown away precious hours . . . only to confirm what we already knew. Nothing can be gained by waiting another full day. If anything, all that will do is give the Americans more time to strengthen their defenses—or to find this warehouse. By now, the Poles must know the methods we are using to avoid detection. The American government will not be far behind."

Shakily, Dobrynin nodded. That part of what Baryshev said was true. The destruction of their Moab air base meant their enemies must be aware they'd been using Regan Air Freight as cover for their operation. And it was only a small step from knowing that fact to zeroing in on FXR Trucking vehicles and facilities as the next logical piece of the puzzle. "Have you cleared this with Moscow?" he asked, still stalling for time.

"Kurakin has my recommendation," the robot said flatly. "No doubt he will dither for a time before deciding one way or the other. But in the meantime, I am the senior officer here. Yes?" The threat in its normally emotionless voice was unmistakable.

"Yes, you are, Colonel," Dobrynin agreed hastily. He had nothing to gain by opposing Baryshev's orders. And everything, including, quite probably, his life, to lose. The only sane action was to play along and load the war machines aboard their three big rigs. By the time they arrived within striking range of Farrell's ranch, Moscow should have made its call. If General Kurakin vetoed an immediate attack, they could always turn around and drive back to San Antonio, with no harm done. And if the RKU chief actually approved Baryshev's request? Well, then, the more darkness they had to operate in, the better. He raised his voice. "Yumashev! Popov! Prep your trucks! We're heading north."

ON THE FARRELL RANCH
A short time later

Aristov wished he could swear out loud without giving away his hiding place. He should have known Dobrynin would buckle if pushed. The KVMs and their increasingly inhuman pilots were too frightening. Now the trucks carrying the robots were inbound—only thirty minutes away at most. If Moscow approved Baryshev's demand for an immediate attack, what was he supposed to do? Stay here and watch from this hillside and hope that no stray rounds came his way?

There sure as hell wasn't time for him to pull back before they arrived . . . not without being spotted by Farrell's security guards. It had taken him half the night to worm his way this close to the governor's ranch house. And once the KVMs did their dirty work and withdrew, what then? Would he be expected to somehow skate away in all the confusion? To where? Did anyone really think Larionov and Mitkin would be foolish enough to hang around and wait for him while every American police and military unit within two hundred kilometers came screaming in with their sirens on and weapons hot?

Pizda rulyu, Aristov thought bleakly, I am *so* screwed.

The noise of a fast-approaching helicopter broke into his despair. Instinctively, he flattened himself, hoping the multispectral camouflage elements in his ghillie suit would prove effective if the Americans already had aircraft up hunting for him. That might only be paranoid thinking, he realized. But with the universe suddenly seemingly stuck in a "let's fuck Kirill over" setting, a touch of paranoia felt apt.

A black helicopter clattered low over his position. Rotors whirling, it swung back toward the ranch house and settled in to land not far from the building. Dust and tufts of grass swirled into the air. Lights abruptly flicked on around the compound. Another couple of Texas Rangers appeared from behind a stable and an equipment shed with their rifles at the ready. Several horses whinnied quietly from a corral outside his view, somewhere behind the ranch house itself. A dog barked off in the distance.

A man Aristov recognized from the pictures and video clips he'd studied as John D. Farrell came out of the house. He was accompanied by a single bodyguard. The Russian stared through the viewfinder of his compact Gen IV night-vision camera, torn between conflicting emotions. Was Farrell unexpectedly leaving his secluded ranch ahead of schedule? If so, Moscow would be furious at the missed opportunity to assassinate him. On the other hand, the Texan's sudden departure would guarantee Aristov's own survival—

Two men climbed down out the helicopter. One of them, bulkier than his gray-haired companion, seemed to move very awkwardly . . . almost mechanically. Farrell strolled over to greet them.

Without waiting any longer, the helicopter

lifted off and flew away to the west at very low altitude, practically hugging the earth as it disappeared into the night.

Aristov triggered the zoom on his camera to get a closer look at these new arrivals. His eyes widened in astonishment as their faces filled his viewfinder. Without thinking, he snapped a string of pictures. The gray-haired stranger was former U.S. president Kevin Martindale, now the head of Scion. The other was a man who had long been Russia's most determined and effective enemy . . . a man his leaders, especially President Gryzlov, believed was safely dead—reduced to nothing more than ashes scattered in the wind.

THE KREMLIN, MOSCOW
A short time later

For a long moment, Russian president Gennadiy Gryzlov stared at the grainy, green images showing Kevin Martindale and Patrick McLanahan shaking hands with Farrell. *This cannot be true*, he thought. *This must not be true*. He exhaled sharply, struggling against a swelling wave of red, all-consuming rage. Closing his eyes, he gripped the edge of his desk, squeezing so hard that his knuckles turned white.

"Mr. President?" Vladimir Kurakin said nervously, backing away a few steps. "Are you all right? Should I call someone? Your secretary Ulanov? Or perhaps your personal physician?"

"That fat American whore Barbeau lied to me," Gryzlov snarled, turning toward him. "She told me her fighter pilots killed McLanahan! She promised me he was dead!"

Kurakin looked down, unwilling to meet his leader's furious gaze. Sweat beaded his forehead. "It is possible President Barbeau sincerely believed that to be the case," he pointed out warily. "The strange exoskeleton the American wears proves that he was badly wounded, perhaps even crippled, when his aircraft went down."

"I don't want that murdering piece of shit crippled!" Gryzlov said through clenched teeth. "I want him torn to fucking pieces!" Gripped by fury, he came around his desk and strode over to the other man. "Very well! Since the Americans have failed so miserably, we'll do the job ourselves."

Kurakin moistened suddenly dry lips. "Mr. President?"

"Are Baryshev's war machines in position?"

Warily, Kurakin nodded. "Almost, sir. His KVM force is assembling on a country road close to Farrell's ranch." He looked even more nervous. "But I strongly urge caution. Without further reconnaissance, we can't be sure how strong the governor's security forces really are. Captain Aristov is the only scout we were able to get into position. Who knows how many troops the Americans may have concealed outside his field of view?"

"You can't seriously be frightened of a handful of cowboys and yokels with small arms?" Gryzlov scoffed.

Kurakin shook his head. "It's not just them. This sudden visit by Martindale and McLanahan could indicate that Farrell's bodyguards have been reinforced by the Iron Wolf machine that destroyed our base in Utah."

"Enough!" Gryzlov snapped scornfully. "You're sniveling like an old woman afraid of ghosts!" He turned away in contempt. "No more delays, Kurakin. We've just been handed the perfect opportunity to kill three birds of ill omen—McLanahan, Martindale, and Farrell—with a single stone. We're not going to waste it. Order Baryshev and his pilots to attack immediately!"

CHAPTER 39

NEAR THE FARRELL RANCH
A short time later

Colonel Ruslan Baryshev brought his KVM's systems to full readiness, transitioning from the power-saving mode used while they were being hauled around by truck. Limbs that had been locked in position whirred into motion. Data from newly energized sensors flooded through the neural link into his mind. It was as though he had been nearly blind and deaf, peering out at a silent world through a tiny pinhole . . . and then, in the blink of an eye, he found himself gifted with senses far beyond those of any mortal man. He felt a surge of exhilaration as the machine he inhabited came fully online.

Bent low to clear the trailer's ceiling, he dropped down onto the ground and then straightened up to his robot's full height. Immediately Dobrynin and the four other ex-Spetsnaz soldiers who served as the unit's drivers and scouts backed away in fear.

Baryshev accepted that as his due. They were right to be afraid. From the dawn of time, myths and legends had spoken of gods and demigods who walked the earth among mere humans—handing down judgment and dispensing vengeance as they saw fit. Now those myths had become reality.

He stepped aside, making room for Oleg Imrekov to bring his own machine out of the semitrailer they shared. Around him, the other four KVMs disembarked from their own transports. All three of the big trucks were parked along a dirt road that wound north from here, paralleling the flank of a lightly wooded rise. His night-vision sensors revealed a jumble of limestone and granite hills and ridges rising in all directions.

"Distance to primary target?" Baryshev queried the robot's computer.

Straight-line distance is thirty-one hundred meters, it replied. Instantly, the computer updated his tactical display with a detailed topographic map. It incorporated the most recent satellite-derived data with new information obtained by Aristov and Larionov during their attempts to infiltrate through the enemy's security perimeter. Icons representing known and suspected sentry posts and electronic surveillance gear speckled the map.

Whoever commanded Farrell's guard force *was* clever, Baryshev admitted to himself. The American had deployed his limited resources to maximum effect—placing almost every possible avenue of approach to the governor's vacation home under some form of observation. Aristov had been lucky indeed to find the solitary weak point in those defenses . . . and even then the gap was one only a highly trained operative like the former Spetsnaz officer could possibly exploit.

He frowned. Those sentries and sensors could not do anything to stop his planned assault, but they would make it impossible to achieve complete surprise. No doubt his KVMs could silence one or two of the guards posted in those hills without raising an alarm. But the security net was too tight. Sooner rather than later, the enemy would know his robots were on their way. And even a few minutes of warning would make the job of tracking down their intended victims—Farrell, Martindale, and McLanahan—that much more difficult and time-consuming. This would be especially true if Kurakin's warning of a possible Iron Wolf CID operating in the area proved accurate. A single enemy combat robot would be no match for his machines, but destroying it would take time.

In the end, Baryshev thought, none of that should matter very much. The nearest American heavy reaction force was stationed at Fort Hood, more than 160 kilometers away. Even if they took off immediately, the AH-64D Apache Longbow gunships based there would take at least thirty minutes to arrive within striking range. Any tanks and infantry fighting vehicles ordered out would be hours behind the gunships. Still, why take unnecessary chances?

With that in mind, he discarded his preliminary plan, which had called for a simple head-on rush by all six KVMs. Quickly, he sketched out an alternate maneuver—one that proposed a converging assault on Farrell's ranch house by three two-robot teams. Attacking nearly simultaneously from three separate directions should split the American defenses and render any escape attempt futile.

Baryshev's computer highlighted one of the assault routes he'd selected in red. It was the one that envisioned two war machines swinging to the right around the southern edge of the ranch. Once in position, they would attack from the east while two more pairs of KVMs came storming in from the south and west. *Early detection on this route is possible*, it declared. *Multiple communications satellite connections identified here.* An icon appeared on his map, on the main north-south road through this area and just outside the ranch's main gate.

"Identify those signals," Baryshev ordered. "Correlate them with the most recent satellite photos."

CNN, FOX, MSNBC, ABC, CBS, BBC . . . the computer reported, listing a slew of different media outlets from the United States and around the world. It pulled up a satellite photo showing a group of vans with antenna dishes in a tight-packed cluster on the shoulder of a narrow, two-lane road. A police car was parked just inside the gate, apparently keeping an eye on the press flock.

The media were camped out as close as they could get to the American presidential candidate's doorstep, Baryshev realized—which in this case was nearly two kilometers away. After so many days stuck deep in this rural backwater, this band of reporters must be growing desperate for some dramatic bit of news to fill airtime.

He opened a secure channel to the other robots in his force. "Specter Lead to all Specter units. Attention to orders." With a flick of one finger, he transmitted his revised attack plan to their computers. Imrekov, Zelin, and the rest radioed their acknowledgment. Their voices sounded avid, as though they were wolfhounds straining at the leash.

The Russian KVM commander bared his teeth in a malevolent grin. Just as in all the old stories of men and women who made deals with the devil, those journalists were about to have their deepest desires fulfilled . . . though not at all in the way they expected and only at a terrible price.

From his concealed position on the hillside above the road, Ian Schofield watched the Russian war machines split up and stride away into the darkness. The men who'd accompanied them were spreading out along the dirt road. His guess was that they were setting up a security perimeter around the three tractor-trailer trucks and a dark-colored sport utility vehicle. He zeroed in on one through the night scope attached to his M24A2 Remington sniper rifle. The Russian was armed with a submachine gun. He also wore body armor and a radio headset.

Seeing that, the Iron Wolf recon unit leader chewed at his lip, wishing he dared to transmit a quick warning to Andrew Davis and the rest of his team. But it was impossible. They had to assume the Russian combat robots had sensor capabilities that matched those of their own CIDs. If so, the enemy would pick up any transmission, no matter how short. Radioing in right now would be like sending up a flare. Not only would doing so give away his position, with fatal consequences for him personally, it would also blow this entire operation.

So instead, Schofield continued to lie low. He hoped like hell this scheme the McLanahans and Nadia Rozek had cooked up on the fly actually worked the way they hoped . . . because if it didn't, an awful lot of good people were going to get killed. Of course, given the odds stacked up against them, that was a likely outcome no matter how things played out.

OUTSIDE THE MAIN GATE
A short time later

Karl Ericson tossed his cigarette butt down and ground it out under his heel. Then he refolded his arms and leaned back against the production truck. He narrowed his eyes against the glare of klieg lights, surveying the gaggle of reporters and cameramen milling around outside the big ornamental wrought-iron gate with undisguised boredom. National Cable News paid his salary as a broadcast engineer. That meant he was expected to be able to install, operate, and maintain all the video, sound, and satellite communications equipment needed by this particular television news crew. It didn't mean he had to pretend that everything they did was important.

"Let's go live to Governor John D. Farrell's country estate, where our crackerjack reporter I. M. Sofullofshit will once again prattle on for thirty seconds about nothing at all," he grumbled to Amy Maguire, his petite, red-haired sidekick. She was the production crew's audio assistant.

She laughed. "I think he told New York we had some really hot breaking news this time."

"Like what, for Christ's sake?"

Maguire shrugged. "Well, that sheriff's car that's been guarding the gate did pull out of here about half an hour ago."

Ericson rolled his eyes. "Seriously? That's his big scoop? A couple of Cowtown cops go off on a kolache and doughnut run?"

"'I'm not saying it's evidence of a black-ops conspiracy, Tom,'" Maguire said portentously, mimicking the earnest, soulful tones favored by their not-so-favorite piece of on-air talent. "'But it could be a conspiracy—'"

And then the darkness beyond the circle of TV lights erupted in fire and shattering noise. A fusillade of high-explosive bullets ripped into the crowd of reporters and cameramen—mowing them down in a flurry of blinding flashes. Parked production trucks started coming apart under the shattering impact of more 30mm cannon rounds.

Wide-eyed with horror, Ericson turned to grab

Amy Maguire and drag her away . . . and abruptly
found himself sprawled on his back several yards
away from where he'd been standing. Flames
boiled off the wreckage of their vehicle. More explosions rocked the ground, but he couldn't hear
anything. Everything seemed to be happening in
an eerie, unearthly silence. He couldn't feel his
legs.

Through glazed eyes, he saw a tall, terrifying
shape emerge from the drifting smoke. Its head,
a smooth ovoid bristling with antennas, spun in
his direction. He opened his mouth to scream as
it raised a metal arm, aiming a massive weapon
at him.

There was a final blinding flash. And the whole
world went black.

Baryshev turned away from the American he'd
just killed. It was time to move on. His audio
and visual sensors weren't picking up any more
signs of life in the immediate area. He strode
back through the tangle of burning vehicles, un-
touched by the searing heat that swept across his
KVM's outer armor.

Another robot waited for him across the road.
*"I don't want to worry you, Lead, but it's possible the
enemy now knows we're here,"* he heard Imrekov say
with dry amusement.

Baryshev laughed, gripped by the sense of fierce
joy he increasingly experienced whenever given
the chance to demonstrate his power. "Much good
may it do them, Two." He switched his attention

to his computer. "Replay radio transmissions intercepted from the enemy compound since we opened fire here."

No transmissions recorded, the computer reported.

He arched an eyebrow in surprise. None? Shouldn't this sudden slaughter have sparked a flurry of radio chatter among the different elements of Farrell's security detail? In fact, triggering such a burst of signals was one of the reasons he'd carried out this massacre in the first place. He'd anticipated learning more about the Americans' plans and current deployment by analyzing their frantic emergency transmissions.

Imrekov confirmed that his computer hadn't picked anything up either. *"Are the Americans so deeply asleep? Or only deaf?"*

Baryshev shook his head. "Neither, I suspect, Two. They are only exercising remarkable communication discipline." Mentally, he shrugged. Let the Americans cower in silence. It wouldn't save them in the end. He opened a channel to the rest of his assault force. "Specter Lead to all Specter units. Commence main attack. Repeat, commence attack."

Joy-filled, guttural voices poured through his headset, acknowledging his order with animal-like glee.

Imrekov's KVM sprinted toward the wrought-iron gate closing off a winding, paved drive that led deeper into Farrell's ranch. Its hands gripped the bars, yanked hard, and with an earsplitting shriek of rending metal tore the whole gate loose from its hinges. Then, like an athlete throwing a discus, the robot spun through a half circle and hurled the crumpled shape away into the darkness. Its head swiveled toward Baryshev. *"What do you think, Lead? Shall we just go strolling on up that road and say hello?"*

The colonel shook his head with a slight smile. "Let's not be *quite* that obvious, Two. Follow me!"

Together, they raced through the opening and ran across a large grazing pasture, angling northwest toward a tree-lined 140-meter-high hill that overlooked Governor Farrell's ranch house from the east.

CHAPTER 40

ON THE FARRELL RANCH
That same time

Inside the cockpit of his CID, Brad McLanahan listened to the quick, staccato *beeps* that indicated the Russian robot pilots were talking to each other. Like the Iron Wolf Squadron, their radio signals were encrypted and then compressed into millisecond-long bursts. Given enough time, his computer might be able to decompress and decipher those transmissions. But time was exactly what he did not have. Nor could he draw an exact bead on the locations of those radio calls. All he knew now was that two of the Russian combat machines were somewhere south of him, two were off to the west, and two more, those that had just butchered the journalists at the main gate, were to the east.

With active data links between his CID and those piloted by Nadia and Whack Macomber, triangulation based on relative signal strength and bearing would have swiftly yielded the positions of those enemy robots . . . accurate to within a few meters. But open data links would also reveal their own existence to the Russians. It was the typical wartime trade-off: Which was most important? Obtaining information about the enemy? Or denying the same kind of information to them?

In this case, given the disparity in numbers, Brad had opted to stay still and silent for now—relying on his camouflage systems to hide from visual and thermal detection, while his passive sensors gathered information about the Russians. His CID was fully prone about a thousand meters south of Governor Farrell's ranch house. Lying flat against the ground meant that only half of his robot's thermal tiles and electrochromatic plates needed to draw power, which significantly reduced the drain on his fuel cells and batteries.

According to their battle plan, Nadia's robot was stationed north of the house, guarding against a possible threat from that direction. And Whack's CID was in position to the west. Brad swore fiercely under his breath. He'd guessed wrong, foolishly assuming the Russians would be unwilling to blow their cover so soon by going after the unarmed TV crews, who would have seen any approach from the east. Innocents had died because of his mistake. And now the enemy had found a gap in their defenses.

Brad checked his display, quickly reevaluating the tactical situation. From his current position, he had a field of fire along part of the road coming from the gate. But if the Russians coming from the east chose to cross that wooded high ground to the north instead, it would be up to Nadia to stop them.

Colonel Wayne "Whack" Macomber hoped his old boss's son wasn't beating himself up too badly for missing a single piece of the enemy's plan of attack. Sometimes the kid forgot that real war was almost always barely contained chaos, not some board game with set rules. As it was, the deployment Brad had selected at least gave them a fighting chance—which was more than a lot of soldiers down through history had ever had, from Leonidas's three hundred Spartans at Thermopylae to Pickett's Virginians stoically marching into the cross fire of more than a hundred Union artillery pieces at Gettysburg.

His CID was stationed near the edge of a thicket of cedars and oaks in a little valley west of Farrell's ranch house. From hcrc, hc had an almost unobstructed view down a dirt track that ran all the way to the western perimeter of the ranch. Spotting enemies moving through the jumble of hills and ridges to his north and south would be a little trickier, but his thermal and audio sensors should still be able to get a read on them.

Warning, Macomber's computer suddenly pulsed in his consciousness. *Movement alert west. Two enemy machines advancing toward our position. Range six hundred meters and closing fast.* Reacting instantly, he slaved several of his visual sensors to the new contacts. The Russian combat robots had just emerged from behind the sheltering mass of one of the neighboring hills and turned in his direction. They were loping along parallel to the dirt track at roughly sixty kilometers per hour.

Macomber eased his electromagnetic rail gun out from under his CID's torso. It powered up with a shrill, high-pitched whine. "*Zdravstvuyte.* Hello. *I do svidaniya.* And, good-bye," he murmured, sighting quickly on the lead enemy fighting machine.

Inside the cockpit of Specter Six, Major Alexei Bragin felt a sharp jolt sizzle across his brain as the KVM's computer sent an emergency alert through his neural link. *Strong electromagnetic signature detected,* it reported. *Unknown type. Range five hundred meters. Bearing zero-nine-two degrees.* A red dot blinked rapidly, centered at the edge of a grove of trees up ahead.

Bragin blinked. What kind of enemy sensor was that? He started to raise his 30mm autocannon—

And then his view of those woods disappeared, eclipsed by a dazzling, sun-bright white flash. One-third of a second later, a small superdense tungsten-steel alloy slug smashed through his KVM's torso at Mach 5. Bragin died instantly, vaporized by the massive impact that ripped his robot in half and sprayed molten fragments high into the air.

* * *

A hundred meters behind the blazing wreckage of Specter Six, Major Dmitry Veselovsky's highly trained instincts kicked in. He spun Specter Five, his KVM, away from the threat, and darted north toward a rocky spur jutting out from the nearest stretch of high ground. While on the move, he triggered a burst from his autocannon—sending a hail of high-explosive, armor-piercing rounds ripping downrange toward the still-unseen enemy. "Specter Five to Lead," he radioed, plunging into cover behind the boulder-strewn spur. "Enemy contact! Six is down. My computer evaluates the weapon used as a rail gun."

"*Engage and destroy the enemy, Five,*" Baryshev snapped. "*That has to be the Iron Wolf machine we were warned about. Kill it while the rest of us destroy the primary target!*"

"Affirmative, Lead!" Veselovsky pushed on, digging his robot's feet deep into the crumbling soil as he climbed fast up a wooded draw that offered him a sheltered route straight to the top of the hill.

Macomber flattened as the stumpy oak and cedar trees around him exploded in a hail of splinters and flying debris—shattered by a sudden burst of autocannon fire from the second Russian fighting machine. *That son of a bitch out there sure has fast reflexes,* he thought. Bits of shrapnel pinged off his back armor.

Minor damage to rear-facing visual camouflage elements, his computer told him. Wood fragments and razor-sharp pieces of shrapnel had slashed through some of the paper-thin electrochromatic plates layered across the CID's rear torso, head, and legs.

He raised up again, just in time to see the Russian combat robot disappear behind a spur of high ground. Quickly, he pulled his rail gun to the right and squeezed off another shot. Hell, who knew, maybe he could punch a round right through that rise.

CCRRACK!

Dirt and shattered rock fountained high into the night sky—spraying away from the deep crater the rail-gun slug gouged out of the hillside. *No hit*, the computer reported.

"No shit," Macomber growled out loud. With one part of his mind, he zoomed in his tactical display. What he saw made him frown. That enemy machine now had a covered route all the way up to the top of the forested hills that bordered this little valley. And from there, it could move swiftly along the high ground to any number of good vantage points overlooking Farrell's ranch house and its outbuildings.

Which left him no choice, he knew. He needed to intercept that Russian robot before it found a clear shot. Moving fast, Macomber shut down the CID's camouflage systems and scrambled to his feet. Broken tree branches and smoldering leaves cascaded off his back. Then he sprinted out of the thicket, thudded across the dirt trail, and started uphill himself, angling toward another draw that climbed out of the valley.

His skin crawled. Apart from a few trees and shallow limestone outcrops dotting the slope, there was no cover here. He'd be a sitting duck if the Russians attacking from the south blew past Brad's position and put him in their cross hairs.

Macomber was about two-thirds of the way up when his computer blared a warning. *Movement alert left front. Range close. One hundred meters.* Swearing, he swiveled to the left, seeing the bright green thermal image of a Russian autocannon protruding from between a pair of weathered boulders perched at the top of the hill. That enemy robot hadn't been heading for the ranch house after all. Instead, it had picked out the perfect spot to bushwhack him. He raised his rail gun, knowing it was already too late.

WHANG. WHANG. WHANG. WHANG.

Armor-piercing 30mm rounds hammered his CID with enormous force—slamming home at point-blank range. His rail gun went flying, destroyed by a direct hit. He tumbled backward, rolling over and over down the slope in a spreading cloud of dirt and gravel as the Russian kept shooting.

Macomber crashed heavily into the scarred top of a rock ledge. The impact stopped his fall. Immediately he scrambled across to the other side and dropped prone. The outcrop provided him with a small amount of cover . . . at least until that clever Russian bastard up there moved over to a new firing position.

Damage readouts scrolled across his displays in a dizzying sea of red and orange. *Severe hydraulic*

*systems damage. Forward thermal and visual camou-
flage tiles off-line. Fuel Cells Two, Five, and Seven down.
All weapons packs and ammunition destroyed. Torso armor holding, but effectiveness significantly degraded.*

"Translation: I am totally fucked," Macomber
said, tasting blood in his mouth. He'd been
slammed around inside the CID's cockpit pretty
badly during that wild-assed tumble down the
hill. He ignored the pain. Whatever injuries he'd
taken would have to wait their turn. Right now, he
needed to assess his tactical situation. Not that it
required any deep thought. Apart from having no
working weapons, no serviceable camouflage, and
no way to run away, everything was just peachy-
keen. Even bailing out of this shot-to-shit tin can
wasn't an option, since it would only leave him
more exposed . . . and he had a serious hunch their
enemies weren't planning on taking any prisoners.

Which left—what, exactly?

Movement detected, his computer reported un-
emotionally. *No visuals from this position. Assessment
derived from audio sensors only.* An icon blinked
into existence on his flickering tactical display. It
showed the CID's estimate of that Russian robot's
position based on the sounds its highly sensitive
microphones were picking up . . . in this case, the
noises made by metal feet cautiously picking their
way down the battle-torn slope.

Macomber whistled softly. That other pilot was
coming straight downhill toward him, apparently
determined to finish off his crippled enemy at knife
range. "Jeez, what a dumb-ass," he said with a slow,
twisted grin.

He ran a quick mental calculation, weighing the speed at which that Russian robot was making its way toward him against the time he needed. Finished, he nodded sharply. What he planned was doable. Calling it "survivable," on the other hand, might not pass the laugh test. Still, any chance was better than none at all.

Macomber took a deep breath, suddenly seeing a vision of Charlie Turlock's bright-eyed face floating before his eyes. She was laughing. Impatiently, he shook the vision away. "Sorry," he muttered. "I really don't need any bad omens right now." Through his neural link with the CID, he ordered, *Initiate self-destruct sequence. Authorization Macomber One-Alpha.*

Self-destruct authorization confirmed, the computer replied. *Thirty. Twenty-nine. Twenty-eight . . .*

Without waiting any longer, Macomber pushed his damaged machine upright. He was less than thirty meters from the oncoming Russian combat robot—which stopped dead in its tracks the moment his CID rose above the shallow limestone ledge. It started to raise its weapon.

"Boo, motherfucker!" Macomber snarled. He lunged uphill, covering the intervening distance in a few awkward, shambling strides. The CID's servos and actuators shrieked in protest. More sections of his system schematics winked out as his computer rerouted most of the remaining power reserves just to keep moving.

Twenty-five. Twenty-four . . . the computer said, continuing its dispassionate countdown.

The Russian robot opened fire again—scoring

more hits on his torso armor. Through his neural interface, Macomber felt the impacts like red-hot daggers plunging deep into his vitals. Groaning aloud, he clenched his jaw hard against the pain.

And then he crashed headlong into the enemy machine. His CID's large, articulated metal fingers curled around the other robot's arms and gripped tight. It stood frozen for a millisecond and then started thrashing around, trying to free itself.

Twenty. Nineteen. Eighteen . . .

Time to go, Macomber decided. He squirmed out of the haptic interface and wriggled around to the hatch at the bottom of the cockpit. *Fingers crossed*, he thought coldly, remembering how Charlie had died when her hatch jammed in a similar situation. He punched the emergency release.

With a grating sound, the hatch slid open.

He squeezed through the narrow opening and dropped out onto the ground. He hit with a *thud* that rattled his teeth and jarred his spine. Without hesitating, he rolled away from the entangled machines, scrambled to his feet, and ran full tilt across the slope—determined to put as much distance between himself and them as he possibly could.

Inside his head, his mind kept up a running count. *Eight. Seven. Six . . .*

Behind him, the Russian combat robot tore one arm free from the Iron Wolf CID's grip and started working to pry the other loose.

Three. Two . . . Macomber dove for cover behind

a boulder and curled up, covering his head with his hands.

With a deafening roar, his Cybernetic Infantry Device exploded. A massive ball of fire ballooned skyward, turning night into day for a split second. A powerful shock wave rippled outward from the center of the blast—toppling saplings and ripping branches off larger trees. The blast wave curled around the boulder, scooped Macomber off the ground, and tossed him against the trunk of a nearby oak tree with enough force to knock him unconscious.

When the terrible noise and light faded, all that was left of the two entangled war machines were burning fragments of metal and half-melted wiring scattered far and wide across the ravaged hillside.

CHAPTER 41

SOUTH OF THE RANCH HOUSE
That same time

Specter Three's pilot, Major Viktor Zelin, saw the green blip representing Dmitry Veselovsky's KVM wink out. He scowled. First, Bragin had bought it—blown to hell by one of those damned American rail guns. And now they'd lost a second combat robot, Veselovsky's Specter Five. How was that possible? The other man had just reported that he was closing in to kill the crippled Iron Wolf machine . . . when suddenly the whole sky over there lit up like the grand finale of a Moscow Victory Day fireworks display. Did the Americans have concealed heavy-weapons units—antitank missile teams, armored vehicles, and artillery—deployed around the ranch after all? Despite what all the satellite photos showed and what that little weasel Aristov had reported seeing with his own eyes?

"*Three, this is Four,*" he heard Captain Sergei Novikov say over their dedicated secure circuit. "*You know, this suddenly looks a lot like a trap.*"

Zelin nodded. "So it does, Sergei." He slowed his pace, seeing Novikov's robot do the same on his display. Up to now, their two KVMs had been advancing at their best possible speed given the rugged terrain, making their way through patches of trees and brush, across open pastureland, and up and over rocky, forested heights. Currently, they were moving north along a wooded valley that ran straight toward the center of the ranch, approximately two kilometers away. Visibility along the valley floor, even with their thermal sensors, wasn't good—limited in most places to much less than a hundred meters. If the Americans really did have antiarmor weapons in place, hidden under anti-IR camouflage netting, say, rushing along practically blind was just asking to be ambushed.

"*Maybe we should swing left, up onto those hills,*" Novikov suggested. The new axis of advance he proposed appeared on Zelin's display. It would take them out onto the slopes of a pair of low, rocky elevations that rose fifty meters or so above the valley. Someone had logged those hills in the past, clearing away everything but a few scraggly oaks and scattered tufts of thick brush and brambles. "*At least that would get us out of these trees. We'd be able to see. And we'd have much better fields of fire.*"

"True, Specter Four," Zelin said tersely. "But the same would apply to any concealed American units with a line of sight on those slopes. We'd be missile or tank cannon fodder out there. So we'll stick to cover for now."

"*Affirmative, Three.*"

Colonel Baryshev's irritated voice broke into their conversation. "*Specter Lead to Specter Three. What's the hold-up? Why are you and Four dicking around all of a sudden?*"

Zelin checked the two blips representing Baryshev and Imrekov on his map. They were still making their way uphill through the dense growth on a ridge east of the ranch house. Sourly, he noticed they weren't advancing much faster than he and Novikov were . . . and that they were even farther from the planned objective. He thought about pointing that fact out to his superior and then decided it was pointless. The colonel had been growing more domineering and less willing to listen to alternate views over the past several days. "You may have missed it, Colonel . . . but we've just taken thirty-three percent casualties, thanks to stronger-than-expected enemy resistance," he said coolly. "And since Specter Four and I would rather kill the enemy than die stupidly for the Motherland, we're playing this our way from here on. Specter Three, out."

"*That's insubordination, Zelin!*" Baryshev spluttered, sounding furious—even in a compressed and encrypted transmission. "*Get your damned KVMs moving faster, or—*"

"Block further signals from Specter Lead," Zelin ordered his computer. "Unless they carry a tactical emergency tag verified by his own robot's software."

Instructions understood, his KVM replied.

Zelin nodded, satisfied. That should prevent Baryshev from bitching at him for no good reason while still allowing two-way communication in a genuine crisis. He supposed the colonel would scream about it to Kurakin later, but at the moment, they were a long way from Moscow. He smiled wryly. Besides, they were nominally "mercenaries" now, right? They weren't supposed to be soldiers locked into a regular chain of command, were they? And anyway, if he and Novikov actually succeeded in killing Farrell, one of America's two major presidential candidates, and then escaping to Mexico without getting caught, no one back home would care much about any minor breaches of discipline.

Staying within sight of each other, the two Russian war machines stalked slowly north through the woods—accompanied by the loud, crackling sound of snapping branches and trampled brush as they bulled their way through places where tangles of interlaced trees, stunted saplings, vines, creepers, and bushes formed an otherwise impenetrable barrier. They stayed off the occasional, meandering horse and cattle trails they crossed. If the Americans did have prepared defenses on this ranch, those narrow paths would be death-traps. Despite the noise they were making, Zelin figured it was safer to stay deep in cover rather than give any defenders lurking up ahead a chance to use high-caliber, long-range weapons against them. In this thick forest, any encounters would take place at almost point-blank range, where their KVMs' agility, armor, and speed should prove decisive.

Brad McLanahan swallowed hard, feeling a painful lump in his throat. That huge blast off to the west could mean only one thing: Macomber's CID had blown itself up. There was no way to tell whether the colonel had been able to get out of his machine and into good cover before it detonated. So all he could do was hope and pray that Whack's name wasn't going to end up on his list of dead friends and comrades, a list that was already far too long. His eyes stung. Impatiently, he shook his head to clear them, but his CID's neural interface material around his head was too tight. Screw it. If he lived through this fight, there'd be time enough to mourn later.

Just now that looked like a mighty big "if."

At least the pair of Russian war robots Macomber had tangled with weren't transmitting anymore. It was likely they were both wrecked, too . . . or at least so seriously damaged that they no longer posed a real threat. Which left four of the powerful enemy machines prowling out there in the darkness. And that meant he and Nadia still faced odds of two-to-one against them.

A map section on Brad's tactical display turned red. *Signal intercepts plus audio sensors indicate two hostiles advancing in this sector,* his computer reported. *Exact range indeterminate, but certainly less than six hundred meters.*

He frowned. Those Russian pilots were coming right at him through the thickest parts of the stands of scraggly, second-growth timber that covered this narrow valley from rim to rim. It was obvious that they were staying well away from any clearings and trails. *Probable engagement range?* he queried the computer.

Less than one hundred meters, it replied.

"Great." He sighed. Their rail guns were the one weapons advantage they had over the Russians. Unfortunately, being forced to fight in the middle of a woodland robbed him of that advantage. Firing *through* those scrub oaks and cedars wasn't the problem. At Mach 5, a rail-gun projectile could punch a hole in the tallest redwood and keep on going. No, what sucked was the fact that he wouldn't be able to get a lock on those enemy machines until they were practically right on top of him. Powering up the rail gun would give his position away, but he should still be able to get the first shot off . . . which meant he could nail one Russian robot for sure. And then its companion would undoubtedly kill him, before his rail gun could cycle for a second shot.

Falling back to engage in more open ground wasn't an option either. The only open country behind him would give those Russians clear fields of fire at Governor Farrell's ranch house.

Ditch the "woe is poor, little me" crap, Brad, he told himself sternly. This was one of those "best-laid plans" deals, where everything went to hell, despite your best efforts. So he was going to have to fight and win right here, in the middle of these woods—or die trying. And since he'd really rather not get killed, he'd better come up with some better options . . . and fast.

Enemy advance continuing, the CID's computer reminded him. *Range to hostiles firming up based on additional audio and signals data. Now four hundred meters, plus or minus one hundred meters.*

The area highlighted on Brad's display shrank, reflecting this new assessment. But he still didn't have enough information to engage at a decent range. Even now, his computer's best estimate of the enemy location only put the two oncoming Russian war machines somewhere inside a moving box two hundred meters wide and three hundred meters deep. Firing blind with his rail gun and trusting to sheer luck to score a hit would be stupid. Nor could he effectively sweep a zone that large with his 25mm autocannon. The odds against destroying or disabling both enemy robots before he ran out of ammunition—or, more likely, they returned fire and blew the crap out of him—were astronomical.

Suddenly he remembered one of Whack's favorite battlefield maxims: When in doubt, smoke them out. He grinned tightly. He had area-effect weapons. It was time to use them . . . even if only to rattle those Russian pilots a little and maybe throw them off their own game plan. *Load thermobaric grenades*, he instructed his computer.

Quickly, Brad selected a series of desired impact points on his tactical display. The "ready" icon flashed. He stood up, unlimbered his grenade launcher, and aimed the weapon downrange, following the cues shown by the CID's computer as it calculated a precise trajectory automatically adjusted for wind velocity and temperature.

He squeezed the trigger. The launcher coughed quietly. He absorbed the minor amount of recoil, swung toward the next aiming cue, and fired again. And then a third time.

Time to go, Brad thought. His first grenade would impact in about three seconds. And when it did, all hell was going to break loose. For once, that phrase would be almost literally true. He started moving to his right, striding through the woods at an easy pace to keep his camouflage systems effective and to stay as quiet as possible.

Through the tree canopy, the sky to the south lit up with a bright orange flash. The sound reached him a second later.

WHUMMP.

"What the devil!" Major Viktor Zelin snarled, caught off guard by the powerful explosion a hundred meters behind him. The blast wave tore past, ripping leaves off trees and sending them swirling into the air. Heat swept across his KVM's armor. He crouched lower, reacting instinctively.

A second explosion shredded the darkness, this time even closer and off to the right. His night-vision sensors stepped down the flash so that it didn't blind him. His machine rocked, hit by another shock wave. The temperature readings outside his cockpit spiked upward again. Burning debris rained down across the nearby woods.

WHUMMP.

A third blast slashed at the forest a couple of hundred meters to his left—sending another ball of fire boiling into the sky. "We're being mortared!" Novikov yelled.

Negative. Weapons are 40mm thermobaric grenades, Zelin's KVM countered. A threat icon appeared on his map, highlighting a clearing about 350 meters ahead of them. *Sound analysis indicates this area as probable firing point*. He grimaced. The Americans must have a bunker or trench complex out there, camouflaged against satellite detection.

He wished again that their robots were equipped with radar. Not only would a counterbattery radar have warned them about the incoming grenades before they detonated, it would also have provided a far more precise fix on that suspected enemy position. Unfortunately, Russia's scientists hadn't been able to reverse-engineer the power-efficient, compact Sky Masters radars built into the Iron Wolf CIDs. And their own active radar systems were too cumbersome and needed too much energy. The passive radar warning receivers fitted into their KVM sensor arrays were a distinctly second-best solution.

"Specter Three to Four," Zelin radioed. "We will advance on the enemy. Lay down suppressive fire on that position!" Acting on his own orders, he rose and stalked forward—firing short bursts from his autocannon into the woods ahead of them. Novikov did the same, going forward on his left while shooting on the move.

Tree trunks started exploding, blasted to splinters by HE and armor-piercing rounds. Tracer rounds slashed through the darkness, corkscrewing wildly into the air as they ricocheted off boulders. Zelin wasn't anticipating they'd actually hit anyone. Right now, he only wanted to lay down enough fire to make the still-unseen Americans keep their heads down.

Brad pressed his CID flat against the ground, hearing 30mm rounds whipcrack past low overhead. Staccato flashes from their weapons showed the enemy fighting machines prowling closer, advancing through the splintered, burning forest. He smiled tightly. Most of their fire seemed to be directed about thirty meters to his left, toward his old position at the edge of a little clearing in the woods. But there were enough shells peppering the general area to make the idea of standing up for no good reason seem distinctly unwise.

Through narrowed eyes, he watched the Russians come on. They were definitely converging on the clearing. More high-explosive rounds slammed into the ground on the far side. Fountains of pulverized dirt and rock erupted.

The nearest enemy robot darted forward into the opening and loosed a long, withering burst aimed low—shredding trees and bushes and blasting more craters in the hard-packed soil. Its autocannon fell silent, with smoke coiling away from its muzzle. Slowly, the robot lowered its weapon. Its antenna-studded head whirred from side to side and then stopped—looking in his general direction.

Abruptly, Brad realized the Russian pilot must have spotted the trail of broken branches and crushed bracken he'd made when leaving the clearing. A trail that would lead the enemy straight to his current position, no matter how effective his camouflage systems were. "Damn," he muttered.

He leaped to his feet, unslinging his own 25mm autocannon at the same time. With a wild, piercing yell, he opened fire at point-blank range. More than a dozen rounds smashed into the enemy war machine—punching through its composite armor in a dazzling shower of sparks and shards of metal and plastic.

The Russian robot froze in midmotion. Tendrils of oily, black smoke poured out through the rents torn in its torso. Flames glowed red through the smoke.

Warning. Hostile to the right, his CID's computer snapped.

Brad glimpsed the second Russian war machine as it crashed through a thicket no more than fifty meters away. It was already shooting at him. Something clipped him in the side, spinning him partway around. Another round slammed into his CID's right arm with bone-rattling force. The hand gripping his autocannon went dead. Red lights flared on his display. *Lower arm actuators destroyed*, the computer said calmly. *Autocannon ammunition feed off-line*.

He whirled aside and ran, racing through the woods at high speed—zigzagging in an effort to throw off the enemy's aim. Shattered branches and torn leaves fluttered in his wake. More 30mm rounds struck his rear armor, cracking thermal tiles and knocking him off stride, but not quite penetrating.

The enemy machine was in close pursuit, firing at him on the move.

Time to go vertical, Brad realized. Running all out, he bounded into the air at nearly forty miles an hour—tearing through the woodland canopy on the way up and crashing back down among the trees. He hit the ground still running, and leaped again . . . soaring even higher and farther this time.

Again, he fell back to earth, thudding down in a huge cloud of dirt and dust. With his CID's left hand, he pried the damaged, still-warm autocannon loose and tossed it far away into the woods. Then he bulled his way on, shoving through saplings, brambles, and past vine-draped oaks without any attempt to hide the signs of his passage. Seconds later, he came out into another small clearing, a roughly circular patch of open ground no more than fifteen meters in diameter. His eyes narrowed. *This would have to do,* he thought. One way or another, he was done running.

Quickly, Brad plunged in among the trees and brush on the opposite side. As soon as he was out of sight of the glade, he cut right and circled back halfway around. He stopped a short distance from the opening and knelt down. *Reengage camouflage systems*, he commanded. Carefully, he took out his rail gun and set it behind the trunk of the nearest cedar tree . . . within easy reach.

Rear torso and right arm thermal and chameleon

camouflage partially compromised, the CID warned him. Several areas on a systems schematic glowed yellow. He edged over a little so that the robot's lifeless right arm was at least partly screened by the same tree. Then, satisfied, he settled in to wait.

Furious, Major Viktor Zelin ran through the forest, heading for the spot where his computer calculated the Iron Wolf robot must have landed after its second bound. He was on his own now. Novikov was dead, cut to pieces inside his cockpit by that sudden, shattering burst of point-blank cannon fire. *So much for Moscow's fucking intelligence reports*, he thought viciously. All those cheerful rear-echelon assurances that they wouldn't have to face more than a single one of the enemy's combat machines had just gone up in smoke and flames . . . exactly like Novikov's wrecked KVM.

At least he'd scored a number of solid hits on the other robot as it turned and ran. That should make the job of finishing it off easier.

Nearing the site, Zelin slowed down. He had no intention of stumbling into another ambush. Damaged or not, that Iron Wolf machine could still have teeth. Cautiously, he approached the place where the other pilot had crashed back to earth. Broken tree limbs and plowed dirt showed the exact spot. He paused, scanning the area with his night-vision sensors and listening for even the slightest sounds.

A long, thin shape glowed green off the woods

on his left. He swung in that direction, ready to fire. *Discarded 25mm enemy weapon*, his KVM's computer reported. Zelin showed his teeth. Nobody dropped their armament without good reason. He must have inflicted more damage on the Iron Wolf robot than he'd first thought.

The major turned back and moved on, following the trail of disturbed vegetation left by the other machine as it fled. He stayed on high alert. The KVM's sensitive microphones weren't picking up any new sounds . . . which meant the enemy had gone to ground somewhere up ahead.

Hostile approaching at nine o'clock, Brad's CID reported.

He held his breath, watching as the Russian war robot stepped warily into the clearing. Its smooth, featureless head swiveled from side to side, almost as though it were a hungry tiger sniffing for the scent of prey. His mouth felt dry as dust.

Come on, he urged it silently. *Just come a little farther. See, there's no one here. Just you.*

Apparently satisfied, the other machine started across the open ground—heading toward the false trail Brad had laid deeper into the woods.

Now.

He grabbed his rail gun from its hiding place behind the tree and powered it up. Alerted by the sudden noise and electromagnetic signature, the Russian robot spun toward him with its 30mm cannon ready.

Too late, Brad thought coldly. He fired. In a burst of bright, white plasma, the rail-gun slug hit the enemy machine squarely and blew it apart.

Awkwardly, he pushed his CID to its feet and moved out into the clearing. Its right arm dangled uselessly. That made four of the Russians down and dead. But with Macomber's machine wrecked and his own seriously damaged, the odds were still against them. He turned right, ready to head north toward Farrell's ranch house to offer Nadia what help he could . . . and saw new explosions rip the darkness to shreds. The harsh rattle of gunfire echoed off the surrounding hills.

Brad felt the blood drain from his face. Desperately, he lurched into motion, already knowing he was too late.

CHAPTER 42

EAST OF THE RANCH HOUSE
That same time

Colonel Ruslan Baryshev pushed his KVM up the steep slope, painfully clawing his way from tree to tree. Loose soil and chalky scree shifted under the robot's considerable weight with every step. He grimaced. He and Imrekov were already several minutes behind schedule, slowed down by his decision to advance over this high ground overlooking Farrell's compound instead of rushing straight up the paved drive from the main gate. His original plan had called for a near-simultaneous assault. Instead, his two-robot teams were engaging the enemy as separate units . . . and paying a much higher price than he'd anticipated.

In their first three attacks against the Americans, none of his KVMs had taken anything more than superficial damage. Now, in a matter of moments, a single Iron Wolf combat robot had apparently destroyed two of them. How was that possible?

Suddenly the beacon representing Specter Four, Novikov's machine, vanished from his tactical display. At almost the same moment, his team commander, Zelin, snapped a terse report that he was in pursuit of yet another Iron Wolf war machine. Over their dedicated circuit, he heard Imrekov's growled oath. "Chert voz'mi! *Damn it! What have we walked into here, Lead?*"

Baryshev bit down on the urge to unleash his own string of profanity. This was supposed to be a soft target, for God's sake! Instead, half of his robots had been turned into burned-out wrecks . . . with their highly trained pilots blown to charred bits. For a split second, he considered ordering a retreat. But then, just as quickly, he discarded the notion as cowardice. This was not a game, and casualties were inevitable in war. Besides, neither he nor Imrekov had yet encountered any opposition. And once they reached the top of this hill, the whole ranch would be at their mercy—laid out before their guns and missiles like a lamb trussed for the slaughter. "Keep going, Two," he ordered. "The American defenses cannot possibly be strong everywhere."

"*Very well, Specter Lead,*" the other man said, after a noticeable delay.

Seconds later, Baryshev made it to the hilltop, joined almost immediately by Imrekov's Specter Two. The two KVMs went forward through the trees and down the other side until they reached a vantage point on the military crest that gave them a clear line of sight across the whole valley. Fires glowed orange in the woods off to the south. Otherwise, everything seemed unnaturally silent.

From seven hundred meters away, Baryshev was puzzled to see that Farrell's large, single-story ranch house was completely dark, without any lights showing anywhere. Nor were there any lights on at the stable, equipment shed, or garage. The sedans and SUVs shown in Aristov's surveillance photos were still parked next to the house. Only the horse paddock was empty.

Movement in the open pastures to the north caught Baryshev's attention. Instantly alert, he swiveled that way, bringing his weapons to bear. *Horses only*, his computer reported, analyzing the fast-moving thermal signatures it detected. *No human riders.*

Ah, he thought, the sounds of battle must have spooked those animals. Well, there was no sense in wasting his limited ammunition on them. He was here to kill two-legged beasts.

"Lead, I'm not picking up any IR signatures in the house or in any of the other buildings!" Imrekov reported, sounding perplexed.

Baryshev turned his own thermal sensors to the task. His readings, or rather, the lack of them, confirmed the other man's findings. He wasn't able to pick up any human-sized heat sources inside the ranch house or its outbuildings. His mouth tightened. Where were the men they'd come to assassinate—Farrell, Martindale, and McLanahan?

He considered the house. Those stone walls were thick. When this battle began, the three

Americans must have retreated to a safe room or cellar deep in the interior. Certainly there were no signs of them on the grounds or even on the wooded slopes rising west of the compound. Anyway, if they had bolted for safety in that direction, Captain Aristov would have spotted them and reported in.

CCRRACK!

Another huge flash lit the woods to the south. Major Zelin's KVM went off-line immediately.

For a long, frozen moment, Baryshev stared at his readouts in shock. Two-thirds of his force gone? Just like that? In a few minutes of battle? For the first time in a long while, he felt the ice-cold sensation of fear crawling up his spine. He and the other KVM pilots had reveled in their strength, confident of the near invulnerability given them by these powerful war machines. But now it was only too clear that this sense of godlike invincibility had been nothing more than a dangerous illusion. They *could* be killed. In fact, they were *being* killed—struck down one after another by enemies who seemed like ghosts, able to move unseen in the shadows.

"*Lead? What do we do?*" Imrekov's tense voice broke through his sense of growing terror. "*Should we withdraw?*"

"No!" Baryshev snarled, shoving his fears aside with an act of will. Retreating now, when they had their target in sight, would be an act of supreme idiocy . . . as well as unforgivable cowardice. "We're not running, Oleg! We're going to finish this now!"

He yanked one of his three Spike fire-and-forget antitank missiles from a weapons pack. Imrekov did the same. Cued by their computers, they fired simultaneously.

Both missiles streaked downslope, punched through the ranch house's metal rooftop, and exploded inside. Windows shattered, blown out by the twin blasts. Thousands of tiny glass shards flew outward, twinkling eerily in the flickering light cast by orange-and-red fireballs soaring through the gaping holes torn in the roof.

They fired again. Two more explosions rocked the house. Fires glowed through the empty windows. One of the outer stone walls sagged inward. Imrekov switched to his 30mm autocannon and started shooting through the mangled rooftop, using incendiary rounds to set more fires among explosion-shattered bookcases and furniture. The colonel held his third missile ready. If Farrell and the others were still alive in what was fast becoming a roaring inferno, they might try to make a last-minute dash for one of the vehicles parked outside.

And then a burst of sun-bright white light flared on the wooded hill facing them. Oleg Imrekov's KVM disintegrated—hit by a metal projectile moving at supersonic speed. Jagged pieces of man and machine sprayed across the slope.

Horrified, Baryshev saw his computer highlight a new target several hundred meters away. He recognized the unmistakable outline of an Iron Wolf CID standing among the trees. *That's impossible*, he thought. One moment, the enemy robot wasn't there . . . and the next moment, there the damned thing was. Without wasting time on further thought, he fired his antitank missile. It slashed across the valley, visibly guiding on the other war machine.

Target destroyed, Major Nadia Rozek's CID computer reported calmly. She laughed in delight—knowing she'd just made sure there was one less Russian bastard to make trouble in the world. She raised her rail gun again, seeking out the second enemy robot.

Her warning system went off with a shrill *BEEP-BEEP-BEEP. Launch detection. Threat axis one o'clock. Missile has IR lock*. She saw a tiny bright dot streaking straight at her, growing bigger with astounding speed. She didn't have time to reactivate her thermal camouflage. "Damn," Nadia said softly. In the last possible instant, she hurled herself to the side—desperately crossing both of the CID's metal arms in front of its torso.

WHAAMM. WHAAMM.

She felt herself smashed backward in a dazzling flash of orange and red light. And then everything went black.

"Got you!" Baryshev crowed, seeing the bright orange burst engulf the Iron Wolf CID. He saw pieces fly off as it flew backward, crashed into a stand of trees, and collapsed in a heap. He turned away, thoroughly satisfied. No robot could have survived the rapid-fire detonations of his missile's tandem warhead—a smaller-shaped charge to strip away any explosive reactive armor and a primary charge designed to penetrate the underlying armor of a modern heavy tank.

His mood darkened again at the sight of the smoldering wreckage of Imrekov's KVM. This victory had come at too high a cost. Filled with wrath, he strode downslope toward Farrell's gutted ranch house. It was time to make sure the men his leaders wanted him to kill were truly dead.

Baryshev switched back to his own autocannon on the move. He came out onto level ground and closed in on the burning building. When he got to within fifty meters, he started circling it—methodically probing the ruins with his visual sensors, microphones, and chemical sniffers set at maximum sensitivity. He found nothing.

The Russian scowled. There should be some indication of dead bodies in there, even if it was only a glimpse of a mangled arm or leg half buried in the rubble or even just the smell of burning flesh. The flames roared higher, fed by cooler night air being drawn into the conflagration.

Unidentified movement. Right rear quadrant, the KVM's computer said. *Range two hundred and twenty meters.*

Startled, Baryshev whirled around . . . and found himself staring at the empty horse corral. Dust kicked low across the bare earth, blown by the wind sweeping in toward the burning house at his back. "Replay your detection footage," he ordered.

Obediently, the computer cycled the brief snippet of video imagery captured by its night-vision cameras across his display. Watching closely, Baryshev saw a patch of ground ripple in the breeze . . . almost as though it were cloth instead of solid earth. An eyebrow rose in surmise. Could that be—?

He headed toward the paddock.

Hugging the dirt with Martindale and Farrell in a shallow scrape near the middle of the paddock, Patrick McLanahan saw the IR camouflage netting stretched over their heads flutter slightly in the wind. Immediately he dialed up the sensitivity of the audio pickups built into his life-support helmet. *Well, damn*, he thought bitterly, hearing the tempo of the Russian robot's footsteps change and grow louder. *That's torn it*. So much for Plan A—which had called for the three of them to hide out here while Brad and the rest of his Iron Wolf team fought it out with Gryzlov's forces. Too bad there really wasn't a Plan B.

He glanced at Martindale and Farrell, seeing their eyes gleaming in the darkness. He put his hand on their shoulders, one after the other, pressing down in a peremptory command to stay *down*, no matter what happened. Tightly, they nodded.

Time's up, Muck, Patrick thought, deliberately using the nickname his friends had given him years ago . . . many of whom were long dead, killed in combat, in air crashes, or by terrorists. It seemed appropriate, somehow, considering he'd probably be seeing them soon. Besides, if he was going to die, he'd much rather meet his end out under the open sky than cowering in a covered ditch.

Quickly, not giving himself time to crap out, he wriggled out from under the camouflage netting. Gritting his teeth, he forced himself upright, ignoring the way the servos in his supporting exoskeleton protested the sudden movement. Then, moving awkwardly, he jog-trotted away across the dusty paddock.

Colonel Ruslan Baryshev saw the strange figure scramble out from under the camouflage net and turn to run. "Identify that man," he snapped.

Profile matches most recent photograph of Lieutenant General Patrick McLanahan, his KVM's computer replied. *Target priority per Moscow's most recent orders is Alpha-One.*

Baryshev nodded. Given President Gryzlov's personal desire for revenge against McLanahan— the man whose bombs had killed Gryzlov's father and led directly to his mother's suicide—that was no surprise. It was certainly a desire he shared. As an officer in Russia's air force, he'd seen hundreds of friends and comrades killed by the American and the forces he'd commanded. He raised his autocannon. His finger started to tighten on the trigger . . . and then it eased off. Why give McLanahan so easy a death? After all, what was it that Gryzlov had said to Kurakin, a message passed on verbatim by the general when he'd ordered this attack? Oh, yes. "I don't want that murdering piece of shit crippled! I want him torn to fucking pieces!"

His lips twisted in a savage grin. Well . . . why not follow those orders to the letter? Turning away from the camouflaged shelter he'd spotted, he stalked slowly after the fleeing American, gliding along like a cat toying with a terrified mouse.

Warning. Warning. Multiple systems failures. Severe damage. Weapons off-line. Sensors at ten percent efficiency. Power supplies at critical level. Warning. Warning. Immediate pilot action required.

Groggily, Nadia Rozek swam back to consciousness, pulling herself away from what had seemed a dark, lightless abyss filled with terrifying creatures. Her CID computer's recitation of its litany of woes continued. The crackling static in her ears and the weirdly shaped blotches obscuring some of the virtual readouts it was sending to her suggested the neural link was damaged.

She shook her head, trying to wake up faster, and winced as a sharp pain stabbed at her. Blood dripped from a gash on her forehead. The bitter odor of burned-out electronics and circuitry hung heavily in the stagnant air. She grimaced. Evidently, her life-support system was dead, too.

Her CID's left arm was gone—blown off at the socket. The robot's right arm was nothing more than a stump. She had a vague memory of desperately throwing them up in front of her to shield the section of torso that contained her cockpit.

Blearily, she realized they must have taken the brunt of that antitank missile's blast.

Nadia strained to get the CID back on its feet. Using the damaged haptic interface made her feel as though she were slogging through hip-deep quicksand . . . with fifty-pound weights fastened to her ankles. Leg servos and actuators screeched shrilly, audibly on the edge of total failure. She gritted her teeth, ignoring both the painful, head-splitting noises and the cascade of yellow and red caution and warning lights that suddenly blossomed on her last working equipment display.

She staggered upright . . . and gasped out loud at what she saw through her only functioning camera: General McLanahan, Brad's much-loved father, stumbling away across a dusty field, with a sleek, deadly-looking Russian war machine in pursuit.

"No," Nadia said brokenly, imagining the sorrow the man she loved with all her soul would feel on learning of his father's gruesome death at the hands of their enemies. The news would pierce Brad's heart like a sharpened sword. She stiffened. "No. I will *not* allow it!"

Doggedly, she lurched down the hill, overriding every one of the dying Iron Wolf CID's fail-safes and damage protocols to move faster.

Laughing now, Baryshev strode on after the crippled American. That odd metallic carapace the other man wore was a pale imitation of the powered exoskeleton at the core of his own KVM. Perhaps he should begin by forcibly peeling those bits of metal away from the writhing, screaming coward, he mused . . . before moving on to wrench off McLanahan's physical arms and legs.

Through his link, the computer tried to attract his attention. *Movement al—*

With an impatient gesture, Baryshev silenced the alarm. This was a moment to savor . . . without pointless distractions. The robot's sensors must have spotted the other two Americans—Farrell and Martindale—making their own futile dash for safety while he chased after this one. *Let them run*, he thought coldly. They couldn't get far. Once he'd finished mutilating McLanahan's corpse, they would become his next quarry.

And then something crashed hard into his KVM from the side, knocking him off balance. Despite his safety harness, the sudden impact was forceful enough to slam his head up against one of the backup instrument panels. His robot stumbled, falling to its knees.

Enraged by this intrusion on his private hunt, Baryshev spat out blood from the lip he'd just bitten. "*Sukin syn!* Son of a bitch." His KVM got back up and spun toward this new attacker.

His eyes widened in surprise as he recognized the Iron Wolf machine he thought he'd killed with his antitank missile. The enemy war robot was a battered wreck, with both arms gone and most of the sensor panels mounted on its weird, hexagonal head reduced to slag and broken bits of circuitry. But the damned thing was still moving somehow . . . deliberately putting itself between him and McLanahan.

Not for long, Baryshev thought viciously. He fired his autocannon—perforating the Iron Wolf CID as it stumbled toward him again. Sparks and smoke danced around the punctures his rounds tore through its already weakened armor. With a harsh laugh, he stepped aside from the other machine's lunge and watched it crumple to the ground.

Triumphantly, he looked back to find McLanahan. The American had stopped running away. Instead, he was rushing toward the downed robot with a look of horror on his lined face.

Grinning, Baryshev raised his autocannon again, taking careful aim.

Patrick McLanahan dropped to his knees beside Nadia's CID. Through his partial neural link, he made contact with the machine's computer. It was failing fast, shutting down more and more core memory and command functions in a futile effort to stay online for its pilot. He had only had time to order it to open the emergency hatch before it went dead.

The hatch cycled. Smoke and the harsh, coppery smell of blood eddied out through the opening.

"Trying to hide, little man?" he heard a cold, synthesized voice say in accented English. "Gennadiy Gryzlov sends his regards."

With a wry smile, Patrick looked up, right into the muzzle of the Russian war robot's 30mm cannon. "Does he? Well, you tell that asshole I'll see him in hell," he said coolly. At a faint glimpse of movement far off in the darkness, well beyond Farrell's blazing ranch house, he smiled more genuinely. "But you know, I have a feeling you'll get there first."

"Brave words for a—"

CCRRACK!

The Russian combat robot blew apart in a ball of fire—hit squarely in the back by a rail-gun shot that went through and through at Mach 5. Its head and broken limbs spiraled away into the air . . . and came crashing down in different places scattered across the dusty corral.

Painfully, Patrick pushed himself back up onto his hands and knees from where he'd been thrown by the blast. He crawled back over to Nadia Rozek's dead Cybernetic Infantry Device as fast as he could. His lips moved silently. Prayer wasn't usually his thing, but right now he'd take any help on offer. Especially when the alternative was watching his son's heart shatter into a thousand pieces.

CHAPTER 43

ON THE FARRELL RANCH
That same time

Brad McLanahan skidded to a stop. He stared down at Nadia's mangled CID, feeling a sudden sense of dread so intense that it drowned every other emotion, even his relief at seeing his father alive and the last Russian war robot scattered in pieces.

Unable to open data link to Wolf Two, his CID computer said unhelpfully. *Damage analysis indicates complete processing unit failure, along with—*

Skip it, Brad ordered harshly, not wanting to hear any more.

Command not understood, the computer replied.

I mean, cancel Wolf Two damage analysis report, Brad said tiredly, kicking himself for forgetting that English-language idioms were not the system's strong suit. He noticed Martindale and Farrell hurrying up to them across the corral.

Slowly, his father backed out of the downed

CID's emergency hatch, carefully dragging a blood-soaked Nadia Rozek with him. Despite the open gash on her forehead, her face was still beautiful, but it was ashen, almost chalk white. Her long, slender legs were—

Hurriedly, Brad averted his gaze from the mess he'd just seen. *Oh, Christ*, he thought, in mingled horror and supplication. Those had been shards of bone glistening white in the middle of all that gore. His stomach heaved abruptly, and he fought against the urge to vomit—swallowing hard against the sour taste of bile. He turned to his father. "Is she—?" He choked up, unable to go on.

"Nadia's still alive, son," his father said quietly, "but she's badly wounded. I can't promise you she'll make it." He looked up and saw the two other men. "Governor," he told Farrell, "we need a life flight here, ASAP."

Farrell nodded sharply. He pulled out his smartphone. "I'm on it, General." He tapped in the emergency number and started talking to the dispatcher—rapping out terse instructions with calm assurance. When he was finished, he glanced back at them. "Fort Sam Houston down in San Antonio's got the nearest decent trauma center. Their ambulance helicopter will be here in about twenty minutes."

Brad saw his father frown. "We need to stabilize Major Rozek before then. And I can't do that with my bare hands."

Farrell nodded again. He swung around to the security guards who were rushing toward them from the other hurriedly camouflaged shelters they'd scattered across the ranch compound. "Jimmy!" he shouted, pointing at one. "Grab that emergency medical kit from the stable! And then get your ass back here, *muy pronto*!"

"Yes, sir!" the guard yelled back over his shoulder, already sprinting off.

Farrell shoved his hands in his pockets and kicked absently at the dry soil of the corral. "I did have another medical kit," he said reflectively. "But that was in the master bathroom over there." He jerked a thumb at the brightly burning remains of his ranch house. "Somehow, I don't figure it's still in one piece."

Martindale cleared his throat uncertainly. "I regret the property damage, Governor."

Farrell shrugged. "Never mind about the house." He knelt down beside Nadia and gently took her hand in his. "People are what count in the end, folks. Ultimately, *things* don't matter a damn."

"Indeed," Martindale said coolly. "I'm sure you're right." He looked at the older McLanahan and at Brad. "In the meantime, the three of us need to be moving. If word of this . . . *incident* . . . isn't already flashing across the Internet and up the chain of command to President Barbeau, it will be soon enough. Before the military and the FBI descend *en masse* here, it would be best if we were long gone."

"What about Whack?" Brad heard himself snap. "And Nadia?"

"I'm sure the governor's security detail will search for Colonel Macomber. If he's still alive, they will take good care of him," Martindale said soothingly. "As for Major Rozek, if she lives, she should be safe enough in a hospital . . . under the governor's protection."

Farrell nodded. "You can rest easy on that score, Captain McLanahan," he assured Brad. "No one, especially not some fed, is going to mess with her on Texas soil. I promise you that."

"I'm not leaving," a firm, matter-of-fact voice said. It was Patrick McLanahan. He stared hard at Martindale. "We've been running from Stacy Anne Barbeau for far too long. It's high time we stopped hiding out and took a stand. The American people need to know what she's done . . . and what she's failed to do."

Martindale snorted. "And just what overoptimistic impulse leads you to conclude that Barbeau will *ever* give us that chance, General? Before we can say boo, she'll have her goons drag us off to some black site—about as far away from the media as the back side of the moon."

"I wouldn't be too sure of that," Farrell said with a sudden flash of teeth in the darkness. "Y'all may have forgotten . . . but those Russians were trying to kill *me*. Which makes this a matter for the State of Texas, not the federal government."

Martindale stirred. "I suspect the president will strongly dispute your jurisdiction, Governor."

Farrell shrugged again. "Sure she will," he agreed. "But it'll make a real dandy court case, won't it? And it would be one hell of a media draw . . . especially coming smack-dab in the middle of a hotly contested presidential campaign."

Despite his sadness and anxiety for Nadia,

Brad felt a sudden urge to laugh at the bemused expression on Martindale's face. It appeared that the master manipulator might finally have met his match—

The staccato chatter of submachine guns rang out, echoing off the high ground to the south.

Brad spun toward the sound of the firing and darted off at full speed, slowing down only long enough to scoop an object off the ground with his CID's still-working left hand.

NEAR THE FARRELL RANCH
That same time

Nikolai Dobrynin frowned toward the Farrell ranch. The sound of firing from over those hills had ended several minutes ago. So where were Baryshev and his damned KVMs? The longer they delayed here, the more likely they would be to run into American law enforcement or military roadblocks on the roads back to San Antonio and then farther south toward the U.S.-Mexican border. "Specter Lead, this is Checkmate Two," he said into his throat mike. "Do you read me? Over."

There was no reply. Only the hiss of static over an empty frequency.

"What kind of game are those bloodthirsty maniacs playing now?" he groused to Pavel Larionov.

The bigger man shrugged. "It's probably better if we don't know," he advised. "If we want to be able to sleep tonight, that is."

Dobrynin winced. That much was probably true, he decided. He'd already had nightmares about the blood and scraps of human flesh coating Baryshev's war robot after that attack out in California. He tapped Larionov on the shoulder. "Let's pull the rest of our guys in, Pavel. I want to get on the road as soon as the colonel and the others return."

The other man nodded. He turned his head toward where the other three former Spetsnaz soldiers were posted, and spoke briefly into his own mike—using their team's own secure channel. One after another, Yumashev, Popov, and Mitkin rose from their concealed firing positions along the dirt road and trotted back toward the three parked big rigs. Finished, Larionov asked, "What about the captain?"

Dobrynin sighed. "If Kirill's smart, he'll hold tight. He's got a good position. Once the Americans make their initial sweep, he might be able to get clear and make it out on his own."

The big man snorted. "You really believe that bullshit, sir?"

"Not really," Dobrynin admitted. "But let's face it. The captain was fucked as soon as Moscow sent that premature attack order." He shook his head. "We just have to hope that he keeps his mouth shut long enough for the rest of us to escape—"

Larionov's head, hit by a 7.62mm bullet, exploded in Dobrynin's face—spraying him with lacerating fragments of bone and teeth. The big man went down in a boneless heap, like a puppet with all its strings cut.

For a split second, Dobrynin stared down at the dead man in openmouthed astonishment. Then he recovered. "Sniper!" he yelled, diving for the ground.

Along the road, Mitkin and Yumashev reacted fast, hitting the dirt and rolling into a shallow ditch beside the road. Popov was slower. Fatally so. A second silenced rifle shot dropped him in his tracks.

"Suppressive fire!" Dobrynin shouted. "At the hillside across the road!"

They opened up with their HK7s, firing short bursts toward the opposite slope—carefully directing their shots at the most likely spots where the unseen sniper could be hiding. Dust, bits of torn brush, and sparks from ricochets drifted downwind.

"Cease fire!" Dobrynin called. "Cease fire!"

Silence descended across the darkened stretch of Texas country road.

"Did we get him?" he heard Mitkin ask.

Another rifle bullet tore up off the dirt beside Dobrynin's face. Frantically, he rolled away and scrambled into cover behind a big-rig truck tire. "Unfortunately, not," he said dryly. He grimaced. They were pinned down. Advancing into the open against that concealed rifleman would be suicide. The same thing applied to trying to drive away down the road in their trucks. No, he thought angrily, they were stuck here until Baryshev's KVMs returned, pinpointed the solitary sniper who'd ambushed them, and blew him away. "Where the hell are those robots?" he wondered aloud.

"Right here," he heard an ice-cold electronic voice reply.

Dobrynin whipped around in time to see a massive shape emerge out of the darkness. Relieved, he stood up, careful to keep the tractor-trailer between him and the rifleman who'd killed Larionov and Povov. "It's about fucking time," he growled . . . and then felt the hairs on the back of his neck stand up when the robot moved closer. It was taller than the KVMs, with a six-sided head. "Oh, Christ," he muttered. "You're not one of ours, are you?"

The Iron Wolf war machine shook its head. "No, I'm not." It tossed an object onto the ground. Dobrynin stared down in horror at the smooth, featureless ovoid that rolled up against his boots. "*That's* what's left of your robots," the CID said harshly. "Now it's your turn. Surrender. Or die. It's your call."

Numbly, Dobrynin tossed his submachine gun aside and raised his hands. He heard the clatter of weapons hitting the ground as Yumashev and Mitkin followed his example.

ON THE FARRELL RANCH
A short time later

Kirill Aristov decided it was time to go. So far, only a single medevac helicopter had landed and taken off. But he could hear more aircraft in the distance, along with the sound of police and fire-engine sirens coming closer. If he waited much longer, the ranch would be swarming with American police and soldiers. And there was no way he could evade a serious sweep by dismounted troops and sheriffs with dogs.

From his vantage point on this low, wooded knoll, it was difficult to know exactly what had happened, but one thing was very clear: Baryshev's attack had run into ferocious and wholly unexpected opposition. He'd seen at least one of the KVMs destroyed—blown to pieces near the top of the hill across from him. And he'd watched another vanish into the darkness beyond the burning ruins of Farrell's ranch house . . . followed soon after by a powerful explosion. That, coupled with the sight of one of those Iron Wolf war machines moving out in the open without being fired on, strongly suggested the colonel and his men had been defeated. But whether they'd won or lost no longer mattered much to Aristov. His only goal now was to get off this ranch and out of the country as fast as possible.

With that in mind, he carefully stowed his night-vision camera and scope back inside his camouflage suit. Then, slowly and cautiously, he wriggled backward, out from between the two gnarled trees he'd been using for cover. As soon as he reached a place where brush and high grass cut off his view of the burning house, he started to get up.

And froze suddenly, feeling the cold muzzle of a gun at the base of his skull.

"I'd sure appreciate it if you'd keep your hands

where I can see them," an amused-sounding voice drawled conversationally. "See, I'm a little high-strung just now . . . and my trigger finger gets kind of twitchy when that happens."

Aristov swallowed hard. He lowered himself back down and carefully spread his hands out, palms flat against the ground. He lay still while the gunman patted him down roughly, but efficiently—swiftly finding and removing his camera and his fighting knife, which was the only weapon he carried.

The gunman stepped back. "You can roll over now, friend."

Aristov did as he was told . . . and saw a grizzled, tough-looking man pointing a Ruger Mini-14 Ranch Rifle at him. The American wore a camouflage suit much like his own. "You have the advantage of me, Mr.—?"

The other man nodded politely. "The name's Davis. Andrew Davis."

Aristov sighed. "And how long have you been watching me, Mr. Davis?"

"Pretty much from the time you crossed Governor Farrell's property line," the American said casually.

"So what happens now?"

Davis grinned back at him. "We mosey on down to what's left of the governor's house." His eyes hardened. "I sure hope you didn't have any real urgent business, friend, like say down in Mexico, or maybe back home in Russia . . . because I'm thinking there are an awful lot of folks who are real eager to have a word or two with you."

CHAPTER 44

THE KREMLIN, MOSCOW
A short time later

Vladimir Kurakin sat in painful silence, watching the evidence of an unmitigated disaster unfold in real time. The big-screen monitor in Gryzlov's private office currently showed a hurriedly called press conference taking place at Governor John D. Farrell's Texas ranch.

The American presidential candidate stood confidently before an array of microphones—looking tired, but otherwise none the worse for wear. "These terrorist attacks against our military and our vital defense industries and scientists . . . and now against me . . . were carried out by Russian mercenaries—mercenaries I'm convinced were acting on the orders of the Russian government itself. Fortunately, thanks to the heroism and incredible self-sacrifice of a handful of brave American patriots and their Polish comrades-in-arms, this threat to our country and to our political stability was stopped cold tonight."

Farrell's mouth tightened. "Despite President Barbeau's earlier repeated assertions otherwise, the evidence of Moscow's involvement in these atrocities is now overwhelming. The pieces of six wrecked Russian war machines, which they call *Kiberneticheskiye Voyennyye Mashiny*, are scattered across my ranch. I have no doubt that careful forensic analysis of these materials and components will prove conclusively where they were manufactured . . . in Russia . . . and nowhere else." For a moment, a bit of mischievous humor peeked out through his serious expression. "And if that's not enough to convince the president and her people of the boneheaded mistakes they've made all the way through this crisis, well, then, maybe interrogating the prisoners we captured here tonight will do the trick."

He looked straight into the cameras. "But whatever President Barbeau does or doesn't do, the evil men responsible for orchestrating these brutal and unprovoked attacks on our country had better get one thing straight: If I win the election in November and become president of the United States, there *will* be a day of reckoning. And that's not a threat. It's a solemn promise—"

Gennadiy Gryzlov snapped off the broadcast with a decisive gesture. Slowly, he swiveled to face Kurakin. "I am shocked, General," he said coldly. "Shocked to the depths of my soul by these terrible events."

Kurakin stared at him. "Mr. President, let me

remind you that the attempt to kill Governor Farrell was ordered *against* my best advice. From the beginning, I was the one who warned *you* that doing so was both hasty and reckless."

Gryzlov raised an eyebrow. "You misunderstand me, Vladimir," he said with a sly smile. Seeing the other man's incomprehension, he sighed. "I'm simply expressing my dismay at learning about the crimes you and these other disgraced ex–Russian soldiers have been committing on foreign soil. I can't imagine how you were able to steal so much valuable state property—like those experimental industrial robots—let alone use it to carry out wholly unauthorized terrorist actions against the United States." He shook his head gravely. "I suspect I'm going to have to clean house at the Ministry of Defense, purging it from top to bottom."

Kurakin turned pale. "But I—"

"You thought I would sanction what you've done, especially after this fiasco? You forget: The core of 'plausible deniability' is the willingness to *deny*." He tapped a button on his desk phone.

The door to his office swung open. Several hard-faced men in police uniforms filed in. One of them, with the two stars of a lieutenant colonel on his shoulder boards, moved directly to Kurakin and laid a firm hand on his shoulder. "Former major general Vladimir Kurakin, by order of the president, I'm placing you under arrest for crimes against the state."

Kurakin sat rooted in genuine shock. His mouth opened and closed uselessly, like a fish gasping for breath after it had been hooked and reeled in.

The officer who'd arrested him nodded to his subordinates. Silently, they closed in, dragged Kurakin to his feet, and then led him, unresisting, out of the office.

Gryzlov stopped their leader with a glance. "A moment, Colonel."

"Sir?"

"Major General Kurakin is a very dangerous man," Gryzlov said mildly.

The lieutenant colonel nodded. "Yes, Mr. President."

"So he may try to escape," Gryzlov went on.

"That is possible," the hard-faced man agreed.

Gryzlov's eyes were icy. "Be sure that he makes the *attempt*." His smile looked as though it had been pasted on. "Do we fully understand each other?"

"Completely, Mr. President," the officer assured him. He saluted and left.

Russia's president sat back with a hooded expression. Snipping off loose ends like Kurakin was easy. Arriving at a final solution for dangerous men like McLanahan and Farrell and their master, Martindale, was going to take a great deal more work.

THE WHITE HOUSE, WASHINGTON, D.C.
Several days later

President Stacy Anne Barbeau glared at the image of her Russian counterpart, Gennadiy Gryzlov. Over their secure video link, he seemed utterly unfazed by her undisguised anger. In fact, if anything, she realized with mounting fury, he looked remarkably pleased with himself.

"You look unwell, Madam President," he said coolly, before she could start in on him. "Have you consulted your doctors?"

Barbeau felt her teeth grind together. Of course she looked "unwell," she thought bitterly. No amount of makeup could disguise the bags under her eyes or the haggard, haunted expression she wore almost constantly these days. With the revelation that the Russians were really responsible for terrorist attacks she'd so vehemently blamed on the Poles and their Iron Wolf Squadron allies, her days in power were numbered. Every poll, every focus group, every high-priced consultant's report came to the same, inexorable conclusion. Politically, she was a dead woman walking. She was going to lose the November election. The only open question right now was by how wide a margin—and how many congressmen and senators of her own party she would take down with her.

"I'm just fine," she lied. "Which is more than anyone will be able to say for you in the not-too-distant future, you arrogant son of a bitch."

Gryzlov raised an eyebrow challengingly. "Is that a threat, Madam President?"

"What else would it be?" Barbeau snapped. "What the hell made you think you could launch a covert war against the United States and stroll away unscathed?"

"Me?" he said with a cold, dismissive laugh. "Have you forgotten the precedents you set yourself? Long ago, you washed your hands of any responsibility for the actions of Scion's Iron Wolf mercenaries, remember? You practically got down on your knees and begged me to absolve you of their sins against my country. And I agreed." He smiled thinly. "Why then should I take any blame for the actions of a few criminal ex-soldiers who acted without any authorization from *my* government?"

For a moment, Barbeau could only stare at Gryzlov, flabbergasted by his sheer gall. "You can't seriously believe anyone will believe that crock of shit?" she demanded at last. "Who are you going to claim paid this General Kurakin and his men? The Chinese? Some criminal syndicate? Little green men from Mars?"

Gryzlov shrugged his shoulders. "Who knows? Life is full of mysteries." His gaze turned even colder. "In one way at least, Madam President, my government has proved itself more cognizant of its obligations under international law than yours. You claimed to be powerless against the depredations of Martindale's Scion. Russia is not so weak or negligent. The deaths of the criminal Kurakin and his closest associates prove that." He showed his teeth. "So you see, justice in my country is swift . . . and certain."

"Knocking a few pawns off the board won't cut it, this time," Barbeau retorted.

"Will it not?" Gryzlov said lazily. Abruptly, he leaned forward. "Don't waste any more of my time with paper threats, *Madam* President. We both know you don't have the stomach for real war. And even if you did, who will follow you into the abyss? You have no allies. No friends. Your own Congress would impeach you, if only to save its own skin."

Barbeau saw red for a moment. *Oh, for a knife and just a couple minutes alone with this bastard,* she thought darkly, clenching her fists below her desk. Out of the corner of her eye, she saw Luke Cohen starting to get up from his chair. Impatiently, she waved him back down. At last, she breathed out, regaining a small measure of self-control. "You really think you've won something here, Gennadiy?" she retorted. "Because from where I'm sitting, you look like a loser."

He only smiled.

"You think I'm wrong?" Barbeau continued cuttingly. "Well, I hope you enjoy reaping what you've just sowed. Come January, you're going to face a new American president, someone who's openly hostile to you and your ambitions. A president allied with Martindale and Sky Masters . . . and"—she swallowed a curse—"with McLanahan."

For the first time, she saw Gryzlov look uneasy. "I do not fear any of them," he said quickly.

"Then you're a moron," she said flatly. "Because you damned well *should* be afraid." Before he could reply, she broke the connection and sat back breathing hard.

Finally, Barbeau turned to Cohen and Rauch. Both men had been listening in on the call. "Did you hear Gryzlov gloating? There's no doubt about it. That son of a bitch is guilty as hell."

"And free as a bird," Rauch pointed out bluntly.

"Because he's right. Unless we're willing to declare war over this, there's not much we can do . . . at least in the short term."

Barbeau snorted. "The short term is all I've got, Dr. Rauch."

"True enough," he agreed. "Fortunately, this nation's long-term interests and security don't depend on any single person—most especially not on you."

Her eyes narrowed. "I'm not sure I like your tone very much, Ed." She scowled at him. "I suggest you leave the half-assed political commentary at the door next time."

"There won't be a next time, Madam President," Rauch said calmly. He stood up, pulled a letter from his jacket pocket, and put it on her desk.

Barbeau stared down at it. "What the hell is that?"

"My resignation," he said. "Effective immediately."

She looked at him with cold contempt. "So you're just another rat leaving the sinking ship, Dr. Rauch?"

"No, Madam President," Rauch replied with equal contempt. "In this case, the only rats here are the ones who're staying."

Then, without another word, he turned and walked out of the Oval Office—leaving Stacy Anne Barbeau speechless behind him.

EPILOGUE

JELITKOWO BEACH, ON THE BALTIC COAST, NEAR GDAŃSK, POLAND
Winter 2021

Major Nadia Rozek loped alone along the wide, windswept stretch of sandy beach. She gritted her teeth against the icy cold, dug into the loose sand, and kept going—striving to master her new prosthetic running blades. They were the last piece of the challenge she'd been wrestling with ever since the surgeons at Fort Sam Houston amputated both of her mangled legs below the knee.

Weeks of agonizing hospitalization in the United States had been followed by months of painful and exhausting rehabilitation at home in Poland. She'd already relearned to walk using other, more conventional prosthetic legs. Now she was determined to prove that she was not a helpless cripple to be thanked for her service, awarded a pension, and then gently set aside. Men like Douglas Bader, the World War II RAF fighter ace, had already shown that double amputees could fly and fight in the air. Her task was to convince her superiors that she was fit to serve, even without her legs, as an active-duty officer in Poland's special forces.

And so every day, in all kinds of weather, she ran up and down this long, empty stretch of beach—rebuilding her strength, her stamina, her agility, and her speed. Already, she was beating the personal records she'd set with two real legs.

But she always ran alone.

Nadia ducked her head and sprinted across the sand, trying to focus on what was just in front of her . . . and not on what might lie in her future. Since she was a child, she'd only really been afraid of one thing—the chance that she might live out her life as a solitary being, alone and loveless. For years, the comradeship of her fellow soldiers had filled the void . . . though only imperfectly. Then she'd met Brad McLanahan, and it was as though a new sun had risen in her world, bringing with it a glorious feeling of warmth and growth and joy.

But now? When he looked at her, would he still see the woman he loved? Or would Brad's eyes be continually tormented by the sight of her scars and missing limbs? He blamed himself for the wounds she'd taken in that final battle . . . as unfair as that was. During his visits to her hospital room and then later in the rehabilitation center, his feelings of guilt and regret had lain between them like the black shadow of the moon as it eclipsed the sun.

If only he'd been free to spend more time with her—learning to cope with what had happened just as she had. But he was a serving soldier in the

Iron Wolf Squadron and his time was not fully his own . . . especially in a world reeling from the aftermath of Gryzlov's most recent vicious schemes.

Right now, Nadia feared she might lose him forever. America's newly inaugurated president Farrell had lifted all of Barbeau's sanctions and threats of prosecution against those who'd served with Iron Wolf and Scion. She'd heard the joy in Brad's voice when he phoned her with the news that he and his father were flying back to the United States to visit with family. Weeks had passed since they'd left, with only an occasional, awkward call or e-mail or text. What if Brad decided to stay in the land of his birth rather than return to Poland? Through all their time together, she'd known in her heart that he'd never fully reconciled himself to the possibility of a life spent in exile.

She knew she was just feeling sorry for herself, that as a member of the military she should expect to make sacrifices. After all, Whack Macomber was also going through his own rehabilitation—in his case for several shattered ribs and badly broken arms and legs. He hadn't suffered any amputations, but the big man joked that he had more pins in him than there had been in his grandmother's sewing kit. Each time they spoke in the hospital or on the phone, the colonel's encouragement in spite of his own injuries had helped her stay motivated. Yet even with her determination to overcome her physical limitations, Nadia felt emotionally raw.

She stopped to catch her breath, staring down at the hard-packed sand in front of her blades without seeing anything more than a blur. *You will survive*, she told herself, *whatever happens.*

Steeling herself to push through the next five kilometers, Nadia looked up . . . and saw a tall, broad-shouldered figure in the dark, rifle-green uniform jacket of the Iron Wolf Squadron. He stood alone on the sand, waiting for her.

With new energy, she sprinted toward him . . . and found herself caught up in his arms. "Hi, there," Brad said. "I'm back."

Nadia looked up at him in wonder. "I was afraid you would go home now that your president makes it possible. Home to America."

Smiling gently, he shook his head. "America. Poland. Anywhere in the world. It doesn't really matter to me. My real home is wherever *you* are, Nadia Rozek. Always and forever."

WEAPONS AND ACRONYMS

96L6E—Russian surface-to-air missile search
   radar
AH-64D APACHE—U.S. Army attack helicopter
AIM-120—radar-guided air-to-air missile
AK-400—Russian assault rifle
ALQ-293—American advanced electronic
   warfare system (SPEAR)
APC—armored personnel carrier
AT-4—Russian antitank rocket
B-1B LANCER—U.S. Air Force strategic heavy
   bomber
B-21 RAIDER—U.S. Air Force next-generation
   stealth bomber
B-2A SPIRIT—U.S. Air Force strategic stealth
   heavy bomber
B-52H STRATOFORTRESS—U.S. Air Force
   strategic heavy bomber
BMP-1, BTR-82—Russian armored personnel
   carriers
C-17 GLOBEMASTER III—U.S. Air Force heavy-
   cargo aircraft
CH-47 CHINOOK—U.S. Army heavy-lift cargo
   helicopter

CID—Cybernetic Infantry Device, manned
combat robot

CIWS—Close-in Weapon System, U.S. Navy
ship defensive weapon

CO—Commanding Officer

DARPA—Defense Advanced Research Projects
Agency, U.S. Defense Department agency
developing new military technology

DEFCON—Defense readiness Condition

DTF—digital terrain following

E-2C HAWKEYE—U.S. Navy carrier-borne radar
surveillance and control plane

E-3 SENTRY—U.S. Air Force radar surveillance
and control plane

E-4B—U.S. Air Force National Airborne
Operations Center, flying command post

E-8 JSTARS—Joint Surveillance Target Attack
Radar System, U.S. Air Force ground
surveillance radar aircraft

F-15—U.S. Air Force air dominance fighter
aircraft

F-15E STRIKE EAGLE—U.S. Air Force tactical
bombing and fighter aircraft

F-16 FIGHTING FALCON—U.S. Air Force
multirole tactical fighter

F-22 RAPTOR—U.S. Air Force fifth-generation
stealth air dominance fighter aircraft

F-35 LIGHTNING II—American multiservice
fifth-generation multirole tactical fighter
aircraft

F-4—American multirole tactical fighter aircraft

FAA—American Federal Aviation
Administration

FSB—Russian Federal Security Bureau (formerly KGB)

FXR—Francis Xavier Regan, multinational business mogul

GLOCK 22—Austrian .40-caliber semiautomatic pistol

GLONASS—Global Navigation Satellite System, Russian space-based satellite navigation system

GPS—Global Positioning System, American satellite navigation system

GROZA-4—Russian Special Forces assault rifle

GRU—*Glavnoye razvedyvatel'noye upravleniye*, Russian military intelligence

GSH-30-1—Russian heavy rapid-fire cannon

HELLFIRE MISSILE—American air-to-ground laser- and radar-guided attack missile

HH-60G—U.S. Air Force special operations helicopter

HUD—heads-up display; displays flight and weapon information in front of the pilot

HUEY—nickname of the American UH-1 Iroquois utility helicopter

HUMINT—Human Intelligence

IR—infrared

JAS 39—Swedish-designed multirole tactical fighter

KH-35UE—Russian air-to-ground attack missile

KLICKS—kilometers

KVM—*Kiberneticheskiye Voyennyye Mashiny*, Russian manned combat robot

LEAF—Life Enhancing Assistive Facility, robotic life-support system

LED—Light Emitting Diode, advanced lighting system

LZ—Landing Zone

M1911A1—American .45-caliber pistol

M1A1—U.S. Army main battle tank

M-60—U.S. Army main battle tank

MFD—Multi Function Display, electronic information system

MP7 SUBMACHINE GUN—German-made compact personal defense weapon

MQ-55—American unmanned combat aerial vehicle

MRAP—Mine Resistant Ambush Protected, American heavy armored personnel carrier

NEXRAD—Next Generation Radar, American weather radar system

NSA—National Security Agency, American global electronic surveillance agency

NSC—National Security Council, American national defense and foreign policy group

PR—public relations

PSS—Russian silent pistol

PZL SW-4—Polish light utility helicopter

RKU—*Razresheniye Konfliktov Uslugi*, Russian mercenary group

RP—reporting point; also rendezvous point

RPG—rocket-propelled grenade

S-19 MIDNIGHT—American single-stage-to-orbit spaceplane

S-300 SAM—Russian surface-to-air antiaircraft missile

S-400 TRIUMF—advanced Russian surface-to-air antiaircraft missile

SAM—surface-to-air missile

SOCAL—Southern California Air Route Traffic Control Center, American air-traffic-control agency

SOCOM—Special Operations Command, American military special operations headquarters

SPEAR—Self-Protection Electronically Agile Reaction, American advanced electronic warfare system

SPETSNAZ—abbreviation for *Voyska* Spets*ialnogo* Naz*nacheniya*, Russian special forces

SPIKE—Israeli antitank missile

STINGER—American shoulder-fired antiaircraft missile

STOL—Short Takeoff and Landing

SU-27—Russian multirole tactical fighter

SU-34—Russian tactical bomber

SU-35—Russian multirole tactical fighter

SU-50—Russian advanced air-superiority fighter

SUV—sport utility vehicle

T-72—Russian main battle tank

T-90—Russian advanced main battle tank

TU-160 BLACKJACK—Russian advanced supersonic strategic bomber

TU-22M-3 BACKFIRE—Russian supersonic strategic bomber

TU-95 BEAR—Russian strategic bomber

UAZ-3163 PATRIOT—Russian SUV

UDAV—Russian 9mm pistol

UH-60 BLACK HAWK—U.S. Army medium utility helicopter

V-22—American tilt-rotor aircraft

VC-25B—U.S. Air Force highly modified version of the Boeing 747-200B, known as *Air Force One* when the U.S. president is aboard

VH-92A—U.S. Marine Corps VIP transport helicopter, known as *Marine One* when the U.S. president is aboard

WALTHER P99—German-made 9mm semiautomatic pistol

XB-1F EXCALIBUR—American optionally manned modified B-1B Lancer strategic bomber

XCV-62 RANGER—American experimental tilt-rotor transport aircraft

XF-111 SUPERVARK—American optionally manned modified F-111 strategic bomber

XV-40 SPARROWHAWK—American experimental unmanned tilt-rotor aircraft

If you enjoyed *The Moscow Offensive,*
look for the next thrilling adventure
featuring Brad McLanahan and
the Iron Wolf Squadron

THE KREMLIN STRIKE

Available in hardcover May 2019
wherever books are sold

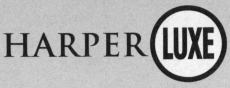